MW00709613

GHOST
OF A
SHADOW

GHOST

OF A

SHADOW

BOOK ONE OF THE SADIE MYERS CHRONICLES

Dear Ethel,
See the magic. Be the magic.
All my best, Andrea

ANDREA ENGEL *AND* LESLIE ENGEL

Dear Ethel,
Always remember what a
special part of this world of ours
you are! Best wishes, Leslie

gatekeeper press

This book is a work of fiction. Names, characters, places, organizations, and incidents are either products of the author's imagination or are used fictitiously to provide a sense of authenticity. Any resemblance to actual events, if not taken from public records, is entirely coincidental.

Published by Gatekeeper Press
3971 Hoover Rd. Suite 77
Columbus, OH 43123-2839

Copyright © 2015 by Andrea Engel and Leslie Engel

All rights reserved. Neither this book, nor any parts within it may be sold or reproduced in any form without permission.

No part of this book may be reproduced in any form or by any electronic or mechanical means including information storage and retrieval systems, without permission in writing from the author. The only exception is by a reviewer, who may quote short excerpts in a review.

ISBN (paperback): 9781619849310
ISBN (hardcover): 9781619849327
eISBN: 9781619849303

Library of Congress Control Number: 2015959097

Printed in the United States of America

For our dearest Gramma Ann,
Our rock and inspiration.
We miss you every day.

For our beloved parents, Irene & Jay,
Whose love and support
Provided us with the confidence to keep going

Table of Contents

Acknowledgments

ASPECIAL THANKS TO our entire family for their time, encouragement, support, and love, including but not limited to our parents, Irene and Jay; our sister and brother-in-law, Marcy and Paul; and our special people, Jon and George, for having our backs throughout this entire roller-coaster ride.

We're grateful for an amazing son and nephew. Jake has conjured many colorful contributions, including naming the land beyond the water. Thanks also to Jake's father, Jim, for his flexibility and warm nature throughout this process.

Thank you, Cousin Amber, who painted our preliminary cover and gave us the gift of seeing Barnaby for the first time. Thank you, Cousin Heather, Aunt Linda, and Tim for reading our roughest drafts of the teaser chapters. We're thankful to Cousins Heather and Aaron for their marketing tips and also to our brother, Henry, for encouraging creativity in the world at large. Thank you, Aunt Ann, for your wisdom and special powers.

Many thanks to Peter of peterdoakglobal.com for his expertise in the world of social media marketing and his cheerful spirit and flexibility . . . and to Michelle Caruso for introducing us to him and her constant support. Thank you,

Joanie Caska, for your longstanding encouragement and ideas about writing and marketing.

Thanks to our first readers, whose support has been unparalleled: George, Mac, Marcy, Stephanie, Dana N., Kathryn, Lily, Nancy, Laurel, Jennifer, Zeau, and Becca.

Much gratitude for the support of dear friends—Pam, Nancy H., Kim, Suzanne, Stephanie, Cynthia, Carrie, Eleanor, Sarafaith, Maria, Thomas, Al, Marta, Emily W., Barbra, Mary Jane, Scott, Linda, Robin Mansfield, Karen Amato, and Judy Toma—for keeping our spirits up and our positivity high with "you can do it" motivation.

Special thanks for the professional insight and support of Dr. Susan Jurish and Jeanne Mulligan Prom.

Rest in peace, Mark Kersey. Thank you for communicating the book's title to us.

A warm welcoming shout-out to the folks at C2Education.

Much gratitude to our talented cover artist/designer, Ana Grigoriu, for intuiting a vision from our squiggly words on the page.

Thank you to our esteemed professional editors, Angela Brown and Veronica Jorden, for their watchful eyes, steady commitment, and creative suggestions. A tip of the hat to Reedsy.com as well. Thanks also to the staff at Gatekeeper Press and Rob Price, our author manager.

A hearty mention for those who have lent their support at Coauthorpreneur Sisters on Facebook, as well as the readers and subscribers of our blog, 2penthrupain.com.

Finally, thanks to all the people who don't know how much they helped us as they crossed our paths without our knowing their names but whose inspiration shows up in this book. We appreciate you.

ACT ONE

The Shadow and the Light

In paths unknown we hear the feet
Of fear before, and guilt behind;
We pluck the wayside fruit, and eat
Ashes and dust beneath its golden rind.

—"The Shadow and the Light," John Greenleaf Whittier

CHAPTER ONE

Earth, Spin: Check

"RUN, SADIE! RUN!" Gramma Rose yelled.

Where's her voice coming from? "I'm running as fast as I can!" I screamed, but the wind swallowed my words. I looked down at my feet; they disappeared into darkness.

Terrorized by the lightning storm overhead, I jumped every time an earth-shaking boom of thunder followed a jagged strike. With the tempest so close, I feared being struck by the next bolt. Sideways heavy rain pelted my face like burning needles, stabbing mercilessly.

"I can't see!" I ran smack into a tangle of branches that formed a maze. Their sharp teeth snapped at me as I crawled through. I knew home was on the other side. I had to get there.

Rumbling peals of thunder cracked, one after the other, shifting the ground beneath me. I pushed my hands hard against my ears to block out the loudest booms. Red lightning jolted my body with electric vibrations. Red flashes strobed all around. I sensed the shadow man behind me, but I couldn't tell where he was.

"Keep running, Sadie!" Gramma Rose called out.

Petrified, I thought this was it: *The End of Sadie Myers.*

"I don't want to die!" I yelled back.

The sound of footsteps squished behind me. I imagined breath on my neck. I felt his fingers graze my hair with creepy restraint.

"*No!* Leave me alone!"

I shot up in bed, glistening with sweat. No matter how many times I told myself I was safe and only dreaming, I couldn't shake the feelings the nightmare left behind.

I'd never been so scared in all my years on earth. This was the first time the shadow man had chased me. He'd never come this close before.

A song trilled at the window. I spotted the goldfinch on the birch tree, singing its clear '*po-ta-to-chip*' call.

Morning eased the tension of my nightmare, and I relaxed a bit. *Okay, Sunday, here I come.*

I headed to the kitchen, where smiling faces greeted me. Mom stood at the center-island stove making waffles, her brown curls bouncing as she spoke. Today, on one of those rare days, her usually dark eyes looked lighter, like milk chocolate. "Here you go, sunshine." Mom handed me a plate while placing a kiss on my cheek. "How did you sleep last night?"

"I had a nightmare. It seemed so real, but now that I'm with you, everything feels safe again."

"I'm glad to hear you're feeling better, though I don't like to think of you having nightmares." She gave me a comforting hug.

I sat next to Dad, who read the paper. He gave me a kiss and a broad smile. He brushed his blond hair away from his green eyes every other second. *Time for a haircut*, I thought. Though he was typically calm, reading at the table with the family brought out the "even more relaxed dad" in him.

He had told me over and over, "Sadie, there's nothing like reading a newspaper to get a sense of what's going on in the world." I would smile and nod, but I preferred fiction.

"Sadiekins, congratulations on completing your summer assignment. Mom told me how much effort you put into it. We're both so proud of you."

Mom squinched her face at me with loving approval.

"And while I hate to lose your company during breakfast, I think Ruby could use a walk. She just mentioned she'd like you to take her." Dad turned another page of his *Evergreen Daily News.*

It didn't take me long to finish those last bites of my waffles. They were that delicious.

"Funny, Dad." I turned to Ruby. "Come here, my special girl. Let's go take a W-A-L-K."

She wagged her tail, her whole body shaking with excitement.

I loved taking my Irish setter out for walks. I didn't like one part as much, though, so I had trained Ruby to poop right into the bag. It made cleanup a snap. It was simple to train her— I'd say, "Ruby, poop in the bag, please," and she did. People commented all the time how shocked they were that a dog would do that, but Ruby and I had an understanding.

One time a woman asked, "How on earth do you get that beast to aim so well?" It looked as though my sweet dog had rolled her eyes right before I did.

That morning after Ruby took care of business, we went for a stroll around the quiet neighborhood. In the bright morning sun with Ruby at my side, I felt my connection to nature, which spread all around our house for many miles. Our rural subdivision of Evergreen Park was well integrated with its natural setting. There were many varieties of birds, animals, and plants to pass, which kept things interesting. I made it my business to wander a little farther each day. When we reached the creek that ran from Deep Lake all the way through town, we turned to head back home.

"Come on, Ruby. I'll race you."

Ruby took her cue, and we ran for the finish line. Completely out of breath, I barely made it to the front porch first.

"I won again, Roo Roo," I teased. Ruby looked up at me, a smile on her adorable face, her tail wagging. I leaned down and hugged her neck. "Ruby, you always let me win."

As we walked through the door, Mom announced, "We're going to your Aunt Sue's today. Gramma Rose will be there too. We'll leave as soon as you're ready."

Dad's sister, Aunt Sue, invited Gramma to everything here in Florida. My paternal grandparents lived far away in California, so Gramma and Aunt Sue had grown close over the years.

"Cool. I don't have plans with Christopher until tomorrow." I raced to get my backpack together, and then we were on our way. The drive to Aunt Sue's was only half an hour. Ruby and I used the time to observe the countryside with its rivers, forests, and gently rolling hills.

"Look at all those horses."

As soon as I spoke the words, the unmistakable warmth of a whisper brushed my ear.

Sweet Sadie.

"Whoa, did you hear that?" I asked.

Ruby nodded; my parents were engrossed in some kind of interview on NPR.

The sky flashed red immediately after, and in the next instant, every one of the horses took off at a gallop across the broad green pasture. Ruby bounced twice on the armrest, shook her head with a soft yelp, and stared with me again. I felt that same excitement as I heard the pounding of their hooves through the ground and up into the car. An earthy mix filled our nostrils.

"Wow, look at that!" I pressed my nose against the window, watching them run.

Ruby acknowledged with one sharp bark.

"What was that, Mom? Dad, did you see that?"

Mom glanced over her shoulder from the front seat. "See what, Sadie?"

"The red flash in the sky? And that whisper . . . Didn't you hear it? Didn't you see it?"

"Sorry, sweetie. I'm not sure what you're talking about," Mom replied.

Dad caught my eye in the rearview mirror. "Yeah. Sorry, honey. I didn't catch it either."

I shook my head and looked at Ruby. "You saw it, didn't you? I'm not losing it, right?"

Ruby yawned then moved to the other side of the car to lie down.

I sighed and slumped in my seat.

Dad changed the radio station. One of our all-time favorite songs, "Loud Harry," came on, and the three of us belted it out together.

By the time we got to Aunt Sue's, I'd forgotten all about the horses and the red streak in the sky. I was excited to see everyone. It had been a few weeks after all.

Aunt Sue's house, a modest Spanish Colonial, displayed a single gable that extended to become the porch roof. Inside, everything was about two decades old in color and construction, but my parents and I found it cozy and inviting. Aunt Sue had downsized after her husband had run off. I can't even talk about Uncle "Whatever His Name Was" anymore. I'll never understand why he left. Aunt Sue was so cute with her black bob and stunning blue eyes, and to leave those incredible girls? They looked just like her.

"Aunt Sue," I called out as we walked into the house.

"In here, guys," she called back.

We headed for the kitchen, our favorite place to gather.

Aunt Sue's loving arms engulfed me. "Hi, Sadie. So happy you came today. You get prettier every time I see you."

"Aunt Sue," I groaned, totally embarrassed. I returned her hug, looking over the top of her head, which was level with my nose. She always smelled like honeysuckle.

"Well, it's the truth, Sadie. You'd better get used to it."

"Sadie will get used to it in her own time. And might I add, she has a lot more going for her than looks alone!" Mom stated.

"Which she gets from you, no doubt?"

"Yep, you know it. Brains and beauty!"

I giggled at their good-natured banter. "You two are too much."

I loved my Aunt Sue. I liked to pretend her twin five year-old daughters, Brenda and Karen, were my little sisters. I taught them new things, like how to do a cartwheel or have a conversation with Ruby, like Gramma had taught me. Their go-to girl, I kept them company when the grown-ups were busy.

"You're excellent with the girls," Aunt Sue often told me. I felt proud to hear her say that.

Gramma Rose came in through the back door. She wore a neon-pink tank top with teal shorts and a pair of jeweled sandals—flats, of course, since Gramma was tall. Not your typical grandmother fashion, but she rocked it. She waited with outstretched arms.

"Gramma!" I hurried over to her, and we gave each other a big squeeze. I felt protected in her arms. "Oh, Gramma, I love you so much."

I loved my mom and dad, but there was something different and special about Gramma. I could tell her anything, no matter what it was. She never made me feel bad or ashamed. That, and she offered the best advice . . . and cookies.

"Thank you, my sweet Sadie. I love you too."

"Hi, Mom," I heard from behind me. "How's it going today?"

"I'm fantastic. How are you today, Tess?"

"Doing great. Thanks for asking." Mom and Gramma shared

a hug then started a conversation as my mind wandered. Gramma was a beauty in her day—and every day as far as I was concerned. I had seen three or four photos of her as a young woman. Her hair was strawberry blond, and her eyes were hazel, just like mine. Since photos of her from those days were in short supply, I'd studied them carefully. My overall expression was similar to Gramma's, but I was waiting for the "beautiful" to kick in. *Any day now*, I hoped.

These days, Gramma remained tall and athletic, swimming every other day. Her shoulder-length hair gradually had taken on a stunning silver and flipped up a bit at the ends. The last time we were together, Gramma had taken me to play paintball. She had taught me well even though she still won every time . . . so far.

Coming out of my reverie, I realized the conversation had stopped, and Gramma and Mom were both looking at me with twinkling eyes.

Such a wonderful day, I thought. *My world is perfect.*

CHAPTER TWO

Dream Crasher

"Sadie . . ."

"Gramma, you sound funny."

"Sadie . . ."

"What *is* that noise?"

"*Sadie!*"

Sadie turned over in bed, backing away from her mother. "Wuh-huh . . . ? What's going on?" Sadie asked, rubbing her eyes.

"Come on, Sadie. Get up. We're going to be late for the doctor." Sadie's mom gave her arm a gentle shake.

Sadie yawned. "Wait . . . We aren't going to Aunt Sue's?"

"What are you talking about? Aunt Sue lives across the country now, remember? So her parents could help out with the twins? Come on, Sadie. Get up."

"Where . . . where's Ruby? Where's Gramma?"

"Oh, Sadie." Her mom's tone softened, as she sat on the bed next to her. "You know Gramma and Ruby both passed away last year."

Sadie snapped out of her fog, and the present came rushing back. "Oh, that's right. We're in Florida, and Aunt Sue is . . . gone. Just like Ruby and Gramma." She sniffled. As she woke up a little more, the memory of her dream left her heart in knots. She threw off her lilac blanket and sat up.

"Come on now," her mom snapped, trying but failing to be patient. "You overslept, and we have to leave for your checkup at Dr. Goldman's office in twenty minutes. Come on! Get up now and get dressed!" Her mom stood and left the bedroom.

What a way to wake up. I want my dream back, please. I want to stay there, back with Gramma and Aunt Sue. Back to the way things used to be, when Mom and Dad were nice.

Exasperated, Sadie grumped out of bed. She dragged her feet toward the bathroom, surrendering to another day. Still groggy from her dreams, she wiped the sleepers from her eyes and splashed water on her face. Way too cold, of course. She brushed her teeth and ran a comb through her uncooperative hair. There was the usual part down the middle, and then came the hair ties.

"Why am I still wearing pigtails when I'm almost fifteen? Oh, well." *Do I really care? It's not like there's anything else to do with this messy hair. Or anybody to impress with it!*

Twenty minutes . . . We have to leave in twenty minutes. Twenty minutes, kept repeating in her head. *Aghhh, why does Mom treat me this way? Maybe she should have woken me up earlier? But no, now it's my fault. Geez.*

Sadie spoke to her reflection as if it would answer. "What's wrong with me? How did this end up being my life?"

The mirror gave Sadie the third degree: "Tell me, when did you last smile? And what's up with your mom and dad? I can't remember the last time they were happy."

"Are you up for an experiment?" asked Sadie. "I heard if I stare at you without blinking, strange things will happen."

After what felt like fourteen hours, Sadie's reflection grew wavy around the edges. *Huh? This actually works?* She blinked, and her image went back to normal. *Darn it! Try again, Sadie. Something definitely happened.*

"I hope you're getting ready, Sadie Ann Myers! You only have ten minutes left!" her mom's voice shrilled down the hall and into the bathroom.

"Okay. I'm coming!" *Not!* Concentrating harder this time, she squinted her eyes without blinking. Her reflection got fuzzy around the edges and wavy throughout. Holding the stare, she didn't move.

It was still her yet somehow different. She looked almost . . . happy. Happy and older somehow? The only time she felt joy anymore was in her dreams. Her mirror image turned and spoke to someone, but Sadie couldn't see who it was.

Sweet Sadie, she heard whispered behind her. Caught off guard, she spun around, but no one was there. She could have sworn she'd heard Gramma's voice.

She'd been hearing the whispers more and more. They seemed so real, but she wasn't sure. It could have been her vivid imagination.

Gramma's unexpected passing had hit Sadie hard. It must have been horrible for Sadie's mom too, who had found her on the kitchen floor, a shattered teacup by her side. Sadie knew her parents didn't want to upset her any more than she already was, but some details had come out as they all wept together.

She looked back at the mirror. "No, let me see more!" Sadie returned to her trance-like stare, but nothing unusual happened this time, and her eyes ached from the strain. All that was left was her disappointed image glaring back at her.

She wondered how much time had passed. For some reason, blue scarves flooded her brain. *Why blue scarves?* Gramma wore those. Pale blue and silky, souvenirs from her travels. They were Gramma's favorite.

Blue scarves floated from the bathroom ceiling. They fell slowly, gently touching Sadie's hair, her face, her arms. Blue scarves piled up around her.

Then she heard it. *Whoosh, shwoo, whoosh.* She recognized the calming sounds of ocean waves hitting the shore. A light breeze warmed her face. She smelled the crisp salt air and felt the ocean mist.

The scarves rose up her legs, where they transformed into water. The bathroom disappeared. She stood in the ocean up to her knees. Fear crept in.

Sadie pinched her cheek, just hard enough to tell it wasn't a dream.

She noticed people standing on the shoreline. *They look familiar,* she thought. *Wait a minute . . . There's Mom and Dad. Aunt Sue's there too.* They had their heads down and arms around one another. Sadie scanned the shoreline and spotted herself standing alone. There were no other sounds but the waves and the cry of a lone seagull.

She realized what was happening. Why they were all there. They had come for Gramma's memorial and had spread her ashes over the water.

Sadie still couldn't look at the ocean the same way, knowing Gramma's ashes were there, changing the tone of their favorite place.

"Gramma!" Sadie called out, but as expected, there was no reply. The day of Gramma's memorial had been the worst day ever.

Tears streamed from her eyes. "No," Sadie protested. "Not again. I don't want to see this again." She shut her eyes, squeezing them tight. "No, *no!*" Her eyes opened, and she found herself back in her bathroom. No more ocean. No more blue scarves. No more Gramma Rose.

"Sadie? Are you all right in there? We have to leave now."

Sadie wiped the tears from her eyes, splashed more cold water on her face, and found her voice. "I'm okay. I'm coming . . ."

CHAPTER THREE

Wake up, Amnesiac!

USING HIS FINGERS, the boy pulled his eyelids apart, as others might gently peel off a bandage so it would hurt the least amount possible. Objects gradually came into focus. Black shadows grew into white surfaces. What were they? The word *wall* appeared in his mind.

Eyes tearing, he looked down and saw that he was lying on a soft platform of some sort. This foreign space enclosed him like a box, and his breathing intensified. *Trapped.* His fight-or-flight response activated his body's fiery nerves.

He stood up, spotting a face he didn't recognize in a piece of glass high up on the wall. He jumped, and his breathing sped up even more. His mind raced.

The boy took a deep breath and let it out slowly. His courage returning, he inched forward and studied the unknown face.

It looked vaguely familiar. Perhaps he'd seen it in a dream? Pale skin, nearly white, adorned dark circles above and below, not quite like blackened eyes.

He concluded this was his own face, long and narrow. His straight hair reached below his shoulders. It was dark brown, and so were his eyes. He looked down to see ribs that rose like mountain ranges on his lanky frame. He was wearing a white T-shirt and slightly loose aviation-themed pajama bottoms.

A flash of white caught his eye, and he looked out the window. As tiny white shreds of clouds fell to the earth, small bumps formed on his skin. Before he could panic, whether from the cold or the surprise, the words and meanings came to him: *Goose bumps. They're okay. And so are these . . . snowflakes.*

The door opened. He looked at the lady who entered. She was at least two heads shorter than him. Her frizzy hair had some pink here and there. She wore thick glasses that sat low on her nose. Her striped dress was partially hidden by a bland sweater.

No recognition sprang to mind. He took a step forward and noticed that she took an immediate step backward. He was the superior animal here. He felt it in his bones.

"Hello, Finn. I'm Miss Beverly," she revealed with the slightest tremor. "I've fixed some tea for you downstairs. I thought I'd see if you were ready."

"Finn? Who's Finn? Where am I? What have you done with my memories?"

"Finn is your name, honey. Finn Montgomery. You're in Colorado, in the home of your new foster parents. You've been here since last night. As to your other question, you have amnesia. We haven't been able to locate any of your family members."

"Finn Montgomery . . ." He chewed on the sounds for a few moments, not feeling any connection. "Amnesia?" Distress settled in. *I don't belong inside this body.*

"It's a condition that strips away your memories. Usually it's temporary. You'll have a comfortable bedroom in which to bring them back, along with hot meals every day. Mr. Felix brought you to us last night after making all the arrangements. He came back to check on you."

He noticed how silly this all was: her acting serious, him being nervous. Somehow he knew he had to stifle back the laughter growing in his throat. She droned on and didn't appear to notice the humor he found in all this.

"How old am I?" he asked.

Miss Beverly paused for a moment, though too long for Finn's growing lack of patience.

"Well, are you going to tell me?"

"We're pretty sure you're thirteen. We don't know the exact day you were born. We only know what Mr. Felix told us. Maybe your birth date will be one of the first things you remember, honey."

Finn grew nervous again. *How did this happen to me?* He didn't trust this Miss Beverly person talking to him. And who was Mr. Felix? He didn't recognize his own name, yet the name "Felix" fluttered through his memory on transparent dragonfly wings.

"Would you like to meet your new foster parents and Mr. Felix before he returns home?"

Without his even realizing it, his head nodded vigorously.

"Yes. Take me now."

CHAPTER FOUR

The Place beyond
Saponi Straime

THELONIOUS RESTED ON the velvet moss. He loved this hilltop, which was alive with the sweetest-tasting air. It was peaceful, and he could see most everything from this vantage point. In the valley below, Saponi Straime wound along its semicircular way, its waters glinting with errant rays of light.

As the breeze changed direction, he sensed the presence of his most trusted ally.

"The sky is magnificent today. There are so many arbanious cloffuls, would you not say, old friend?"

"Yes, I have to agree with you, Thelonious. Mesmerizing as always but many more cloffuls than usual."

They didn't always agree with each other but did more often than not. They had experienced many challenges over the eons, so they remained alert despite the recent years of calm.

The cloffuls parted to bright sunshine. The light revealed the glimmering essence of Thelonious's old friend, though his body remained across the straime.

They enjoyed the view of the silken cloffuls and their

forever-changing shapes and colors. Directly above, a brilliant blue-and-green clofful rippled into the shape of a human. Yes, it was definitely forming a young one they had seen on earth, the place beyond Saponi Straime.

"Interesting," Thelonious observed. "Now that I recognize the child, it makes sense. Our last opportunity was so long ago. This could mean it is time again."

"If that is true, we may have another chance, except this time it must work."

"Wait. Hold on." Thelonious pointed toward a darker one on the horizon. The fiery red-and-orange clofful headed their way.

"I see it, Thelonious. It looks like it is turning into . . . but you know that cannot be."

"Of all the things we have seen in our lifetimes? Even that is possible."

CHAPTER FIVE

Through the Muck and the Myers

S ADIE THOUGHT OF little else besides those dreams, the sleeping ones and the waking one in the bathroom. *What's going on?* she wondered. Usually she forgot her dreams, but these had come alive, staying with her long after waking.

The doctor's appointment and Mom's errands couldn't wrestle Sadie away from her inner world. For one second in the doctor's office, she considered sharing her recent odd experiences and getting his opinion. Immediately, however, she realized how it would sound and changed her mind.

Hours later, it became necessary to recharge in the sanctuary of her room with her books, her window seat, and most important, her door.

It was getting harder to tell the difference between dreams and reality and even harder for her to pretend everything was okay around Mom and Dad.

Not that they're paying much attention to me anyway, unless Mom needs something done . . . like every other minute.

She picked up her current read, *Death Moon*, a dark mystery novel set in Atlantis, and sat on her window seat.

"Sadie!" called Mom from the kitchen. "Come help me with dinner!"

"I just started reading. Can't it wait a half hour?"

"Sadie Ann Myers, get in here right now!"

"Okay, okay. I'm coming."

Sadie scanned the last paragraph on the page and sighed. What she wouldn't give to spend the entire day lost inside a story so far from her own. *Why Mom thinks we need two hours to get dinner ready is beyond me.* She put her book on the bed and left her room.

Mom was barely visible, halfway in the refrigerator. Most of the salad ingredients were on the counter, but when she emerged she handed Sadie a bag of carrots.

"You know how your father is when he gets home from work, Sadie, and if dinner isn't ready, he'll be annoyed."

More than usual? Sadie didn't dare say that out loud. Dad was hardly around, and when he was, she didn't want him to be. *He's always so cranky!*

"Your father breaks his back at work every day for us. Do you think advertising at McCruder and Doyles is easy? It's a longer drive for him now that his office is all the way in Clarkson City. His stress keeps him up most nights, so don't upset him with your nonsense when he comes home."

"I won't," Sadie said quietly. *Then there wouldn't be room for your nonsense.*

She sat at the table and peeled carrots. Her mother continued talking, but Sadie only caught every few words.

"Have you heard from Christopher lately?"

Even though Sadie half listened, that name came through loud and clear. It squeezed her heart.

"No. Not lately."

"Hmm, I'm surprised."

You're surprised? "Not as surprised as me," she muttered.

Sadie's mind flew back to one of the first times Christopher had come to her house.

The doorbell had rung. Mom had gone to answer it while Sadie hid at the end of the hallway. She didn't want to seem too eager, so she had waited out of his sight.

"Hi, Mrs. Myers. How are you today?"

"Very well. Thank you. And how are you, Christopher?"

"Oh, I'm always happy when I see Sadie."

She saw Mom smile at that.

"Sadie, Christopher's here," her mother called out.

"Coming." She couldn't get to the door fast enough. "Bye, Mom. See you later."

"Don't be home too late, Sadie. Couple of hours tops. We have things to do."

"Okay, Mom. See ya."

Beaming, Sadie held on to Christopher's hand as if she were afraid she would float away. She adored him. He had dark-blond hair and crystal-blue eyes. Eyes she thought could see right through her.

They strolled to a secret place Sadie had found on one of her walks with Ruby. Hidden on the other side of the neighborhood, among the elms near the playground, it had a clear view of the sky. She and Christopher liked to lie on the grass and look at the clouds.

"Hey, that one looks like Mrs. Tansner."

"Hahaha, you're right, Sadie. Can't mistake that huge head with that awful bun she wears every day. I think the hump gives her away the most, though."

"That's terrible, Christopher. How can you say that? Mrs. Tansner is so nice to us."

"Ah, what can I say?" Changing the subject, he pointed to another cloud. "Hey, look . . . that one over there looks like an elephant with a really long trunk."

"Oh, it does. Hmm, that one looks like a ghost," she said, pointing.

"A ghost? They all look like ghosts if you think about it. White and fluffy."

"These are happy ghosts. I hope all ghosts are. It would be tragic if they weren't."

"Just think they are, and they will be." Christopher propped himself up on one elbow and looked at her seriously. "You know there aren't such things as ghosts. Right, Sadie?"

"Oh, I don't know about that. I hear lots of stories where people say they've seen them."

"I think it's their imagination. Really, if there were ghosts, I think I would've seen one by now."

"Yeah, I guess you're right. You usually are."

He shook his head and pursed his lips. "Come on. That's *so* not true." Nevertheless, a wide smile spread across his face, and in an instant he tickled her relentlessly.

"Stop it, stop it. You'll make me pee myself!" Sadie managed in the spaces between fits of laughter. They both giggled at that. Little did he know she wasn't kidding.

Christopher eased up, and they resumed their cloud watching. It relaxed her after the torturous tickles. The hours melted away, with the conversation drifting from one subject to another, or nothing in particular, until the mosquitoes woke up and started their feast.

"I guess we'd better get out of here!" urged Christopher. He jumped to his feet and helped Sadie stand.

They hated when it was time to go. They walked slowly, hand in hand, back to her house.

"Until we meet again, m'lady."

She loved when he called her "m'lady," but it made her blush every time. They gave each other a tight hug and exchanged good-byes.

Sadie lingered on that hug. Though it was two years ago, she could still feel his arms wrapped around her.

Flash. She turned but didn't see anything. Back to peeling carrots. A few moments later, she felt something underfoot. Blades of grass came up through the kitchen-floor tiles as if they were in a time-lapse video. Shiny pebbles pushed their way up, bumping against her toes. The grass shimmered, as if drenched in morning dew, and Sadie felt cool moisture on her bare feet.

She pushed backward. "What the what?" popped out.

"Sadie! Are you even listening to me?" Mom snapped, standing there with her hands on her hips and eyes of fire glaring at her.

Sadie dropped a carrot as she whipped her head up. "Uh, yes. Of course I am."

"Then what did I just say?"

"Uhhh, umm."

"Never mind. Go set the table."

Sadie surveyed the tiles, but the grass and pebbles were gone. *Hmm. Another trick? They seemed so real.*

She helped her mother bring dinner to the table. *Yuck, meatloaf.* "Do I have to eat that?" she asked, her nose scrunched up at the thought of the first mushy bite.

Mom turned around and growled, "I'm not running a restaurant. You eat what I make."

Sadie shrugged. "Whatever. You don't have to get all huffy about it."

"Sadie," Mom snarled, "you'd better cut that out, or your father will hear about it when he gets home."

"Fine. I'll eat it. You don't have to say anything to him."

Speak of the Devil! She heard Dad's key in the door. A few moments later, Mom tried to kiss him hello.

"Do you think you could give me five minutes to walk in the door? Geez, Tess. At least let me take my jacket off."

"Sorry, George," Mom conceded, choking on her obvious disappointment.

"Hey, Dad," Sadie offered. It grew tougher by the day to speak with him.

"Hey," was all he could muster.

I can see dinner is going to be fun again tonight. Awesome.

Gramma Rose's passing last year and Dad's new job had started a downward spiral in her parents' lives, especially at dinnertime. Turned out those two had been the glue that had kept everyone from spinning out of orbit. Not having Gramma around made it difficult to communicate. Dad used to keep things light, but not anymore.

I miss the way things used to be, Sadie ruminated.

She sat in her usual seat in front of the kitchen window, with her mother at one end of the table and her father at the other. Mom was silent. Her head lowered until all Sadie could see were her defeated curls. *I guess Dad really hurt her feelings. I almost feel sorry for her.*

Sadie remembered when dinner was one of the happier times of her day. She looked at Mom. Once slender, her mother had noticeably put on weight during this last year. Then she observed her father: once toned, now downright skinny. She barely recognized either of them anymore.

As she studied him, Dad grew increasingly distant and strange. His head split into two distinct dads. One looked like last year's dad: kind and gentle. The other wore lines of worry and anger.

She blinked nonstop, trying to determine what was real.

"Sadie, is something wrong with your eyes?"

"No, Mom. I'm okay." She pinched herself. It stung. *I'm awake.*

Then Kind Face spoke. "Hi, honey. How was your day?"

What's going on? He doesn't speak that way anymore. Should I answer? Mom is speaking right over him!

"So, George, how was your day?" her mother asked robotically.

Grumpy Face spat out, "The usual," as he continued eating, head down.

Kind Face asked me what I wanted for my birthday. I don't know how to respond. I'm just gonna put a forkful of mashed potatoes in my mouth.

"Sadie!" Grumpy Face scolded. "Stop scraping your teeth along your fork! It's driving me nuts!"

At the same moment, Kind Face asked, "How's your dinner, Princess?"

"Huh?" Sadie looked back and forth between the two of them, uncertain which one to address. She chose to answer Grumpy Face, for fear of angering him.

"I didn't realize I was scraping my teeth. Sorry."

Grumpy Face shook his head. "Of course you didn't realize it. You never realize anything."

With that, Kind Face dissolved back into Grumpy Face. Crabby won.

Defeated, Sadie asked, "May I be excused?"

"No, you may not be excused until we're all finished," Dad spat.

Sadie sat back, arms folded, and waited for her prison sentence to end.

CHAPTER SIX

What Do You Mean, No Mr. Felix?

F INN BURST OUT of his bedroom and pushed past Miss Beverly. He felt a surge of confidence along with his desire to meet this Mr. Felix. Something about the man he couldn't remember or didn't yet know poked at his brain like a needle. He barely noticed the thought before it dipped back under the waves of his subconscious.

He descended three steps on the simple wooden staircase then slowed to a halt. His senses on fire, he prepared for any action necessary then continued down the steps with a raptor's keen eye.

When he reached the landing, he came to such an abrupt stop that Miss Beverly collided with him, nearly pushing him over. Without thinking, Finn turned and snarled at her.

Miss Beverly took a step back. An automatic response from the reptilian part of her brain, it didn't go unnoticed. Finn nearly clawed the air for emphasis, but at that moment he heard voices from elsewhere in the house. His orientation immediately turned toward them. He crept across the front hall to the doorway of a large parlor, where he spied a couple sitting on an ugly green brocade sofa.

The woman was bony. Curious, he leaned forward to see if one of the bones might pop out. *Nope.* He didn't get his wish. Her hair was reddish-brown, done up in tight curls piled high on her head. *Surely one of those springy things will escape?* When it didn't, he turned to the man, whose hair was the opposite. It was lighter and tight to his head. Shiny too. He was also in danger of losing buttons from an expansion around his gut. He watched, confused, as they leaned toward each other and then away. *What are they doing?*

"Frank, I can barely contain myself. I can't wait to meet the boy already! Go fetch him."

"Sure thing, Marj. I'm on my . . ."

The couple turned their heads in concert as Finn entered the room. He felt a little dizzy and reached out to the wall for support. In a barely controlled growl, he declared, "My name is *Finn*, not 'boy.'"

The couple stiffened, the woman patting her chest with an audible intake of air. Their faces softened after a moment. She stood up and took a step forward. "I assure you, we mean no harm, Finn."

The shorter man beside her offered a tentative smile. "Of course your name is Finn. Hello, Finn. I'm Frank, and this is my wife, Marjorie. We know your last name is Montgomery. Ours is Reid." His smile melted into a look of concern. "How are you feeling?"

"*Finn* is feeling . . ." He searched for the word, which eluded him. " . . . feeling . . ." He looked around the room. It was dim. All the shades were pulled, and he realized that he felt, as he had upstairs, strong in himself. Finn stretched up to his full height. "You want to know how I'm feeling? I'm feeling 'Where is Mr. Felix!'"

"I'm afraid you just missed him, sweetheart, but—" the woman started.

"Are you torturing me on purpose, or are you simply deaf?" Finn's voice grew louder, and his nostrils flared. "I want Mr. Felix now! I know you're hiding something. What have you done to me? Get him for me now, wherever he is. Do it."

Marjorie shook her head. "But we can't, Finn. I'm sure you can understand that he's a very busy man. Once he leaves, he has to call on us. We can't—"

"I don't understand, and I don't care. You'd better find him for me." Finn drew whatever calm he could from the darkened room. "I might look like a peaceful person, but I can make you hurt if I want to."

Marjorie and Frank exchanged glances, eyes wide. "Miss Beverly, a word in the kitchen, please?" Marj indicated the direction with her shaking hand.

Before Finn could blurt out anything else, Frank told his wife, "You go, sweetheart. I'll keep our guest company."

Marjorie guided Miss Beverly through the swinging kitchen door.

Finn heard whispering with periodic crescendos. His brain switched to another sector and ran through possible scenarios. His current behavior created something that, in his vulnerable state, might not be in his best interest. At worst his present tactic could cause him great harm.

At this thought, a Voice emerged quietly from between his ears. *Hold up there, Finn. And please answer me in your head rather than aloud, so Frank won't get involved.*

Finn shook his head and tilted it, smacking one ear with his hand as if to balance excess pressure in the other. *What was that? Who are you? More important, are you real?*

Frank leaned in and put a hand on Finn's shoulder. "You okay there, Finn? Do you have an earache or something that needs tending?"

"Yeah, I'm fine."

Yes, I'm real enough. Never mind that now. You have to be smarter than them. You are smarter than them. You know that, don't you?

Well, I sort of figured, Finn answered. *I have so many questions—you might be able to help me.*

Sorry, kiddo. There isn't time for that. They're in the kitchen right now, deciding your fate.

What do you mean? I'm in charge of my fate!

Well, that's our goal, but right now you're stuck with them because you don't have any resources. Resources are necessary. Get it?

Um, yeah, Finn thought. *So what do you think I should do? Run out of here before they get back? Get resources?*

No. They're part of the solution if we play our cards right. If you want the best resources, you have to know how to play the game.

Play what game?

Think, Finn! You have to talk the way they talk. Pretend to be kind and courteous. They'll eat that up with a big fat spoon.

Finn had noticed the way these people interacted with each other with certain words and tones. He found he had a selection of these stored away, and better than that, he had access to them. But kind? Courteous? These words disturbed him.

The Voice responded, *It'll only be for a little while. You'll see. I'll help you. Do you know what it is to cry?*

Frank interrupted their internal conversation, cautiously asking, "Is there anything you'd like to talk about, Finn? Anything I can help you with? We're on your side."

Finn could see that the man carried some genuine concern for him, and in that moment he knew exactly how to use it to his advantage.

"Please help me speak to Mrs. Marjorie, Frank. I'm afraid I said the wrong thing, but I hope you'll understand that I'm upset. Things come out of my mouth, but I don't honestly mean them. I want to get along with everyone. That's all I want," Finn pleaded with an increasingly rising tone that led to tears. "If I could only talk to her again, I'm sure I could do better," he added, sobbing.

Frank placed a comforting hand on the boy's shoulder once more. "I'll see what I can do. Please wait here. I'll be right back."

"Thank you."

The Voice immediately returned once Frank left the room.

Perfect performance, kiddo.

Yeah. I thought so too.

You're on your way now.

What can I call you? Finn asked. *When can I call you?* But there was only silence.

When Marjorie emerged from the kitchen, followed by Miss Beverly and Frank at a bit of a distance, she also had tears in her eyes.

"You wanted to say something to me, Finn?" she asked with care.

Finn could feel her surrender through the hesitation in her words. Also, now that he understood more about the power of tears, he knew she was ready.

"I'm so sorry. I don't know what came over me. Please give me another chance," he begged. "It'll take some time to adjust, but I'll do my darnedest." He presented her with his best pleading eyes and practically felt Marj's heart melt.

Frank put his arm around his wife. They smiled at Finn while Miss Beverly watched, nodding. Finn continued to pump out a few tears, but inside he felt pleased with his manipulation and the new help that had spoken to him at the perfect time.

And so it was decided. Finn would stay on probation for the next three months. If there were no further incidents, he would be welcome to continue living with the Reids.

* * *

Three months passed faster than anyone could have expected. Finn shot up in height and remained lean. He was everywhere at once, offering to help, staying out of the Reids' way, smiling to gain advantage and trust. And gain it he did. Still, not a single memory returned.

By the end of the probationary period, all three of them nearly forgot that it had come around, since things were going so well. But March fifteenth was circled on the calendar to remind them. Marj prepared his favorite lasagna dinner that night for a surprise celebration.

Finn watched the long arc of cheese stretch from the pan to his plate as she served him the first piece. They had no idea he had executed all this to ensure he'd be able to stay. Smiling, he took the first bite of his dinner. It was all too easy, but how long could he keep up this charade?

CHAPTER SEVEN

Dear Rufus

WITH DINNER FINALLY over, Sadie escaped to the solitude of her bedroom. She couldn't stop thinking about what had happened. The kitchen floor turning into their backyard. Her dad's head splitting into two faces. *What's going on?* she wondered. *Was it real, or am I hallucinating?*

Okay, not going there. I need a distraction. It's time to take matters into my own hands again. I need to get away from this place, if not physically then at least mentally.

Sadie looked around her room. *Reading isn't going to help. It takes too much concentration.* She stood in front of her bookcase and noticed some shiny plastic. *Hmm.* She took out the unwrapped journal she had received for her last birthday from Aunt Sue. *I never thought I'd use this, but maybe tonight's the night. It seems like the right time, I guess. When really is the right time to write all my secrets on paper?*

Sadie climbed onto her plush, purple window seat. She loved it—and like the bed in the Goldilocks story, it was just right. The stiff new journal smelled a bit like plastic, but she was ready to give it a go.

"Dear . . . Hmm, what do I call you? 'Dear Diary' sounds so common. How about 'Dear Rufus'? Yeah, I like that . . ."

Dear Rufus,

Today is my first attempt at writing things down. I never thought of doing this. I always thought it was silly, but then I read that Antoinette Barrows in Mystery at Harmony Lake (that's my favorite book right now, Rufus) did it, and she said it made her feel better. It helped her say things she couldn't say to anyone else, even the awful people in her life. Things would be worse if I told everyone what I really thought of them. I'd better find a safe hiding spot for you. I definitely don't want anyone (aka my parents) reading this. I mean, it'll probably be mostly about them.

"Okay, let's start for real this time," she proposed.

Dearest Rufious,

"No, seriously, I'm going to start now."

Dear Rufious von Doofious,

"Wow, even when I'm upset I can still crack myself up," she snorted. "Okay, start now . . . start . . . *now.*"

Dear Rufus,

My parents never let me say good-bye to Ruby. They knew she was sick. I knew she was sick, but they never told me how sick she really was. All I know is I came home one day from school, and Ruby was gone. They could have waited until I got home. They should have waited until I got home. They didn't have to bring her to the vet while I wasn't there. They said it was better that way. Said I would get over it.

*Well, it's a year later, and I still haven't "gotten over it."
She wasn't just any dog. She was my dog. Ruby was different.
She was special. She was a present from Gramma for my
first birthday. She had a certain look in her eyes every time
I confided in her, and I knew she understood me. She did
everything I asked her to do—and even things I didn't, like
bring me my socks on a chilly morning. We were the same
age almost to the day, and she slept with me every night
since I was small. When no one else was around, I had her
company. Everyone loved Ruby. How could I not have been
allowed to say good-bye? It's not fair.*

   *I pretended I had one last day with her. I gave her one
last hug, one last "Good-bye, Ruby. I'm so going to miss
you." Oh, Rufus, I miss her so much! I miss her every day.*

   *Wow. Sorry to bum you out on your first day. I'll try and
cheer you up next time.*

   *I never told anyone about that, so thank you for listening,
Rufus. I'm still sad, but hopefully I'll feel better soon.*

   *I think that's enough for today. Until we meet again . . .
Darn, that just made me think of Christopher . . . again.*

CHAPTER EIGHT

It Was the Best of Times

S ADIE CLOSED RUFUS and placed him on her lap.

Christopher. Your name brings back so many memories. I have to stop thinking about you. I've been doing so well, but now I've thought about you twice today. I have to stop doing this to myself.

She allowed herself a satisfying stretch on the window seat. Then her eyes turned toward the night. She looked up at the full moon, its soft yellow glow illuminating a vast expanse of the sky as well as the ground below.

The moonlight hit the yard just right. The view was marvelous. There were still woods behind her house. The oaks, magnolias, and cypresses integrated to form a thick treeline. These were the trees the construction workers hadn't knocked down. They hadn't destroyed these surroundings yet like they had in some of the other towns her family drove past. When she and her parents had first moved here, the woods ran as far as she could see in every direction. Sadie felt sad whenever they chopped a tree down. Her heart ached when she felt their hurt, their sadness. *Why can't they leave the trees alone?*

Sadie imagined a whole world out there, where hares, armadillos, and panthers spoke civilly to one another, where she understood what they were saying. She had felt that way back when Ruby was still with her, like she grasped everything Ruby thought and vice versa.

Then, as often happened, she thought of Gramma Rose.

I miss you, Gramma. It's not as bad as it was, but it still hurts. I miss our perfect days together. I miss going on long drives in your convertible to the ocean. I miss camping and hiking and our long talks. I especially miss all the movies we went to and talked about afterward. My sleepovers with you were some of my most memorable experiences ever. I wish I had that escape right now.

One sleepover in particular stood out from all the rest.

"Sadie, Gramma's here," her mother had called out.

"Okay, Mom. Coming." Sadie ran over to Gramma Rose for a hug and said good-bye to her parents.

"Have a fabulous time, honey."

"I will. I always have a great time with Gramma."

Gramma had brought Barnaby along for the ride as usual. He was the only cat Sadie knew who acted more like a canine than a feline. Balancing his back two paws on her thighs and front two paws on the dashboard, he watched everything that happened as they rode along.

His coat shone a wondrous iridescent navy. Everybody thought he was gray, but Sadie and Gramma saw him differently. Barnaby was one cool kitty and never got distracted from his sightseeing. As Sadie's nails scratched behind his ears, he purred along happily . . . in total bliss.

As Gramma turned left onto her block, Barnaby seemed to be checking out the street sign. Sadie couldn't be sure. She never knew if he was really doing these things or whether she imagined them. He felt human, like a family member hanging out with her and Gramma.

As they pulled up the driveway, Sadie could have sworn she

saw a dark cloud cross her grandmother's face. *That's weird*, she thought. It was only for a second, but the cloud had been there.

"Is everything okay, Gramma?"

"Of course, Sadie! What could be wrong on such an enjoyable day when we're together?" She winked and climbed out of the car.

Sadie knew she saw something, certainly the concern on Gramma's face, but she let it go and followed her inside.

Gramma's home was completely different from Sadie's. It was two stories, unlike the ranch house where she and her parents lived.

Gramma Rose said Grampa Henry loved their antique furniture, but once he'd passed, she needed to remodel. The Scandinavian furniture had clean lines and fit Gramma's personality better. The two things she saved for sentimental reasons were the high-backed chairs. They resembled thrones made of purple velvet and were decorated with carvings. Sadie felt like royalty sitting on them. She was happy Gramma didn't give those away.

Mom and Dad, on the other hand, had changed their modern furniture as often as they could afford to. It was as if they didn't know what they liked. One couch would be too firm; the other had that sinking feeling.

Gramma's entryway displayed a grand staircase, adorned with pictures around its curve. Photographs filled nearly every room. She and Grampa Henry had been United States Peace Ambassadors and had traveled the world frequently. These days, Gramma chose to explore many places she hadn't seen closer to home. She started with her own state first, leaving for weeks at a time and surprising Sadie with souvenirs upon her return.

As Sadie settled into the familiar surroundings, she spotted Gramma taking an extra moment to look at the photographs.

She looked as though she were reliving beloved memories. Her face wore a mixture of longing and serenity. In the next moment, however, she was her usual cheerful self.

"It's always such a special day when you're here, Sadie. We have a lot on our fun-time schedule, starting with Barnaby feeding."

Sadie smiled. *Gramma is the silliest.*

"Come on, Barnaby. Lunch time," Gramma sang.

Barnaby came running and gave Gramma a sideways look.

"Yes, I know, Barnaby. We're running a little late today. You saw the traffic on the way over."

Her explanation seemed to pacify him. Gramma placed his salmon and peas in his favorite bowl on the floor, and he dug in. Barnaby loved to eat.

"Look how Barnaby loves his salmon and peas, Sadie."

"Are you sure, Gramma? I wouldn't like that combination if I were him."

"Meow." Barnaby lifted his head, squinted, and made moony eyes at Sadie.

"See, Sadie. Barnaby's seal of approval."

After he finished, there was always some mushy food left on the bottom. Sadie knew how ridiculous it sounded, but every time she looked in his bowl, she saw pictures of another cat, a tree, a bird, or something else. Always something other than leftover cat food.

"Gramma, do you see that face in the bottom of Barnaby's dish?"

"Of course, honey. Barnaby's quite the Pawcasso."

Sadie's smile grew. "Ha-ha, Pawcasso. That's funny, Gramma."

Gramma smiled too. "Yeah, you know me, Sadie. I'm a laugh riot. Now that Barnaby's fed, how about we take care of ourselves? Would you like that?"

"Yes, Gramma. You know I love everything you make." Sadie

hopped up on the kitchen counter and pulled a wooden spoon from the canister near the cooktop. "What are we making today?"

Gramma knew how to cook and bake everything, and Sadie loved to help.

"I thought we'd make stuffed crepes. How does that sound?"

"Awesome."

Making the batter took a few minutes, and Sadie gave the bowl a final stir before settling in to watch her favorite part. Gramma tilted the pan, poured in the batter, swirled it around, and then, as each one started to form, she flipped it over.

Sadie watched with awe. After Gramma had cooked all the crepes, they sat at the table and stuffed them. They had their choice of sweet fillings of blueberries, sweet cherries, chocolate chips, cotton-candy cream, and sprinkles. Sadie knew Gramma had provided the creative choices just for her. After they rolled the crepes tightly, tucking in the edges, Gramma put them back in the pan until they were golden brown. Topped with hot fudge and whipped cream, they were unbeatable for taste.

"Go on," Gramma offered. She always let Sadie take the first bite.

Without hesitation, Sadie pressed her fork into the crispy crepe, which contained a little of everything, and heard that perfect crunch. Next she mopped up the toppings with the first bite.

She closed her eyes, sighing as she chewed. These crepes were more delicious than the last time she'd had them.

"Wow, Gramma. You've outdone yourself."

"Perfect." Gramma brightened. "I'm so pleased you like them."

"Mmm. How could I not? You're the bestest cook ever."

"I don't know about that, but thank you." Gramma handed Sadie a napkin and poured her a glass of milk.

"What would you like to do now?" she asked after they finished eating. "Watch a movie?"

Sadie nodded.

"What would you like to watch?" Gramma asked, already knowing the answer.

They laughed after they'd both proposed *Willy Wonka* at the same time.

"Jinx." Sadie giggled, crossing her fingers.

Gramma chuckled. "Don't you ever get tired of that movie?"

"No, it's my favorite. "I love Charlie's relationship with his grandpa. Then the end of course, when Charlie gets the factory by giving back the candy. I love that something like that could happen when you do the right thing."

Sitting on the sofa with a big bowl of buttery popcorn between them, Sadie and Gramma Rose crunched their way through the movie.

"Do you think you'd give back the candy like Charlie did?" asked Gramma.

"I hope so. I'd like to think I would, but you never know what you'll do until your integrity is tested. I'm sure you've always done the right thing, haven't you, Gramma?"

Gramma laughed and turned slightly to face Sadie. "Nobody's perfect. It's from our mistakes that we learn the most, but I think that once a lesson is learned, or if we reach deep inside ourselves when faced with a tough decision, we can somehow do what's right for all involved. Do you understand what I mean?"

Sadie nodded. "I think so. I always want to be like Charlie."

Gramma put an arm around her granddaughter. "Do your best. Try to be kind to everyone, Sadie. We all make mistakes, my girl. It's part of being human."

Sadie jumped at the sound of the doorbell after dark, and Gramma dropped the empty popcorn bowl on the coffee table. Barnaby rushed from upstairs to accompany her to the door.

Sadie listened, but the conversation was muffled. She glanced over her shoulder and saw a black hat hovering behind Gramma's head. The visitor wasn't invited inside. In fact, there was an intensity to their short discussion. The deeper voice remained calm, but Gramma's sounded abrupt and raised. "Not now. It's the worst possible time. No, I haven't. Thank you. Good night."

Sadie knew by Gramma's tone that she was upset. "Who was that?"

"Just a salesman. They come at all hours. It's annoying." She paused for a moment then continued. "Sadie?"

"Yes, Gramma?"

Gramma twisted her wedding ring round and round on her finger before looking into Sadie's eyes. "Please come upstairs with me. There's something I need to show you."

A heaviness settled in the pit of Sadie's stomach. "Is everything okay?"

Gramma nodded with a half-smile before climbing the stairs. Sadie followed.

"I'll wait in the bedroom while you brush your teeth and put on your pajamas," directed Gramma.

After Sadie finished getting ready for bed, she went into the bedroom she always stayed in at her grandmother's. Then she crawled into the bed next to Gramma, who sat there wearing an unusual expression. Her eyes focused on Sadie. Though she'd said she was okay, Gramma seemed sad and concerned.

She waited to speak until after Sadie had settled under the blankets.

"Look, my girl," Gramma said, pulling something out of her pocket. A different "Gramma voice" emerged—one Sadie never had heard. It was serious and soft, as if she didn't want anyone else to hear. "Sadie, I have something for you."

"Really?"

"Yes. A present. A very special present that you must keep safe."

"What is it, Gramma?" Sadie wondered as she sat straight up.

"Do you promise you'll always keep it safe?"

"Yes, Gramma. Always. I pinky swear. Is this why you seem so serious?"

"Yes, a little bit. I don't want you to worry, but you have to know that it's important."

"I understand, Gramma. You can count on me."

"Okay then, Sadie. I trust you'll keep this treasure safe. Thank you." She handed Sadie a small music box.

A perfect purple rose sat atop the ornate golden box. It played a sweet and gentle song. Sadie recognized it as "Lara's Theme," the one Gramma always hummed.

"This is an incredibly rare music box. In fact, it's the only one like it in this world. When you play it, I'll always be with you.

Sadie whistled, surprising herself. "Gramma, I promise. I'll keep it safe."

"You'll see its abilities grow as you do."

Sadie looked confused. "What does that mean? How can a music box have abilities or even grow for that matter?"

"You'll know it when you experience it, Sadie. Take care of it, please."

"It's enchanting. Can I show it to anyone, like Mom and Dad? Is there anything I need to know? Like where it came from?" A shiver ran up Sadie's arm, the one holding the gift.

"For now I'd like you to keep it to yourself. If that changes, I'll let you know."

"Okay, Gramma. Thank you so much. I love it, especially the purple rose on top." Sadie hugged and kissed Gramma before running her fingers over the tiny flower. Then she opened the lid. She listened to the song a second time then placed the music box on the nightstand.

Gramma tucked her in. Sadie hummed the song from the music box. Then Gramma planted a kiss on her forehead. "Good night, my sweet Sadie. May you always live with peace and love in your heart."

As long as Gramma was with me, I always did.

Sadie shifted her neck from where she'd been staring out from the window seat. It was bittersweet to snap out of those memories, the last one being the echo of Gramma's footsteps on the stairs. She rose to retrieve her music box and listen to its song. She hardly noticed Rufus falling to the carpet. *It's surprising how strange that conversation with Gramma still* seems, she thought. *I never did get the chance to ask her where she got this music box.*

CHAPTER NINE

Guilty or Gardening?

Frank Reid crawled out of bed and pulled the covers up around Marj, careful not to wake her. She'd been up late, looking over Finn's homework in preparation for his home-school tutor. Frank was glad she liked doing it, as it wasn't his favorite chore. He woke early, as he always did on Saturdays, enjoying a few leisurely minutes over a cup of coffee before taking on the rest of the day.

He shuffled downstairs in his robe and opened the front door to fetch the paper. Spring had arrived in full bloom, and though it was only the second week of April, they were already enjoying the glorious wash of color in Marj's immaculate flower garden.

He picked up the *Hallstown Gazette* and stopped short. Dozens of bright-yellow daffodils, orange tulips, and fragrant lavender hyacinths littered the yard, torn up from the roots and tossed into the grass like weeds.

Frank went back inside the house, closed the door, and tried to shake off the image he'd just seen. He began over again, opening the door, sure that it had all been a mirage.

But it wasn't an illusion. Someone had ripped out all of Marj's flowers. Frank reentered his home in time to catch Finn's gleeful eyes spying on him from around the corner by the stairs. Something wasn't right.

"Finn, do you need something?"

In a singsong voice oddly out of place, Finn hummed, "No, no. Nothing at all." He plopped onto the living-room rocking chair and gave it a push.

A slow shiver began at the bottom of Frank's spine and worked its way up to the hair on his head. He looked at Finn, who was happily rocking away. *No, it can't be. I need to talk to Marj.*

With halting steps, Frank climbed the stairs and entered their bedroom. He hesitated before waking her, but a quick glance out the window to the mayhem below set his resolve.

"Dear?"

"Yes . . . What is it, Frank?" Marj mumbled groggily.

"Marj, we need to talk."

"Now? Are you serious?" She yawned then sat up and wiped the sleep out of her eyes.

"Yes, I'm afraid I am. You might want to splash some water on your face first." Frank sat on the bed next to her, pulling her close for a sideways hug. His expression transformed from one of compassion to fear.

Marj, brow furrowed, sat up and searched her husband's gray eyes. "Frank, what's wrong? Are you okay? You don't seem yourself."

"I don't know how to say this, but I think Finn might have pulled up all the flowers in your garden."

Marj's light-brown eyes grew wide as she got out of bed. "What are you talking about? The flowers are still in the garden, surely?"

"I was just outside. Every last one was yanked out of the ground. I hate to tell you, and I hate even more to implicate Finn, but—"

She shook her head. "Finn? It can't be Finn. I don't believe that for a second. I *won't* believe it. Did you see him do it? Do you have proof?"

Frank sighed. "I don't have any proof, just a feeling. When I came back inside, he was watching me. It was like he was waiting to see my reaction."

"I think I could use that cold water now, if you don't mind." She hurried to the bathroom.

Frank waited for the water to stop. "Is there anything I can do to help, love?" After twelve years together, he didn't need to hear her response to know the water hadn't helped. Concern etched itself across her forehead in ever-deepening creases.

"No, I'm okay," she reassured him, tightening the belt around her terrycloth bathrobe. "I'm as ready as I'll ever be. Let's continue this conversation downstairs."

The door still had that squeak he needed to oil. It sounded louder than ever. He would fix it today, he decided. They walked outside, and Frank stood beside his wife as she took in the complete destruction of her carefully planned garden. He wrapped an arm around her shoulders and waited for her to speak. All her hard work and pleasure in the results . . . gone overnight.

In a barely audible monotone, she droned, "Frank, please ask Finn to come out here for a second."

"Are you sure, Marj? Are you up to confronting him right now?"

"Yes, dear. I don't believe it was him."

"But—"

"Just wait. We'll see soon enough."

Marj scanned the other houses in their neighborhood. Their garden wasn't the only one vandalized. Mrs. Mulvaney's prize begonias were strewn across the sidewalk, and Old Man Garfinkel's rosebushes had been trampled.

"Who would do such a thing, Frank?"

Frank walked inside shaking his head. A few moments later, the front door squeaked again as he and Finn joined Marj in the front yard. He wore the face of innocence.

"Finn, dear, do you know anything about what happened to my flowers?" Marj asked. "To our neighbors' gardens? Did you see or hear anything during the night or morning?"

"I don't know anything about it. You don't think I did this, do you?" Hurt crept into his voice, and a crop of tears filled his eyes.

"I don't, sweetheart. I just wanted to find out whether you knew anything about it. Maybe you saw something through your window. It does face the front after all."

Finn shrugged. "No. I just woke up."

Marj smiled at him and pulled him in for a warm hug.

Frank looked on with a queasy feeling brewing in his stomach.

"I didn't mean to upset you. I'm sure it'll all get sorted soon." Marj ruffled Finn's hair and touched his cheek. "Go get ready for your Spanish tutor, and make sure you brush your teeth."

"*Si, si,*" Finn sang, and went inside, softly humming to himself.

Frank wanted to apologize to Marj for accusing the boy, but a lingering doubt hung in his chest. He said nothing as he retrieved his paper and headed for the kitchen.

CHAPTER TEN

The Mist Rose Alone

SADIE NEARLY TRIPPED over Rufus. *Oops, almost forgot to hide you.*

Once she had hidden Rufus, she went back to the window seat, all but ready to fall asleep.

Some movement in the backyard caught her attention. Wispy clouds drew close and gathered together, low to the ground. Sadie looked to her neighbors on the left and right but didn't see anything unusual in their yards. What started as a ball of fog stretched slowly, from bottom to top, thinner as it climbed. It swirled and spun as it drifted closer to the house. It never left her yard.

Even as tired as she was, Sadie stared, unable to blink. Now she saw a distinct head and arms. What should have been legs was more like floating, formless mist on the bottom. *Shape-changing fog. That's a new one.* The top half grew more defined, and Sadie leaned closer for a better look. "It can't be!" She put her hand on the window. The cold of the glass shot up her arm and through the rest of her body.

With a sharp breath of air, Sadie's cry of "Gramma..." echoed in the room. *I'm seeing things that just can't be,* she thought. But then the sweet scent of roses enveloped her.

"Oh, Gramma, I miss you."

The apparition nodded. Then, as if its sole purpose were to wait for Sadie's recognition, it blended into the night as if it never was.

Sadie took another deep breath and sank down on the window seat, her eyes still searching the moonlit lawn. Goose bumps were the only remaining evidence that the apparition had been there at all. Relief mixed with sadness during every heartbeat. *Why did Gramma Rose come here? Was she trying to tell me something?* "Please come back!" she cried out. "I need to know more!"

Head bobbing, Sadie gave in. She knew another sighting wasn't going to happen tonight. Within seconds she fell asleep.

CHAPTER ELEVEN

Just Journaling

MARJ REPLANTED HER garden without further incident. Though it never regained its springtime magnificence, it did earn an award from the local gardening club. Summer was quiet and filled with sprinklers and weekend trips to Tivern Lake. Finn's home-school grades made Marj proud. He caught up and even surpassed his grade level. With autumn approaching, all seemed well, though Finn's memories still hadn't returned.

Even though Marj saw the strained relationship between Frank and Finn, the boy proved himself trustworthy, and the warm, loving father she knew her husband could be returned.

It was rare that Marj had the house to herself on a Saturday, but Frank had promised Finn a round of miniature golf and ice cream afterward. With the last few days of a Rocky Mountain summer upon them, she urged them to go have fun.

Marj took the opportunity to catch up on chores. She folded a basket of Finn's laundry and carried it upstairs to his room. She balanced it on her knee and turned Finn's doorknob with her other hand. She looked around and smiled. She never once had seen a boy be so tidy with his room. Put that together with his stellar grades, and she couldn't ask for more. She might try talking to Frank again about the adoption, later when they had some time alone.

As Marj put away his clothing, she admired the awards Finn had won from their municipal chess club. Marj went to every practice and match. She was his most avid fan.

The trophies were arranged on his shelves along with his prized mystery novels. All that remained to put away were his jeans. She tucked them in and closed the bottom drawer. That's when she heard it: a clunk and a thud.

What was that?

She reopened the drawer. The clothing now slanted, she took it out and placed it on the bed. *I'll have to get Frank to fix this when he and Finn get home.* She touched the raised side, and something slid.

Hmm. She moved the bottom of the drawer back and forth until it broke free in her hands.

"It's fake!"

Confused, she pulled up the fake bottom and immediately saw the lime-green journal underneath. At first she didn't know what to do. Finn deserved his privacy as much as she would want hers. She went to put it back, but that little voice inside urged her to take a peek.

As she turned page after page, her heart pounded in her chest. One tear and then another streamed down her cheeks. She couldn't stop looking, her horror growing with each new entry.

Amid violent drawings of what obviously represented Finn, red splashes adorned most of the pages and covered two prone bodies—one male, one female—lying at his feet, flowers strewn around them. What few words were written were like knife wounds to her heart.

They will die!
They must die!

How long must I endure their nauseating presence?
My day will come!
Why won't you speak to me?
I've been waiting all these months for you to come back.
    Where are you?!
Tell me when to do it already!

The book dropped out of her hands as she followed it to the floor. The room spun, and she had no sense of time as she lay there.

When she came around, she didn't think. She acted.

CHAPTER TWELVE

J'Accuse!

*B*UZZZZZZ!

Ugh, morning already? Is it a school day? I think it is—crap! I thought a good night's sleep and Gramma's visit would help . . . but no. I'm not sure what I despise more: being home or being at school. There's nothing for me now. I'm just going through the motions. Thank goodness for my books, or I'd really be in trouble.

Sadie moped to the bathroom. Not fully awake, she sleepwalked through her usual routine: brushing her teeth and quickly running a comb through her hair. At least her comb didn't meet any resistance. Today's date wormed its way into her consciousness: October eleventh. Two beats later and she realized it: not only had everyone else forgotten her birthday yesterday but so had she. *That's a lifetime first.*

Heading off to the kitchen, she glanced at the happy family photos that dotted the walls. *What a crock. Are they ever going to take these lies off the walls? I don't know why they keep them up there. It's ridiculous.*

Sadie walked into the kitchen; no one was there to happily greet her with breakfast. *What a shock.* She couldn't remember the last time she'd eaten a cooked breakfast. Her father always left for work before sunup, and her mother rarely made an appearance from her room before Sadie had to leave for school. It was always the same. *Mom still in bed . . . surprise, surprise. Crappy cereal and crappy orange juice with crappy pulp. Good morning, Sadie. Here's your trifecta of crap. Doesn't she care that I can't stand pulp?* Sadie retrieved the strainer from the drawer and poured the juice through it into her glass. She took a tentative sip. *Relatively pulp free,* she thought, carrying it to the table.

She quickly ate, started to clean up, then stopped. She usually did her own dishes, but today she didn't care.

"Sorry, Mom," she said, and tossed her bowl and spoon into the sink.

I know you're going to be pissed when you finally wake up and see the messy kitchen, but I really don't care how you feel. You forgot my freakin' birthday—how could you?

Sadie caught the reflection of her sour face in the window. *I don't think even I want to be around myself today.* She tried on a smile, but it only lasted a few seconds. She didn't have anything to smile about. She had betrayed herself just like everyone else.

I am not going to play this smiley game. If it's time to drag myself through another dreadful week, then I'll do it, but I don't have to be happy about it. How did Monday get here so fast?

Her walk to school was uneventful. Growing more miserable with every step, she looked down at the gray sidewalk under her feet and counted the cracks. Although she heard birds chirping in the trees, she wasn't able to appreciate them. Head down, she kept plodding forward.

As she got closer to school, she heard the bell ring. *Oh, well, I guess I'm late. Big deal. I'll add this next pink slip to the pile of them in my locker.*

Sadie shuffled up the steps, took her time turning the

combination to her locker, then trudged down an empty hallway toward her first class.

"Come on, Sadie. Have a seat. I need to get started and can't wait for whenever you decide to grace us with your presence," said Mr. Blanc, her homeroom teacher.

She mumbled an incoherent apology and slid into her seat. Then she pulled out her notebook and started doodling, a daily ritual. She knew she could always catch up with her schoolwork on her own. She would read the night before her tests and still get A's. She did her homework during lunch and study hall. It was the only reason she wasn't in trouble at school.

After lunch was gym class. *Could they have picked a worse time for gym? Here—eat food then go run around outside. How many kids have to throw up on the blacktop before they figure this out? Eat and run, tons o' fun.*

As Sadie's classmates headed out, she had no desire or energy to keep up with them. She waited until they had crossed the first set of basketball courts, and then she took the shortcut to the sprawling, green soccer fields. After that she turned right and followed the yellow line that circled the entire blacktop.

Ten minutes later, she finally joined her classmates.

"Where were you, Myers?" asked her gym teacher, Mr. Wagner.

"I . . . I was cold so I went back to my locker to get my jacket."

"You aren't allowed to just take off without permission."

Everyone gathered around.

Can't they just mind their own business? "I'm sorry, Mr. Wagner. It won't happen again."

"It had better not, Myers." He blew the bright-silver whistle around his neck. "You can thank your fellow classmate for this one, girls. Give me two laps around the field everyone."

"Seriously? Do we have to? Come on!" groaned her classmates.

"You know the answer! Get moving!"

"Nice going, Sadie," Cathy Sanders shouted in her ear.

Sadie made a face and started to run, her school-lunch tacos grumbling miserably in her stomach.

Twenty minutes later, Mr. Wagner blew his whistle a second time, ordering everyone back to their lockers.

Sadie, still panting from her run, changed back into her regular clothes and hurried to her English class. *They don't even give us enough time to get cleaned up after gym. We smell like a zoo.*

She plunked into her seat and rummaged around in her bag, pulling out a pen.

"Where is it?" shouted Kylie Robinson.

Kylie wore a floral shift dress with a cropped cardigan sweater. The blooms on its pattern complemented the caramel shade of her perfect skin. Petite, she had striking amber eyes now full of tears, ready to fall.

"Where's what?" asked Kenny Barker. Kenny, perpetually sunburned, had red hair and piercing green eyes. He hovered over Kylie's desk.

"My monarch butterfly pin. It's missing! I set it on my desk while I put my sweater on the back of my chair. How could it just disappear? It was only a few seconds. Oh, no! My mother gave it to me. I can't believe it's gone."

Kylie wore that pin every day. Pink jewels sparkled on baby-blue wings, and it was as light as a leaf.

Kylie put her head on her desk and started to cry. She was popular, so no one made fun of her. "Oh, Kylie, don't cry. We'll help you find it," assured Kenny.

Sadie stayed in her seat while everyone looked around; it wasn't long before people noticed.

"Why aren't you helping us, Sadie? Is it because you have it?" Kenny accused her.

Sadie pulled her shoulders forward and frowned. "Why would I take it?"

Alex Chen pointed at her. "I saw you do it." He had jet-black hair, shaved close to his head, and cinnamon-brown eyes.

"How did you see me, Alex?"

"I looked over at Kylie and saw you take it."

Sadie glowered at him. "I was busy getting ready for class. I don't know how you have time to see what everyone else is doing."

"You sit right next to her. It has to be you!" roared Kenny.

Some other kids nodded, and the circle around Sadie grew tighter.

"Leave me alone." She folded her arms and sunk down in her seat, avoiding all eye contact. Beads of sweat formed on her forehead.

"We're going to keep our eyes on you, Myers," Kenny informed her. "You won't get away with this."

Sadie picked up her pen, waving it in front of her eyes until its line became blurry. It helped her ignore them.

Kenny glared at her. "Just wait until Dave finds out."

The meanest kid in her year, Dave Jablonsky, was out sick. He probably would have held her down and had the other kids search her. The thought of him getting involved made her sick to her stomach. As if in response, it started gurgling. One loud one seemed to go on forever, and she wondered whether anyone else could hear it.

"What's all this?" a voice asked, punctuating the question with a pile of books hitting the front desk. Her English teacher, Ms. Argello, had come in without anyone realizing it. The crowd quickly backed off and sat down.

A few minutes later, Sadie stole a glance at Kenny. He made a motion with his hands, pointing at his eyes, then at her. He mouthed the words, "I'm watching you." Sadie shook her head and turned back around in her seat. She kept her eyes on her notebook for the rest of the class.

Even without knowing what had transpired, Ms. Argello somehow knew not to call on her.

CHAPTER THIRTEEN

You Screwed up, Kiddo

Finn waited in silence, hands cuffed behind his back. He sat on a curved, hard-plastic chair that made it impossible to get comfortable due to its awkward shape and unyielding construction. He longed to be elsewhere.

Why am I here? he wondered.

The room was empty but for the lingering cigarette smoke. Tendrils of tobacco burned his nostrils. The police officers had intimidated him, but he'd succeeded in shutting them down. Frustrated, they'd finally left him.

Finn was self-amusing, running revenge scenarios through his mind one by one. First he would kill this chair, which ate into his spine with relentless fury. He had no idea what was going on or why he was here. No one told him anything.

Where are those Reids? Supposedly they care about me . . . whatever that means. They're always going on about it. Though he watched and waited, they never showed.

Last he knew, he and Frank were having "fun" together. *What went wrong? I had it down to a tee. Something or someone got in my way, and when I find out who it was, it'll be dark days for them.*

How did THAT turn into THIS? Finn took a mental tour

through the events of the day, putting remembered pieces of experience into place.

Finn and Frank had laughed and joked as they'd driven home after a "father and son" outing. Ice cream cones in hand, they had turned onto their street.

Finn had sat up straighter when he noticed the flashing lights ahead.

"I wonder what's going on down there?" asked Frank. "I hope everyone's okay. Wait! Are they in front of *our* house?"

Finn watched as Frank's hands shook, followed by the rest of him. Frank's cone fell into his lap, which amused Finn. The car screeched to a halt, and Frank ran out, driver's door still open. Finn saw what was going on. It was hard to hear, so he got out and stood next to the car.

Two policemen guarded the front door, blocking Frank's way, while two others moved quickly toward the car . . . and Finn.

"Marj! Marj! Are you all right?" Frank yelled, trying to push past the officers at the door. "Let me in. I'm her husband. This is my house. Please let me see her," he begged, sobbing.

The police blocking Frank looked toward the car, where their colleagues held Finn by both arms. That's when they'd allowed Frank to push past them and into the house.

Hey, there, kiddo, Finn heard, as he sat in the hard-plastic chair. *It's a pleasure to see you again . . . and in such a royal setting as well.*

"Hello? Are you really here? I've called and called for nearly a year, and now you come back?"

That's how I roll, buckaroo. Better get used to it.

"Do you have any idea what I'm doing here instead of being in my own room?"

Sure do.

"Well, spill it then."

Silence.

"Please?"

That's better. I know you have the game down.

"Yes, I know . . . I'm quite the actor, but why am I here? I did everything you requested!"

Not everything. I advised you to be smarter than they were. It turns out you're worse than stupid at hiding your journal of pretty pictures.

"I *am* smarter," Finn growled with shrinking conviction. "Wait, what about my journal? They couldn't have found it. I took care of that."

Then why are they the ones comfortable at home, while you're at the police station in serious trouble?

Finn didn't answer. If this was the way the Voice meant to talk to him, then the Voice could just piss off.

The Voice, whatever it was, took the hint . . . and Finn was alone again.

CHAPTER FOURTEEN

Best Friends Forever

*T*HANK GOODNESS TODAY *is over.* Sadie shuffled toward her locker. *I don't think I could have taken one more second of English class. It's bad enough just being at school. Now I have to deal with more trouble, just like at home.*

She turned the combination for the umpteenth time that day and shoved her books inside. Lockers opened all around her, many of them decorated with a blur of bright colors and photos, things she couldn't see clearly.

She spotted a realistic charcoal drawing of a windmill the next locker over. She reached over to touch it with her fingers but then thought better of it. She recalled when she used to place her art on her locker door, back when school was fun. She remembered looking forward to study hall so she could hang out with Melanie Greene and their friends.

I can almost touch that time, and I miss it. I miss you, Melanie.

"Where should we go today, Sadie?"

"Let's go to the swing tree."

Melanie and Sadie had hopped on their bikes and raced down their street toward the tree.

Legend had it that a mysterious stranger had tied the tire swing to a hundred-year oak so the neighborhood kids could play. Everyone remembered that he wore a funny black hat—that was the only detail anyone ever gave of the man.

It was just an old tire swing, but all the kids were drawn to its enchantment. Today Sadie and Melanie got lots of time in without anyone else there. Later, when a few others came, that was their cue to leave.

"Okay, Sadie, let's get back. Dad should be home soon, and I don't want him to worry."

"Can we make caramel corn and milkshakes when we get back?"

"But of course, Noodle Head."

Melanie called Sadie "Noodle Head" because of her ever-present pigtails.

"Lead the way, Melbell," Sadie chirped as they both climbed back on their bikes.

Melanie got her nickname from the bell-shaped birthmark on her neck—plus it rhymed.

They headed toward Melanie's house. "You make the best caramel corn. I could eat it every day."

"Then you'd be ginormous, Sadie. I wouldn't want to have to change your nickname to 'Six-Ton Sadie.'"

Sadie rolled her eyes. "Nice, Melanie. Real nice."

They both laughed. Melanie and Sadie had been best friends since age five. Melanie was slim, leggy, and almost as tall as Sadie. She had cropped blond hair and sky-blue eyes. Her family had moved into the neighborhood, and the instant the two little girls had met, they had become a pair, going everywhere together. When Melanie's mother passed away after a long battle with cancer, their friendship grew even tighter.

"Hey, you staying over tomorrow night?" Melanie asked, after they'd gorged themselves with caramel corn and chocolate shakes.

"Just need to check with Mom, but it should be a go."

"Cool. See you tomorrow then, Six-Ton."

"Hope you forget about that one, Melanie, or I'm gonna have to give you a new name too. Be afraid . . . be very afraid."

"Ha-ha. Okay, Sadie. You win . . . this time. See ya."

The next night, after dinner, Sadie headed over to Melanie's. Sleepovers at her house were the best, especially because her dad was really nice. He would set up a movie screen in the backyard when the weather was clear.

"Melanie, you're one lucky girl," Sadie confided, as they sat in lawn chairs, waiting for Melanie's dad to set up the screen.

"I know, Sadie, but so are you. You have both your parents."

"Yeah, I know." Sadie wanted to say something helpful but didn't have the words. "What are we watching tonight?"

"I think Dad said *Princess Bride*."

"Oh, great. I love that movie."

They all watched the movie, reciting favorite lines along with the story. At the end, they rose to their feet with a round of applause.

"It reminds me of *The Love Story of Christopher and Sadie*," Melanie teased, once her father had gone into the house.

"Yeah, sure. I just need to get Christopher to say all those things to me and I'll be set."

"Ha, I'm sure you can, Sadie. He's totally into you."

Sadie blushed then turned away, but in the next moment she was back, smiling.

It was a calm night by the fire pit, so they hung out and talked for a while.

"So, Noodle Head," Melanie said, "I heard two weird stories about the Fletcher house all in one week."

"Tell me." Sadie leaned closer.

"I heard another family lived there before the Fletchers. A family nobody talks about."

"Really? Sadie asked, her eyes larger. The pitch of her voice rose higher. "Who were they?"

"There's not much to tell, only that they died in a car crash right outside of town."

"That's disturbing. How come this is the first we're hearing about it?"

"Don't know, Sadie. That's all I could get out of Dave."

"You'd think he'd know more about it. He knows everything about everyone."

"Not this time." The girls got up and collected their empty cups and plates.

"It's funny," Sadie mused. "The Fletchers have been gone for a long time, and I still can't call it anything but the Fletcher house."

"Gone? That's putting it mildly!" Melanie exclaimed. "Mr. Fletcher lost his mind after their son disappeared."

Both girls found their seats again.

"Then he shot her in the head and shot himself. Nobody found them for days until the mailman called the police. Apparently there was an awful smell coming from the house and a pile of mail stacking up."

"Kids are always talking about how that house makes people do strange things." Sadie shivered, hugging her knees to her chest.

"Yeah, I stay way clear of that house." Melanie shuddered slightly as well.

"Me too. For sure."

The old Fletcher house, as it had come to be known, stood at the loneliest corner of its triple-acre lot. It was past the cul-de-sac, after the modern-day neighborhoods ended. The wooden slats barely hung together in most places, and errant tree limbs had broken some of the windows. It once had been a respectable farmhouse, but long lacking in care, it was now worn down.

The woods behind that house appeared to go on forever. No one in the neighborhood really knew how vast they were.

Parents were too busy working to care. Kids didn't have the nerve it took to explore and find out just how far back those trees extended or where they led.

"Anyway," Melanie went on, "the last I heard of anyone living there was this group of girls about ten years ago. They were from out of town, and they rented the place for that summer. They had no idea what they were in for, but I overheard my sister telling my mom that she was at the grocery store the other day, and one of the girls came back to town and spoke with the cashier about her experience there." Melanie paused to catch her breath, then continued.

"She hinted that some really weird things happened, and did he know anything about the house before or since? The realtor never mentioned a thing to them. The girl was curious now because back then she was too afraid to ask. So the cashier told the renter girl about what happened to the Fletchers, and my sister said the girl turned white as paste."

"And then what happened?" Sadie prodded.

"The cashier asked her what was wrong, and she told him that all the girls had heard strange noises and felt cold breezes blowing past them throughout the house. One night, while she slept on the couch, she woke up and saw an old man's face floating right above her. It was craggy, bearded, and half its face was missing. She said it looked like it was about to speak."

"Wow. That's creepy."

"I know," Melanie agreed, inching back a bit from the fire. "She said she screamed until she couldn't scream anymore. Then it disappeared. She thought she was dreaming, but now she knew she wasn't. She said after that happened, she couldn't go back in the house or anywhere near it. Now, years later, curiosity got the best of her, so she came back to town to find out about the house's history."

"So weird. I've never heard that story before, but I've

heard about people staying overnight on a dare. They threw parties and wrecked the inside. But eventually they stopped going."

Melanie raised her eyebrows. "So . . . I'm thinking we should go check out the house."

Sadie shook her head. "Uh, no way, Melanie. Are you out of your mind?"

"Sometimes, ha-ha."

"Yeah, me too, but not that much." Sadie couldn't tell whether Melanie was relieved that she'd said no, or if she was trying to think of a way to convince her to go.

"Well, speaking of ghosts, how about some Ouija?" Melanie suggested.

"Ooh. Okay. I'm up for that."

"Are you sure? You still look pretty scared. I've never seen you that shade of pale before, and it looks like you're sweating up a storm."

"I am not. I'm not scared. I'm sitting up straight as straight can be. See?"

"Oh, we'll see about that all right . . . after some Ouija."

The girls got up and went into the living room to say good night to Melanie's dad.

"Good night, girls."

"Good night, Dad," they replied in unison.

They headed upstairs, took out their sleeping bags, and set up their bedroom camp. Then they sat on the floor with the board between them.

"I wonder who we'll be talking to tonight."

"How about Mr. Fletcher?" asked Melanie.

"Oh, I hope not. I heard he wasn't very nice to begin with. And if the house did make him psycho, I definitely don't want to talk to him."

"Well, then, I'm gonna say 'some nineteenth-century dude.'"

"I don't think they called them dudes back then," Sadie quipped.

"No? I thought guys were always dudes."

"Ha-ha, that's funny, Melbell."

"Okay. Let's get serious," Melanie proposed, her smirk transforming into a straight line.

"Okay. Let's."

They placed their fingers on the pointer.

"No pushing."

"I never push."

"Uh-huh."

"Really. No pushing."

"Geez, Melanie. Just say it already."

"Okay, okay. Spirits from beyond . . . what message do you have for us tonight?"

The big lights were off, so they used a small desk lamp. They wanted it to be super spooky in the room. They always freaked themselves out, but it was still fun despite their fear.

First letter: *H*, followed by *E*, then *L*. Melanie and Sadie looked up at each other, outwardly nervous. The pointer zoomed straight for *P*.

"'Help.' You promised you wouldn't push, Sades."

"If I was pushing, the last letter would've been *L*. So there."

"Very funny. Ha-ha. Okay, I guess it really is 'Help.' Hmm."

Shaking a bit now, Sadie had trouble holding her fingers steady on the pointer. "Uh, okay, spirit. What are you trying to tell us?" Fingers back on the pointer. First letter *I*, then *A*, then *M*.

"'I am' what, spirit?" Melanie asked.

The letters started flowing again: *A*, *T*, then *T*, *H*, *E*.

"'I am at the . . . '? Where are you, spirit?"

Once again the pointer took off in short order: *B*, *O*, *T*. It paused before it quickly zipped to *T*, *O*, *M*.

"'I am at the bottom . . . '"

They looked at each other nervously, thinking the same thing: *Should we finish?*

They didn't realize they hadn't spoken that out loud; then Melanie answered the unspoken question. "I think we have to now."

O, F, T, H, E. "'I am at the bottom of the . . . '" After some hesitation, they put their fingers back on the pointer. The flurry of letters now in the past, the pointer moved excruciatingly slow. *B, E . . .* They were sweating now. Cemented in place after what seemed like an interminable moment, they watched as the pointer landed on *D* then stopped.

"*Bed!*"

"Oh, my God. He's at the bottom of my bed! Ahhhhhhhh! Hurry, Sadie. Get up!"

Sadie froze in place. Flashes of red that looked like heat lightning appeared by her feet and nearly struck her toes.

"Come on, Sadie! Run!"

Sadie couldn't move. "*Sadie!*" Melanie grabbed her shoulders and shook her out of her trance.

They both screamed and ran out of the room . . . right into Melanie's dad.

"Okay, girls. Calm down. Get back to bed."

"I don't know if I can," gulped Melanie.

"You girls are always scaring yourselves. Come on. I'll take you in."

Melanie's dad looked around the room. "See? There's nothing here."

"Buh . . . but you didn't look in the closet, Dad."

He opened the door. "Look, nothing's in here."

"Are you sure?" Melanie asked, as she peeked around her father's broad back.

"Yes, Melanie." Her dad sighed. "All's well. Time for bed."

"Uh, okay, Daddy."

Once he had gone and they had settled into their sleeping bags, Melanie flipped on her flashlight, shining it directly at Sadie, and whispered, "Sadie, what happened? It's like you weren't even here. Do you remember anything?"

Sadie put a hand in front of her eyes to block the blinding beam. "I remember seeing the red lights."

"I have no idea what you're talking about. Red lights? What red lights?"

"There were red flashes at the end of the bed. You didn't see them?"

"No, I definitely did not. I think the Ouija board messed with your head, Sades."

"Yeah, I guess you're right." Sadie stared at the floor at the end of Melanie's bed, thankful the red lights had vanished but frustrated that Melanie hadn't seen them.

"Come on. Let's try to get some sleep."

"Okay." Sadie's voice quavered as she hunkered as far into her sleeping bag as she could.

"Good night, Noodle Head. Sleep well."

"Good night, Melbell. You too. No scary dreams for us."

"Yeah. No scaries allowed."

A short while later, Sadie heard Melanie's breathing change and knew she had fallen asleep. She wasn't as lucky. Even though she'd said so, she wasn't sure the red lights had been her imagination.

The locker in front of Sadie slammed shut, and she was jolted out of her daydream.

It was Melanie and her new best friends. Their own friendship had ended a few weeks after Gramma had passed. Melanie had been there for her a little while, but then things had taken a bad turn.

"Come on, Sadie. Snap out of it," Melanie had told her. "Are you just going to sit here in your room all day? All the time? I know what happened to Gramma Rose has been awful. Believe me, if anyone understands what it's like to lose someone, it's me, but you have to come back. Let's go for a walk. We can go to the park or the swing tree. Anywhere but here in this room. It's been weeks, Noodle Head." She sat on the bed beside Sadie and hugged her neck. "Come on, Sadie. Let's get out of here."

"Leave me alone. Please just leave me alone," Sadie begged, pushing her friend away and lying down again, her back to Melanie.

"Sadie, look at you. You can't keep going on like this. Everyone at school is talking about you . . . about how you've 'weirded out.'"

"I don't care."

"Well, you should care. Everyone talks about how strange you are. You bump into desks and people. You knock over their stuff and never pick it up or say you're sorry. You never smile or talk anymore, and when you do speak, you're always sarcastic. What are people supposed to think? You've alienated everyone. I've tried telling them that you aren't like this, but they don't want anything to do with you."

"I don't care about anything," Sadie said into her pillow. "Not that horrible school. Not those stupid kids and not stupid you!" She sat up, grabbed the nearest book, and threw it at Melanie, barely missing her. "Go! Just go and leave me alone!"

"Geez, Sadie. You really are a freak." Melanie left the bedroom, slamming the door behind her.

Sadie crawled deeper under her covers, crying uncontrollably. "I don't care about any of them. They can all just leave me alone . . ."

Sadie's locker reverberated from the force of Melanie's slam. "What's the matter, Sadie? You've been staring at your open locker for like ten minutes. Were you dreaming that Christopher is coming back to save you from yourself?" The two girls next to her laughed.

Since their falling out, Melanie had become glued to her new best friends, Ronnie and Jade. She'd turned hostile, and those two had been more than willing to be her backup. Sadie couldn't speak; it broke her heart every time she saw Melanie. She knew it was her own fault but couldn't think of any way to fix what had happened between them.

"Come on, girls. She's useless. Let's go back to my house. My dad promised he'd set up the movie screen for us tonight."

Their voices trailed down the hallway. Sadie worked to block out the rest of their conversation as best she could until they were gone, all the while biting her lip to keep the tears at bay.

CHAPTER FIFTEEN

Take Your Medicine Like a Good Boy

STRAPPED TO A gurney in a too-white room with the now-familiar instruments of invasion, Finn still managed to fidget. He was more than halfway through the dozen shock treatments demanded by the screaming orange chart that hung from the end of his transport. It taunted him, but he didn't care. They always made him wait like this until Demon Doctor, his Royal Highness, Dr. Llewellyn, deigned to make an appearance. As always, his simpering servants in blue caps and long uniforms accompanied him.

Fine. Let them take forever. He tried to shield his eyes from the bright light, which focused its white beam on his face. There was no escape, even with his lids closed, as the horrid thing never requested permission.

That freaking burns. I'm not sure whether I'll live through this, but somehow I'll get my revenge. In this world or the next, I will have it.

Stay focused on the here and now, Finn. Remember everything you can, warned the familiar Voice in his head, who'd advised him when he'd first arrived.

Some advice, No Name. Soon they'll come in and make me fall into that black pit of theirs so they can perform their evil electric waltz.

Finn recalled being dragged from the police station and tossed into the back of a nondescript white van. He'd waited alone for someone to tell him what was going on, but when they had come for him, they hadn't said a single word. He had tried screaming and spitting and kicking, but he was outnumbered and alone. They were large brutes, and he was a lanky fourteen-year-old.

He remembered the pain in his arm, and how he'd screamed for a full minute as it worsened. "What are you doing to me? I demand to know!"

The fools looked at each other. Maybe they were expecting a different response? Wasn't I entitled to ask questions?

"Calm down now. You're beginning to feel sleepy a bit, yes?" one of the blue-sleeved trolls had asked.

"No. Are you?" And he had spat once more while imagining what it would feel like to kick her in the teeth.

That had resulted in extra-thick straps for his arms and legs, as well as a gag to cover his mouth. Finn smiled when he thought about it. It had taken six of them to accomplish the feat.

Then he had been on a moving trestle of some sort. It had squeaked as it rolled him along. He had turned his head and had seen the nasty tiles and grouting go by. He'd wound up in the too-white room. They left him alone then. He wondered what would come next.

But that was the beginning, and he'd since learned the score.

He heard the footsteps now, coming down the hall. He could identify each person by his or her own set, those imposters.

"Hello again, Finn. How are we feeling today?" Dr. Llewellyn boomed.

The doctor reminded Finn of one of the lunatic doctors in

the black-and-white movies he'd watched with Marj and Frank. The ones wielding their scalpels in the air and pulling down levers as they created their monsters.

From behind his gag, Finn tried to hurl swear words regarding his hate and their ineptitude, but it came out sounding muffled even to his ears. *What a shame. They really should hear this. It might teach them a thing or two.*

"Mfff mmmm bwnllll."

I know all about what you're trying to do, you ants! Do you really think you've helped me with what you call the "violence and compulsions"? You should get to know me better before making hasty decisions like that. Ironically you're helping me but not in the way you imagine.

"Okay, Finn," the doctor said, "here's a little prick, and then you won't feel anything more for a while. You're in good hands, as you already know."

The Voice spoke to him. *Hey, kiddo. There's some serious stuff going down here. I'll protect you, but we have to work together. Whatever they think they're doing, I'll make sure it comes out to your advantage. I'll see you on the other side, but be prepared to go back into "performance mode." This will have to be your best yet.*

There wasn't enough time to answer. Finn began his descent into the abyss . . . into the cold, bright water where he couldn't breathe at all.

CHAPTER SIXTEEN

When David Met Sadie

"Hey, Sadie. Wait up."

Oh, no, not Dave. Sadie walked faster down the hall.

She had done a good job of avoiding him all day, but he'd finally found her.

"Saaaaydeeeee. Come on, Sadie. Slow down. I just want to have a little chat."

Sadie kept walking as Dave finally caught up to her. He was now at her side.

Dave Jablonsky was at least twice the size of Sadie, in every direction. He had wavy hair that refused to behave, like its owner. It barely hid the nastiness behind his almond-colored eyes.

"So, Sadie, I heard there was a little problem at school yesterday. I heard you took something from my girl. You know we can't have that."

"Leave me alone, Dave. Go away."

"I heard someone saw you taking my girl's favorite thing—well, aside from me, that is."

"Kylie isn't your girl."

Dave shrugged. "Not yet, but one day she will be."

"Whatever. No one saw anything."

"Sadie, just confess, and I'll make it real easy on you. Give Kylie back her pin, and it'll be 'end of story.' You can give it to me, and I'll tell everyone I found it, or you can leave it in the classroom, and I'll make sure someone finds it. No one will ever know. The whole incident will go away like it never happened."

Sadie kept walking past the endless line of lockers. "Dave, you'd never just drop it. You never drop anything."

"No, seriously, Sadie, if the pin is returned, I swear this matter will be dropped. We can just go on ignoring you as usual. We'll completely leave you alone. If you choose to refuse my generosity, however"—Dave stepped in front of Sadie, blocking her path, his determined eyes locked on hers—"things will get real hard for you around here, Myers. By the time we're done with you, you'll wish you lived two thousand miles away."

Sadie shrugged. "I already wish that, Dave."

"I'm serious. This is your only warning. You have until the end of school tomorrow. Do you understand?"

Sadie tried to ignore him.

"I asked if you understood me, Myers," he sneered, more forcefully now. "Do you?"

Sadie nodded to end her discomfort.

"Good, I'm glad we settled the rules here. Just so you remember: until the end of school tomorrow, last bell. I hope you make the right choice and make my girl happy again. When she's not happy, I'm not happy, and believe me, I like to be happy. Got it?"

"Yes. I got it. Loud and clear."

"Good, Myers." Dave started to walk away. "There may be hope for you yet . . . on Mars."

Sadie, relieved he was gone, couldn't move for a few moments. "Come on, Sadie," she coaxed herself aloud. "Get it together." This rallied her enough to finally exit the building.

On her way home, the scene with Dave replayed in her mind. His threats, his beady eyes staring at her. It was hard to shake off. She increased her pace, looking over her shoulder every now and then to make sure he wasn't following her. School was supposed to be a respite from the misery at home; now it felt more like a second prison.

CHAPTER SEVENTEEN

Are We There Yet?

THE SUN SET over the eastern mountains. The cloffuls were larger and more colorful than usual, with many varieties of blues, purples, and then warm yellows toward the horizon.

"Should we step in yet, Thelonious?

"It is almost time, Let us hold out a little longer and see what happens. What do you say?"

"Think of the possible consequences, Thelonious. You saw what is coming."

"I remember my oath. It is almost time but not yet."

"Well, if you are certain, Thelonious, then I will agree with you. I do not think it can be too much longer, but we will see."

"Yes. We will wait a little longer, my friend. Keep your eyes open. We have to be able to make those impossible decisions this time."

CHAPTER EIGHTEEN

My Name Is Mud

"Hey, guys. There she is. Let's help her home." Dave and his followers, Kenny and Alex, surrounded Sadie.

"Oh, come on. Just leave me alone." As brutal as they'd become in the classes they shared, Sadie had managed to avoid them after school for longer than she'd expected. She'd made it all the way to Friday, but her time was up.

"We can't do that, Sadie. I have to keep my promise, or else who am I? Once you make up your mind not to do what I say, there are repercussions. You know that."

Sadie shrugged. "I don't know what you expect me to do about your promises."

"Now we have to make sure all our stuff is safe from you, Sticky Fingers Sadie."

Are there any names they haven't called me?

She lowered her head and kept walking.

"We're giving you an escort home." Dave smirked. "You should feel honored. Better than walking alone. By the way, when was the last time you weren't alone? Been a long time, huh? Wouldn't you like some company?"

"Not from you jerks."

"Aww, come on. Don't do us like that, Sadie."

Dave took a step in front of her and stopped short. She shifted her weight and tried to step around him, but a quick push from behind sent her sprawling to the ground, face first off the sidewalk and into a giant mud puddle.

"Yug! Threally?" She pushed up onto her hands and knees and spat out a mouthful of mud. A dark-brown slobbery trickle added to the stain on her once-white T-shirt. *Oh, my God! This really happened.*

Sadie sat awhile longer in the mud as her tormentors loomed and laughed all around her.

"Nice lil piggy. Right in the mud where you belong. You should be happy and comfortable there. Have a fun bath. We'll see you Monday, if not sooner," Dave jeered, as he blew her a kiss good-bye.

Sadie couldn't imagine what other terrific things Dave and his buddies had in store for her.

She continued to sit there, knees in the mud, stewing in her misery until long after the boys had gone. It took all her remaining energy to extract herself from the sticky clay. *I heard people pay a lot of money for mud baths, but I'm not impressed.*

Looking down at her ruined shirt, she saw the first hint of light. Then another. She held up her mud-caked hands as sparks, the colors of soap bubbles, flitted from finger to finger, leaving trails like fireworks on the Fourth of July. Eventually their lights dimmed, and Sadie was finally able to blink and close her mouth. She came back to herself, amused by the encouraging light show. She slung her backpack over her shoulder and headed home.

She sighed. *Should be fun showing up at home looking like this. I wonder what Mom will say this time,* she thought, as she pushed open the front door.

"Sadie? Is that you?"

"Yes, Mom," she answered quietly. She tried to sneak down the hallway to the bathroom, but her mother caught her halfway there.

"Sadie Ann Myers, what in the world have you been up to?"

"Oh, nothing. Thought I'd go for a swim. Then I realized we don't have a pool."

"Not funny. You're dragging mud all over the place. What really happened, missy?"

"Just the cheerful neighborhood welcoming committee walking me home and showing me the sights, face first."

"What did you do to them?"

"What? *Me* do to them? Really, Mom?"

"Why can't you be more like your friend Melanie? I haven't seen her in ages. She was always so nice. Where's she been?"

Sadie shrugged. "I think she moved to Albuquerque."

"Albuquerque, huh? Why can't I ever get a straight answer out of you? Maybe if you tried to make friends and not be such a smart aleck, you'd have a better chance of getting along with people."

"Uh . . . thanks, Mom. Thanks for all your support." Sadie wanted nothing more than to wash away the dried mud, which made her skin itch. *Just let me go, Mom. You don't understand what it's like.* Sadie couldn't get away fast enough.

Her mother ran a hand through her dark-brown curls. "What? What did I do this time?"

"Never mind. Just drop it. I'll clean up and be out of the bathroom soon."

"Yes, you'd better be out soon. We have a ton of things to go over."

Sadie rolled her eyes. "Great. I can't wait."

She hurried into the bathroom and locked the door behind her. She couldn't believe what she saw in the mirror. The mud had dried, and her hair felt like straw.

The dirt on her face and hair reminded her of another time. A time when she wasn't alone. A time when she had someone who protected her.

"Isn't it terrible, Christopher?" Sadie had asked. "I'm so upset. I don't understand it, and I can't get it out of my head."

Some neighbors had found the mutilated body of a little black-and-white cat by the storm drain at the end of Sadie's street.

"I know, Sadie. How anyone can hurt an animal, or anything for that matter, is beyond me."

"That poor cat. I don't even want to think about it."

"I know a way to get your mind off it." He reached out and took her hand. Her knitted brow softened, and she started to relax. "Let's take a walk," Christopher suggested. "We can look at the trees and watch the birds. That always helps me."

"Sounds good."

They strolled around the block. When they were almost at the creek, they ran into Jeremy Stevens, the neighborhood bully. He was older than them by two years and must have been at least six foot tall. He'd never grown out of his towhead coloring. Sadie had no proof, but something in her gut told her he was responsible for the cat's death.

"What are you two doing in my neighborhood?" Jeremy demanded. His voice sounded as if he always had a cold.

Sadie rolled her eyes. "Last I heard, no one owns neighborhoods."

"Well, you heard wrong. You're in my space, and if you don't turn around, there's going to be trouble."

"The only trouble will be for you," Sadie fired back. She stared up into his nearly transparent eyes, which had an unearthly glow. "Why don't you just crawl back inside that hole you live in?"

"What did you say?" Jeremy grabbed the front of Sadie's

jacket and knocked her down. He pushed her face hard into the dirt with one hand.

As Jeremy stood up, Christopher rushed him. He swung his right leg around, sweeping Jeremy at the knees.

The bully crumpled to the ground, and Christopher jumped him, his forearm pressing against his throat. "You'd better get the hell out of here so I don't have to *really* hurt you."

Jeremy put his hands up in surrender. Sadie didn't think he'd ever been challenged before. He scrambled to his feet and ran away.

Christopher held out a hand to help her up. "You okay, m'lady?"

"I am now." She brushed a bit of dirt off her sleeve. "How did you know what to do?"

Christopher picked the bits of grass and dried leaves from Sadie's braids then took her hand. He shrugged. "My dad taught me how to take care of myself."

"Yeah, I can see that," Sadie said admiringly.

She let him lead her back toward the street. "Can we walk for a little while longer?" she asked. "I don't think I'm going to feel okay for a while. He's so rotten. I've heard stories at school about what he's done to some of the other kids. I can't imagine how they must feel."

Christopher squeezed her hand. Her nerves started to settle, but the more she thought about Jeremy's other victims, the sadder she felt for them. "I hope someone sticks up for those kids like you did for me. I hope one day no one has to deal with his crap ever again."

"Me too."

"I'll never forget what you did for me, Christopher." She let go of his hand and reached up to hug him. She smelled spruce in his hair and felt the warmth from his ear. He always made her feel safe. "I'll never forget you either."

"Forget me? Why would you forget me? I'm right here. I'm never leaving you, m'lady."

Sadie smiled. He was perfect. He smiled in return and touched her cheek, and then he kissed her softly.

She sighed. "I never want this to end."

"It never will, m'lady."

"Promise?"

"Cross my heart."

Those words haunted her now. Sadie stared at her mud-caked reflection and blinked away the tears. She was alone, truly alone. She had no one.

I guess there's no getting around a shower. When she turned on the water, she heard yelling on the other side of the door.

"You'd better clean up that mess when you're done. And don't clog the tub. I don't want to see any evidence of dirt anywhere."

Sadie tried to ignore her.

"Did you hear me, Sadie?" her mom yelled louder.

"Yes, yes! I heard you. I'll clean it up!" *Geez. Can I please be transported anywhere but here? Anywhere? I hear Albuquerque is phenomenal.*

CHAPTER NINETEEN

A Shocking Reminder

Darkness faded. Light stabbed through Finn's eyelids. No matter how tightly he squeezed them, he couldn't shut it out. He placed his hands over them, but they did nothing. The penetrating rays worked through every crack between his fingers. They tortured him, trying to scald his brain. They came from everywhere. He was certain once the blazing light gained entry, it would tear through his entire being.

He felt something under his arms, working against gravity, pull him up.

Floundering in liquid space, Finn tried repeatedly to free his arms and legs. His strength waned, and he had no choice but to give in, letting whatever it was do its thing. His lungs burned; he longed for huge gulps of fresh air.

The slamming of the metal door ended the pain, and he drew a deep breath. He was back in his cupboard of a room, another shock treatment over and done. He knew it, even though he'd received no communication to that effect. Experience was a good teacher.

He thought back to the light and liquid space, and let the feelings overtake him again. They were neither dreams, nor side effects, but actual memories. The strength of this knowing was clear and visceral. He was finally remembering things!

This is good! This is a step forward, and I'll use it. It could be the answer to so many things.

He jumped to his feet, but the throbbing in his head forced him to the floor, where he resembled a crime-scene chalk drawing.

From that position, he did what any sane person would: he laughed. He couldn't wait until his next treatment, when more memories might come.

Not so fast, kiddo. It's time to roll on down the road. Let's make like a tree and leave this place behind!

You again? You know you're not all that bright. I could do with a little less you, Mr. Helpful.

Not all that bright! And as far as helpful, why do you think you're so happy right now?

I was until you showed up.

Nice socks, the Voice told him. *Meant to tell you. Now on to the real work. Remember when I explained how you'd have to perform after your treatment? Well, it's show time, buddy! It's the only way we're going to get out of here.*

Are you kidding? I remembered something real. Finally . . . for the first time—and you want me to leave here now?

It's time to get us the hell out of here, and to do that, you have to play normal. Think you can do that for us?

What's this "us" about? And why would I want to get out of here now, when I'm just starting to remember things?

Listen up—I'm only going to say this once. All we needed was to kick-start your memory. Now that it's happened, any more will damage you and ruin your chances to take control of things. Get me, buddy boy?

Finn had some choice responses he wanted to voice, but he couldn't doubt the truth he heard.

Yeah, I guess. So now what?

Good. Just do normal. You've done it before; now do it again. Break a leg and see you down the road a piece.

When? Finn thought, too eagerly, but the Voice was gone.

He knew how to do this. He'd played "their normal" for the parent people. He'd known just what they wanted and how to deliver. But this time he couldn't screw up. These were "professionals." It was the tiny details they liked.

The steel door creaked. A nurse stood in the archway, checking her chart, while two bulky aides stood behind her.

"How are you doing today, Winn?"

He bristled. "My name's Finn . . ." He took a deep breath before adding, "Ma'am. I'm doing well. Thank you, Nurse . . ." He quickly glanced at her badge. "Tindle. Nurse Tindle. How are you doing today?" He smiled, forcing his teeth to show a bit. *I hope this isn't too much.*

Nurse Tindle's eyes grew large. She looked from one of her aides to the other, then back to Finn. "I'm fine." Her tone suggested she wasn't sure of him yet. "Thank you for asking, Finn. I'll be back to check on you this afternoon."

"Okay. See you soon," and he waved a little. *Not too much.*

Idiots. Take that, Mr. Helpful. I'd like to see you perform half as well!

CHAPTER TWENTY

Field of Rose

Early Saturday morning, Sadie's mom, hands on hips, fussed at her husband and daughter to hurry up and get in the car.

"Tess, do you really think this is a good idea? It's not the best time for me. A whole weekend away makes it hard to catch up with work!"

"George, your saying it's not the best time shows me it's the perfect time. We need this. Sadie and I hardly see you. You've been working practically round the clock."

Dad grumbled something unintelligible under his breath, caved, and slouched into the driver's seat.

"Okay, then, chop, chop." Mom tossed a large canvas bag stuffed full of beach towels into the back of the car. She flashed her best cheerleader smile.

Sadie gave a small smile in return and did a quick double check of the contents of her beach bag. *I almost admire her hope, but let's be honest. We all know this is bound to end in a big pile of poo, just like all Mom's brilliant ideas. Flip-flops: check. Book: check. Misery: check.*

My music box! Oh, no, I left it in my room. "Mom, I'll be right back."

"What now, Sadie? It's time we got on the road."

"I know, but I'll be back in one minute. I promise!"

Thank goodness I remembered about my music box before we left. I hate going anywhere without it. Except for school. I never would bring it there—everything is too messed up there now.

Sadie ran all the way to her room, seeing the state her parents were already in today. *At least Mom puts her annoying qualities out there—it's ridiculous . . . But Dad? There's something about him that makes situations like this a little scary. Who knows what he might do at any given moment? I can't help feel bad for him somehow, though. If I could only tell them about the music box, they might be calmer somehow.*

Ever since Gramma gave it to me, I've used it to bring her closer to me, and it's worked. I've sat with it almost every day. When I do, I feel her around me and hear her whispers. That music box was part of her—I've heard her voice singing its soothing song to me whenever I've played it.

Sadie used her stepstool to reach the top of the bookshelf, where her music box hid behind her volume of Shakespeare. With the predictable discomfort she was surely in for this weekend, she needed it with her.

Grabbing it quickly, she brought with it a sheaf of artwork, which fluttered all over the carpeted floor. *I don't have time for this! It looks like a rainbow puked all over the place.*

She glanced out the window in the direction of her parents, toes tapping by now, she guessed. Then she looked at the mess. "Ughhhh!" Steam practically blew out of her ears as her frustration increased. She tucked the music box into her pocket, got onto her knees, and put page after page back into the art folder.

The last page was so familiar that memories of that day rushed forward in her mind, and they were as clear as those of the day before. She was in kindergarten. Tanner had painted his arms instead of the paper. Lily had run Steven over with the plastic tricycle, and Dillon had sat in the corner, talking to a spider. She remembered when she had taken the piece of paper and sat down. In the center of the paper stood a tall tree with golden branches and leaves like waterfalls. The tree held hands with an alligator that stood straight up on its hind legs. A strong wave of déjà vu washed over her.

The reptile wore a trench coat of all things and had the coolest sparkly eyes. Sadie recalled the care she'd taken to add just the right amount of glue before dusting on the silvery glitter.

She was the proudest of that picture, more than any she had painted that year. When she was older, she always wondered, *Why the coat? It doesn't seem to fit . . . an alligator anyway!* Sadie could still hear her mother's voice asking her, "Why the golden leaves?" which made her a little sad.

As she stared at the picture, more memories of that kindergarten day returned. Though she had painted the tree and the alligator, they had come alive, appearing between her desk and the chalkboard. She had asked her classmates if they could see them, to which they all replied, "Of course, Sadie. They're right there on the paper!"

Sadie smiled and shook her head. *How could I have forgotten that? It was absolutely real . . . I guess?*

After adding her rendition of the tree and the alligator to the folder with the rest of her artwork, she laid the entire lot on her desk and ran down the hall.

Mom stood in the doorway, tapping her watch. "Tick-tock, Sadie! Come on already!"

With her precious music box tucked inside her hoodie pocket, where it wouldn't be seen, she climbed into the backseat of the car. While Mom locked the front door, Sadie continued her reverie. Still vivid in her mind was the portrait of the tree and the alligator, two friends she thought she knew. Thinking of them gave her comfort.

Sadie fastened her seat belt, knowing it would be a grumpy ride. In a little more than an hour, they would be at Hunter's Point Beach. She could almost feel the sand between her toes.

Mom, the frustrated passenger, and Dad, the distant driver, were in the front, barely talking to each other. Mom at least tried for a while until she gave up with a heavy sigh. Next she flipped on the radio and tuned the dial to an oldies station. The familiar sound of the Beatles filled the car.

"Can't Buy Me Love" reminded Sadie of beach trips they used to take when she was younger. The whole family would pile into their old van. Gramma and Aunt Sue sat in the middle row, while Sadie and the twins camped out in the back. Everyone laughed and joked during the whole ride.

Sadie stared at the back of her parents' heads. *I wonder if they remember how happy we used to be. I can barely remember it anymore myself.* She sighed. *Mom and Dad were still kind of normal then.*

Dad switched the station to the local news and mumbled something about traffic reports. Though Mom didn't say anything, Sadie felt the tension thicken in the car. After ruffling around in her bag, she pulled out her copy of *Cat's Cradle* and put on her headphones so she could listen to the band, Blind Faith. *We're not even halfway there, and I already don't want to be here. Honestly, what was Mom thinking? What exactly does she expect from us? Is it Sunday yet?*

Sadie turned up the volume and tried to focus on her book. A few minutes later, Mom tapped her on the knee and made the universal sign for "Take the headphones off."

"Sadie, the volume on that thing is way too loud. I called your name five times."

Sadie sighed. "Sorry, Mom,"

"Turn it down, okay? Now take a look to your right. Look how lovely it is!"

A huge field of flowers stretched out for acres and acres on the right side of the road. Astonishing blooms of many different colors and shapes. Sadie spied the long, delicate vines of her favorite purple morning glories and, behind them, rows of roses. *They look so out of place. I don't remember ever seeing this before.*

Mom pointed to the side of the road. "George, pull over. I want to get a picture."

Grumbling, Dad maneuvered the car onto the wide shoulder. Sadie climbed out after her mother. The air outside was warm, humid, and thick with the perfume of thousands of blossoms.

From their vantage point, Sadie saw pink, red, white, and yellow roses, all in full bloom.

They make me think of Gramma.

Then came the familiar whisper.

Sadie smiled. Gramma's soft voice called out again, *Sweet Sadie.* She was getting used to hearing that phrase.

Just behind a row of bright-pink blossoms, a fine mist swirled and took shape. Sadie recognized Gramma Rose's silhouette. The shape of her face became clear, as did her smile.

Sadie glanced at her mother and wondered what good could come of asking her if she could see Gramma. She wanted to but decided it best to keep it to herself. She'd made the mistake of telling her mother she'd seen Gramma a couple of weeks after the funeral. Mom had freaked out and promptly made an appointment for Sadie to see Dr. Goldman. By convincing Mom it was all a misunderstanding, Sadie had squirmed out of the doctor visit.

Mom snapped several shots with her camera then motioned that it was time for them to get back in the car.

Sadie glanced over her shoulder and made a faint waving motion. Gramma still watched.

"Wow, Mom. That's incredible. How come I don't remember seeing it before? We've taken this trip dozens of times."

Mom shrugged. "I've never noticed it either, Sadie. Not one time."

"Huh . . ."

Gramma always knows when I need her. It's good to know she's not gone. Maybe she'll actually talk to me one of these days, instead of just whispering.

Climbing back inside the air-conditioned car sent a quick shiver down Sadie's back. She fastened her seat belt once more then took a last look at the field.

As Dad pulled back onto the highway, Sadie whispered, "Good-bye, Gramma. See you soon."

Mom put the lens cover back on her camera then turned around to face Sadie. "That's the first time I've seen you smile all morning, Sadie."

Sadie nodded and smiled again. As they approached a bend in the road, she took one last glance to see Gramma still there, waving.

CHAPTER TWENTY-ONE

Off the Charts

D R. LLEWELLYN STOPPED outside the heavy door behind which patient 58210, Finn Montgomery, was most likely still sleeping. The doctor had just come on shift and wanted to get Finn's charting done first thing, since it was the boy's last entry. Beds were needed, and it was a good feeling to move another improved patient to the next stage of care.

He glanced at page one to remind himself of Finn's condition upon arrival.

16 September: Finn Montgomery, patient 58210, age 14, admitted under duress. Complaint details written threats and disturbing drawings of violent fantasies of harming foster parents. Intake interview was difficult in the extreme. Patient is violent and abusive. Patient kicked and screamed. Refused to answer questions. Maximum security required. Restraints imposed. First diagnostic meeting scheduled with psychiatrist tomorrow, 9:00 a.m.

Dr. Llewellyn flipped to the back of the chart. He read his last few notes prior to adding the final entry.

28 June: Finn Montgomery, patient 58210, still under observation during therapy. More civil and even friendly on occasion during social interactions. Remains calm in all settings. Schedule includes daily meetings with doctors and group therapy twice per week.

Other entries were fairly repetitive. *Interesting,* Dr. Llewellyn thought. *There hasn't been much to say since the end of August.* Finn apparently had hit a therapeutic ceiling. He was highly functioning at this point. It was time for him to leave.

22 October: Finn Montgomery, patient 58210. Thirteen months after initial intake interview. Recommend transfer to Hanover's secured juvenile detention facility.

CHAPTER TWENTY-TWO

Gramma's Library

THE TRIP TO the beach was a bust. No one talked to each other for most of the weekend. The little talking they did was more in the way of grunts and mumbles. Sadie brought enough books and music with her for just this type of emergency. The interminable hours finally came to an end. After dropping Dad off at home, Mom and Sadie headed for the store to restock the fridge.

"Wait, Mom. Stop the car. Stop!" Sadie opened the door as the car rolled to the curb.

"Sadie, what are you doing? You're scaring me half to death!"

"I saw Gramma!" Sadie jumped out of the car and ran after her.

"Sadie. Sadie!" Mom called.

Sadie had a hard time keeping up. "Gramma! Wait!" Sadie followed the quick-moving figure ahead of her. Gramma darted up alleyways, swiftly turning corners. She appeared in pale blues, purples, and fuchsia. Her feet reminded Sadie of cartoon takeoffs leaving a trail of steam behind. Every time Sadie thought she got a little closer to her, the figure accelerated and rapidly disappeared.

"Gramma! It's me, Sadie. Why are you running away?"

Sadie kept following, trying to keep up. She couldn't stop, even though she was getting tired and her feet were burning. She wasn't sure where her mother was and could no longer hear her calls. She knew she'd catch hell from her mom, but she couldn't miss this opportunity to see Gramma again.

Gramma entered through a door up ahead. Sadie hurried to the same spot and read the sign over the door—PAPYRUS STREET BOOK EMPORIUM—before following her inside. Sadie had been in this store before. It was an old bookstore and had the distinct mustiness that only old bookstores have. Even after all the big chain stores had come to the outskirts of town, the emporium, with its rows of old and out-of-print books, had managed to stay open.

The store was dimly lit except for the light sneaking through the front windows. Sadie scanned the darkened space as she stepped over short stacks of books and maneuvered down the aisle marked art history just in time to see Gramma turn the corner. She followed her as fast as she could, reaching the back of the store in a few seconds, but no Gramma. *Where could she possibly go?*

"I know I saw her," she whispered. Blue and green flashes strobed by the time Sadie's voice died away. They were strong and vivid at first, but after several moments, the flashes began to fade. A few moments more, and they were gone. Sadie's whole body slumped in disappointment, and she leaned against a bookshelf. "I must be out of my mind," she muttered.

Nearby, a rickety table was covered with stacks of newspapers. Although Papyrus Street Book Emporium specialized in old clippings, this part of the store was only a destination for students researching local history. The faded sign identified this section as, OLD TOWN NEWS.

A faint blue spark danced atop one of the stacks. Sadie took a step forward and shook her head. *Why am I here? It can't be to read some stupid old article.* She would give it one more minute, and then she was out of there.

She picked up the article on the top of the stack. Despite the plastic sleeve, the paper had yellowed with age. A picture of what appeared to be an incinerated car sat over an ominous headline: "Family of Four Dead, Burned in Grisly Car Accident." Sadie read on. Investigators determined that a mother, father, and two children were on their way home from the Eagle Lake Country Club when their car careened off Clover Bridge and exploded. Forensics deemed the evidence unidentifiable, and the case was closed.

How sad, she thought. *It happened right off the main highway on the other side of town.* It was only a few miles from where she stood right now.

Sadie sat on one of the wobbly chairs flanking the table. Farther down in the article was a picture of the family, their smiles radiating into the present. Sadie was intrigued by their old-fashioned clothing: bow ties, suspenders, gloves, and long dresses included. She sighed. *I should stop complaining about everything in my life. A story like this shows me how lucky I am.* She looked at the mom's smiling face.

"Mom!" she exclaimed. "She's going to kill me." Sadie could picture the look on her mother's face; she was probably frantic with worry. She dug into her jeans pockets, hoping to find enough money to buy the article, but only found a quarter and an old gum wrapper. She left the store just as her mom's car pulled up.

"How did you find me?" she asked through the open window, passenger side.

"You're lucky I did, young lady," Mom yelled. "I've been circling every block in this town for the last fifteen minutes, trying to track you down! Thank goodness I found you!"

Sadie got in the car, and that's when she saw the tears on her mom's face.

"Oh, Sadie, I was so scared." Her mother reached sideways and held her so tight she couldn't breathe.

Sadie wiggled out of her grasp. "Geez, Mom. I'm not a kid anymore. I know I shouldn't have run off like that, but why were you so afraid? It's only in our little town."

Sadie's mom bit her lip then hugged her again. "Honey, please don't do that to me again, okay? Why on earth would you run off like that?"

"Sorry, Mom. I thought I saw Gramma, but I guess I made a mistake."

"Aww, Sadie. I know how much you miss her. Sometimes I think I see her too."

Sadie's eyes went wide. "Really? You've seen her?"

Her mom never had told her that before.

CHAPTER TWENTY-THREE

Dear Christopher

Dear Christopher,

I can't believe it's already been a year since I last saw you. I can still hear you calling me "m'lady." I can feel your hand in mine as you showed me so many things I'd never seen before. I never want to explore the world with anyone else but you.

I remember how you told me you would never leave me—how one day we would get married and always be together. I remember all those things, and it hurts my heart so much. I still see you everywhere I go.

The other day I almost went up to someone I thought was you. Imagine how embarrassed I would have been. You would have laughed about it, teasing me. Making me giggle about how funny it was.

I still can't get over you not being here with me. How you left and everything fell apart. How within two months of you leaving, I lost my Ruby and then Gramma Rose.

You loved Ruby and Gramma too. How could you not be with me when I needed you most? You weren't here to comfort me like you always did, to tell me everything would be okay.

Nothing is okay. I have no one now. My parents hardly talk to *me, and I guess that's a good thing because I don't want to talk to them.*

Why did you stop writing? What did I do?

I miss you so much. It feels like you leave over and over again. I have no friends now, and everyone is so mean to me. When are you coming back? You have to come back.

Please come back.

I have nothing.

I am nothing.

Dear Rufus,

I never sent that letter. I just couldn't. It hurt too much. I mean, I wouldn't want Christopher to laugh at it. To laugh at me. That would be the worst. It's been so long I'm sure he has someone else now. Someone else to call his lady. I'm sure he doesn't think about me at all.

Thank you, as always, for listening. xoxo

CHAPTER TWENTY-FOUR

Juvie, Juvie, Juvie

FINN RODE ON the blue-and-white school bus, staring at his seat. It was made of standard-issue green plastic, meant to feel "leathery." His had a hole in it. He doubted it was made by a cigarette. *Not on this bus. Too many guards.* More likely it was caused by some deadbeat rider picking nervously at it until the surface wore away, exposing the cotton beneath.

The stench of mildew assaulted his brain. He gazed out the window, breathing mist on the cool glass, leaving a damp layer thick enough to write on, but he was too bored to follow through. The sunset grabbed his attention. He guessed it would be a while before he saw one again. For lack of anything better to do, he took over for the previous rider and picked at the green-and-white scab. Soon it was three times the size, all the way around. In his stupor he didn't hear the jeers coming from outside until this minute.

Finn's seat was on the side of the bus closest to all the noise. He looked out and noticed a group of boys dressed in bright-orange jumpsuits, leaning up against a high barbed-wire fence, aiming unintelligible insults at the newcomers. Annoyed, he decided to turn it all . . . *off.*

Later, when he turned it back *on*, he was in a tiny room on the top bunk. He glanced around quickly to gather clues. An odor of gym socks prevailed. The space was barely large enough for a single set of bunks, let alone the kitty-corner toilet and sink and each boy's small storage trunk. He shared the space with a slight blond boy who looked to be half his height. The kid wore the same orange jumpsuit he'd seen on the other boys when he'd arrived. Looking down, he noticed his new attire matched. *Perfect. Part of a team.*

His cellmate sat in the middle of the floor, staring up at him. He made Finn think of a cherub at a graveyard. Small, tousled hair, but thinner. Much thinner. His pale-green eyes took on a faraway look, giving Finn time to scan the blond's posture. The boy's blank expression, along with that black eye and hunched demeanor, led Finn to a swift conclusion: he was juvie's punching bag.

"Didn't you know it's not polite to stare, kid?"

"I wanted to see what you were all about, Finn."

"How the hell do you know my name?"

The boy shrugged. "You told me."

"Well, there's no way to know anything about me from merely looking. And who dressed you today? The jumpsuit clashes with your face."

In a voice hardly audible, the boy ventured, "Someone woke up on the wrong side of the bed."

"Where have I landed? Cliché Palace?"

"No." The boy stood up and crossed his arms. "It's called juvie. Hanover Juvenile Detention Center. And the outfit is something everyone wears. Have you ever been before? To juvie, I mean?"

"No. Have you? Why are you here in the first place? I doubt you could pull anything off."

"'It was a case of mistaken identity,' my lawyer told me. 'Wrong place at the wrong time, son. They've ruled against you, so I'm afraid there's nothing more we can do for at least a couple of years.'"

"That was boring. How about a name?"

"Um—"

But Finn cut him off. "It hardly matters, as from now on you'll go by the name I give you: Beagle. Good boy."

"But I wanted to tell you. My real name, I mean."

"No need. It's all settled now. So tell me everything I need to know about this place, Beagle. Start with how the food works."

The boy stood there, his mouth open and head shaking from side to side. Then it was over. He accepted his new name: Beagle. It didn't take long for him to go over what he knew.

The kid is concise, Finn thought. *I have to give him that much.* "Good job, Beagle. You'll make an excellent attaché."

Beagle lost a little of the hunch in his shoulders. "Does that mean you'll watch my back if I watch yours? I know things. I'm good at watching even though sometimes I get hurt for it."

"Never mind that now. It's early to bed for you, Beagle. Rest up while you can. We have work to do."

CHAPTER TWENTY-FIVE

Orange Cone of Shame

"SADIE, COME BACK here, please. It's cold out today. Wear the hat I made for you."

"I don't need a hat, Mom. Don't we live in Florida for a reason?"

"Must you debate everything I say? It's cold out, and you need one. Wear it."

"Ugh. Fine!" *It's sixty-five degrees out, Mom. Not exactly a frozen tundra out there.*

Sadie had mixed feelings about the hat. Did she like it? No. Did she care about it? Yeah, sort of. Why? Because it meant so much to Mom. It was the first and last thing her mother ever had done with yarn and a pair of knitting needles. Besides that, she couldn't stand arguing over every little thing.

No one wore bright orange at school. *It would be a nice hat if it wasn't orange,* Sadie thought. *Orange, really? What's the matter? They run out of crap brown or puke green? Might as well be one of those two. Anything's better than a hat that can be seen from outer space. "Mission control, mission control, come in, please. We seem to have a problem in sector six. A blinding orange light has surrounded us, and we can't see where to put the next* satellite. *Do you think you can get down there and remove that horrific orange beacon from that Sadie Myers girl?"*

She usually took it off immediately. Today, however, she was halfway to school and still had it on. *I'm still wearing it!* Probably because the weather was chilly this morning. It was past time to take it off, so she yanked it.

Oh, no. Here comes Dave. This isn't good. He had kept his word. Kylie's pin didn't reappear by his deadline, so he and his buddies tormented her daily.

Before Sadie had a chance to hide the hat, Dave came running up to her. "Nice hat, stupid. Where'd you get it? The circus?"

Wow, that's the best he could come up with? He's usually much better at this. He must be losing his edge.

Keeping her head down, Sadie continued walking.

Dave wouldn't let up. "Here, let me help you with that traffic cone you call a hat. It really brings out the ugly in your eyes."

Sadie groaned.

He grabbed it right out of her hand. Taunting her with his hyena laugh, he ran the rest of the way to school. She watched as his form grew smaller.

By the time Sadie got to school, a line of kids waited in the front hall. They all pointed and laughed at her. The line parted, and there, in the middle of the floor, was her sopping-wet orange embarrassment.

"There you go, Sadie," Dave crooned. "I gave it a nice bath in the toilet for you."

All the blood rushed out of Sadie's extremities, and she went limp. She took a deep breath, pulled herself together, and silently headed to her classroom. A marching band of laughter followed right behind her.

With pangs of guilt, despite the punishment she'd endured, Sadie was relieved that the glowing orange hat was no more.

CHAPTER TWENTY-SIX

It Is Time

"I T IS UNUSUAL to find you on this side of the straime. What brings you here this day, Thelonious?"

"Have you been watching the signs?"

"Yes. Are we thinking the same thing?"

Thelonious nodded. "We are. She cannot fail. The stakes are too high.

"So, is the time now?"

"Indeed. It is time."

"Then I will send the messenger."

ACT TWO
Walk on Through

Is it firelight or morning,
That red flicker on the floor?
Your good-by was braver, sweetheart,
When I sailed away before.

— "The Shadow Boatswain," William Bliss Carman

CHAPTER TWENTY-SEVEN

Who's Afraid of the Fletcher House?

For the first time in her life, Sadie Myers took a permanent marker to school property. She couldn't face another soul, and this was the best time of day for using the "secret bathroom" on the second floor. Hardly anyone ever used it. The door's lock gave it a unique benefit but was also a gamble. Sometimes the custodian locked it, but other times she didn't.

It was like playing Russian roulette with her sanity. If the lock opened, she would win the solitude she needed to make it through the afternoon. If it was locked, she'd have no choice but to return to class and the onslaught of humiliation.

What would be the outcome this time?

Thank goodness it's open. That's the only good thing about today. save yourself! She found the message she'd just written on the bathroom tiles philosophical in nature. She hadn't thought about leaving school early, but fate had made plans for her. She looked at her handiwork with approval. She would leave the communication there as her legacy. It might be helpful to another student sitting in similar misery.

After half an hour of sitting and standing, she grew restless. It was either now or much, much later. Once the halls grew silent, she had her best chance of escaping the building unnoticed before last period ended. On the other hand, she could wait until the building was completely deserted. She opted to go now, collected her scattered books and papers from where she'd thrown them, then opened the door a few inches. The long hallway was deserted.

Unnoticed, Sadie ran down the stairs, slipped out the side door, hurried down the steps, and crossed the street. She glanced over her shoulder to make sure no one saw.

She was tired. Tired of hiding from Dave and his friends. They'd been at it nonstop for more than a week. Even without Dave, the whole school thing was a colossal waste of time. And she was tired of having no friends. She was exhausted from watching Mom and Dad act like they were the only ones who had lost something. But more than anything, she was angry at the world—no, the universe. How much would she have to endure before she caught a break?

She reached the crosswalk that would take her home. She couldn't bear to go there. She needed to be alone. Since all the pedestrians around her were turning left at the first intersection, she turned right. One foot went in front of the other, eventually parting the various grasses. Sadie headed to the one place she knew no one else would go.

Cutting across yards and open spaces, she wound up at that old subdivision, the last one before the forest. No one in the neighborhood had any idea how far back these woods went. Within minutes she stood in the cul-de-sac where the rundown home stood. She felt drawn to the Fletcher house in a pleasant sort of way. There was a peace about it that pushed the earlier tension gradually away.

It was the only house she knew of that had its own name: "the

Fletcher house." She took in the sight of it and its surroundings. Like all the kids around her neighborhood, she'd heard those stories for years, but somehow, now, she wasn't afraid.

It was a two-story white house, simple in construction, though "rundown" was putting it mildly. The porch appeared dangerously unbalanced. The paint was scratched and weather worn. The shutters hung askew or were off completely. Some of the shingles had fallen off, which had led to the roof's decline and allowed every form of weather inside. Still, it was a place where people had lived. It was once somebody's home.

The interwoven cracks in the pavement created a black-and-gray repeating pattern up the driveway. Its surface rolled up and down with crumbly ridges and valleys that made walking treacherous. As Sadie walked across the uneven asphalt, a sweet buzzing filled her ears. It reminded her of springtime in Gramma Rose's garden and the bees that hovered from flower to flower.

She walked through the front yard, its grasses brushing her knees, releasing their green fragrance each time she stepped down. It was hard to tell where the yard gave way to the thick, impenetrable forest behind it. The scent of ozone came on the breeze, and she knew it must be raining nearby.

The buzzing grew louder. It called her closer, friendly and familiar. Sadie's hand met the railing with trepidation, and she carefully climbed the front stairs. Seeing the house up close, she easily saw why this was the same place that had inspired nightmares and made those who claimed they'd visited get all wobbly kneed. Oddly enough, Sadie felt comfortable here.

She looked at the first window she came to: cracked glass and a few slats of wood across it. There wasn't much to see on the inside either, just enough to know the place was deserted. So much dust floated in the air that she could see it in the rays of sun coming down through the roof. A few filthy blankets sat in one corner, and an old-fashioned table lay tipped over near the entranceway. *Feels like no one has lived here in a thousand years.*

Backing up and retracing her steps, she felt something soft brush against her leg and looked over in time to see a navy-blue tail disappear around the corner of the house. *It couldn't be . . .*

Sadie heard a faraway meow. She hurried to follow it past the side of the house and into the backyard. She explored for a good five minutes before finally spotting a cat's blue tail swinging back and forth under some bushes. As she got closer, the navy blue intensified and turned iridescent.

"Barnaby, is that you? How can it be possible? No one's seen you since Gramma died." *It's not for lack of looking either,* she thought.

The cat responded to his name, and by the time he reached Sadie's outstretched arms, he purred up a storm. He rubbed against her fingers and sat down as she scratched behind his ear. After a moment, he meowed loudly then took off toward the woods. Before Barnaby crossed over into the dark, dense vegetation, he stopped and looked back, as if waiting.

"Barnaby, where are you going?"

Sadie followed him, pursuing the blue tail through the slanted sunbeams, struggling to maneuver through the brush as it grew thicker. She eventually wound up crawling on her hands and knees. The undergrowth, full of brambles, gripped her clothing and hair. *Is that a wild rose up ahead?* Its perfume traveled on the breeze in her direction. She had to pick up her pace, as she couldn't chance losing Barnaby. Scraping her arms and legs along the way, she followed the bushy tail of Gramma's cat.

The thick wall of leaves and thorns began to thin. The bushes and trees grew farther apart, and Sadie was able to return to her feet. The obstacle course of branches and vines gave way to a patch of lush green grass that climbed a small hill. At the top of the hill sat a fallen cedar, the perfect spot to sit and catch her breath.

Sadie willed herself up the steep incline and tossed her backpack to the ground. She sat on the moss-covered bark and picked half a dozen burrs from her jacket and several leaves from her hair.

When she looked down the hill, her breath caught in her chest. It was worth all she'd endured.

The most breathtaking turquoise stream meandered through the shallow valley below. Forgetting her fatigue, Sadie walked down toward the stream's bank, Barnaby at her side. She'd never before seen water this clear. A cool mist settled on her skin. Smooth, white stones speckled the stream bed, while brightly colored fish swam through patterns of light.

I don't see any evidence of people . . . It's remarkable! Compelled to see where the stream led, Sadie followed its moss-covered banks. When the sun sank to five fingers from the horizon, she saw, wearing the stream like a shawl, a lone majestic tree of a type she'd never seen before. It was taller than any tree she'd ever known, its roots spreading out in a perfect circle around the trunk. Strangest of all, its long, breezy branches grew down rather than up.

How cool is that? The space underneath those branches is like a cave, but one made of green-and-golden light. Once sunlight filtered through the branches, it remained, reflected by a gentle ricochet. The towering tree silently called to her, its magnetic force drawing her in. Light as air, Sadie literally floated on her tiptoes until she stood in front of the ancient-looking bark.

Coming out of her hypnotic state, she asked the tree, "What was that? Did you do it?"

She pressed her palm against the trunk. The tree's energy surged into her hand, tingling along her fingers and up her arm.

The feeling had the same quality as the musical buzzing she'd heard earlier at the Fletcher house, only a trillion times stronger.

At first it overwhelmed her. She couldn't keep her hand still for more than a second at a time. She stepped back but not out of fear. She knew to give herself a minute, somehow, so she could align with its melody. She didn't know how she knew, but this tree deserved respect. The energy, having made itself known, now diffused.

After a moment, she decided to try again. This time she knew what to expect. She eased her hand to the trunk and was able to keep it there.

Sadie sat down in a small hollow at the base of the tree, her back pressed against the smooth bark. As she sat quietly, she experienced the charged exchange. Barnaby joined her, curling up in her lap. She petted him and listened to him purr. "Barnaby, your fur is as silky as I remember."

Barnaby butted his head against her hand, and the corners of his mouth lifted.

It was getting easier to allow the tree's energy to flow among all of them. Feeling the warmth in her heart and the soft melodious bells in her ears, she knew the spot under this tree was meant for her.

They sat together for a while. She knew she'd be back. It was okay to go home now.

CHAPTER TWENTY-EIGHT

Pudding, Punch, and Pie

"THE PUDDING LOOKS exceptional today, doesn't it, Beagle? It's got that three-inch skin on it you like so much."

The muffled sounds ahead made the boys in line behind Finn bob and sway as they tried to get an eyeful of the commotion, but it didn't succeed in pulling Finn's attention away from the chocolate dollop that filled the small bowl on his dull metal tray.

Meals at the detention facility were served in an industrial cafeteria. The walls were pea green and mustard yellow, while the floor was a multicolored linoleum disaster. There were twenty tables, able to seat ten boys each. The room was in constant motion as the swarm got their food, threw rolls, and stole what they could off each other's trays.

"I like your sheen," Finn said to the pudding, but nobody, including the dessert, paid the least bit of attention. "What's that you say, Beagle?" he asked, staring straight ahead at the glass shelf. "Speak up, man! And clearly, please. You don't prefer the pudding today? Okay, we'll move on then."

Even though Finn joked, it wasn't like Beagle not to respond by the time his last syllable sounded. Finn glanced to his left. No Beagle. A short, pudgy boy stood beside him and pointed to the front of the line. Beagle had gone on ahead and gotten into a difficult pinch.

His Beagle was surrounded by a group of three broad-shouldered thugs, infamous for roughing up anyone who looked vulnerable in the slightest. He'd heard tales of them tormenting his little friend, but that was before he'd arrived. Finn's hands tightened around the edges of his tray, the glistening pudding momentarily forgotten as he focused his attention forward, letting his internal pressure cooker build up more steam.

"What? Are you firsty, dog face?" one of the boys taunted Beagle.

"Yeah, don't you know you can only drink out of a special bowl?" the smallest of the three jeered him.

Finn noted the security guards absorbed in their card game, laughing it up behind the Plexiglas in the back.

"On the ground, puppy! That's so you can drink properly with your tongue."

The third boy to speak was the tallest of the three and stout too. He knocked Beagle's knee out and shoved him hard, making him lose his balance and land face first into a puddle of thick sludge near the drain on the floor.

Beagle got up.

Finn could practically smell the sourness dripping down Beagle's cheek. It was an odor and taste he didn't envy his tiny attaché.

The instant it turned physical, Finn broke from the line and approached the bully standing between the other two. "Are you the boss here?" The moments ticked by. Finn cocked his head when there was no reply.

The middle kid opened his mouth, but before he could answer, Finn shifted on his heel, gracefully bringing his tray around as he turned. The largest boy soon met with a pudding-and-metal combination smash to the head. He went down. A loud, sickening crack sounded as his knee met the floor. Not content to leave it there, Finn completed the job with a fierce kick to his shoulder. Head met floor, which seemed to say, *You're going to be here for a while.* Finn stood, with tray in hand, over the prostrate body as if it were a prize he'd won in a carnival game.

A visible energy rolled off the tray but more so from Finn's body. It shrieked a warning that spread throughout the room, rattling the tables.

The usual loudmouthed banter and chewing ceased. For a moment the room sat suspended in the silence of awe. Someone clapped, and then a few others joined in. Several boys stood on their chairs and let out hoots and whoops. Within seconds the entire room erupted in cheers and applause.

The guards ran out of their protected room and looked ready to roar, but when they saw who fell, they bit their lips and shook their heads.

"Okay, okay, everyone. Have a seat," the husky guard hollered, "and by that I mean sit on them."

"Yeah," barked the one with the bristly mustache, "you've had your fun. Hope you enjoyed it while it lasted."

Two of the four guards picked up the semiconscious boy from the floor and inch-walked him out of the hall as quickly as his deadweight allowed.

The remaining two guards continued herding, but it didn't help. Everyone talked over one another, and it took five minutes to settle the room again.

Finn placed the tray back on the rails and picked up two servings of pudding and napkins. He felt everyone's eyes on him as he crossed the room with Beagle at his side. He handed the smaller boy one of the puddings and a napkin. "Wipe your face. It's starting to crust over."

"Thank you, sir."

Finn gave Beagle a distracted nod as he listened to all the whispers: "Who's that kid?" "Where did he come from?"

He was pleased, smiling on the inside, as he stood near the cafeteria exit, spooning shiny chocolate pudding into his mouth while observing his new domain.

Finn dropped his tray into the bus bucket, and he and Beagle headed back to their cell. Beagle didn't take his eyes off him. Finn continued his silent pacing once the door had closed.

"Sir?"

Finn continued to walk, tapping his fingers against each other in quick succession.

There wasn't the slightest change to indicate he'd been heard, so Beagle gave it one more try, a bit louder this time.

"I don't mean to bother you, sir, but I didn't want you to have to come to my rescue like that. I didn't mean to cause any trouble." The boy drew a deep breath and let it out as quietly as he could.

Finn stopped, parallel with Beagle. One second later, Finn's giant face loomed an inch from his.

"You've done me a service, Beagle, though you might not realize it. I won't forget it." Finn's hand rose then turned into a fist. "However, my boy, if you go on ahead of me in line like that again—*ever*—it will be the last thing you do in this lifetime."

Beagle shivered, nodding. He dropped his gaze, no longer looking Finn in the eye.

"It's past time for your punishment, but it'll be meted out at the appropriate moment, I'm sad to say."

"Why? I'll never do it again, as you said," Beagle ventured quietly, on the verge of tears.

"Because, Beagle. Because. He and I have talked about it, and now I've told *you*. Stay close or you will die."

Beagle shifted his weight from side to side. His mouth hung

open a few seconds before he spoke. "I *will* stay close. Who is 'he,' sir?"

Further irritated by this question, Finn shouted, "Why does that matter to you? Mind your own stinking business and be silent! No more words from you today!"

Beagle cried in earnest now, evidenced by the regular rise and fall of his bony shoulders as he curled tighter into a ball. He whimpered, his back to Finn.

Finn stood up and resumed his finger-tapping walk.

The next day, lunch was quite different. The guards watched for a few minutes. The cafeteria was orderly, and they returned to their cards.

Two empty seats had been left at the end of many of the tables, should their occupants be lucky enough to host the new celebrity.

Finn scanned the room and selected his seat. It didn't matter that a boy already was sitting in the place he chose.

The greasy-haired blond kid in the seat stood as Finn approached; in fact the boy nearly tripped over his chair as he hurried to pick up his tray.

"What's your name?" Finn asked the departing one.

"Alistair."

"I won't forget this small act of respect, Alistair. Off you go. Come back in ten."

Finn cleared his throat and eyeballed the kid with the tightening jaw who sat across the table. "We'll need that seat too, I'm afraid."

There was no movement in the ensuing seconds. With a cheery smile on his face, Finn reached out, quicker than light, and bent the boy's fingers backward. There were a couple of pops and one possible crack.

Before the kid could scream, Finn put a finger up to his own lips, commanding silence. With tears streaming down his cheeks, the kid struggled to pick up his tray with his good hand and scurried off to another table. Finn hadn't bothered to ask his name.

Beagle sat down in the vacated chair.

Over the next half hour, Finn sat and held court, welcoming many guests. They came to thank him and bring small offerings. They even brought cigarettes, which traded like gold in the bustling contraband market of the detention center. Finn sat silently and received them.

Leadership is rightfully yours, Finn, bestowed the Voice that kept him company in his mind. *They're wise to seek your approval.*

The only time he was anything other than magnanimous was when a giant of a boy came up to him.

"Get on the ground," he commanded.

Beagle stiffened.

The boy began, "Just who do you think you're talking—" But his words were cut short in the unwavering power of Finn's steely-eyed stare. First his hands, next his arms, and then his whole body visibly shook. "What's happening to me?" he asked, in a voice an octave higher. His body quaked until he knelt as originally commanded.

On his knees, the boy stared at Finn, even after the unknown pressure had compelled him to yield.

"What's your name, man?" Finn asked.

"Fred," the boy croaked out. He remained on his knees, his eyes now directed at the floor.

"Rise now, Fred. Will you join us?"

"How did you do that to me?"

"I did nothing. I'll ask you one last time: do you accept this honor of joining us?"

Fred stood. Seconds seemed like hours. Finn thought the boy looked as though a war were waging inside.

Finn rolled his shoulders back and straightened up further. "Taking a moment to think there, Fred? Smart man. I appreciate thoughtful commitment."

Fred's once-defiant expression changed to concession. "Yes. I will join you."

"Have a seat with us." Finn pointed to the chair next to Beagle, which was occupied at that moment. Without another word, the boy vacated the chair, and Fred sat down, resting his beefy forearms on the table.

Finn intermittently acknowledged those who came to welcome him, but most of his attention stayed with Fred, Beagle, and Alistair, who'd since rejoined them. "I want each of you to find the best someone to recruit and make up our gang. Do you need to know the specific qualities?" Finn leaned toward them, grasping the table's edge in front of him until his knuckles turned white.

They all shook their heads, just enough.

"Good."

Pushing himself up, Finn stood and raised his arms above his head to draw the attention of the room.

"Are you listening?" his voice boomed.

For the second time in two days, the room was silent.

"I recognize you all for what you are. How nice to be welcomed in this manner." There was a syrupy tone to his voice, yet it allowed no opposition. "You may come again tomorrow, but this is it for today."

Finn got up to leave. Beagle, Alistair, and Fred followed him out. They headed down the hallway to their various cells.

"Later. Keep an ear to the ground, everyone," Finn called after them.

"I'll keep you updated," Alistair responded. "At lunch tomorrow unless I hear something before that."

"See you then," Finn confirmed.

Finn and Beagle continued to their cell. Finn watched out of the corner of his eye as Beagle struggled to keep up.

Are you having fun? inquired the Voice that came from within.

"I can't talk to you now. I'm busy."

You'll talk to me whenever I appear. Don't fool yourself, pal.

Even at the peak of his glory, Finn decided not to argue.

Do you know what you're meant to do up ahead? Do you know why you're collecting them?

I felt it was the thing to do, Finn thought.

That's because I'm always here, prompting you, even when you don't realize it. Don't forget that. When I call in my chips, you must obey.

Finn paused then thought, *It's for Beagle to do my bidding, not for me to do yours. I'm in control. My orders must be obeyed.* He waited for Beagle to catch up then turned to look at him. "*I* must obey?" He laughed under his breath. "We'll see about that." Finn's pace quickened, as did his temper.

"Sir? Obey? But I . . . What?"

Yes, we'll see, said the Voice. *Unless you do what I need you to do, this will come to an unsatisfactory end.*

So you say, but what proof have you offered?

I don't need to provide any, but I can. I am you, idiot. I can hurt you more than you can imagine. Would you like your proof now, Finn?

Finn felt a stab behind his left eye. A poke on his nerves that was impossible to ignore. His face contorted, and he bent over, distressed. A long moment later, the pain finally eased.

Openmouthed, Beagle leaned toward Finn then backed away, shaking. "Are you okay, sir?"

Fine. You proved your point. Now leave me alone. I've got things to do.

"It's been a long day, Beagle," Finn decided. "I need to lie down."

The lunchtime ceremony continued for several days. Finn ordered Beagle to bring a large paper sack with him each day as they took their place at the far end of the room, against the wall. Visitors lined up, far enough away to provide Finn privacy. They dropped their cigarettes, candy, soap, and an occasional magazine or deck of cards into the bag as they sought Finn's counsel.

Though the room still hummed with various conversations, the once-raucous din had quieted, thanks in part to the disappearance of the metal lunch trays. Their replacements were made of dull cardboard. It was a silent acknowledgement from the officers who patrolled the room to the newest resident who had come out of nowhere.

CHAPTER TWENTY-NINE

Enter the Jennifer . . . Joie de Vivre!

*B*ANYAN . . .

Sadie heard the whisper and twitched, causing Barnaby to jump off her lap. "Did you hear that too, Barnaby?"

The cat gave her a blank stare, turned, and sauntered off without even a good-bye.

"Fine. Be that way. I know I heard a name." Sadie stood next to the tree and placed her palm against it. "Is that what you'd like me to call you? Banyan?"

She closed her eyes and waited for an answer.

Banyan, replied the wind.

It had taken a week of daily visits to find out his name. By researching trees, she had learned he was a weeping willow. She didn't think it was possible, but every day brought her more connection to her secret place. She never knew when Barnaby would show, but she loved when he did.

"I'll be back tomorrow. Thank you for telling me your name, Banyan."

She headed home, away from the Fletcher house, making

sure no one saw her leave the woods. She was almost there when she saw a moving truck pull up to the house across the street.

New neighbors. Huh. Interesting. I wonder if they have any kids.

She headed over to investigate.

Sadie observed her new neighbor for a few minutes as she took some things out of the trunk of a car. The girl had a ton of curly brown hair and appeared to be around her age.

Sadie walked up the driveway—so new it was a bit sticky.

She spoke first. "Hi, I'm Sadie. I live across the street in that white ranch." She turned around and pointed. "Nice sticky driveway you got there."

"Hey. My name's Jennifer, but you can call me Jennifer. Oh, the driveway? Yeah, isn't that nice? It was a parting gift from the people who lived here before. We just moved here from Chicago. It's pretty dead around here compared to what I'm used to." She tucked a bit of her wild hair behind her ear. "Aren't we supposed to shake hands or something?" Jennifer noted, looking up at the taller girl.

Sadie shrugged. "We can if you like."

Jennifer put out a hand to shake. When Sadie joined in, Jennifer wrapped her thumb around Sadie's and flittered the rest of her fingers away like a wing. Sadie couldn't help but smile.

She helped Jennifer with a few more bags from the trunk and carried them to the front door, where Jennifer's mom greeted them.

Jennifer's mother looked like she had stepped out of a fashion magazine. Despite it being moving day, she wore a belted dress and knee-high boots. Every wave in her chestnut hair was perfectly placed.

"Hi, I'm Mrs. Hunt, but you can call me Carol."

"Nice to meet you, Mrs. Hunt."

"Didn't I just say to call me Carol?" She winked and went

back inside, returning with a man who was equally well dressed. "Honey, this is Jennifer's new friend, Sadie. Sadie, meet my husband, Tom."

They both said hi at the same time. Tom gave Sadie a charming smile before heading back into the house.

"Your parents are so friendly."

"Yeah, they're okay. Hey, thanks for helping with the bags," Jennifer told Sadie. "You should come back on Saturday. I'll give you the grand tour. We can hang out. You can have dinner over, maybe watch a movie with me?"

"Don't you need to ask your parents?" Sadie could only imagine what her own parents would say if she invited someone over without a formal request.

Jennifer rolled her eyes. "*Please*. My parents pretty much let me do whatever I want. As long as I don't set the house on fire, they don't care what I do."

Sadie agreed on the spot. *Yeah, why should I ask my parents?* She felt daring.

"Okay, see you then."

Sadie waved from across the street and headed inside. *Everything feels right. Could be a new start.*

*   *   *

After the doldrums of her daily classes and doing her best to avoid Dave and his cronies all week, Friday afternoon finally had arrived, bringing a sense of relief. Sadie kept an eye out for Jennifer but hadn't seen her at school. *Maybe her parents gave her the week off?*

With her anticipation, it was harder than usual for her to fall asleep that night. Despite that, she woke the next morning feeling rested. *This is going to be a good day. I can feel it. Haven't had one of those in a really long time.*

Sadie got ready then inhaled her cereal, barely chewing it.

"You're going to choke. Take it easy over there." Her mom touched her daughter's shoulder then handed her a glass of juice.

"Mmokay, phMom," Sadie mumbled through a full mouth.

"Sadie, don't talk with your mouth full," her mother scolded, shaking her head.

Sadie didn't let that bother her. She gulped down her pulp-laden juice and, while clearing her plate, blurted, "I'm having dinner and watching a movie over at Jennifer's tonight. See you later, Mom."

"Well, I guess that's okay, Sadie. It's about time you made a new friend. See you later." Mom stood, arms crossed and winked. "Have fun."

"Later." She ran out the door.

The last time she had visited a friend was back before the Dark Ages.

Jennifer's house was a split-level with three floors. When Sadie came over after breakfast that day, she looked around, following Jennifer as she indicated the rooms with game-show-model flair.

"We have a secret den on the bottom level," she said conspiratorially, "plus a huge basement where I'm going to throw lots of parties."

Sadie was intrigued; she definitely was interested in going to parties again.

As Jennifer showed her around the house, Sadie noticed that her new friend laughed a lot, especially at herself.

"Look at these cheesy paintings I did years ago. My parents save everything and hang it up—I think to humiliate me!" Jennifer cackled, throwing her head back. "It's so ridiculous. I think I painted this one with my hands behind my back and the brush between my teeth. Come on. Let me show you something." She took Sadie's arm and led her upstairs and out the back door.

They half walked, half ran through a few of the neighbors' yards and finally up over a hill. Sadie never had wandered to this side of the hill before. As they crested it, she stared with her mouth open. An untouched field of dandelions stretched out for half a mile. Almost every yellow flower had given way to soft white puffs, ready for wishes to be made.

"Uh, you might want to close your mouth before you start catching mosquitoes." Jennifer pointed and made a funny face with her mouth hanging open.

Realizing how she must look, Sadie closed her mouth and hung her head a little.

"Oh, come on, Sadie. Can't you take a joke?" Jennifer lightly punched her in the arm.

"Oh." Sadie smiled, and they both laughed.

They ran midway into the field of dandelions, sat down, and thought of wishes. Sadie's allergies made her nose twitch, but the fragrance was worth it. It reminded her of sunlight—if sunlight could have a smell.

"I know!" Jennifer said, closing her eyes tightly. "I wish I had straight hair down to my butt."

"Oh, that's a good one, but I love your curly hair."

"You do?" she asked, opening one eye first then the other.

"Yeah, it's so pretty. My hair is always so straight, and I can't do anything with it. That's why I always wear it in pigtails."

"Oh, you shouldn't think like that, Sadie. I like your hair. It's really nice."

Sadie blushed. "Thanks."

"What are you going to wish for?" Jennifer asked.

"I wish I was a princess." As soon as the word left her lips, she was mortified.

"A princess? What are you? Six years old?" Jennifer roared hard at that.

Embarrassed, Sadie thought quickly. She had no idea where

that wish had come from. "I'm just kidding. Can't you tell I'm joking?" Sadie questioned with a bit of nervous laughter.

"Oh, yeah. I could tell," mocked Jennifer. "So what are you really going to wish for?"

Sadie thought for a moment before she answered. "I wish I could be with Gramma Rose again. I miss her."

"Why can't you be with her? Where'd she go? Did she move away?" Jennifer raised an eyebrow.

"She passed away last year."

"Oh, I'm sorry to hear that." Jennifer plucked another dandelion. "I wish that no one we love would ever have to die . . . and that I marry a super-handsome, rich actor when I grow up." She giggled then blew until every last seed departed.

Sadie laughed too, and they spent the next hour whispering back and forth, making wishes.

"C'mon," Jennifer coaxed. "Let's head back to my house. I'm thirsty. Who knew making wishes was such hard work?"

When they got back, Jennifer pointed at the hose. She twisted the spigot, pressed the nozzle trigger, and took a long drink. She offered the hose to Sadie, who swallowed big mouthfuls of the cold water.

Without warning, Jennifer grabbed the hose back. Nodding with a mischievous look, she goaded, "That's right, I'm going to . . ." and squirted Sadie in the face.

Reflexes took over. First Sadie covered her face, and then, without even thinking, she grabbed the hose back, retaliating with a direct hit into Jennifer's open mouth. "Now who's catching mosquitoes?"

Jennifer snarfed the water then bent over, choking.

"Are you all right?" Sadie asked, growing concerned.

Jennifer fell to the ground, her eyes rolling back in her head.

Panicked, Sadie dropped beside her and shook her. "Jennifer, are you okay?" She got no response, so she shook her harder. "Jennifer, wake up!"

Jennifer's eyes snapped into focus. "Boo!"

Sadie screamed, falling backward onto the wet lawn.

Jennifer rolled onto her side, laughing until tears formed.

"How could you do that to me?" Sadie demanded, keeping her voice even, but within seconds Jennifer's laughter grew contagious. Sadie bent over laughing, holding her stomach. "I . . . bwhahahaha, can't . . . hahahahaha . . . breathe . . . hahahaha." Tears of silliness ran down her cheeks.

When the two girls finally calmed down, Jennifer playfully punched Sadie in the arm. "Sadie, you're all right. You're a lot of fun."

"Thanks," Sadie replied, rubbing her arm. "You are too."

They recoiled the hose then headed inside.

"You're just in time for dinner, girls," Carol called from the kitchen.

Sadie licked her lips at the sight of beer-battered fish and chips. *Fantastic!* They all sat down and dug in.

For dessert, Carol presented the girls with sundaes with extra hot fudge.

Sadie took a big bite. She leaned over so the sauce wouldn't get all over the table. *So amazing.* "Yum." *This is too good to be true. I never get to eat like this at home.*

Next on the agenda came hot cocoa and a movie. "Mmm . . . hot cocoa," Jennifer cooed. "Good any time. Wouldn't ya say, Sadie ol' chum?"

"Why, yes, Jennifer. Indoobidablee. I would have to agree with you on that. Cheerio!" They chuckled at their unsuccessful attempts at British accents.

Sadie finished her drink, tapping on the bottom of the mug to get every last drop. She couldn't remember the last time she'd had hot cocoa, especially on such a humid day.

A shimmer at the bottom of the mug caught her eye. A face formed from the tiny drops of remaining cocoa, and it looked a whole lot like Gramma, but then it started to change. She grew younger. Gramma was gorgeous. *This is unreal. It can't be happening.* Then Gramma grew younger still, until she looked around Sadie's age.

The face was rising now. In soft wisps the image swirled up to the top of the yellow mug, her arms down, her hands gripping each side of it.

"Um, Jennifer . . ."

Before Jennifer could turn around, the ghostlike girl brought her index finger to her lips. Sadie could have sworn she heard her whisper, "Shhhhhh."

"What you want, Sadie?"

Sadie looked back inside the mug, but all she saw was the last dried bits of cocoa. "Uh, never mind. I was going to show you something, but it doesn't matter now."

"Dang, Sadie," Jennifer teased, "you're one weird girl, but I like ya anyway."

Sadie laughed that off. *I'd better keep stuff to myself before she thinks I'm nuts.*

When the movie, *Jaws*, was over, Sadie carried her mug to the kitchen. Then she thanked Carol and Tom, hugged Jennifer, and crossed the street to her home. She basked in the glow of her perfect day and evening until she walked through the front door.

"Hi, Mom. I'm home." She felt the change in atmosphere as soon as she entered. "I had an awesome day. I'm going to bed."

"Okay, Sadie," Mom muttered, sitting on the sofa, watching the news. "Sleep well. See you in the morning."

That night, Sadie lay awake in bed, thinking of the hot-cocoa Gramma ghost girl. Even the ghost had more expression than her mother.

CHAPTER THIRTY

Release the Hounds

FINN RAN HIS fingers through his hair and pursed his lips the second he heard the Voice.

You got everyone you need. You found that guy, Fred. What a keeper he is. And who expected an extra from that little Beagle? Now it's seven, a lucky number if ever there was one.

"What are you driveling on about, Mr. Oh-So Helpful?"

Once again it's time to pack your bags. You know, buddy boy, I shouldn't have to tell you these simple things anymore. You're all grown up now. Or are you?

Ignoring that last taunt, Finn shook his head. "I thought I'd stay for my birthday. It's only a few more weeks."

Stop whining. Who gives a rotten banana about your birthday? Time to go. Snap, snap! Are you sure everyone knows where to meet? At the halfway house?

Finn rolled his eyes. "Of course. What a stupid question. Everyone's already there except Beagle and me. There's Fred and Alistair, Carl, Ben, and Patrick. Beagle's getting out next month, so I'm sticking around to wait for him . . . you know, make sure he's okay."

This is where we disagree. Big time. Let that pup use his big-boy pants and do one thing on his own. He'll be the better for it.

"I think I'll stay, if it's all the same to you."

It's not up to you. You're leaving today. I saw the papers, signed and sealed.

"What are you talking about? I'm leaving next month with Beagle. It's been arranged."

No. You're not . . . and no, it hasn't—not anymore. You'll get a kick out of this, tiger. They're giving you an extra month of half freedom in addition to your early release for good behavior. That makes seven months off your two-year sentence . . . again, a lucky number. Either your psychiatrist put in a good word, or more likely they need your bed for a new kid.

Finn picked up a book and hurled it across the room, just as two guards strolled up to the door to his cell.

"Get your stuff together, Montgomery," one of them commanded. "You're out of here by the top of the hour."

Finn looked at Beagle, who had crammed himself in the corner by the far side of his pillow. The boy whimpered as big ploppy tears rolled down his cheeks.

"Listen up, Your Majesties," Finn growled. "My release date is in a month."

"You know the rules, Montgomery. It doesn't work that way. You do what *we* say." They left before Finn's second statement formed on his lips.

It was too late, yet he repeated it: "My release date is in a *month!*"

He changed his tone with restraint and gently sat on Beagle's bed. "It's only a month, Beagle," he reassured the boy. "You can hold it together. You have to. I'll see you then."

Beagle turned his face toward the wall as Finn packed what little he had into a grocery sack and was escorted from the cell.

* * *

The month passed slower than Finn could stand. He paced the claustrophobic kitchen of the halfway house on the second floor. The bedrooms on the third floor were nearly as small as his cell at juvie. All the rooms were white, except for the living room, which was an obnoxious shade of pumpkin. Three floors of white walls. He wanted so badly to write all over them, but now wasn't the time. There were more important tasks on his mind. He could hardly take this place for one more second, but he had to wait for their seventh member before busting out.

He thought he'd be in a better mood. Beagle was joining them today. But the Voice in his head constantly chided him about that, telling him not to get his hopes up. *What the heck does that mean?* Finn wondered.

One of his crew came up to offer him a can of soda. Finn grabbed it and crushed it against the boy's skull. Foamy, sticky liquid sprayed everywhere. Finn didn't even notice his own wet shirt.

"Clean up this mess," he barked. "All of you! It's disgusting in here! I want this floor so clean that you can eat off it, because—believe me—you're going to later tonight. I *cannot* believe how you've kept this place. It's a pigsty!"

"What, is the queen coming today?" joked Fred.

"Are you freaking kidding me, Fred? You dare to *joke*?"

Finn howled as if the full moon had walked right through the door. "Awwhoooooo!" He stomped one step closer, and Fred got busy cleaning on his haunches, cringing.

Finn advanced on the cowering boy-giant, prepared to give him a full-on beating, when he heard a car idling outside. Next came the sound of a door slamming out front. The group froze. Fred dared a furtive glance at the window. Finn fastened "The Eye" on each of them in turn. Each stayed put, quickly returning to their cleaning efforts.

Finn arrived at the window in three long strides and parted

the dingy curtains. There he saw the small blond boy, arm in a sling, limping toward the front door with a guard for a companion.

Blood dripped slowly to the floor as Finn's anger forced his fingernails into the tender flesh of his palm. Alistair rushed to clean it up.

"Carl. Ben. Bring Beagle to me," Finn ordered in a monotone voice.

"Sure, boss."

Finn stared at where his Beagle had walked a moment before. When he got his hands on those who had hurt him . . . He could already hear their screams.

Finn was not pleased. Not happy at all. Even the air could tell.

CHAPTER THIRTY-ONE

Where Oh Where Has
My Christopher Gone?

S ADIE WALKED OVER to Jennifer's house after breakfast. "I had fun yesterday. I don't know how we're going to top it."

"Hmmm," mused Jennifer, rubbing her hands together. "I know. Let's make some money."

Sadie's left eyebrow rose. "Okay. Tell me more."

"How about we go door to door with a fake collection box and say we're taking donations for charity? I've done it before with great success. No one will ever know. And I already have a box I've used upstairs in my room."

Sadie didn't feel at all comfortable with this proposition. "Are you sure that's cool, Jen? Sounds wrong to me."

"Yeah, it's fine. Come on. It's all good."

Sadie hesitated. She finally had a friend and wanted to give her a real chance, but on the other hand, this was messed up. *Maybe I'll just keep her company?*

Jennifer dashed into the house then came back a minute or two later with a box marked, "UNISELF," which looked *almost* totally official. They walked down the street and talked. "So what are the boys like around here?" asked Jennifer.

"Well, the ones in my classes are a bunch of jerks," grumbled Sadie. "They never shut up, and they're always on me about something. I keep as far away from them as possible." She considered mentioning the missing pin and what had come after but decided it best to keep quiet. She didn't want to scare away her new and only friend.

"Are they cute at least?"

"Yeah, kind of, but they're awful. I'd stay away from them if I were you."

"Well, obviously I'm not you, Sadie. They won't be mean to me. I do pretty well with the boy population, if you know what I mean."

Sadie nodded. "Okay, but don't say I didn't warn you."

"I won't. So have you ever had a boyfriend, Sadie?"

"Two years ago I had an amazing boyfriend."

"Really?" Jennifer sounded curious. "Tell me more."

"His name's Christopher. He told me that one day we would get married and always be together. He was perfect."

"If he's so perfect, where the heck is he? Should we go knock on his door? Come out, Christopher Charming. Come out, come out, wherever you are."

Sadie heard Jennifer's laughter, heard the teasing, and although she continued to walk with Jennifer, it faded in the distance. Her mind was with Christopher and the last time they were face-to-face.

Christopher had held Sadie's hand and led her along the tree-shaded path that ran around the perimeter of the neighborhood park. "Sadie, I have to talk to you about something important," he'd said. "I don't know where to start."

"Uh-oh. That sounds serious. Did you run away from prison or something? Are you in trouble with the law?" Sadie teased.

He offered her a half smile, but his expression soon grew grim. "I have some bad news. I don't know how to tell you this."

Sadie saw he was serious. He wasn't teasing her. "Oh, okay. What is it? You can tell me anything—you know that."

He stared at their hands, his head slowly shaking. "I know, Sadie, it's just that I don't want it to be true. If I say it out loud, then it's for real and I can't take it back."

Sadie squeezed his hand. "Whatever it is, just tell me, please. You're scaring me."

"Okay, come sit with me over on the grass." Still pensive, Christopher finally began. "I found out last week that my father got a new job."

Sadie's head canted to one side. "But that sounds like good news."

"No, it's not. He got a job in New York City. We're leaving tomorrow morning."

All the blood drained from Sadie's face. Her heart sped up, and she felt like she might pass out. "Tomorrow? How can that be? That can't be right. It takes time to do these things. You have to pack the whole house and find a new place to live. No one leaves that fast."

"Not with this, Sadie. His new company is taking care of everything for us. We're flying out tomorrow."

This can't be happening. It's too soon. I'm not prepared to say good-bye. "You knew last week? Why are you just telling me now? All this time you've known, and you didn't even seem a bit upset. Are you upset at all?"

A sorrowful expression draped down his face. "Of course I am. I didn't know how to tell you. This is a really good opportunity for my dad, and it's New York City. You know I've always wanted to live there."

Cracking at first, Sadie's voice grew emphatic, "Yes, of course, but in like ten years . . . and with me!"

Agitated now, Sadie waited for him to clear up his obvious mistake.

"I know, I know. It's going to be really hard, but we'll write all the time, and you can come visit me whenever you want."

Sadie's gaze trailed off; she felt tears forming. She wrapped her arms around Christopher's neck and hugged him. "I'm going to miss you so much. I'm not ready for you to go."

"Neither am I. It'll be okay, though. You'll see. It won't be as bad as you think. We'll figure something out. Don't be sad." He brushed away her tears with his thumb. They sat for a few minutes longer, but even as he stroked her hair, she felt him pulling away.

He glanced at his watch. "I need to go. Mom wants me home for dinner and some last-minute packing."

They stood. "I guess this is it for now, Sadie. But you have to promise me you won't worry. You have to believe that everything's going to be okay."

She hugged him tightly as a fresh round of sobs racked her shoulders. She didn't want to let go. Her tears soaked his T-shirt.

Christopher gently pulled her arms away and took a step back. His eyes were red and puffy. She could tell he did his best to hold it together. Choking on his words, he managed to get one last sentence out: "Until we meet again, m'lady."

Sadie had stood rooted to that spot until she could no longer see him. She had pressed her hand to her chest, certain her heart had shattered.

"Earth to Sadie," Jennifer teased. "Seriously, where does this perfect prince charming live? I think I need to meet him."

"No, you can't." Sadie put her head down, still shaken. "Christopher and his family moved to New York City. I couldn't believe it: one day he's here, and the next he's gone. I walked by his house every day for months, still looking for him. I swear I could still see him in his backyard, shooting hoops. Sometimes I still feel his hand in mine, still hear his laugh. He has the best laugh. You'd like him."

"Oh, my Gah, Sadie, really? You went to his house every day, even though you knew he wasn't there?" Jennifer couldn't stop laughing. "Stalker much? Oh, Sadie, you could still see . . . hahaha . . . him in the . . . hahahaha . . . backyard?" she mocked between bouts of laughter. "Do you kiss your pillow at night too, imagining it's him?"

Painful memories of her lost love spurred such heartache that Jennifer's ridicule couldn't take hold. The last time she'd heard from Christopher was a year ago, but he'd written in one of his few letters that he would come back to her one day. Sadie shrugged and tried to hide her true emotions. "He was a great guy, Jennifer. What can I say?"

"Whatever, girl. He's just a boy. Come on. Let's get going. We have work to do and moolah to make."

Sadie walked quietly as she half listened as Jennifer went on and on. Flashes of red . . . Sadie snapped her head to the right. Again, flashes of red . . . She looked all around.

"What, Sadie? What is it?" Jennifer asked.

"I don't know. I thought I saw something."

"Well, the only thing I see is an empty collection box. Let's start making some cash."

Sadie shook her head. "I don't really feel comfortable with this."

"Oh, come on. You don't even have to say any actual words."

They walked up to a two-story beige-colored Victorian with purple shutters and a perfectly manicured lawn.

"This looks like a good place to start," Jennifer nearly sang. "They can certainly afford to give us a donation."

"So you really think this is a good idea? I mean—"

"Oh, come on. It's fine. They'll never know what we're up to."

They climbed the stairs up to the front door. Jennifer knocked.

"Coming," called a voice from inside.

Sadie started sweating. The wind kicked up, rustling in her ears as it whipped up her pigtails. She turned and looked behind her. Several trees gave shade to the front yard of the house, but not a single leaf rattled in the breeze.

Sadie rubbed her right ear. *Weird. Where's that coming from?*

An old woman answered the door, her Siamese cat wrapped around her stockinged leg.

"Yes? What can I do for you young ladies?"

Sadie frowned and stepped backward. *This doesn't feel right at all.*

Jennifer launched into her pitch, and then Sadie heard it. A whisper.

And what do you think you're doing, Sadie?

Sadie felt all her muscles contract, especially the ones in her face. Her right eye twitched.

You're better than this. Make a decision right now.

She had no idea where the voice came from or if it was even real, but she knew what she had to do.

"I'm sorry, ma'am. We didn't mean to bother you." She took another step back, pulling Jennifer with her.

Jennifer shot her a death-ray glare. "Uh, Sadie, what are you doing?" she seethed out the side of her mouth.

"Saving us," she whispered back. Then louder she added, "Sorry. This is the wrong house." She turned to Jennifer. "Come on. Let's go find the right one."

Their eyes met, and for a moment, she worried that Jennifer wouldn't relent, but Sadie had left her little choice.

"Oh, yeah, you're right. Wrong house." Jennifer turned and gave the old woman a winning smile. "Sorry to have bothered you, ma'am."

The confused woman smiled, "No bother at all girls." The cat winked at Sadie, and a sense of familiarity swept through her.

When they reached the end of the driveway, Jennifer

punched Sadie's arm. "What the hell, Sadie? She was such an easy target."

"I know you said it wouldn't be a problem, but I can't do it. And may I just say, '*ouch!*'"

"Fine, be a chicken. I'll do it on my own. See you later. Bawk, bawk." She moved her arms like wings as she walked away.

Sadie stood at the end of the woman's driveway, fuming. She knew she had done the right thing, but it would have been nice to have kept a friend.

Even if it was Jennifer.

CHAPTER THIRTY-TWO

Shocked through a Canyon

*D*EAR RUFUS,
There's been a lot of things happening lately. I think they're finally looking up . . . well, except for the nightmares and Jennifer and school and my parents.

First things first. The good stuff:

I found an incredible place, Rufus. I don't want to go into detail just in case anyone other than me reads you, but I think you know what I'm talking about. I needed this.

Here's the so-so news:

You know that new friend of mine, Jennifer? Well, scratch that. She's turning out to be not so nice after all—in any way. I'm finding it takes more than parental freedom to make a good friend. I might try one more time. I'm not sure.

Now for the bad:

The pièce de résistance: I had another nightmare last night.

It was about him again. The creepy shadow man. I see him more and more now. I don't know why or what it means. Who could he be?

I watched through the woods. I saw him slinking down the sidewalk. It was daytime, but he was still dark. His shadow trailed behind him, like smoke from a candle, swirling as he walked. All I could make out in his darkness were those piercing scarlet eyes.

He walked in front of a tall brick wall, and it was crumbling as he passed it. Strange, huh? When it was all knocked down, an empty room appeared behind it. No windows, no doors, but I could see into it from where I stood. Then suddenly I was inside it. I opened my mouth to scream, and it shook me awake. When I opened my eyes, I was facing my window, and an arm reached in from outside then sped toward me. It looked like the images on a movie screen at high speed, and it reached all over the place. It stopped short of my bed, but then it kept moving all around, like it was trying to grab at me. All of a sudden, it burst into roses. Bright-red roses, blooming so fast I could hardly count them. They were like red-rose fireworks. I watched for at least five minutes before they faded.

I know what I saw has to do with Gramma, but yet again, I'm not sure what she's trying to tell me. After that I finally went back to sleep, and the dream didn't return.

Weird, huh, Rufus? I know Gramma Rose watches over me, and that makes me feel safe, even though I'm afraid. With all these things happening around me, it might be some time before I get a chance to write to you again, but I really want to thank you for everything you've done for me. You were there when no one else was. Thank you, my dearest friend. I'll never forget you.

Good-bye for now.

* * *

A thousand miles away, a cry echoed through the woods. The gray-haired man screamed as he woke, his mind twisting in pain.

She's here again. She stares at me with those blinding eyes. Accusing me. Who told her? How could she know?

CHAPTER THIRTY-THREE

The Gang's All Here

FINN SAW ONLY white. The light from the overarching skies, he guessed. There was a strange star, so close and directly overhead. It seemed to be the cause of all this brightness. They had lifted him out of the water onto dry land. His head swam with the cartoon standards for his experience: little tweeting birds and stars zipping and twirling until the oxygen returned to his brain.

A voice that wasn't his own spoke softly. "What happened?"

He urged his mind to focus on the source of the words. White hair, a female voice. He could see her hair but not her face. A cloying wind blew strands of it around. The distinct, putrid scent of rotting meat drifted down to him.

"He was in the water. We lifted him out," explained a deeper voice.

Finn shivered. His wet clothing clung to his body but provided little warmth. A bright, glowing form caught his eye, but it was closer to the ground, not in the sky as the natural order dictated. It had what resembled petals stuck around its circular edge. He wanted to say something, but his mouth was still full of that disgusting liquid. For all he knew, he had worms swimming around inside. He rolled over and spat out the slime as quickly as he could.

Claustrophobia set in as the silhouettes of three beings surrounded him. Though he couldn't explain it, he sensed that he knew them and that he'd been in this place before. Bile rose in his throat, turning to hatred as he focused on the two figures to his left. The one on the right, however, was in sync with him and didn't burn like the others.

Finn's eyelids fluttered as the forms took more definite shape, their images growing clearer and distinct. He couldn't hold on. In the next second, they were sucked backward and away.

He sat up in his bed, fully awake, right where he'd gone to sleep at the halfway house. His boys were in their rooms across the hall. The light, the voices, and the disgusting smell: those had all been a dream.

He got up and splashed water on his face. It had been a long time since he'd dreamed of anything at all. As he recalled the shapes and images, a wave of familiarity struck him.

He sensed that it hadn't been a dream but a memory. *How could that be?* It didn't make any sense or fit in with what he saw day to day, especially the images strongest in his mind now: the sun—a strange sun—strung on a chain of pearls, he now remembered, along with a flower he couldn't name. More details flowed in as he concluded it was real. There were silver streams of light around him. He couldn't forget them.

With another splash of water, he felt awake enough to tackle the first item on his agenda: talking to Beagle.

Yesterday, Finn had insisted on commandeering one of the rooms on the first floor as a makeshift infirmary. He was the only one who could make Beagle feel better, he had argued with the administrator. He won permission to keep Beagle isolated from the rest of the boys until he fully recovered. The last thing Beagle needed was all their crap.

Finn had watched the triage nurse escort Beagle back to his room late last night. The nurse had insisted on no visitors, and Finn allowed the boy to rest undisturbed for the night. This morning, however, was an opportunity not to be wasted, so he snuck down the hall to where Beagle's name adorned the wall next to the door.

Finn knocked gently and whispered Beagle's name. He waited, but no one came, so he took a chance and turned the knob. There was only one occupied bed, and he recognized the tuft of blond hair peeking out from beneath the covers. He closed the door quietly. It made a soft click as it fell back into place. A set of pale-green eyes peered up at him.

"Beagle, I would appreciate it if you'd answer the door whenever I knock, should I deign to do so."

"Sorry, sir." Beagle could barely get the words out.

Has he been crying? Finn sat on the bed and leaned toward Beagle. "Speak up, man! I can't hear you when you whimper."

"I said, 'Sorry, sir!'" He made a small attempt to salute.

"Are you getting snippy with me, pup? Is that what a month away from me does to you?"

"I'm in a lot of pain, sir." The boy winced as he spoke. "I'm trying my best. Honestly I am."

"Who did this to you, Beagle?"

Beagle pulled the covers back a little but made no effort to sit up. "You know that guy, the big one?"

"Which one? There are several."

"It was the famous one from Pudding/Tray Day. Do you remember, sir?"

"How could I forget? That sniveling idiot. I put him on the ground, where any snake must crawl."

"Once you left, sir, there was no order. He took over, saying he would restore it, but things got even worse. I was first on his list of examples."

Finn ground his teeth so hard that his jaw muscles ached. "What did the nurse tell you?"

"That I should rest and not do any of the house duties for a week. Plus, they gave me a fancy sling for my arm. It has cartoons on it."

"Well, put it on immediately, Beagle. Stop wasting time. I need you to get better as quickly as you can."

"Yes, sir. I'll do it. It's good to see you again." Beagle finally tried to get up but couldn't. He fell backward so quickly that Finn feared he might hit his head on the wall. A gasp almost escaped Finn's lips, but he reeled it back in before any harm was done.

Finn stood. He coughed a couple of times while the words came out: "Rest up. I'll be calling on you soon."

Once outside the door, Finn leaned against the wall, his hands on his knees. He was pretty certain that anyone who came around the corner would be able to see the steam coming out of his nostrils. *Someone will pay for this.*

Ben's timing was impeccable, if not serendipitous for Finn. The boy rounded the corner and soon found himself on the floor after a body slam smashed him into the wall. Finn didn't wait to see the outcome and was soon back in his room.

* * *

Another season was on its way out, but it already had done its damage. The Voice had told Finn about the meetings and grumblings of his men not once but four times over the past four months.

"Men?" Finn laughed. "Do call them what they are."

I wouldn't blow this off if I were you. There's danger out there if you're not careful.

"Sure, sure. I don't buy it. They're mine. In my pocket so to speak."

Finn wanted to be free of the Voice yet still have all its knowledge. He waited for more words; nothing but silence followed. The Voice had wisdom, though Finn felt loath to admit it to anyone, including himself.

He decided to heed its advice for once. He changed course to go through the kitchen and see what his lackeys were up to this morning in the dining room. Ignoring the disapproving expression on the cook's ruddy face, Finn positioned himself near the dining-room door, tucked behind the doorframe—hidden but well within earshot. Even with the ruckus of food preparation, he tuned in to the voices in the next room.

"This has gone on long enough," griped Patrick.

"We do everything he says, yet what do we receive but abuse for our troubles?" Ben chimed in.

"He's the only one who knows where our stash is located. In what universe is that fair? We all put our butts on the line, yet he claims to be the 'sole caretaker'? I don't know about you guys, but when we get out next month, I'm done," bleated Patrick.

"Guys, I wouldn't be so quick to write him off. Finn's got reach. You remember Tray Boy, don't you? The one who beat up Beagle? I heard he had an 'accident' going down the stairs. We could be next," Alistair reminded them.

"Yeah, we'll have to disappear all right . . . if we decide to leave, I mean. Tray Boy is dead. No more Tray Boy. Kaput. Buried. Gone. I'm too young to wear a toe tag," whined Carl.

Finn could see that Beagle squirmed in his seat, while the others leaned forward, arms on the table. After all this talk, Beagle whispered more vehemently than the others.

"Guys, you're missing the point. Have you forgotten all that Finn's done for us? He's set us up for when we get out of here. He's the one who thought of daytime house invasions as a good stream of income. Think about how our heists have increased our skills. He takes care of us. We're completely protected but only as long as we're with him. Think about it some more before we talk again."

"I agree with Beagle and sort of with Patrick on this, guys. Once we're out of here, we can see what happens, but for now? In this little house? We need to stick together. We're the Golden Boys after all!" bragged Fred.

"Hello there, my loyal crew of men. How goes it today?" asked Finn, strolling through the door. Looking around he noticed there never was a more bloodless pack of specters at their dining-room table. Alistair actually backed up into space and fell on the tan linoleum. They were all pale except for his loyal Beagle, rosy cheeked as ever. He was also the only one who didn't jump like a guilty schoolboy when Finn arrived.

The others recovered from their alarm pretty quickly, as Finn was in one of his more reassuring moods. They glanced from one to another yet refrained from catching his eye.

Finn clenched his jaw. His smile froze on his face. His eyes flared. As soon as this happened, he turned toward Beagle and winked. A small wink but unmistakable.

Finn watched as Beagle did everything he could not to breathe, swallow, or move any bone in his body, trying not to show a reaction.

Good boy. Good, loyal Beagle. You'll live. With you serving at my side, we'll go far. You'll see. You might even grow a few feet taller. Anything's possible.

CHAPTER THIRTY-FOUR

Dawn on the Rocks

SADIE SPENT SATURDAY morning reading her latest mystery, *Killer Looks Can Kill When You're Not Looking.* With school and trips through the woods to visit Banyan, she hadn't had much time for this favorite activity.

Someone knocked on the door. Dad was working, as usual, so that left Mom.

"Come in."

"I'm heading out now to pick up some groceries and do a few errands, but I should be back by three. Is there anything you need from the store?"

"I'm good. Nothing I can think of right now. Thanks. See you then. I might go out for a walk, but I should be home by dinner at the latest."

"How's that new friend of yours? Are you going to see her today?"

"I'm not sure. I'll report in later." Sadie wanted to get back to her novel.

"Bye, Sadie." Mom waved and closed her door.

She spent another hour reading until it was time for a stretch. She grabbed a snack and decided it was time to see Banyan.

Making sure she had her keys and some money, she locked the door behind her.

Thank goodness it's the weekend. Too bad it didn't work out with Jennifer. That whole situation was like icing on my life's cake o' crap. I'm grateful for Banyan and Barnaby time. What else do I have to look forward to really?

Sadie hoped she could get past Jennifer's house without running into her. That was the last thing she wanted after seeing how awful she had behaved. She was almost in the safety zone when she heard that grating voice.

"Hey, Sadie! Where you been?"

Sadie kept walking, head down. For all Jennifer knew, she might not have heard her.

"Come on, Sadie! Don't be that way!"

All right. There was nothing to do but talk to her. *I have to sooner or later. Might as well do it here than at school.* She turned to face the voice.

Jennifer was hunkered down at the end of her driveway, her hands covered in suds on the far side of the family sedan.

Sadie ventured a monotone. "Hey, Jennifer. How you been?"

Jennifer stood up and smiled. "Doing okay. Wanna hang out today?"

"Nah, I'm just going for a walk, and then I need to be back to help my mom."

"Oh, come on, Sadie. I'm sorry about the other day. Really, I am."

Sadie looked in the direction she'd been heading a moment earlier then back at Jennifer. Something inside told her to keep on walking, but she thought it might be worth giving this friendship another shot. "Well . . . I guess an hour or so would be okay."

"I just have to finish up the car. You can help if you want. It's actually fun."

They wound up chasing each other around the car, doubling back to avoid getting hit with each other's wet sponges. Once they'd settled into a rhythm of focusing on the car instead of each other, it was done and rinsed in no time.

"That looks pretty good, don't you think?" Sadie asked.

"It really does. Thanks for the help."

"You're welcome."

Soon they were sitting and laughing together by the car, as if they hadn't been estranged for the last week.

The little girl who lived next door to Jennifer played in her yard while they worked, but once they finished, she came over to Jennifer's house.

"What are you guys doing?"

"Hi, Dawn." Jennifer grinned. "We're just hanging out."

"Oh. Can I hang out too?"

Sadie patted the ground beside her.

Jennifer leaned over and whispered, "I'll be right back. I'm going to get her a snack."

"Okay," Sadie replied, and turned her attention to Dawn.

"How old are you, and what grade are you in, Dawn?" Sadie asked.

"I'll be seven next Tuesday," she answered with obvious glee. "I'm in first grade!"

"How fun! Do you like school? Do you like your teacher?" But before Dawn could answer, Jennifer was back with a plastic bag in her hands. Tousling Dawn's short hair, she handed her the bag of raisins.

"Thank you," Dawn said, and tossed a couple into her mouth. A strange, pained look came over her face, and she spat them out. "You hurt my mouth!" the girl cried, her hand covering her frown. She dropped the bag and ran away. Jennifer bent to pick it up, but Sadie snatched the bag from Jennifer and took a closer look. More than half the "raisins" were actually pebbles.

"Jennifer, how could you do such a horrible thing to a little girl like that? To anyone?!"

"Calm down, Pollyanna! She'll get over it, and besides, it'll teach her a valuable lesson: don't take food from strangers."

In that moment, Sadie realized Jennifer didn't even know she had done anything wrong. She took no responsibility and showed no remorse.

Forget this. Being alone is better than being in this kind of friendship.

"Dawn might be able to get over it . . . *if* you didn't damage any of her teeth," Sadie snarled, "but I'll never forget. You did something awful . . . again. I'm done."

"Oooh, Shmadie's done. Run on home. I'm *so* upset." Jennifer made an overly dramatic sad face then smirked. "Take it easy, Polly. Enjoy your boring life."

Sadie ignored Jennifer's continuing taunts and resumed her original plan for the day. She started to walk in Banyan's direction when *Music box* chimed in her mind, and she listened. Jennifer's obvious plea for attention continued. Sadie hurried across the street to grab Gramma's gift before heading toward the Fletcher house.

Before stepping onto her lawn, Sadie took one last look across the street. It might have been the sun, but she thought she saw a glint of tears in the corners of Jennifer's eyes.

Well, there's another friendship down the toilet, Sadie thought. *I don't think it's me, but maybe I'm missing something.* She noticed her own tears only when they were halfway down her face.

Not even being near Banyan could make her feel better. Sadie cried as she nestled into her favorite spot between Banyan's roots. She tried to calm herself and connect with his warm, comforting energy, but not much changed.

She thought she heard a whisper nearby. She stopped crying and listened closely. She heard it again.

"Try not to worry. Everything is going to be okay."

Sadie sat straight up and turned toward the sound. She didn't hear anything. Nothing at all. *It must have been my imagination.*

"Everything is going to be okay."

There it is again. "Is someone here?" she called out, but the only sound she heard was the breeze. A prickling sensation crept up her arms, and she huddled closer to Banyan's roots.

Flashes of red sprang up in front of her. She pressed back against Banyan, looking around for more. They were gone, but her fear remained.

Still unnerved, Sadie stood up and walked around Banyan, looking for signs. After a few minutes passed without incident, she turned to her music box for comfort. She held it in her hands and lovingly admired its unique facade. After turning it over, she wound the tiny key beneath then opened the lid. The harp-like music soothed her. She relaxed, listening to the song and staring up into Banyan's swaying branches. After a few moments, she closed her eyes, and a soft smile reached her face.

Flashes of bright green sparkled in her mind, and her eyes opened hesitantly. Heavy, they closed again.

Flashes of blue. "Okay. What's going on?" She braced herself against Banyan's roots. "I'm starting to freak out a little here." No answers came.

Her body tingled. Colorful lights flashed, now visible even with her eyes open.

"Everything is going to be okay," she heard again.

"Something very weird is definitely going on here, and it's not my imagination. Who's out there?" Sadie scanned her surroundings. Then she spied him.

Near the stream stood a man wearing a long, shimmering coat over a navy suit. His black hat sat low over his brow, making it difficult for her to see his face in full. He was lean, tall, and his wingtip shoes were polished to a high shine. In his left hand, he carried a walking stick with a bright-blue stone at the end.

Sadie's heart pounded. She jumped to her feet and hightailed it around the back of Banyan for some imagined distance and safety.

I thought this was my place, Banyan. How does HE know about it?

"Your friend, Banyan, is a friend of mine too."

Whoa! What the what? He read my mind!

Sadie pressed a hand against Banyan's smooth trunk. *Banyan, if you've got anything to say, now would be the time.*

"Don't worry, Sadie. You have nothing to fear." The man's voice sounded familiar.

"Wait, it was you back at that old woman's house, wasn't it? The voice, telling me I was better than stooping to Jennifer's level? I thought I was losing my mind. Now you're here? Is it too much for me to ask what's going on? How do you know my name? Who are you?"

The stranger maintained his distance. "Forgive me if I intruded. It is only fair that you should know my name as well. I am Mr. Felix, and I have come to visit my friend, Banyan. It is Thursday after all."

A tenor, his voice was neither deep nor piercing. "You call him Banyan too? And what do you mean, 'It's Thursday'? It's Saturday."

"Young lady, it is always Thursday somewhere, and of course I call him Banyan. That is his name. Even you know it."

Sadie didn't appreciate his tone. He was too matter-of-fact about too many things. On the other hand, she didn't have the slightest idea what was going on. When he wouldn't answer any of her questions, she crossed her arms and rolled her eyes. "Let's back up a bit and start at the beginning. Where did you come from?"

The man smiled slowly. It was the only part of his face she could see from beneath his hat. He polished the blue stone with the edge of his sleeve. "I come from a place nearby. It is here but not here exactly." He leaned forward on his walking stick. "Banyan and I grew up together. He is one of my oldest and dearest friends."

Sadie gave him a skeptical look. "You don't make much sense, do you? It's Thursday, but it's not. You're from here but not exactly. What does it all mean?"

"You will see, in time."

Sadie hesitated then stepped out from behind the tree. "If you and Banyan are such good friends, how come I've never seen you before?"

"You were not ready."

Sadie cocked her head. "Ready? Ready for what?"

"Ready to learn."

Her arms tensed with perceived insult. "I don't need to learn anything from you," she huffed.

Mr. Felix smiled again, shook his head, and turned away.

"Wait, where do you think you're going?" She took a few steps forward but stopped when he turned back to face her.

"That is enough for today. I will see you in your dreams." And then he vanished.

Sadie rubbed her eyes then scanned the bank of the stream for as far as she could see. "Banyan?" *What the heck just happened?*

CHAPTER THIRTY-FIVE

Save the Date

M R. FELIX CAME back exactly seven counts after Sadie took off. This time he came in gradually. He saved the instantaneous dissolves and appearances for grand gestures.

It was a singular time of day. The setting sun hit the stream with glints in the water's movement, as if a stone of light perpetually skipped from here to there.

Mr. Felix knew that the sight of the sun on water warmed Banyan's heart. The glow spread naturally to his roots, branches, and leaves. He was able to look at the impressive old willow and hear meaning inside his own head.

Barnaby curled up for a catnap in the crook of one of Banyan's arms. He always chose that one branch. It was level with the ground, and there was an easy route up and down. He deserved a nap, even if it was with half an eye open, after all the work he'd done that day.

Mr. Felix cleared his throat to get everyone's attention, though it was hardly necessary. It was just one of those weird quirks about being human.

So, my friend, how do you think that went? Banyan's voice slid into Mr. Felix's mind with a smooth timbre.

You know how these things go, Banyan. It is a delicate process, especially with a strong personality such as hers. It is all necessary. It takes extra care.

My concern is the timing. I do not want her to feel pushed, as you know.

Nor do I, of course, and yet, Banyan, we're working with a limited amount of time.

What do you propose? Wait, I know. Let's just call her in. She has embraced me, so that bodes well for her embracing the shift. What do you think?

Mr. Felix chuckled. *She didn't embrace me too well, though, did she?*

We are on this side after all. And seeing how the connection will be through that box, it should ease any jet lag.

So the only question is when to issue the invitation.

You read my mind, Banyan replied.

It is what I do . . . and by the way, sir, so do you.

Ahhh . . . how true.

You were talking about the invitation before that bit of fun. Maybe we should move tonight?

Mr. Felix winked now. *I'm sure our old friend will provide a warm welcome.*

Tonight it is then. Sometimes I wish I were able to make popcorn.

If I didn't know you were teasing, I would bring some for you myself, Banyan.

CHAPTER THIRTY-SIX

Parting Makes a
Sweeter Tomorrow

F INN PULLED A folded piece of paper from his pocket and smoothed it open on the dining-room table. He could sense their nervousness, hear their minds wondering how much of their conversation he'd overheard. Their insolence would not go unpunished, but for now he needed them to focus.

"Here's the house we'll meet at during Choice Time." Finn pointed on the paper. "The southwest side of the house and the facing side of the house next door have no windows. There's a door there, and the tree coverage is also excellent. It's a perfect place for us to meet."

The gang, or the Golden Hounds, as they'd come to call themselves, looked from one to the other, but no one spoke up.

"Are you all going to sit there looking at each other like a bunch of idiots, or are you going to study the plans and prepare?" Finn crossed his arms, his piercing brown eyes sliding from boy to boy.

Patrick spoke first. He cleared his throat then leaned over the map. "Yes, of course. Excellent rendering, as usual, sir."

"Sure thing," Carl piped up, nodding slowly.

"Okay then," said Finn, "this heist should give us the financial resources we need in full. If we score this house, we'll have enough to leave Halfway Hullabaloo forever."

Carl asked, "Have you had a chance to scope the place out yet, Finn?"

"What do you think I am, as dumb as you? Of course I've been there. Every day this week."

Carl returned Finn's glare for about half a second then slumped down in his chair.

Finn resisted the urge to smack the spineless lump of Carl onto the floor. "That's why I'm in charge, and you would do well not to forget that." They never would be anything more than pathetic followers who required instructions for how to do everything.

Finn leaned across the table and continued. "Check out at the front desk, same as always. Meet me there at one o'clock this afternoon, and don't make it obvious. We've done this countless times before, so I trust that you all know what you're doing. Quick in, quick out. The best way to accomplish this is the following: we split up, and that way we'll have more coverage. Fred, Carl, Ben, and Patrick—you take the four upstairs bedrooms. Alistair, take the office downstairs. Beagle, you're on watch outside, while I explore the open spaces and the cookie jar. I wrote your assignments on these papers. On the back of page two, pay extra attention to the escape route. Study them."

Everyone dispersed quickly after this conversation, but Finn raised a hand and motioned for Beagle to stay.

"Have I ever told you, dear Beagle, how much I appreciate your loyalty, how you're always by my side when I need you?"

"You don't have to do this, sir. I owe you my life."

"Well, I did it. I want you to remember it always, because I might never actually say it again."

Finn watched as high color and a smile graced Beagle's hollow cheeks. "Thank you, sir."

"Never mind the thank-yous. There's work to be done. Go."

As Beagle ran off, Finn appreciated the momentary glow his power to give and take away feelings gave him. That was the best he could do with the warm and fuzzies, which usually left a bitter taste in his mouth and an irritating tingle on his skin. But this time it was tolerable . . . but only because it was Beagle.

*   *   *

Finn checked his watch for the umpteenth time in the past hour. The simple wristwatch read 12:30 p.m. *Those morons better not be late.*

He evaluated the key areas of the house from his position across the street, half concealed by a small grove of red oaks. Although several low-hanging branches already had begun to redden, their deep, sunset color didn't move him in the least. He leaned against the brown bark. All he had to do now was wait.

Everything was set for the party. He had picked the lock and placed the supplies inside the side door just after noon and left the house unlocked so it would be easy for the crew.

Sure about this, kiddo? It's one of those steps you can't take back, you know.

Finn pursed his lips and forced a long, slow breath between his teeth before he replied to the Voice. "Of course I know. Are you implying something?"

The good it'll do won't last. I'm telling you, but it's your decision, obviously.

"How kind of you to finally acknowledge the truth. I have no further use for you today, so if you don't mind, skedaddle. I see my boys coming up the road." Finn shifted his stance then shook his head. "Morons! I told them to come separately." *On any other day, they'd feel my disappointment on their faces, but that'll have to wait until later.*

For the last time, Finn, I urge you to reconsider. If you choose to go forward, I have no choice but to issue this ultimatum: I will take my leave of you. You will no longer have access to my knowledge, nor will I provide guidance. I will never return.

Finn shook his head. "I don't believe you for a second. You've always been too preoccupied with everything I do and bossing me around. You need me more than I need you."

The Voice did not reply. For a moment a strange pain pierced Finn's chest, one he'd never felt before. As the feeling dissipated, he shoved what was left of it down then stood up. He brushed off the seat of his corduroys and walked toward the street to meet his "pals."

The two-story colonial made for an easy mark. From the fancy semiprecious door knocker to the grand piano, it was a first-class dwelling ripe for dismemberment and sale.

Upon entry the gang dispersed to their assigned rooms. The boys went right to work. As usual, Finn sent Beagle outside to keep watch.

"Don't forget, three loud knocks on the side door if you see anyone. Then run as fast as you can to the rendezvous point. If anything goes wrong, I'll meet you there."

Beagle nodded and scampered toward the door.

"I mean it, Beagle: knock and run. Don't come in. Your job is to monitor the outside and the outside only."

"Got it," he replied, then disappeared through the oak-paneled door.

Finn began his inspection of the crew's work. Once they were finished, he passed quietly from room to room. He had to admit he'd trained them well and timed this perfectly. It was almost a pity, but all things must come to an end. He checked his watch. It had taken them exactly half an hour to accomplish their final mission.

He stepped inside the last room at the end of the hall and did a cursory inspection. Nothing of value was left to take, and no evidence of him or any of his crew had been left behind. After closing the door, he checked his watch again then cast a glance over the open stairway to the side door. Several small canvas bags waited for him there, each filled with easily transportable treasures. Everything from jewelry to rare coins and other small items that would be easy to pawn.

The street was always quiet in the early afternoon, as he'd seen from a week of observation. Today was no different.

When he was halfway down the grand staircase, the side door opened. "Sir? What's happening?"

"Beagle! I told you to stay outside!"

"I know, but then it got so very quiet. The crew hasn't come out yet, and we're ten minutes overdue for departure. I had a bad feeling. I wanted to make sure you were all right."

Finn watched Beagle's pale-green eyes pan across the foyer to the formal dining room. The long mahogany table was now attended by the rest of the Hounds, each of them duct-taped to one of the high-back chairs. Their mouths were also covered, their eyes wide with fear. Well, all except for Carl's, whose throat was slit and bleeding profusely. His head lolled back. Blood spatter adorned his neighbors' faces with red flecks, and the odor of iron traveled through the air to where Finn and Beagle stood.

Finn sighed and shook his head as he slowed his pace, lingering on each step he took until he stood in front of Beagle. He heard the other members of the pack squirming, smelled their terror as they stared at the empty cans of gasoline scattered about the room and on the highly polished dining-room table.

Beagle pulled on Finn's jacket, something he never would have done before. "Sir, please. You can't do this!"

Finn shrugged. "That's the thing, Beagle. I can do whatever I want. Haven't you learned that by now?"

Finn stepped forward and placed his hands on Beagle's shoulders. He looked at his attaché's pleading eyes for a long moment. "My Beagle . . . I told you to stay outside. I warned you not to come in. If only you'd listened to me. You know disobedience cannot be forgiven."

"I'm sorry, sir. I meant well. I was worried. I'll never do it again!"

Heartbroken, Finn gently held Beagle's cheeks in his palms "If only you could take it back . . . but you can't."

Beagle gave a look of panic. "Sir? I can. I promise."

"Oh, Beagle . . . I'm so sorry about this. Once again you're in the wrong place at the wrong time."

Finn turned his head to the side so as not to watch his own actions. With one swift movement of his hands, he broke Beagle's neck as if it were nothing more than a twig. The small blond body crumpled to the floor.

The pain in Finn's chest returned and intensified. Then he felt it hit him. Everything *Beagle*—all his memories and emotions, the way he saw Finn and looked up to him—it all entered through his mouth. He tasted peaches and smelled fresh-cut hay. It came to him as a trail of smoky visible energy. He swallowed. Pain struck first and then a kind of euphoria and strength.

He couldn't dwell on the motionless form that once had been his loyal brother-in-arms. There was no time. He turned his attention to the remaining four boys at the table, who were now even more active in their restraints.

"What were we talking about before we were so rudely interrupted? Any volunteers can raise their hands. Oh, wait. You can't.

That's okay. I remember anyway—something about going your separate ways? Breaking up the band? Well, good news! I agree!"

Finn took an antique Zippo lighter from his pocket. He'd taken it as a souvenir from their very first job together. Caressing it—and the memories it produced—he dramatically shook his head. "Nothing too good for my boys!" Finn laughed irreverently, and then his smile turned icy. "I don't think so. Not for traitors!" After placing the lighter back in his pocket, he grabbed a pack of matches.

Finn lit a match and dropped it at the head of the gasoline stream. It bloomed at once into angry flames that chased the shiny liquid across the floor and up over the mahogany table. The room grew hotter by the moment, which was Finn's cue to exit. As he heaved the five bags of loot over his shoulder, he heard the boys' muffled screams, barely contained by the duct tape, rise in a ghastly crescendo. He glanced down at his Beagle one last time. Before heading out the side door, he felt the essence of each member of his one-time gang enter him, elbowing one another to find a new home inside.

The moment he was back in the safety of the trees, he dropped the canvas bags and took a slip of paper and a pen from his pocket. With the kind of satisfaction that comes from the mostly successful execution of a well-thought-out plan, he crossed another line off his list. Only one thing left to do before he could mark through the final goal. It was written in big, bold letters and circled.

"See, Mr. Helpful? You didn't think I could do it, but I did. It wasn't that hard, now was it?"

There was no response, not even a breeze.

"I know you're not going to be able to stay away, so you might as well cut this act out right now!"

Nothing stirred.

"Mr. Helpful?"

CHAPTER THIRTY-SEVEN

Love at First Like

I KNOW YOU CAN'T *hear me this far away, Banyan, but I'm so glad to know you.* Sadie felt like a part of something now that she had Banyan, Barnaby, and her own private oasis. *It has to work out. If it weren't for that rude Mr. Felix, I'd still have you all to myself. Who knows how often Thursday comes around in his head? We have to work this out because being with you is the only way I can feel happy. How can Mr. Felix be your friend? He doesn't even make sense.*

Still steaming from the distinct displeasure of meeting that awful Mr. Felix, Sadie grabbed her ten-speed from the garage without stopping in the house to say hello. Her only other thought was to be off the street before Jennifer showed up.

She rode over to the bike path beyond the creek. She passed close by the field where she and Christopher used to meet. *Will I ever get over you, Christopher?* she wondered. *It would be nice if today was the day.*

No sooner had the thought faded when Sadie noticed a moving truck up the street. *I wonder who's coming to the neighborhood this time. I'll be more careful about who I become friends with next. I don't need any more drama in my life.*

As she rode, the moving truck grew larger. *I'll take a quick peek and be on my way.* She dismounted and stood next to her bike. When she looked over, in her line of sight stood the most handsome boy Sadie had ever seen. His olive skin complemented his wiry but muscular body, which she could see because of his shorts and sleeveless basketball tank.

Wow, I can't look away. Good thing he isn't paying attention to me, and then he saw her. Embarrassed, Sadie managed to avert her eyes.

"Hey . . . hey you." He started to walk over.

Oh, no. Sadie didn't know whether to take off or not. Her body wouldn't let her escape, so she took a deep breath, smiled a bit, and waved. She was sure she must have turned firehouse red.

Feeling wobbly kneed, she walked over, using her bike for stability, and met him halfway. She could see his eyes now. They were the deepest shade of brown she'd ever seen and matched the color of his wavy hair, which hung just below his neck. *He must be six inches taller than me, at least.* Feeling weaker still, she gripped her bike tighter.

"Hi. My name's Sam Perez." His smile shone wide and bright. "What's yours?"

"Umm, Sss . . ." She thought quickly. "Annie. I'm Annie Cooper." She used her middle name and Gramma's last. Her gut told her to do it.

"Nice to meet you, Sss . . . Annie." He laughed a bit.

Sadie blushed again. "Yeah, sorry about that. I was thinking of something else, and it sort of came out weird."

"That's okay. I do it all the time."

She doubted that; she knew he must have told her that to make her feel better. *Careful, Sadie. I mean, Annie! Take it easy. Don't overdo it. Is there such thing as love at first sight?* She'd heard of it, but even with Christopher it hadn't been immediate like this. *Christopher.* A tinge of guilt struck her. *But I wasn't the one who stopped writing.*

"It's a little cooler out today, isn't it?" Sam noted.

"Sure is." *Who am I kidding? I'm sweating like an animal. Can someone find me an air conditioner?*

"So, Annie, do you live around here?" Welcome and warmth reflected in Sam's eyes as he waited for her answer.

"Umm, I live across town a ways."

"Oh, secretive, huh? Okay, I'll let you get away with that for now." Sam laughed as he teased her. "Where do you go to school?"

"Just over at the high school. Are you going there too?"

"Nah, my parents are making me go to the prep school the next town over. It's on the other side of Oak Street. Do you know which one I mean?"

"I think so. Is it St. Vincent's?" Sadie was relieved he didn't go to her school. *I'm so glad I gave him my middle name.*

"Yeah, that's the one. They think I'm going to be some famous doctor or something. Maybe I'll be the next Doctor Dolittle. Do you have any animals you'd like me to talk to for you?"

"I wish, but sadly no." Sadie turned away for a moment.

"Yeah, me neither."

"Do you really want to be a veterinarian, Sam?"

"I'm thinking about it, but it's hard to know for sure. I do love animals, but I don't know if I could stand to see them in pain."

"I can understand that," Sadie agreed.

"How about you, Annie? What would you like to do?"

"I've always wanted to be a diplomat like my grandparents. Growing up, I heard stories about their time overseas and the differences they made. I'd give anything to do that."

"Wow, that's deep."

Sadie blushed. "I know. It sounds silly."

"No, it sounds perfect." Sam smiled with sincerity.

"Thank you, Sam. That's nice of you to say. So where did you guys move from?" Sadie asked, changing the subject.

"We came down from New Jersey."

"New Jersey? I heard it's nothing but highways and pollution."

Sam shook his head. "Oh, then you heard wrong, dear Annie. Jersey is a verdant state from the top to the bottom. Sure, there are a few not-so-nice spots, but doesn't every state have those? We lived in horse country. Not much left of it anymore, but we were lucky enough to be there for a while. My dad decided it was time for a change of scenery, so here we are in the Sunshine State."

Well, thank you, Daddy. Sadie blushed and hoped he didn't notice. "Nice. Welcome to the neighborhood." Sadie didn't want to push. "I'd better head back now."

"It was nice meeting you, mysterious Annie. Don't be a stranger."

Oh, don't you worry. I won't. Where's this coming from? Good thing he can't read my mind.

"Nice meeting you too, Sam. See you on my next ride." *Like tomorrow.*

CHAPTER THIRTY-EIGHT

The Bogeyman

THE LITTLE BELL over the door of E-Z Pawn tinkled its welcome tune. A paunchy man in an undershirt looked up at the sound.

"Hey, slim. What do you have for me today?"

Finn lifted his duffel. "Packed to the hilt with the good stuff."

"Better come around the back then, my man." Bogey flipped the OPEN sign to CLOSED and locked up the store for "lunch."

Finn walked around to the alley and met his partner in slime. "One hand washes the other, right, Bogey?"

"You know it. Come on in so we can see the goods."

Finn followed the obese man who always smelled of sausage and onions, his shirt sporting the grease stains to match. "Let's go downstairs, shall we? And there we can lay it all out. I tell you, slim, I can almost stay in business just by what you bring in alone."

The narrow wooden stairs from the outside were rickety and led to an unfinished basement that smelled of mildew and garlic. A single light bulb in the middle of the room cast the shadows of Finn and Bogey on the corner safe.

They had an arrangement. Finn would take out Bogey's

trash—human trash, that is—and he always gave Finn top dollar on his packages in return.

"Where's your little guy today?"

Finn stiffened and held back his first response in order to think for a moment. "He's visiting his grandmother in Topeka. They haven't seen each other in a long time. It's quite the reunion. He's staying with her now."

"Ah, too bad. I like the look of him, know what I mean?" Bogey made several shallow thrusts with his hips, and Finn buried his hands in his pockets to keep from bashing the man's teeth through his brains.

This would be the last time he'd ever let anyone speak that way about his Beagle—*anyone*, no matter how valuable they might be to his enterprise. Right now, however, he needed Bogey, so he made the best of it.

Soon, a variety of diamond necklaces, rings, gold chains, bracelets, an unparalleled coin collection, and miscellaneous trinkets covered the table under the light. Bogey whistled as he weighed the pieces and examined them with his loupe. He abandoned calculating the total in his head and brought out his adding machine. "I think this is the biggest haul you've brought in so far, slim. There's even coins here from the early nineteenth century."

"Good. That's what I like to hear. Enough to buy a car?"

"Enough to buy three or four luxury-mobiles, I'd say."

"Excellent."

Finn looked around at Bogey's odds and ends, while the latter went to the wall where he kept his safe. With his back to Finn, he turned the dial with fat sweaty fingers, finally opened the door, then counted out each bill as though it were worth ten times as much. He licked his fingers to peel off the last bill just as the crowbar made contact with the back of his skull.

Finn let the crowbar fall to the floor and took back his

duffel. It was never part of the deal anyway. He used it to take everything he'd originally brought plus all the cash in the safe. He gathered the handful of bills that had scattered across the floor near the body, save the ones already saturated by the growing pool of blood.

What a shame, but it had to be done. The man had been kind to Finn, but he couldn't let the comment about his Beagle stand. *Tragic mistake, Bogey.* Finn didn't particularly need too much blood on his hands, but principles were important. He felt the moment of death, and he inhaled as Bogey's essence entered through his nostrils. He shuddered. There were those sausages and onions again.

Instead of going back out the way he came, he climbed the stairs to the shop and gave it the same once-over he'd given the basement. He could have taken anything he wanted, but it was time to get going. The rest of what he now needed was all around him. From lighter fluid behind the counter and the many wooden trinkets and statuary, there was more than enough to build a campfire in the middle of the shop. *S'mores, anyone?* He waited for a laugh from Mr. Helpful, but none came.

A porcelain statue caught his eye. He took the tiny beagle and slid it into his jeans pocket.

He used three cans of lighter fluid to douse the floor and walls. He went back to the basement with another can and used the entire thing to saturate Bogey's body. He lit Bogey first, waited until the flames licked the corpse from head to toe, then hurried upstairs to light the shop. With his duffel in hand and a new pair of designer sunglasses, he headed out.

Two blocks over stood a used car lot, which shared the same seediness as the pawnshop. Finn browsed the small lot then settled on an older silver Cadillac. A salesman sauntered over and introduced himself. Both ignored the billowing smoke behind them, as well as Finn's overflowing duffel. Finn watched

Leonard, whose eyes were wide. He saw drool forming at the side of the salesman's mouth as he stared at all the cash. He wanted the man's attention to stay on the money rather than his partially shaded face. It worked.

Finn climbed behind the wheel. He loved the red leather interior, though he could do without the tobacco infusion. As he took off his sunglasses, he caught sight of his face in the rearview mirror and gripped the wheel tighter. Something was different. There were loose folds under his eyes, as though he hadn't slept in a month. *I have to get going,* he thought. *No time for distractions.*

Considering that he didn't have his license, he started the car and backed out without a hitch. It took only five turns and two miles before he was both a proficient driver and cranking it on I-25 North. He knew exactly where he was going but put the *Thomas Guide* street map on the seat beside him as backup.

By his calculations, he would arrive at 11:30 p.m. Perfect. He couldn't have planned it any better.

CHAPTER THIRTY-NINE

Dream a Little Dream for Me

SADIE SCARFED DOWN her dinner, even though it was her favorite meal, eggplant parmigiana. She usually took her time to sop each bite with adequate sauce and cheese, but tonight she had experiences to share with Rufus. She needed to talk to him now.

She ignored the surprised looks on her parents' faces when she politely asked to be excused. Once she was out of earshot, she ran all the way to her room, shutting the door behind her and securing herself within the confines of her own personal space.

"Oh, Rufus, keeper of my secrets, where might you be?" she called out. "Of course! Right where I left you, in the closet under my art supplies. Mom wouldn't think of looking here." She smiled so wide it hurt her face. "I know I said good-bye to you less than a week ago, but it was never meant to be permanent."

Dear Rufus,

I rushed through eggplant parm to talk to you. I'm so excited. I can't believe it. I met someone. His name is Sam. Even though he doesn't go to my school, talk moves pretty quickly, so I told him my name is Annie. I know that was wrong of me, but I want a real chance, you know, Rufus? Just a chance without Dave and the others changing his mind before he gets to know me.

He's really nice, Rufus. He lives a couple of blocks over. I was riding my bike, and I saw him in his driveway. He's perfect. I don't know what gave me the courage to stop, but I did.

I can't believe I actually feel this way again. I almost feel a little guilty—I mean, he's not Christopher, but this feels so strong, Rufus. Could this be real love? Sam listened to me. Even though I only introduced myself, I know he heard me. I felt important to him when we were talking. The way he looked at me when I spoke.

He has an easygoing confidence, and he's interesting. He doesn't seem hung up on himself. This is the first time I've met a boy like that since Christopher . . . and I like it.

No, no, no . . . I promised myself I wouldn't do this. I don't want to get hurt again. But, hey. What can I do? I can't think of anything but Sam.

Awesome, right, Rufus?

I'll try and get used to the name Annie for a bit. Maybe I'll ask Mom to call me that for a little while so I'll remember. I'll tell her it's for a school project. That everyone needs to go by their middle name for a week. She's so busy with other people's problems anyway—I can't see her checking up on something like that.

What do you think, Rufus? Wait, don't tell me. I think I know.

I have a feeling I'll be talking to you again soon.

Thanks for everything, Rufus!

Until next time,

Sadie, aka Sss-Annie

Sadie closed the diary and tucked it back into its hiding place. She lay on the bed, staring at the ceiling. A quick glance at the clock told her it was time for bed, but she was too wound up to sleep. The only cure for this was on top of her bookshelf: Gramma's music box would do the trick.

She lay back and wound the box; its soothing melody helped calm her. As the first refrain ended, the lights flickered. Barely paying attention, Sadie wrapped herself in Sam's imaginary arms, dancing to the soft music.

The lights flickered again. Bright blue and green, they bounced around the room before zooming to the ceiling. From overhead they flashed repeatedly. As the entire room sparkled, Sadie sat up. The rug beside her bed expanded, turning its thick beige fibers into bright-green grass. Sadie looked at the carpet in astonishment.

Vines crawled up her bedposts and across the top of her bookshelf before twisting their way down in front of her door, barricading her inside the room. Sadie dug her nails into the bottom of her foot, hoping to wake up. She wrapped the blanket around her, allowing one eye to peek out. Fresh, thick shoots sprung from the main vine and knocked over her night table, though delicate curling tendrils caught her lamp before it shattered on the floor.

She burrowed deeper under the blanket, though she couldn't look away. The bookshelf began to crack where it connected with the wall. Books tumbled to the floor. Her art portfolio followed. A single picture caught an invisible breeze and landed at her feet. It was that alligator-and-tree picture, now much more familiar than the last time she had looked at it.

She heard her name.

Sadie.

It didn't sound like her parents, though she couldn't imagine why they wouldn't be at her door with all the ruckus.

The side wall of her bedroom collapsed, sending a cloud of dust across the rest of the room. Sadie brought the blanket over both eyes as if it would protect her. After several moments, the noise and dust died down. She peeked out from under the covers. Gone were the vines and fallen books. Sadie stood outside in vibrant, humming woods. *What the heck is happening? I'm still awake.* The setting was like the woods behind her house, only different.

Sadie had no words for what she sensed all around her. There was a gentle buzzing in the air, reminding her of what she'd heard at the Fletcher house. There was a breeze that smelled like Gramma's butter cookies mixed with peppermint. *I want one of those,* she thought, *whatever they are.*

Colors were brighter. Everything glowed. She caught a flash of purple near her shoulder. It turned out to be her own hair, changed. It now glowed electric violet, long and flowing free. Her signature pigtails were gone.

"Oh. My. Gosh!" she cried, then laughed out loud. "This is awesome!"

She walked farther into the woods and met someone who resembled the alligator from her childhood drawing, but it wasn't an alligator. He had scales all over and three spikes that poked up from his tapered tail. His hide resembled a color pallet with varying shades of blue. Brightly shining jewels set them off, changing the tone of his skin from moment to moment. He was exquisite, sparkling brightly.

She wasn't afraid; in fact she was drawn to him immediately. He came toward her, walking upright into his own light with each step.

"Well, hello there. It's about time. Welcome to our world, Sadie."

His voice sounded smooth. Though deep, it was gentle. "Do

I know you? What is this place? How do you know my name? Why is it about time, and who are you?"

"Whoa, whoa there, Miss Sadie. There will be time enough for many questions and answers, but let's move naturally through them, okay?"

"What should I call you? May I ask that first?"

"My name is Thelonious. My friends call me Thelo. Please count yourself among them. You, Sadie Myers, have been given the gift of Mystashan. That is what this place is called."

"Why me? Though I do feel like I know you. When I look into your eyes, it's like being with someone familiar. I feel connected, even though I can't explain it."

Thelo smiled as only one of whatever he was could. His teeth resembled a wolf's, with a rounded quality at their tips. "I have been watching over you your whole life, and you have known it, maybe not consciously until now. Remember your artwork from kindergarten?"

"Oh, yes! Isn't that something? I can't remember being with you before, but I do remember drawing that picture of you and Banyan, I guess."

"Follow me, Sadie. I have something to show you."

Thelo offered her his arm, and Sadie took it. She felt grateful, as she had no idea where she was going or which direction they were heading. Her questions still lingered, her curiosity growing as they walked along the well-kept path toward some unknown destination.

The unmistakable babbling melody of flowing water grew louder. The light around her shifted from silver to a golden radiance. She blinked as her eyes adjusted to the change. When she could see clearly, a familiar form rose up in front of her.

"Banyan! I knew it was you!" Sadie looked more closely at her transformed friend. Every leaf gleamed gold, and an underlying copper tint shone through the branches. They reached out toward her in welcome.

His kind, smiling face nestled in his glimmering trunk. She glanced at Thelo before racing over to her dear Banyan, embracing him with a big bear hug.

"Hello, my Sadie." Banyan's voice sounded like swirling leaves being swept through the breeze.

"Hello, my Banyan." Sadie's tears of joy rolled down her cheeks.

She walked over to Thelo and hugged him too. He wrapped his arms around her shoulders, and she closed her eyes. For the first time in a long time, she felt safe and wanted. "Thank you so much for bringing me here. I'll always be grateful."

*　*　*

Sadie opened her eyes. She was back in her own bed with the morning light shining on her desk. Everything was as it always had been. The woods were gone, as were Thelo and Banyan.

"Oh, man, it was just a dream." She sighed and rolled over. On the nightstand beside the bed, a spark caught her eye. "What's this? Wow!" she gasped, stunned by the sight of the shimmering rock. It was clear and had flat sides across its surface.

"It wasn't a dream," she whispered. The rock vibrated with a cool, uplifting energy. Without being told, she knew it was alive. As she turned it, the light hit each facet with differing effects. On the underside, a single word was carved into its smooth surface: APPRECIATION.

"Hmm, I don't understand. Why this word?" She thought about it, but the scent of bacon and pancakes was too strong. *Mom's making breakfast?*

Sadie stretched then climbed out of bed. She dressed quickly and hid her gift at the back of her sock drawer for safekeeping before heading downstairs to the kitchen.

Mom flipped a batch of silver-dollar pancakes. She smiled. "Good morning, sweetheart. I hope you're hungry." She reached for a plate from the cabinet next to the window then paused. "Come here, Sadie. Look at how pretty the garden is today." Mom's smile turned into a frown. "Well, all except that bunch of drooped-over flowers on the right."

Sadie joined her at the window. "Mom, they're as lovely as the others. Maybe they're saying good morning to the lawn?"

In that moment, Sadie understood that she was like the droopy flowers—as important as everyone else in their own way, even when life was difficult. A warm feeling of appreciation spread through her. "Oh, now I get it."

Her mother looked at her funny, but she laughed a little as she handed Sadie her pancakes.

"Thanks for breakfast, Mom," Sadie said with a smile.

CHAPTER FORTY

Open the Basset File

FINN PARKED AROUND the corner. He sat for a moment in the quiet, instantly missing the vigorous growl of the Cadillac's engine. He grabbed his roll of duct tape and the flashlight from the seat next to him. His new black suit jacket had roomy pockets, perfect for hiding all the tools of his trade.

The house hadn't changed a bit, and he had a feeling the inhabitants within hadn't either. Lights out was 10:00 p.m. His watch read 11:34 p.m. He was right on time. They were heavy sleepers and would be out of it by now. He headed toward the back door, skirting the bright halo of light that pooled under the streetlamp.

Finn used the picking set he had received from the gang on June eleventh, his last birthday. He released the lock and entered, carefully shutting the door behind him. He removed his shoes and straightened the hanky that was in the top pocket of his jacket. The long mirror at the end of the hall provided a darkened but sufficient reflection of his new ensemble.

The fine Italian suit was from last year's collection, and the pants hung just a tad too long, but he had no time for tailoring. He almost laughed as he recalled the look on the gas station attendant's face when he'd emerged from the dank, dirty restroom impeccably dressed, with his hair slicked back. This day had been long in coming, and he wanted to look the part.

Climbing the stairs to the bedrooms, he avoided the third step from the top. It always had been a squeaker.

From the streetlights' glow through the cracks in the window shades, he clearly saw Frank and Marj, sleeping deeply. They were slightly older but still the same lying, manipulative fakers they'd always been.

"Wakey, wakey, Franky Frank." Finn slapped the man's face on either cheek to speed up the process and get to the good part.

Frank's eyelids fluttered but didn't open. He mumbled something in his sleep and rolled onto his side.

Poor Frank has no idea what his future holds. "I said, 'Wake up!'"

Frank's eyes flew open. His blank expression revealed no recognition.

Marj remained motionless, still asleep.

Finn bent over to look the man in the eyes. Less than an inch separated the tips of their noses. "What? You don't remember me? Don't recall the last time you saw me? Well, I do. Every day of my life for the past three years, I've lived for this day. Care for some ice cream?"

Five minutes later, Finn sat down in the wing chair he had positioned across from the one in which Frank was now duct-taped, with an additional piece for his mouth. *Duct tape. Nothing in the world is quite as useful.* "What's the matter, Frank? Don't you recognize me, your one-time buddy? That's all right. Maybe Marj will." Finn could see that remark hit home with Frank as he struggled in his seat.

Finn walked over to Marj's side of the bed. He couldn't believe she slept through all this, and then he noticed the bottle of sleeping pills on the nightstand. The glass of water next to it came in handy. Finn picked it up, holding it right over her face for a few moments, then let the drips come out slowly. Drip, drip, drip.

In a barely audible groan, Marj mumbled, "Fank, I fink therf's fumfing wron wif the roof." She turned her back to Finn.

Finn poured the rest of the glass on Marj's unsuspecting head. Her usual springy curls were now flattened against her pillow. "Come on, Marj. We don't have all night. I'm on a tight shed-u-al."

Marj's head whipped toward him. Recognition turned to terror, filling her tearing eyes. "How—?"

Before she could finish her sentence, Finn slapped a piece of duct tape across her mouth—something he had been dreaming of since he'd left this awful place several years ago. He wrapped it around her head to ensure its staying power. "Marj, I have no desire to hear that screechy voice of yours. Believe me, your caw has been stuck inside my head since the first time I heard it."

She scrambled across the bed, away from him, but she was no match for Finn's speed. He grabbed her ankles and pulled her back toward him. All her jerky movements and kicks were useless. He let her fall to the floor. She crouched and tried to crawl under the bed.

"Oh, no, no, no, Marj. You can't get away from me that easily." He pulled her up from her middle and spun her around toward him as if it were part of their ballet. With one hand, he dragged her over to the chair across from Frank, and with the other, he grabbed the roll of tape off the dresser. Her muffled screams went unacknowledged, and her kicking was pointless. Her light frame made it easy for him to hold her down in the chair while he duct-taped her to it.

All the while, Finn kept an eye on Frank, whose sweat visibly ran down his face and through his pajamas. His gray eyes were shifting back and forth, looking from Marj to Finn and back again.

"Don't worry, Frank. It'll be quick. Well, maybe. It all depends on how long you and Marj can hold your breath." He watched in delight as the tears flowed freely down the faces of Marj and Frank. Their heads were hung low, shaking in disbelief.

Finn grabbed the two clear plastic bags from his jacket pocket and exaggerated the opening of each of them for full effect. They crinkled and crackled as he waved them through the air.

"Okay, we have to pick up the pace. I can't say this hasn't been fun, because it's been exceptionally entertaining. Thank you for playing. I'll leave your parting gifts at the door. Oh, wait, those are mine. Sorry about the mix-up, you two. Okay, places, everyone. Good. Are you ready with your lines?" He paused. "That's right. Thankfully you don't have any. I've written you out of the rest of the scenes. A wise choice on my part. I could do this all night, but I really have to be going. Plus, we have that bonfire we all need to get to."

Finn put a plastic bag over Frank's head and then Marj's, then sealed them with duct tape. Eyes wide and nostrils sucking in plastic, the two kept their eyes on each other, no longer turning toward Finn. "You know, you really do make a cute couple. Take care of each other. I have to leave. I hope you don't mind. Please feel free to die. Thank you and farewell." Finn pulled up the collar of his long suit coat, puffing the tails out behind him, as he made his grand exit.

A sound came from down the hall. He heard it clearly. It sounded like something rolling over the wooden floor. *What's that?* he wondered.

Finn sneaked quietly in the direction of the sound. *There it is again.* It came from the other bedroom, the one where he used to sleep. *Did Frank and Marj try to replace me? How dare they!*

Finn continued toward the bedroom. The floor creaked, but he didn't try to avoid the squeaky spots now that Frank and

Marj were out of the way. Forever. He knew they were gone as surely as his whole body shuddered, soaking in their energy as they departed.

He listened outside the door then slowly opened it and turned on the light. The room was decorated in a western theme, with cowboys and horses wallpapered on one wall, while the others were painted a dark blue. A cactus-shaped night-light cast a soft, yellow glow on the rustic, rough-hewn furniture.

"Wow, you must really rate to be given such atmosphere." Finn let out a whistle. "When I lived here, I had nothing but white walls. It's kind of a pity to have to destroy this room."

Finn heard an intake of air, and a marble rolled from the right-hand corner bookcase toward the bed.

"Okay, you can come out now." Finn saw the source of the noise. A young boy cowered in the corner. He wore pajamas with lassos and stallions on them, fitting with the room's motif. His small hands gripped an overfilled blue plastic bowl of marbles. "Looks like you had a bit of trouble keeping your marbles together. Come on out. It'll be better for you in the long run."

The boy stayed behind the bookcase. He shook, and a puddle collected around his footie pajamas; the acrid smell of urine filled the air.

"If you come out quickly, I won't hurt you. If not, you'll know the meaning of true pain. Heed my warning. Come out now!"

The boy crawled out from behind the bookcase, shaking too hard to stand.

"Come, come. It's okay. You'll be fine. You'll see." Finn helped the boy up. He was used to the fear he saw in his pets.

The boy couldn't be more than seven or eight, with closely cropped brown hair. He looked thin and pale. Finn patted his head. "It's okay. You'll be fine." Finn showed unusual restraint for a first meeting. It was a different feeling for him to actually employ his patience so quickly. It bothered and intrigued him at the same time.

"What do they call you?"

"Deh . . . Deh . . . Derrick," whispered the young boy.

"Well, not anymore. From now on your name will be . . . Hmm, let's see . . . Your name will be Basset. From now on, I'm the only one you need to know. What's your name?"

"Derrick."

Finn stiffened, squinted his eyes, and looked hard at him.

Derrick's tears ran freely once again. He whimpered, "Sorry, sir. I . . . I meant Basset."

"Very good, Basset." He patted the boy's head. "You'll like this name much better."

CHAPTER FORTY-ONE

One Wave at a Time

Dear Rufus,

So many surprising things are happening. I hardly know where to begin. First off, there's you-know-where, and I know you do! Second, I might be going to a dance! I'm so excited! Actually, I AM going to a dance! I'll have to tell you more. You remember, of course, that kid I met? Sam? Well, I saw him again today . . . purely by chance (wink, wink). He took me to meet his mom. She's a little shorter than me and has red hair and green eyes. She's friendly and kind. She sells houses for a living and loves it. She told me she's so glad that Sam's made a friend already, especially someone as wonderful as me.

Can you imagine? I'd love it if MY mom talked to me half as nicely. How hard would it be? She used to do it.

Anyway, she and Sam and I were in their kitchen, drinking lemonade at the table, and she told me she talked with some of the other neighborhood moms, and they were all excited about getting their daughters dresses for the autumn dance.

She said to them, "Oh, there's a dance? My son's school doesn't have dances."

She told me they said, "Well, if he finds someone from our daughters' school to go with him, then he can go. Then she turned to me and said, "You and Sam should go together. What do you think?"

I must have turned five shades of red—and maybe even purple—because I can't remember ever being that embarrassed . . . and you know that's saying a lot.

I wanted to crawl under the table and disappear, but then Sam said, "That's a great idea, Mom. Annie, would you like to go to the dance with me at your school?" He totally rescued me, and how awesome is that? And how incredible is it that he thinks of someone besides himself first, and this is the first time this school year that someone's treated me that well . . . well, besides you, Rufus, and guess what I answered: "Yes. Yes, of course I'll go to the dance with you." There I go again with run-on sentences, Rufus. Ms. Argello would have my head right about now.

Anyway, he asked me, so we're going. When it was time to head home, I let him walk me to the end of the street. He told me how pretty I am and gave me the best hug. Isn't that sweet, Rufus? I haven't been called pretty since you-know-who. And did I mention he smells good too? Like butterscotch and vanilla with a fresh laundry twist. Mmm!

As soon as I got home, I told Mom. I didn't want her to ruin anything, so instead of telling her I was going with Sam, I told her a bunch of kids from my English class were meeting there. (Ha-ha, what a joke, right?) She's taking me to get a dress on Saturday. She's excited. She said it's about time I went to one of the dances at school instead of staying home and hiding with my books every time. Nice, right? It's like she doesn't even hear what she's saying to me.

I haven't really thought about what'll happen once we get there, but I don't want to. Dave and his goons could cause trouble—a lot of trouble—but at least it's a masquerade and mustache party.

They decided to do this instead of the usual Halloween dance. Maybe I'll get my wish and just go and have a nice time and pretend everything is normal. Just for one night.

Okay . . . over and out.

Until we meet again.

Until next time, Rufus.

Sadie closed Rufus and put him back in the closet, her smile practically glowing.

* * *

More than a week had passed since Sadie had spent time with the golden tree. She longed to see Banyan—and Barnaby, for that matter—but she'd made up her mind to avoid Mr. Felix at all costs, and she didn't want to risk the chance that he might be there. Any other time she would have been lonely, but Sam was fast becoming a good friend.

She couldn't understand why or how it happened, but every other time she walked, rode, or drove by his side of neighborhood, there was Sam. Sam waving. Sam saying, "Hello!" Sam asking whether he might join her for a walk to the park.

On the rare occasions when Christopher did come into her mind, the image of him was quickly replaced by Sam's face. As the week went on, she barely thought of her old love at all.

Sadie just finished giving Sam the tour of the wooded area that led to the creek when she heard it. At first she ignored the sounds, thinking they could be products of her imagination, but finally their persistence won out.

Sadie, it is time to come back. You have had a few days off, but it is time.

Sadie listened, trying to think of a way to answer Thelo without talking out loud to a bodiless voice only she could hear . . . with Sam a foot away from her.

The only solution was to leave.

Oh, and bring your music box with you, Sadie.

Sadie thought hard inside her mind: *Yes, I'll bring it,* and the conversation ended. Big sigh.

"Sam, I have to go," fretted Sadie.

"What, Annie? Now? We just got here, and it's terrific!"

"Yeah, sorry. I'll show you more next time . . . Soon, I mean."

"There you go, being all mysterious again." Sam flashed her one of his "melt me now" grins, his perfect teeth a glimmering white.

As hard as it was, she shook it off. "I forgot that I have to do something back at home. I'm sorry."

Sam sighed. "It's okay, Annie. Let's see each other soon."

"Yeah, of course." *He's so understanding.* She gave him a quick kiss on the cheek. "I'll see you later, I promise."

After a quick stop at home to retrieve the music box, Sadie raced to the Fletcher house. She was careful to avoid any streets Sam might have used to travel home from the woods. *Success!*

She imagined there might come a day when she could tell Sam about the music box and Banyan, but for now he would just have to think she was mysterious, if not a bit odd.

She hid her bike in the Fletchers' backyard and secured the music box under her arm. As she approached, the dense vegetation parted, leaving a makeshift path to the other side. With her first step on the trail, she already heard Banyan talking inside her head.

Good day to you, Sadie. How are you?

"I'm fine. Thanks for asking. How are you?"

As well as ever. Welcome back. It's good to see you again.

Sadie smiled as she took a moment to take in her statuesque friend. "It's good to see you too. I've missed you."

Come . . . have a seat.

Sadie faced Banyan and sat down in front of where she'd

seen his face during her first visit to Mystashan. Though the
hidden hollow behind the Fletcher house was a special place,
she couldn't see his face here in the traditional sense. But in her
mind she could see him, golden leaves and all.

Sadie heard crackling from above. She shielded her eyes from
the glare between the leaves. Noticing a pair of large green eyes
peering at her, she called up. "Hi, Barnaby. How're you doing?"
He rubbed the side of his cheek along Banyan's trunk and scaled
his way down headfirst, landing beside her.

Barnaby placed a paw on her leg and tilted his head,
requesting permission to come aboard.

Sadie petted him as he curled up on her lap.

You settled in, Barnaby? May we proceed? Banyan asked.

Barnaby blinked once and laid his head back down.

*Today, my dear, you will be entering Mystashan on your own.
Well, not entirely. I am glad you brought your key.*

"My key, Banyan?"

*The music box, of course. I'm the gatekeeper, and the box is
your own personal key.*

She beamed. "Ooh. I feel official." In her mind she saw
Banyan's kind, etched face stretch into a smile. "What do I do
first?"

*With your back against me, try to relax. Hold your key out in
front of you or on your lap. Open it up, and you will be on your
way!*

"All right. Here goes nothing."

Sadie had opened her music box hundreds of times without
giving it a second thought. This time, however, she felt every
moment; from holding it in her hands to opening the lid, every
action played in slow motion. She heard the soft creak of the lid,
and then the sweet song began to play. She felt Barnaby jump
off her lap. The blue and green flashes swirled, surrounding her.
The lulling melody eased her into a restful state. The landscape

around her faded; even she was fading, becoming translucent. She was between here and there. Euphoria swept through her. Above her, Banyan's green leaves turn golden, and then she was simply there, in Mystashan.

Jumping to her feet, Sadie couldn't hold back her yawn and stretch, as if she'd woken from a full night's sleep.

Thelo stood waiting for her, his long tapered tail waving hello. "Welcome, Sadie. How was your ride?"

"Hi, Thelo. It was fantastic! I'm glad to be back . . . and relieved I didn't run into Mr. Felix."

"You shouldn't worry about Mr. Felix. He means well."

"That may be, but even though I can't quite put my finger on it, I don't like him. He's not like you and Banyan."

Thelo laughed. "I suppose that is true, but I believe you will come to like him in time. He is always busy, and you will not likely see him often, but I assure you, he is a good man. But we can talk more about him later. Now it is time for your next lesson. I am going to bring you through Saponi Straime."

"What's that?" Sadie asked.

"In your world it would translate to 'Sea-pony Stream.' It is the tunnel to our island."

She looked around. "Island? What island? There's no island around here."

"Maybe not in your world, but here there most certainly is. I could tell you all about it, but it is better if you see for yourself." Thelo looked like an orchestra leader, waving his large scaly arms in front of the water.

Sadie turned to the stream and watched as the water drew up from the banks until it towered over them, then arched across the span and rolled back under itself. It reminded her of one of the giant surfer waves she had seen on TV, but these weren't crashing to the shore. Instead they were creating a continuous wave tunnel.

"Go on," prompted Thelo, gesturing for her to step inside. "Do not worry. You will not get wet."

Sadie turned to Banyan, whose kind face gave a slight nod. This was Mystashan after all.

"It is okay, Sadie. It is safe," Thelo reassured her.

Sadie took a deep breath then stepped hesitantly into the water tunnel. She felt a tiny spray from the water, but it was dry inside. The water shimmered with a bright turquoise light but remained perfectly clear. The tunnel teemed with hundreds and hundreds of what she instantly knew were sea-ponies. They resembled the seahorses she'd seen at the aquarium last summer. The difference here was that each had a cobalt-blue head and body with a long teal mane that flowed all the way down to its curled tail.

They smiled at her and giggled a recurring, "Hello, Sadie!" all the way through the tunnel.

"Hello, friends," she said with a smile.

Sadie still didn't know why she had been brought to this realm, but she knew how lucky she was as she made her way through the tunnel to dry land. Disappointed, she realized right away that it was the dull-tan carpet of her bedroom.

One step at a time, Sadie.

Why would Thelo take me all the way through only to lead me right back home? "I'm not happy about this, Thelo!"

CHAPTER FORTY-TWO

Grueling Downhill, Doggone It

"THIS SAME SLOP again! Have I not told you and told you and told you again?"

"But Mr. Finn, it's not the *same* slop. I hoped you'd like the subtle combination of flavors in this new recipe I'm trying out."

"Don't you ever say 'subtle' to me again, Basset!"

"I'm sorry, Mr. Finn. I only meant—"

"I don't care what you meant. If you understand that, you'll do much better with life in our world."

"Yes, Mr. Finn."

Although Finn noticed the dejected look on Basset's face, it didn't stop him from continuing the rest of their lunch in silence. He didn't care. *Who is he, always thinking he can take my Beagle's place?*

Basset took their bowls to the sink.

"Basset, clean up the rest of this mess you made and get to the store. We need supplies. There's a storm coming; I can feel it."

"Of course, Mr. Finn."

Finn sat back and scowled. He watched Basset work, the younger man's timid hands carefully removing their leftover lunch. *Runt of the litter, can't even grow facial hair properly. And I expected more height from you after all these years. You've disappointed me in every way possible, and you did it on purpose. Look at you with your perfect hair. Don't you know it's out of style?* Finn made disapproving clucks and growls under his breath, but he couldn't be sure whether they were inside his head or coming from his mouth.

As Finn unconsciously changed positions, his back rounded as he rested his fists under his chin. *Why doesn't Beagle ever visit? He never used to leave my side, not since I told him to keep close.* Finn didn't look up again until he heard the door close softly.

Finally! Some peace. I can hear myself think again. It'll be well after dark until that imbecile returns. Basset indeed. Basset hounds are loyal and faithful dogs, but look how he's turned out. It makes me want to wring his scrawny neck.

Finn looked to the ceiling, his eyes narrowing. "Why did you send him to me? First you took my Beagle, and then you had the audacity to remain quiet for twenty years. *Twenty!* Don't think I can't count, Mr. Helpful. Why won't you answer me, you big chicken? I know you said you would leave, but how could you? You were supposed to help me, thus the name!"

As with the thousand other requests of his one-time mentor, the same reply came: silence. Finn could no longer remember the last conversation he'd had with the Voice.

He paced. It was his nightly routine. This time he didn't wait for dark but moved around the room quickly. He could sense there was a reason he needed this time alone. It was important. But why?

A tone sounded inside his head like a tinkling bell: *Hello, Finn.*

"What? Who's that? You're not Mr. Helpful!"

You might not remember me yet, Finn, but you will in time. I'm not sure who your "Mr. Helpful" is, but I can help you.

"I should trust you when you don't even say who you are?"

In time you'll remember on your own. It wouldn't serve any purpose for me to try to explain it. Just know that I'm here for you. I have to go; they're coming. Good-bye for now, Finn.

Perhaps because he was surprised by the entry of a new voice, a hatchet-like pain pierced his right temple. It was the last thing he needed, another migraine. He retrieved the aspirin from the bathroom. Back in the kitchen, he poured water from the gallon jug into his mug, which had a big *F* for Finn on it. He glugged it down quickly then sputtered, choked, and found that he couldn't catch his breath. Affected, he held on to the counter for support. Lights flickered in his vision, and he couldn't stop coughing. Water gurgled in his throat as though he were a drowning man. The flickers of light grew into a blinding flash.

He was back in his nightmare . . . underwater and fighting for his life. The flashes moved to the outside. His cough eased. He was coming back to himself.

That's when he saw her.

She was right outside the living-room window. Finn knelt on the couch to get a better look.

Her braids bounced as she ran in bare feet. The girl didn't seem to be aware of him. She looked down and plucked something from the ground. She held it up, as if for him to see. He inched closer. She lifted her head and looked him straight in the eyes. Hers flashed a color so bright he shielded his own. When he looked again, she was gone.

"Wait! Come back!"

He waited, but neither the light nor the girl returned. There was something so familiar about her. He couldn't quite place it. "I said, 'Wait!'

How dare she disappear like that? Either show me what you have for me, or don't come at all!" *Who does she think she is? She has no idea who I am, clearly.*

What Finn recalled most, later, was the light that shone from her form, as if she existed in a season overlapping his own.

What are these? From each eye, a trickle of water flowed. This experience was so far back in time that it frightened him. But Finn didn't get scared. Not this Finn. Fear turned to anger. He grabbed the large *F* mug and hurled it across the room. It crashed into the corner and shattered into a half dozen pieces.

Thump.

Finn's curiosity shook him from his anger. *What was that?*

He moved to the corner, toward the source of the noise. Among the shards of ceramic lay a book he recognized, large and red. The closer he came, the more it was in focus. The front cover had gold letters that spelled, "RECIPES."

Hmm, why is this all the way over here? He had noticed Basset before with that book. *Always that book. Why?* Finn picked up the recipe book and walked over to his chair.

It was a disorganized mess, filled with torn papers slipped between the book's pages. *Sloppy! This is unacceptable.*

Finn picked up one of the sheets of paper, fully expecting to find proof that one of the latest atrocities Basset called dinner was actually a recipe for wallpaper paste. But the words on the paper surprised him. There were no measurements or ingredients. Instead, Basset's childlike handwriting was scrawled across the page.

I been gone a long time. I don't know how long. I know it not summer. It is colder. I miss Mr. Frank and Miss Marj. I have to be careful he does not find my notes. Miss Marj told me I need to write about me and always show her so she knows how I am doing. I like to write. It makes me not alone.

"Those idiots. Do I really need to read about them? I think not, Basset. Let's see what else you have to say for yourself."

Mr. Finn keeps calling me "Beagle." I don't know why, but he gets really mad at me. He punishes me. He hurts me with that hickory switch. I am sorry I did something to make him so mad. I don't want to. I try to do everything he asks and be a good boy, but he still gets so mad at me. I think he hates me.

Finn knitted his brow as he moved on to the next slip of paper in the book.

Mr. Finn said he is going to teach me how to earn an honest living. He said people need to get rid of their things, and we are helping them. I told him it is stealing, and he smacked me hard across the face. I will do what Mr. Finn wants me to. I don't want him to hit me again. He is very strong.

"That's right, Basset. I am strong, and you will do everything I tell you to do, like the obedient puppy you are."

I am small enough to fit into the bathroom windows that people leave open. I can also get through the basement windows. This pleases Mr. Finn very much. He said I make a good assistant, and he will let me stay.

A slight smile hit Finn's face but quickly vanished as soon as it appeared.

"Okay, I've had enough of these strewn-about pages. Do I

have to read every piece of nonsense you spit out?" Finn went over to the garbage can under the sink. He opened the book all the way and shook it over the bag. Roughly three dozen slips of paper freed themselves and fell into the trash. "That's better. Organization, Beagle. B . . . Ba . . . Basset. Organization, Basset. We must be orderly at all times," and his voice broke off.

Finn, unnerved by his mention of that name, returned to his seat and shakily opened the now-tidy book.

November 13: We've settled into a cabin in the Ozark Mountains. Mr. Finn says we have enough money now after fourteen years of helping people get rid of their things. Mr. Finn told me today was my twenty-first birthday. I know it's not my birthday for real, but whatever Mr. Finn tells me is correct. I like this date much better anyway. It suits me just fine. It was hard for me to keep track of the days since he never let me out of his sight. Mr. Finn told me that since I am so loyal, he will teach me how to drive and let me go to the store alone. That is how I got this recipe book. It feels good to write in a real book and not on whatever pieces of paper I can find. He says I am his most trusted servant ever, and I am. I would never leave Mr. Finn. I do my best not to anger him, but sometimes I can't help it. He still calls me "Beagle" every now and then, and that's when he hurts me. I know he doesn't mean to. I know he doesn't want to hurt me. I know it's all my fault. I will never leave Mr. Finn.

"I'm getting bored." Finn flipped through the next few pages.

August 16: Mr. Finn hasn't left the cabin since we got here. I am worried for him. I hear him talking to himself. Asking questions to no one. I am afraid for him. I try my best to stay out of his way. I try to cook him new things to cheer him up, but that only makes him madder. I only want to please him. I don't like when he isn't happy.

"What drivel. You do as I say, and everything will be in perfect order. All this thinking will only get you into trouble." Finn flipped to the last written page.

November 6: Today makes six years since we came to live in the mountains. I don't mind not having anyone but Mr. Finn. In fact he tells me I prefer it, so I do. I worry about Mr. Finn all the time. He still won't go outside. He still is very angry at me, but I love him very much, so I must try harder to please him. I heard Mr. Finn talking in his sleep last night. Someone was chasing him. He kept telling her to leave him alone. I can't remember her name, but he sounded afraid.

It was after dark, but Finn hadn't bothered to turn on any of the lights. He sat in one of the worn armchairs in the corner of the living room, the recipe book in hand, and waited.

The cabin door creaked open, and he almost smiled when Basset flipped on the switch and jumped, dropping the car keys.

"Are you okay, Mr. Finn?" Basset whispered as he took a step backward.

"Come in. Close the door, Basset. You look as if you're about to leave again."

"No, I was just taken by surprise, and then I saw you had my book."

"You mean *our* book?" Finn asked, as he fanned the pages from front to back before closing it sharply. "Yes, it makes for a highly unusual read. One thing, though, my loyal ward, you will never keep anything secret from me again. Do you understand me?"

"Yes, Mr. Finn. I will never do it again."

"Good. I'm glad we're in agreement. I see no need to punish you . . . this time." Finn smacked the switch on the floor. "You will make my dinner now. I have to head out for a few hours. They're calling to me, Beagle."

CHAPTER FORTY-THREE

Stuck on You

I CAN'T MOVE. *WHAT'S going on?* Trying not to panic, Sadie looked around as best she could, only able to use her peripheral vision.

I'm stuck. I'm stuck in this doorway. Where am I? I can hardly think. Wait, I'm on the wall. No, no, I'm . . . I'm the door. How can I be the door? I'm dreaming. This must be a dream.

Wake up, Sadie. Come on! Wake up!

I must . . . pull . . . out of this.

With all the power she could muster, Sadie willed herself and pushed. One shoulder emerged from the flat plane, but it didn't feel like her shoulder. It felt like a thick piece of plastic coming off in a section. She remained connected to the door, but at least she had one shoulder free.

Keep going, she urged herself. *Push harder.*

She grunted and pushed as hard as she could. She couldn't remember ever having to exert so much energy for anything in her life. She felt like a fly trapped on sticky paper.

Her head broke free, followed by her arms and the rest of her upper body. As each limb escaped the archway, a sound like a plucked rubber band echoed in the room.

Okay. Right leg out. She was still connected but in sections, like origami unfolding. She had one more leg to free. *Okay, puuhhh . . . lll. Pull!*

Free, I'm finally free!

Her relief quickly evaporated.

Something's still not right. I can't stand up . . . I can't catch my balance . . . I'm falling.

Sadie swung her body around and slammed into the wall.

Holy crap, I'm flat!

She lifted a hand from the wall and examined her two-dimensional fingers.

Panic set her heart racing. She tried to lift her head, but every muscle in her body screamed with fatigue. *I'm so tired. I need to rest.*

No, Sadie, Gramma Rose's voice whispered in her ear. *There's no time to rest.*

But I'm so tired.

Sadie, I know you can do this.

Okay, Gramma. I'll try. Just tell me what to do.

Push slowly. Slowly off the wall.

But I'll fall!

No, you won't, honey. Trust me.

Sadie nodded then slowly pushed off, and as she came away, she started to come back into her whole body. The flatness of her arms and legs began to expand like a slowly filling balloon.

Clapping. She heard slow, exaggerated clapping. And then his voice.

"Very strong, girl. Very strong indeed. No one's ever escaped before."

Sadie turned toward the voice but didn't have to see to know who it was. A set of scarlet eyes stared out of the darkness.

She shivered. "Gramma, help me."

Then she was back in her bed.

Sadie closed her eyes and let out a long sigh. Her pulse

galloped, but she was home; she was safe. "Thank you, thank you, Gramma. Do you know that man with the strange eyes? Please tell me!"

No one answered.

"Gramma?"

She glanced at the clock on her nightstand. It was just after two in the morning.

With another sigh, she flipped on the light. "There's no way I'm going back to sleep tonight. I might as well read."

She fetched *Matilda* from the shelf and crawled back under the covers. Eventually her body relaxed, and somewhere between pages forty and forty-one, she fell asleep.

CHAPTER FORTY-FOUR

It Was the Weirdest of Times

"GOOD MORNING, SADIE," said Mom's sideways head. "You up?"

Sadie sat up with her signature yawn-and-stretch combo. "Mom, you're freaking me out. I had the weirdest dream, and you kind of look like it. Will you come in already?" She put the book she'd been reading the night before on the nightstand and checked the clock. "Geez, Mom," she groaned, and fell back onto the pillows. "It's Saturday . . . and not even seven a.m."

Mom stepped into the room. "Well, your school dance is in a few weeks, so I thought we'd go shopping for your dress today. Paper says they're having a sale at the mall."

"Yeah, about the dance . . . I'm not sure I should go."

"What? I thought you were excited about it, and besides, I think it's a fantastic idea for you to get out there again. You can't stay holed up in your room all the time. It isn't healthy."

"But there's too many things that can go wrong, Mom."

"There's a lot that can and will go right. Don't be so negative."

Sadie rolled her eyes. *Don't be negative? That's rich coming from her. She has no idea what's going on at school. I would have told her, but that would actually mean having a conversation with her about something important. And she might not take me seriously anyway.*

"Look, Mom, I don't even know how to slow dance. What if somebody asks me? I'll make more of a fool of myself than I already do."

"Nonsense. I'll teach you."

"You? That's funny. *You're* going to teach me? I don't think I can handle that."

"Oh, come on, Sadie. It'll be fun. We hardly spend any time together anymore."

Sadie thought about: *a) spending so much time with Mom; b) slow dancing with Mom; c) having to talk to Mom; d) having Mom try to teach me something; and e) ugh. Do I really have a choice? Sigh. If I'm going, I really do need to learn how to dance.*

"Fine. I guess I don't have a choice. You can teach me."

Mom crossed her arms. "I don't want to force you to do something you don't want to do. If you don't want me to teach you, then just say so. There are a thousand other things I can do with my time."

"Oh, come on, Mom. I'm sorry." Sadie sat up and tried to look contrite. "Will you help me . . . please?"

Mom hesitated for half a second before offering a genuine smile. "Yes! I'd be delighted to help. Now get up and get dressed. The stores open at ten, and I want to be there as soon as they do."

The ride to the mall was uneventful and thankfully absent of any conversation. At the first store, Teen Blitz, they made a beeline for the sales rack. Within minutes Sadie knew the sale was a bust, but Mom wouldn't be deterred.

Half an hour later, they were back in the car with the best of the worst wrapped in plastic and draped over the backseat.

"You could say, 'Thank you,' you know, Sadie. I was only trying to be helpful in a budget-conscious way."

"I had no idea my choices would be limited to peach lace or gray stick-to-my-body microfiber!"

"I said we could go to the next store on my list if you weren't happy."

"Let's forget it, okay? I'm happy with the gray, Mom. Honestly."

"When we get home, we'll get started on the dance lessons."

"Great," Sadie replied with as much enthusiasm as she could muster. "How long do you think it'll take?"

"You can't put a time limit on these things, Sadie. Let's just get started, okay?"

"Yeah, whatever."

Once they were home, with the dismal, hip-hugging gray dress hung safely in her closet, Sadie dragged herself to the living room. Mom had pushed the couch and coffee table to the back wall to clear a space for them to dance.

"So first, you and your partner are going to face each other. Well, you'll face me for now. Then there's a certain etiquette that you observe . . . just a way of behaving on the dance floor. Always introduce yourself and thank your partner."

"Um, Mom, most of us have been going to school together for how many years now? I think I would already know my partner, and he would know me, so I think we can skip that part."

"Okay, then forget about that. Now you're ready for the four hand placements—one: palm to palm; two: palm to shoulder blade; three: elbow to elbow; and four: palm to neck. In addition to that, there are five foot positions, six dance positions, seven essential dance steps, and eight directional possibilities . . . and don't get me started on leading!"

Sadie stood unimpressed and regretted letting Mom teach her. The feeling intensified with each passing second.

It was an hour later by the time they touched briefly on each of those "basics." One very tiring hour.

"Okay, let's try to put it all together," Mom suggested. "Stand here, and put your hand on my shoulder."

Sadie did as instructed, but as Mom counted out the beat, Sadie pushed away.

"This is just too weird! I don't know if I can do this with you, Mom."

In an instant, the look of enthusiasm on her mother's face shifted into one of sadness. "But Sadie, we used to do this kind of stuff all the time. Don't you remember? I used to pick you up and swing you around." She reached out and tucked a wayward strand of Sadie's hair behind her ear. "We'd sing songs and laugh until our stomachs ached."

Sadie nodded, then shook her head. "I kind of remember, but that was so long ago. I'm not a kid anymore, you know."

"You'll always be my little girl." Her mom lowered her deep-brown eyes and sighed. She was far away in thought and time. "I remember it like it was yesterday."

"Weird, Mom. Like I said, weird."

"Come on. Give it another try. Don't think about it so much."

"I'm sure I won't be the only one who doesn't know how to dance properly. You act like I can't do anything. I'm sure I'll figure it out."

"Oh, come on Sadie. You know I don't think that."

"Really? I think you do."

"Well, that attitude isn't going to get us anywhere. Come on. Let's continue."

Sadie let out a groan. "I think we've done enough for today. I've got geometry homework to do. Maybe we'll try again later, okay?

Mom's shoulders slumped. "Of course. It's just that this is the first time in a long time that I have your full attention. I was enjoying our moment."

Sadie shrugged. "Well, the moment's passed. Thanks for

the lesson, Mom. See you later." She walked down the hallway. Before entering her room, she turned to see her mom staring at the floor. Her expression gave her sadness away. Sadie hesitated. Part of her wanted to go back but also didn't.

CHAPTER FORTY-FIVE

A River of Golden Fire

"**M**R. FINN, ARE you okay? You were yelling. You were yelling at that girl again. Telling her to stop staring at you."

Finn pushed Basset off him, ignoring the worried look written all over the younger man's face.

"I'm fine! I'm fine. I don't need you clawing all over me. Always asking me how I am. Always asking me where I've gone. It's perfectly obvious I'm right here."

"But Mr. Finn, I never know where you are half the time. After all those years of never leaving the cabin, all of a sudden you've started disappearing for days at a time, leaving me alone to worry."

"Nonsense. I only ever go for a couple of hours at most."

Basset dropped the subject . . . again.

Finn got out of bed and walked to the bathroom, shoulders slumped, dragging his feet. A lot had changed over the many years since he had first seen the girl outside his window. She came to his dreams often. Staring at him. Laughing at him. But this time, it felt different. He was shaken.

He stared at himself in the mirror. More than three decades had passed since they had come to live in the cabin. Lines flooded his face now. Gray covered his head. There was a tremor in his reflection too.

Fire swirled up behind him. The muscles in his back tightened and flexed in anticipation of the searing heat. If this was his final exit, he preferred to see it coming. He turned to face the inferno but was met with only the white tiled wall of the cramped bathroom.

There was no heat. No searing flesh.

He turned back to the mirror. This time he saw a towering tree in the distance, rising upward, its trunk expanding until its chest burst open. A flash flood of golden lava emerged, rushing down the hill through the trees. Nothing burned in its path. It glowed its fiery light all the way down to level ground.

The girl peered from behind the tree. "Finny," she sang to him.

Shocked at hearing her call his name, he almost lost his balance. He held on to the sink for stability.

He stared at the mirror, looking to see what she would do next.

"What did you do to me, Finny?"

The piercing light from her eyes zapped through the mirror and knocked him over. Finn banged the back of his head on the towel rack on his way to the floor.

"Mr. Finn! Are you okay?" called Basset from the other side of the door.

"Yes, Basset." Finn felt the back of his head where his thin hair was now matted, sticky with warm blood. He heard a high-pitched beep, barely within his range of hearing. He sat up and smiled. "I'm more than okay. I'm perfect."

Finn rushed out of the bathroom. "Pack a bag, Basset. It's time to leave."

"Leave, Mr. Finn? What do you mean 'leave'? When will we be back?"

"We aren't coming back. It's time to move on."

"I don't understand. What happened? Mr. Finn, you're bleeding. I don't think this is such a good idea."

Finn looked down at his bloody hand. He brought it up to Basset's chest and pushed him hard against the wall, holding him there. "I know I've given you a lot of leeway over the years, but I don't need your questions, fleabag. Do you understand? You'll do as I say. Remember your station."

Basset opened his mouth, but no words came out.

"I remember now. I remember everything they did to me," said Finn. "They won't get away with it."

Finn's eyes blazed into Basset's. He loosened his hand on Basset's chest, and the younger man fell to the floor. He got up, frantic, unable to look Finn in the eyes.

"Yes, Mr. Finn. I'm sorry. I was out of line. It will never happen again."

"It'd better not. We have a lot of work ahead of us, and we can't go about it in a haphazard fashion. I need you at your best. Can you be that?"

"Yes, Mr. Finn. Of course. I'll do anything you ask me."

"Good. That's settled. Let's get out of here. I want to be there by morning."

* * *

They traveled down Route 63 until only fumes remained in the beat-up Ford truck. The engine started to knock.

"I need to pull into that truck stop for gas," Finn said. "If you need to go about your business, make it snappy. We don't have time to waste."

"Yes, Mr. Finn. I'll be fast."

Ten minutes later, Basset emerged from the mini mart, a big bag of barbecue potato chips in hand. As he climbed into the truck, Finn snatched the bag.

"You weren't going to eat those, were you?" Finn asked, yanking the bag open and releasing the pungent aroma into the cab.

"No, Mr. Finn. They're all yours."

"Yes. They are, aren't they?"

At the next gas station, Basset came back to the truck with two bags of chips. He handed one to Finn, who stifled a smile. *He's obedient but brave. I'll give him that.* Basset stood with the other bag in his hand, looking at Finn.

Finn rolled his eyes. "I suppose I'll let you keep one."

They drove through the night, stopping only when necessary to refuel or answer the call of nature. Finn took the first stint, driving for four hours before relinquishing the driver's seat back to Basset. It was just past three in the morning, after several hours of the best sleep Finn had in years, when he settled in for the last leg, his destination firmly in mind. "Rest up, Basset. I need you on your toes when we arrive."

Dawn announced itself with a whisper. Low-hanging clouds, gray and foreboding, flew southward in a hurry.

"Wake up. We're here."

"Where's here, Mr. Finn?"

"Back where it all began . . . and now where it will end."

CHAPTER FORTY-SIX

Butter Flutter Flies

"WHERE IS IT?" Sadie pulled the clothes from her drawers, looking for her appreciation stone.

She'd seen a flash of its light and felt peculiar twinges during the dance lesson with her mother. *It's gone. It can't be gone!* "Oh, come on. Don't take it away from me."

She also felt a twinge of guilt.

Sadie knew she wasn't exactly nice during the lesson, but she couldn't help it. Her mother got under her skin. Sometimes every word was like a banshee's piercing wail. How could anyone bear that?

Fifteen minutes later, exhausted and defeated, she gave up on her search and lay down for a minute.

*   *   *

Make it go away! The thunder's so loud. How can it be this loud inside the house?

Sadie was in that familiar place, caught in the shadow nightmare, as incessant thunder rolled overhead.

She crouched on the floor in the kitchen. The booms were the loudest she'd ever heard. She crawled under the table and covered her ears. It was no use. The refrigerator knocks were muffled but not the thunder.

Crack! Ow. It's inside my head. How's that possible?

Rrrip. Sadie discovered the source of the noise. The roof unhinged as if it were a zipper tearing apart. Red eyes stared from above. They were large, like those of a giant.

"Make it stop, Sadie!"

The side of the house blew away. Sadie peered out, stunned by Mom's presence. *What's she doing in the rain? And barefoot?* Mom stood immobile in the mud. Her clothes were soaked.

"Help us, Sadie!" Mom cried.

The twins materialized, cowering in a huddle with Mom.

"Why aren't you helping us, Sadie?" they screamed.

Red eyes blazed at her from above with rumbles of laughter. She was more terrified for Mom and the twins than she was for herself.

"Why won't you make it stop?" they pleaded.

Sadie's eyes opened. There was finally peace although the thunder in her head still reverberated. *I've never heard it inside my mind before. Why were Mom and the twins there? What did they have to do with anything?*

Her breathing slowly returned to normal.

I can't think about this now. Whatever that was, Sam will help me forget.

For more than two weeks, Mystashan had been quiet—no calls or nudges and no recent visits—but it lived in Sadie's thoughts every day. It felt good to have Sam to keep her company. He seemed so charming. Spending time with him helped her gain distance from the misery of school and home, providing a much-needed distraction from her longing for Mystashan.

Sadie walked over the little footbridge to where Sam stood. It was their favorite spot this week. They met there as often as they could.

The bridge overlooked one of the creeks that wove through the neighborhood. They sat on a bench watching the water rush through the rocks. Sometimes, when the water was low enough, they used those same rocks to navigate to more private places. With welcome chivalry, he offered his hand to help her cross.

They set up a picnic under the comforting shade of the laurel oaks.

"Hey, Annie. Take a look at this," Sam said, pointing.

"What is it?"

He grinned. "See for yourself."

Sadie looked over the railing, and there, on one of the smaller trees, were about two dozen butterflies. They flitted with graceful abandon, wearing combinations of sapphire, hot pink, and deep purple among others—colors so alive she wondered whether her recent trip through the Saponi Straime had something to do with it. Because of their dazzling movements, she was unable to count all the shades, tints, and hues. She glanced at Sam, who also seemed caught up in this moment of awe.

"Oh, wow! That's so cool. I love butterflies."

"Who doesn't love butterflies?" He nudged her with his elbow and winked.

Her face reddened, but she looked at Sam and smiled. "I could stay here and watch them flutter all day and never get bored. Especially if I was with you." She blushed again. She hadn't meant to say that. She didn't want to scare him away. It had kind of slipped out. They were only friends after all.

Sam held the back of Sadie's hand in his palm. With both their palms facing up, they reached out together toward the butterflies. She watched his face and couldn't turn away. She felt the warmth of his skin.

He smiled. "Watch."

A single butterfly flew up to greet them. It settled on Sadie's palm. The butterflies in her stomach fluttered in harmony with the gentle tingling on her skin. The tiny breeze from the flapping tickled, but Sam held her hand steady. It was as if the tiny being knew it was safe with them and would only fly away when all three were ready to let go.

After their once-in-a-lifetime moment, the butterfly lifted off just a little, hovering before it took off in earnest.

"Thank you for showing them to me, Sam. That was . . . I don't even have the words."

"Of course, Annie. I want to show you lots of things. Are you ready for the dance? I'm excited about going with you."

"It's gonna be a lot of fun," Sadie agreed as casually as she could. *Until you meet all my "friends" and find out I'm not exactly who I say I am.*

They walked back to the street corner where they always met and said their good-byes.

"See you later, Annie." Sam bowed and lifted Sadie's hand to his lips.

"Until next time, Sam." Sadie smiled, no longer caring about the heat in her cheeks. Then she headed home.

Tomorrow would mark the beginning of the third week since her ejection from Mystashan. She'd been over and over her last visit in her mind. *What did I do wrong?* She couldn't figure it out. As far as she was concerned, Thelo either didn't hear her or didn't care.

Her stubborn streak didn't allow her to approach Banyan about this abandonment. She wanted more than anything to go back. Knowing that Mystashan existed—that so many of her guesses about the mysteries of her dreams and the universe were true—gave her a sense of hope.

It also didn't hurt to have someone else to talk to. Someone who was as kind, curious, and yes, yummy, as Sam. But he couldn't be around all the time, and in truth, she grew bored sitting in her room alone.

She thought about this afternoon with the butterflies. How warm and caring Sam's touch had been. Calm seeped in and took the place of her tension and anxiety. *What's up next on the Sadie agenda?* she wondered.

She checked out her book collection. It was the one resource she always turned to that never let her down, no matter what trials plagued her life. She'd only read from one book since her return from Saponi Straime, which was highly unusual.

She approached the wall of books, running her fingers over the well-worn spines, thinking maybe she would choose by color, when she spied a book she didn't recognize.

This is strange. What's the title? Dark Secrets. *Hmmm . . . intriguing.* She flipped to the first page. *"Written by Mr. Felix."*

The book dropped to the floor, the binding side up, as Sadie took a few steps back.

Wait. What? She moved cautiously back to where the dark-blue spine waited. *Am I reading this correctly? Yep. That's what it's called.* She rubbed her eyes. *Ohhh . . . not Mr. Felix—Matt Helix. Get a grip, Sadie. Get a grip.*

She picked up the book and brought it with her to her window seat, which was, hands down, the best reading place of all time. She flipped through the pages to get a sense of its essence, when her finger stopped with random determination on page sixty-three. *Weird. Sixty-three. That's how old Grandma Rose was when . . .*

At the top of the page were some handwritten words. Examining them, she saw they were in Gramma Rose's own hand: "Only Rose knows." She read over the simple phrase a few times. The ink faded soon after.

Sadie frowned. "Why does this keep happening? What are you trying to tell me? And how am I supposed to figure it out if every time I see traces of you, they disappear?"

She realized she was getting upset. She stood up and paced

the length of her room, back and forth. *What is it with all the mystery, everybody? You take me here. You send me there. You put a book in my own personal bookshelf, yet you tell me nothing, and you do it with words. Who the heck does that?*

On her third lap, she spotted the music box. Thinking of Gramma Rose brought tears to her eyes, but they didn't fall. She remembered how Gramma's house always smelled like butter cookies and chocolate. Thinking about her baking, she walked back over to the window and picked up the book again. She ran her fingers over the space Gramma's words had occupied. Sadie closed it and placed it back on the shelf. "I'll figure it out, Gramma. I will. Don't give up on me, okay?"

Leaning against the wall, she took a huge breath and let it out slowly. Her thoughts were calm now. Pleased with herself for not losing it, she reflected on what just had happened. She smiled. In the past, Sadie might have thrown something across the room. This time she dealt with her frustration much differently.

Sadie felt a tug on her light-purple hoodie. She reached into one of the pockets and smiled. It was another clear stone. *They didn't forget about me*, she thought.

Turning it over, she read, PATIENCE.

"Really? Me?"

Sadie, it is time to come back. Please bring the music box.

"Okay, Thelo. I'm coming. And don't worry—I'm not even upset with you anymore."

I do not worry.

As with everything in Mystashan, the colors were deeper, richer. Everything gave off a brighter light than Sadie remembered seeing in her whole life, except for maybe the butterflies. The colors also reminded her of how paints blended together in layers, the way they created vivid hues, brightening even what she knew to be shadows. The nearest she could come to comparing that part of it would be how her black light in her bedroom made different colors—only the colors here existed without the darkness. There were shining dots with a luster that she imagined to be tiny star shepherds whispering encouraging tunes to all the plants around.

There were fragrances here she'd never dreamed of before. They were the best parts of vanilla, cinnamon, roses, and a touch of something completely unknown. They all mixed together in a new way, without a name. It smelled delicious here, indescribable.

Sadie couldn't believe she had made it this far, passing through Saponi Straime on her own. She walked between the massive stands of trees that wove through Mystashan. They looked like beech or elm trees from back home, but with something extra, be it bright colors or sparkling trunks. A whole rainbow of otherworldly watercolors stretched far beyond where their trunks were planted.

"What in the world?" Sadie stared at the sky. Lengths of silky fabrics floated, rippling as though they were clouds as far as she could see. But they were neither clouds nor fabric. Their colors in broad daylight changed constantly, encouraging subtle shifts in mood. Shades of pinks, blues, greens, and purples—each brought a feeling of calm. They reminded her of the green and blue flashes from her music box.

A soft, repetitive squeak filled the air. At first, Sadie couldn't tell where the sound came from, but she soon realized it was from the plants themselves. Lush varieties of low-to-the-ground cover and flowers grew everywhere, familiar in a way but distinctly Mystashan. She took care to step between them rather than on them.

As she grew accustomed to the squeaking, she deciphered another tone, sounding in unison. A distinct humming persisted all around her, like the sound of thousands of tiny insects. She closed her eyes and focused on it. Almost instantly it became more distinct. The humming wasn't humming at all but *words*.

High-pitched, fast-talking voices wove in and through one another and carried a melody too. And then she understood. The lilies spoke to marigolds as easily as petunias hummed at roses, and Sadie understood them all. Of course! They were Mystashan varieties—that made all the difference, she supposed.

She took off her shoes and let her bare feet show her the way. They directed her to the midst of a field of finely colored wildflowers in a valley.

A deep voice behind her asked, "How are you today, my dear girl?"

"Thelo!" She ran over and gave him a hug.

"I am glad to see you too . . . and happy that you heard me and came through okay."

"Why didn't you let me through the last time?"

"It is interesting that you ask me that. Have you asked yourself yet?"

Sadie felt for the stone in her pocket and realized she already knew the answer. She gave Thelo a cheeky smile. "Yeah. I hear you."

She felt something flutter by her ear. It was too quick to spot. A warm wind picked up and brushed her hair against her cheek. She couldn't help notice the electric violet of her now-longer hair. "I *love* this color, by the way!"

"I am glad you like it," Thelo said. "You should see your eyes."

"My eyes. I haven't even thought about my eyes. What color are they?

"That is something you will have to experience for yourself."

"Really? You're going to leave me with that?"

"Some things one cannot describe. You must experience them on your own."

Sadie shrugged. "Well, if you say so."

"Yes, I say so. Let's go, Sadie. There are some people here in Mystashan I would love for you to meet."

CHAPTER FORTY-SEVEN

Whiskers and All

THEY WALKED ALONG the narrow dirt path, Thelo leading the way, pointing at various landmarks of Mystashan history. The one that struck Sadie the most was the place where the elders met. It had its own vibrating energy. Sadie felt invigorated as they passed the round structure made of silver gray bark.

"Who are the elders, Thelo?"

"Over time, as Mystashan grew in population, we decided to create a council. Not that there was a need, but should any dispute arise. The years were peaceful, for the most part, but we saw how life evolved elsewhere and decided to be proactive. At first it was composed of representatives from different groups, but a few other individuals were appointed later. You will meet them one day."

"What exactly is Mystashan, Thelo? Is it like another world? A world, you know, like earth is a world?"

"My answers might seem confusing at first, but the more you visit us here, the easier it will be to understand. My answers are, 'Mystashan,' 'sort of,' and for your last question, 'yes' and 'no.'"

Sadie stopped and faced him. Her eyes narrowed. "Huh? I'm not sure I get it. How can something be both yes and no?"

"The worlds, to use your word, whether it is here or on earth, are more complicated yet simpler than you might think. You will come to see in time."

"O-kay . . . for now. I don't see any other humans here . . . you know, people like me. How come?"

Thelo took a long pause—too long, Sadie thought.

"First, let me explain. Our time runs differently from yours, Sadie. The question is 'How *much* faster or slower?' I have noticed that whenever you are here, your earth clocks run much more slowly.

"We translate time through our Velluminator, but that discussion might be best saved for another day. What I will say about it, though, is that it allows us to see things on earth in the present and past. Only the cloffuls can see into the future. Sometimes they share with us what we need to know. Other times we must run the course of fate. That completes my answer to your question about why you are here."

Sadie's eyebrows scrunched up, and she gave Thelo a skeptical look. "Sorry? Run that by me again?"

"No need."

"No! I mean, I don't understand most of what you said. What are cloffuls?"

"Oh! You have already seen them." He pointed up at the sky.

"You mean those fabric-cloud things?"

"What are clouds to your skies are cloffuls here," Thelo explained. "We in Mystashan have learned to read ours. Maybe earth clouds are trying to give you messages too. Have you ever tried to understand them? Our cloffuls can do incredible things. We saw you in them and knew you were meant to come here."

"Wait a minute . . . you saw me?"

"I am afraid I do not have an extra minute, my dear. I am just about to leave you in the hands of one you know very well but whom you may not recognize in Mystashan."

Thelo took a step back. Sadie looked past him at the radiant being now approaching. He strode down the surrounding hill. The word *regal* whispered in Sadie's mind, followed by *poised* and *attentive*. For a moment she thought she saw one of the Arthurian knights.

The once-small figure on the hill was now life-size, standing a couple of feet in front of her. She felt his energy before he spoke. Although it was familiar, she couldn't quite place it.

"Hello, Sadie. Good to see you again so soon. If you don't mind, please take care next time to scratch me a little more behind the left ear. Right over here." He demonstrated. "I like that the most."

"Huh? Did you just ask me to scratch behind your ear?"

"Yes, and while I'm at it, I really don't like the food offerings in your world. Who do people think I am? A pet? Do you think you could help me out in that department? A little fresh fruit now and then wouldn't be unappreciated." He winked at her.

As he winked, Sadie was drawn to his golden eyes. She noticed his pupils were vertical. Just like a cat's. She looked closer and saw a shimmer of blue around him with a familiar essence. *No. It can't be. Could it?* "Barnaby?"

"The one and only."

"But . . . you look human."

"Funny. You sort of do too." He shot her a sly grin.

Sadie flushed. Barnaby was handsome. He looked somewhere in his late twenties. He wore iridescent blue riding pants and a brocade vest, with a cream-colored silk shirt.

Thelo piped in, "Barnaby, I called you earlier, but I could not see or reach you. Were you busy?"

"I didn't hear your call, Thelo."

"That has never happened before, Barnaby. I will have to look into it."

"Yes. You should definitely look into that, Thelo."

"You look like a prince over here," Sadie admired, still staring.

Barnaby wore a headpiece. The closer she looked, the more she realized it might be part of him. The shapes that rose from the "crown" were set about a half inch apart and resembled the cardamom leaves her father used to show her in their herb garden back when he used to be "Kind Face." Barnaby's were straight up and waved about lazily in the breeze.

"Are those attached? Can I feel them?"

"Yes, Sadie. In fact, you have for years. Why stop now?" He lowered his head so she could reach.

She touched one of Barnaby's "leaves" between her fingers. She couldn't believe how velvety soft they were. They even changed shades of blue like the cloffuls. "Amazing. This is incredible, Thelo." She turned toward him, but he vanished. "Where did he go, Barnaby?"

"Thelo? He does that. And just to prepare you, so do I."

"Oh, great. When do I get to do that?"

"One day maybe, but not today." Barnaby pointed to the hill and offered Sadie his elbow, which she gladly took. "Come with me, Sadie. I want you to meet someone while we're here. We're heading toward the village. There are many places to be in Mystashan."

They crested the hill to find huts spread throughout the area below. It didn't take long for them to walk down the hill, where they were greeted by a stunning woman with a headpiece and features similar to Barnaby's. Her crown and damask gown, however, were opal in color. Their pearlescence made their shimmer more obvious.

"Sadie, this is my sister, Penelope. We're twins."

Sadie immediately felt drawn to her.

"What an exquisite pendant you're wearing, Penelope. I love how it seems to change colors."

"Thank you, Sadie. It was a gift from the Habnaws. One of

them found this stone underground and thought of me. You'll be meeting them before long, I'm sure." Penelope winked as she turned to her brother. "You were absolutely right, Barnaby. Sadie does look just like Rose."

"Wait. You both knew Gramma? I knew Barnaby did, of course."

"Yes, I knew her too. It was a long time ago. She was a lovely woman."

"I hope we can talk more about her sometime, Penelope." *Is there anyone else Penelope knows on earth?* Sadie wondered. "Thanks so much, Barnaby, for introducing . . . uh . . ." And Barnaby wasn't there.

That will definitely take some getting used to. Sadie shook her head.

Penelope explained, "We use our minds differently in Mystashan. Sometimes we're needed elsewhere and must take our leave."

Sadie laughed. "I get that, I guess. I just wish it came with some kind of warning signal so I don't end up talking to myself."

As Penelope led Sadie to the village, they passed a shade tree on a knoll surrounded by boulders. She saw that the woven huts were open to the sky. *What do they do when it rains?* They were well spaced, not on top of one another, with plenty of room for self-expression. She saw many banners flying and blankets on looms, showcasing the full spectrum of Mystashan's textures. There were luxurious gardens everywhere, lush with green growth. Again Sadie thought it was unusual that there weren't any people about, as the plants and flowers were so well tended.

"Where is everyone, Penelope? I've only seen the three of you so far."

"There's a big meeting in the Atrium for some. Others are engaged in various activities, either for service here or on earth, or simply for fun."

"Oh, cool. What's the Atrium, if you don't mind my asking?"

"I don't mind, but I know Thelonious wishes to show it to you soon."

Penelope and Sadie talked about everything and nothing, as they were also comfortable with the silences. Sitting on the soft Mystashan ground, Sadie felt comfortable playing with the blades of grass around her. In Penelope's company, she felt completely at ease. Even though they'd just met, she thought she could tell Penelope anything. She imagined it was like having a sister.

"Penelope, do you have a mother?" asked Sadie.

"I had a mother once. She's around here somewhere. After her first year with us, we only got to see each other once in a while. Plus, my mother was also an elder since before Barnaby and I were born. He and I had to leave the den early due to our roles and responsibilities. Barnaby and I do a lot of . . . how would you say it? Earth work. Barnaby gets to see her more often." Penelope turned toward the cloffuls and then back to Sadie, refocusing her attention.

"That must be something, Penelope. Hard but important. I'm glad you still have her. My mother talks and talks and talks. Sometimes I can't keep up with what she's saying. She's either telling me what I did wrong, telling me what chores I still have to do, or telling me what she did with her boring day."

Penelope expressed earnest understanding; she placed her long arm and elegant sleeve over Sadie's shoulders.

Sadie continued, "Mom tells me about how she has to go grocery shopping for hours, though I think it takes more time for her to tell me about it than to actually do it. She recounts in endless detail how it took her so long to pick the right ice cream for my dad and me because one was on sale, but he likes the other brand, and of course I like caramel swirl. It goes on and on from there. I can't take it. My brain shuts off before it explodes, so I can't hear her once I reach that point. I get so wound up that my heart starts to pound, and I feel tiny dots of fire all around my body. It's too much."

Sadie turned to Penelope, who nodded in understanding. "Your openness and observations will serve you well, Sadie. Unfortunately I must take my leave now, but I have a feeling you'll run into friends here soon."

"Wait . . . don't go!"

CHAPTER FORTY-EIGHT

A Hunting We Will Go

"I'M SURE SHE'S around here somewhere. I don't know how it's possible, but something's fishy."

"What do you mean, Mr. Finn . . . and who is 'she'?"

"Never mind the particulars for now, Basset. The signal brought me here, and it'll show me—I mean *us*—the way."

They sat in the Ford, parked outside a discount warehouse store in Florida, but it quickly became too hot for comfort once Finn had turned off the engine.

"What signal, Mr. Finn? Maybe I can help if you tell me a bit more."

"Maybe so. I think you can be a helpful pooch if you listen to each of my directions carefully. First off, we need supplies. More than you used to get at the cabin. We might be in the woods for much of our time here, until I can narrow down where the signal is leading us more clearly."

"May I ask a few questions first, Mr. Finn?"

Finn shook his head. "No, that's for later. The days are short, and there's much to do before dark."

"Just one then?"

"Don't push this good thing we've got going here, Basset."

"Yes, Mr. Finn."

Getting out of the truck, Finn felt the stinging sun on his skin. Each burning ray scorched his flesh. Now that his memories had returned, this unpleasant side effect had come back too. He hurried toward the relative darkness inside the store with Basset close on his heels. He heard the squeal of metal drilling into his skull as the automatic doors opened. He shook it off. He had work to do.

"Basset, stay close until we get the list down, and then I'll have you do most of the legwork."

"Sounds good, Mr. Finn, especially after so many hours in the truck."

"Yeah. Whatever. Get all the things you usually get for the cabin but about three to four times as much. Nothing perishable unless you want to eat or drink it now. It's so hot in this horrid state."

Basset nodded. "Okay. Is there anything extra that you want . . . to fill in for those perishable items?"

"Use your brain, and only this money I give you now. Take it and put it out of sight immediately!" They both turned toward the wall as the dollar transfer was completed. "Keep track of what you spend so you won't bring attention to yourself fumbling about at the register. This is pretty much what we have left. Remember to use it wisely."

Basset pulled a cart from the corral near the door and headed down the dairy aisle.

Finn sighed. *I just told him no perishables.* He waited until Basset turned the corner and was out of sight; then he hurried to the other end of the store. He easily found the camping and hunting section. *The weather may be abominable, but at least this store is well stocked.*

Finn knew just what he needed. Those old magazines in the cabin had made good research material. He scanned the racks for the perfect blade, the perfect ending for that beast. Not just any blade would do. He stopped in his tracks. Eyes closed, he concentrated. "I hear you," he spoke to the air. A steel blade called out to him. He walked over to the display case at the end of the aisle, where the middle-aged salesman stood.

The knife had a sawback design that curved toward the end with a strong, sharp tip. "Will this blade be good for digging rocks out of the hard ground?" Finn asked the man.

"Yes, of course," answered the salesman. "It's made from the finest steel on earth. This is the best hunting knife we carry."

Finn, pleased with his purchase, slipped the blade into its ankle sheath and secured it under his pant leg. He picked up a few other camping necessities as well. Then he met up with Basset and his huge, well-balanced cart on the far side of the registers. They left the building and headed back to the truck.

There's that ghastly sun again! The beast always said I was too sensitive, but I think we know by now how wrong "His Majesty" was about everything! How can anyone live here like this?

Finn and Basset loaded their equipment and food into the back of the truck. "Good job, Basset. It looks like we have enough food and water to last us several weeks, although it'd better not take that long."

CHAPTER FORTY-NINE

Freanweas

PENELOPE DISAPPEARED EVEN as Sadie watched. *Now what? I don't know what to do next.* She stood up, brushed the grass off her jeans, and headed back toward the village. *Wait, it wasn't this far on the way here,* she realized after she'd been walking for a while.

"*Aaachhhooo . . . zzzzzttt . . . hahahahaha.*"

Sadie jumped as a zap of electricity shocked her shin. "Ouch! What was that?" She ran into a group of knee-high, bright-eyed, furry pink people. They were as wide as they were high.

"*Aaachhhooo . . . zzzzzttt . . . hahahahaha.*"

"Ouch! Stop it. That really hurts." A dozen more little electric shocks pricked her skin. It reminded her of how she felt when her mother talked to her nonstop.

"I told you to stop! Do you mind?"

"Yes, actually. We do. We Freanweas had to sit and listen to you whine to Penelope. The least you could do is say, 'Zap choo you.'"

"Zap what now?" Sadie asked in complete confusion.

"It's the proper thing to do when one zapchoos." The tallest one reached out and touched her again.

"*Aaachhhooo . . . zzzzzttt . . . hahahahaha.*"

One Freanwea turned to another and chortled, "Zap choo you."

"Why zank you very much. Hahahahaha."

Sadie didn't know what to make of this bunch. Honestly, they were really getting on her nerves.

She couldn't get Penelope's sudden departure off her mind. *Did I whine? I don't think so. I only told her about my day. I deserve my time to vent as much as anyone.*

"*Aaachhhooo . . . zzzzzttt . . .* hahahahaha."

"Cut that out!"

"We can't help it," one of them confessed. "Sure, we love to zapchoo, but we don't do it on purpose. Take a deep breath and relax when you hear it coming, and it won't hurt so much. That's what the others tell us they do. They tell us they smile, breathe deeply, and the pain's gone in a flash."

"The air makes our noses feel tickly funny," said another Freanwea.

"My nose is just fine," Sadie insisted. Totally exhausted, she took a seat on the ground. "*Aaachhhooo . . . aaachooo . . . aaaachoooooooooo . . .*"

"Achoo you," a Freanwea told her.

"Uh, thank you?" Sadie stood up and realized the air felt different. "Your air is unusual down there," she told them.

"*Aaachhhooo,*" belted out a younger Freanwea.

Sadie, now understanding, took a deep breath and smiled.

"*Zzzzzttt . . .* hahahahaha."

"Zap choo you," Sadie said to the smaller Freanwea. Despite the zap, they were right. It wasn't as bad as before.

"Why, zank you very much."

"Hmmm, let's see if I can figure this out." Sadie walked away from them for a minute to avoid any further shocks and took a good look around. She heard a faint clinking sound, like when she was younger and she and her family were at the beach. She would put some dry sand and pebbles in a can and shake it all around. It would go, *Tink, tink, tink.*

On her search she found a small field of plants. They each had a cylinder at the top with small holes. Whenever the breeze blew, the plant leaned over, and Sadie could see something shake out.

She put her hand out to catch some of the dust. Holding it to her nose, she smelled it. "*Aaachooooo.*" *Pepper.* They were pepper plants. *That makes sense.*

"Okay, guys," she called to the Freanweas. "You need to avoid these plants."

"Oh, the pepper plants?" they asked.

"Yes. You know what they are?"

"Of course we do. What else would they be? They're our delicate pepper plants."

Oh, boy. "Okay, well if you want to stop zapchooing, just move a little to the right."

All at once, the group twirled to the right until they were out of the direct line of the pepper wind. Immediately they stopped zapchooing.

"Thank you, Sadie," they replied in unison. "Thank you for helping us. It was a bit much at times. Not all the time, though." With that, one of the Freanweas jumped to the left and zapchooed Sadie unexpectedly. They all started giggling again.

She hadn't had time to try her "smile and breathe" trick. "Ow," Sadie gasped, but with a giggle in her voice now too.

Still rubbing her zapped leg, half sore, half smiling, Sadie found herself standing in front of Banyan. "How did that happen? Abrupt much?" Sadie placed her palm on her friend's trunk.

After a few moments together, she stepped out from beneath his branches to look at the sky and double-check. *Clouds.* "Okay, I'm back. I guess it's time to head home. See you tomorrow, Banyan."

As soon as she got home, Sadie glanced at the clock while her mother started talking.

Ugh, here she goes again. What time is it? Seriously? I was gone only thirty minutes? I spent a whole day in Mystashan—well, five or six hours at least. It feels longer listening to five minutes of Mom.

"So today I had to go to the grocery store. I must have been there for two hours. I had to make sure I picked up all the snacks you like. Then I had to go to the post office to pick up a package your Aunt Sue sent you and then to the dry cleaner to have them hem that skirt that's too long on you. Next I did the laundry. You put a red shirt in with the whites, but I didn't notice until it was too late. It turned all of your dad's underwear pink. I just knew he was going to be upset. I tried to get it out, but I couldn't, so then I went to the mall and bought him some new ones. Then I came home and had to wash them . . ."

On and on. Sadie felt her temperature rising, and the fire prickles came as a shock to her system. *Hmmm, like a shock to my . . . oh.*

Smile and breathe. Smile and breathe. It started to work. She began to relax. She heard more of what her mom actually said. She was able to listen a bit longer without getting upset.

Dink. Sadie felt the weight of a stone and sneaked it out of her pocket. Glancing down, she saw that it read, TOLERANCE. *Smile and breathe.* Words her mother had recently uttered were coming back to her: *Snacks you like. Picked up Aunt Sue's package for you. Your skirt to the dry cleaner. Wow, Mom did all that for me today? Smile and breathe.*

"Thanks for doing all that stuff for me today, Mom."

Her mother took a step back. "What? Oh. You're welcome, Sadie. Your sweet words made my day." She smiled.

Dink. Was it another stone? She took it out. A grin spread to the far reaches of her face. *I missed you*, she thought. APPRECIATION was back.

CHAPTER FIFTY

Finn Zeroes In

Though the bags they'd bought were in the truck bed, Finn fancied he could smell oranges in the air-conditioned cab. He didn't know how Basset could tolerate the disgusting odor.

As if on cue:

"Don't they smell wonderful, Mr. Finn? From what I read in one of those tourist brochures, Florida oranges are considered some of the best in the world." Basset's expression of enthusiasm, in full flower, was soon quashed.

"Smells like rotting plant material," Finn scoffed. "I wish you wouldn't purchase them ever again."

Basset was usually quick to agree, but he sat quietly this time, head hanging low on his chest.

"What? Did I say something to offend you? Speak up, pup. There's no need for pouting."

"Yes, Mr. Finn."

"Yes, you understand, or yes, there's no need for rancor?"

"Whatever you choose, Mr. Finn."

"Speak up! Let me see that backbone of yours, Basset. I want to know it's there. Turn around and point to it!"

"Yes, Mr. Finn," and Basset rearranged himself in his seat.

"Seriously? You're as dumb as you look, Basset. Sheesh!"

"Please, Mr. Finn. I don't want to argue."

"Then do as I say. Stop buying those stinking oranges! Now step number one," Finn continued, "is to find a good base camp as soon as possible so we can unpack and get settled. I have good intel that our new residence is around here somewhere."

Basset's eyes widened. "Intel? From who, Mr. Finn? Someone in the store?"

"It happened back in the cabin, but never mind that now. Don't be nosy."

After another hour of driving around in circles, Finn was nearly out of his mind with frustration—this was meant to be easy. But he was Finn after all; patience had its limits. He took it out on the steering wheel as they continued going around corners in this monotonous neighborhood. He was about to include Basset in the "conversation," when a sharp pain stabbed his left eye and hijacked all his brain's senses.

Two young girls appeared in the distance. As his brain came back online, he grew increasingly aware of the coincidence. His pain arrived with the appearance of the girls and grew as they came closer. Pangs of recognition dawned on him. It was the blonde in the pigtails. His signal surged.

"There she is. I knew I'd find her." As the girls passed by, wrapped up in their own world, his temperature rose, and the tightening in his jaw was almost too much to bear. Almost . . .

Finn pulled the truck over to park. His pain subsided. As subtly as possible, he got out, using the stealth that came so naturally to him. He didn't want them to take notice. Not yet. They appeared so involved in what they were talking about that there was no need for him to worry.

He hid behind a huge maple and watched them. Snippets of their conversation drifted his way. The pain in his eye returned as they drew closer. He closed his eyes to steel himself against the throbbing. When he opened them, the blonde stared at him.

Don't you know it's rude to stare? he thought.

He leaned back, pressing himself against the tree and out of sight.

"What, Sadie? What is it?" the dark-haired girl asked.

"I don't know," the blonde one said. "I thought I saw something."

"Well, the only thing I see is an empty collection box. Let's start making some cash."

Finn peeked out again after the girls resumed their conversation. They walked toward an old two-story, beige-and-purple "fancy house." *What a waste of space*, he thought.

He waited until he could no longer hear their voices, then returned to the truck.

"All right, Basset. Good news. We've found the key. We need to watch her. See where she goes and what she does. We'll find her next time more easily now that I have this signal leading me toward her. That should cheer you up, pup." He threw his head back and laughed giddily, a rare thing for him. "Oh, I never get tired of saying that."

CHAPTER FIFTY-ONE

Eye Kaleido Spied

Sadie walked from school to the corner by the footpath that led back to the creek. Even before she crossed the street, she had a clear view of their meeting place. Sam was already there, sitting on the curb. He stood up and waved with gusto, and she returned the greeting.

"Hi, Sam." Sadie put her hand in his. He was so kind and open, yet she couldn't even tell him her real name. "So what do you want to do? Walk along the creek, maybe?"

"Or . . ." He leaned down so she had no choice but to look at his face. "You could take me to your house. Introduce me to your parents, let me see your room."

For an instant, Sadie considered it. Maybe it would be better to get it over with now. She thought of her mom, as well as Dave and the others, and felt the guilt creep up from her gut into her face. *Two more days, and the dance will be over and done with. And then I'll come clean; I'll explain everything. He'll understand.* She forced a smile. *I hope he'll understand.*

"Hey, you okay? It was just a suggestion. We don't have to go to your house. We can go anywhere you want." His smile brought a bit of relief to Sadie's churning stomach.

"It's a mess there now. We're cleaning up from the destructo phase of the remodel, and that's the worst. It's so dusty, but it should be over in a few days. If you just give me until after the dance that would be better. Things should calm down by then."

Sam opened his mouth to say something but obviously thought better of it. "Okay, Annie, that's fair, but I eventually would like to meet your parents and see where you live . . . Oh, wait! I know what we can do. There's something I've wanted to share with you since we met."

"Oh, yeah? What's that, Mr. Perez?"

"Ooh, being formal, Ms. Cooper? You'll see soon enough." He gently pulled her forward, leading her down the well-worn footpath toward the creek before veering left and over a small embankment.

"Can you give me a clue?" Sadie asked. "Are we heading toward it now?"

"So many questions. So little patience." Sam smirked.

She saw the familiar twinkle of light that shone from his deep-brown eyes. She couldn't help but get lost in their depth and knew she was falling hard for him. She never would have thought it possible, but the truth of it opened her heart more every time she saw him. Even though this made her happy, it also scared her. She'd felt the same way about Christopher during their time together, and what did he do? Despite all his promises of their shared future, he had left her.

But he's not Christopher, she reminded herself. *He's Sam. Even more perfect. Stop it. You're not helping yourself at all.*

As they walked together, Sadie stuffed down her guilt and basked in the wonderful comfort that was Sam. He held her hand as they walked through the woods, stepping over roots and stones along the way, and lent his support as they forded their favorite creek.

They walked up to one of the tall oaks on the far side. "We're here, Annie."

"Here? Where's here?" She looked around but only saw the woods that were now familiar to both of them.

Sam pulled something out his pocket, and she recognized it as a pocketknife with all the attachments. He squeezed her hand briefly then walked over to one of the ancient oaks flanking the creek. He pulled out the short blade and began to carve.

Wait, is he really doing what I think he's doing? I always wanted Christopher to do this for me, but it never happened. Is it finally going to happen? Sadie's excitement continued until she remembered. *Ugh, he thinks my name is Annie. Crap.*

"I hope you don't mind, but I want this to be our tree, our place. I want to mark this moment in time with our names."

Maybe YOUR name . . . crap again.

All Sadie could do was smile and nod. In the end, it didn't really matter that it wasn't her name. He was doing this for her, *with* her.

As Sam started to carve the *A* into the tree, she thought she heard something—maybe a groan. *Huh?* She listened harder but heard nothing. He continued with the *C*. *There it is again.* It sounded like the wind moaning but with a lower tone and no breeze.

"Hey, Sam, do you hear that?"

"Hear what?"

Sadie closed her eyes and listened. "Never mind. I guess it's nothing."

Finished with her initials, he started carving his. First an *S* and then the *P* in the bark of the old tree. For the finishing touch, he made a huge heart around them.

He reached out for Sadie's hand, and they took a step back to admire his work.

That's when she felt it, an ache in her chest like she'd never felt before. It was similar to the pain she'd felt when she lost Gramma. A sadness that was beyond words. She felt awful . . . and afraid.

She looked at the tree, and hundreds of eyes appeared, staring back at her. Glaring. Accusing.

What have you done to me? the tree shouted in her head.

She couldn't move. She felt those eyes burning into her. *Oh, no, what have we done?*

The seconds ticked by in silence. "Annie? Don't you like it?"

Sadie struggled to take a deep breath. She could see the hurt in Sam's face. "It's lovely," she remarked. "I love it. I do. It's just . . . I'm not feeling well all of a sudden. I need to go home. I should rest, especially with the dance coming up."

"Let me walk you there."

She looked up at his face and saw his concern. "No, please, Sam . . . I appreciate it, but I'll be okay. I just need to lie down, I think."

"I don't like you going by yourself if you don't feel well. At least let me walk you to the corner."

Sadie nodded.

When they reached the corner, Sam wrapped his arms around her and hugged her tightly. "Be careful, okay?"

"I will. I promise." She pulled away and turned toward home. Looking back over her shoulder, she offered him a smile. "I'll see you tomorrow, Sam."

He waved, and she quickened her pace.

All Sadie wanted to do was get her music box and see Banyan. She was so worried: What would he think of her after the tree carving? What did the tree feel? How badly was it hurt? When she'd walked a couple of blocks, she looked back and saw that Sam hadn't moved. She felt awful in every way.

Once Sam was out of sight, Sadie ran the rest of the way home, picked up her music box and played the song that would take her to Mystashan. After telling Banyan she would talk to him on the other side, that is.

When Sadie arrived in Mystashan, the sky was blue, as was

the straime, but it was almost as if the sun had disappeared from the sky. As with mountainous areas, perhaps gateways between worlds had their own weather systems too?

Banyan, standing tall in his timeless manner, closed the gate behind her. She could sense the energy field connecting Earth and Mystashan snap shut. Sadie stood in front of him, looking up into his thick, golden branches even though it brought tears to her eyes.

"Banyan, please forgive me for not stopping Sam from carving our initials in that tree. I felt it hurting, Banyan, and it was awful. It felt as if it were happening to me too, though I knew my pain wasn't as bad as the tree's. I'm so sorry."

There's nothing to forgive, Sadie. From my point of view, neither of you realizes the pain that trees have endured . . . and continue to endure.

Sadie hugged him with all her might. She knew it wouldn't hurt him. "See you soon, Banyan. Thank you for always being there."

Every time she went to Mystashan, it was both different and the same. The difference mainly had to do with how much easier it was getting from one side to the other. What was the same was the fact that she never lost her fascination and wonder for the beauty and energy of this place. In many ways, it felt more like home than the one where she ate her meals and slept. The beings here felt more like family than her own . . . lately anyway.

Sadie was proud that she remembered her way into the village, and she walked there now, waving and whispering hellos to anyone she saw along the way. She kept her eyes out for Thelo, Barnaby, and Penelope.

Eventually Thelo emerged from a simple blue cottage near the center of the village. He looked as regal and radiant as the moon with its mantle of stars. His gems were brilliant by the sun's light, and his eyes emanated peace.

Hugs were shared. Then Thelo walked Sadie over to an unusual-looking structure at the heart of the village and the island.

"This is the Atrium, Sadie. It is a special place, and I want you to spend time getting to know it. Its guidance and wisdom will be a compass should you ever need it."

Sadie's lips tightened, and without realizing it, she hugged herself. "Are you trying to tell me something, Thelo? Will I be needing 'a compass' anytime soon?"

Thelo shrugged. "Who can say? Best to be prepared. This place houses our most precious crystals. You can feel their energy even as you approach."

"Crystals?"

"Yes, you have three of them already."

"Oh! You mean those see-through stones with the words inside?"

"Yes . . . crystals, of the type found only in Mystashan. They are alive. Treat yours well. They can come and go, as you already know."

"Yes . . . About that . . ."

"Let us go in, shall we?" The two walked toward the round building and entered. Columns made of crystal, smoother than marble, continued until they disappeared into the cloffuls. They were a little more than a foot in diameter, with five feet between each one.

From inside, Sadie saw the elaborate construction, whereas from outside the structure appeared simple. Flexible vines wrapped themselves around the columns, from the base to as far up as she could see, then one to another, creating delicate green walls.

Sadie spun as she took in the majesty of the expanse. She strode into the center of the grand space and looked up at the sky. Cloffuls floated up and down lightly, shifting from pink to green to blue and back again.

"When Mystashan was first created, these pillars drew up from the earth. This place is the oldest structure we know of."

Sadie turned around. "But who built . . . Thelo, where are you?"

"I am here, of course." Movement near the door caught Sadie's attention. Thelo was still standing at the entrance.

"But I can hear you so clearly. It's like you're standing right beside me."

"I can hear you as well. I told you this is a special place. You can stand anywhere inside the Atrium and be heard. It is remarkable, yes?"

Sadie could only nod.

"Come with me," Thelo invited. "There is much more I wish to show you, starting with the Velluminator."

Sadie rejoined him, and he led her to the left, where she saw a crystalline archway, allowing entrance to a cave beyond. A waterfall separated the two sides. As they approached, the water parted like a red curtain in a movie theater. Soon a crystal screen revealed itself, and then an image formed on it: Mom was cleaning up from breakfast. When she finished, she sat down at the kitchen table.

A family photo album was open, and she was looking at Sadie's baby pictures. As each page passed, so did the years. Her mother gently felt each photo as if her fingertips were somehow absorbing what was happening in the pictures.

"This is the Velluminator I mentioned before, Sadie. It can show us what is happening on the earth realm, be it past or present."

Sadie nodded, but her eyes were transfixed on the screen, on her mother. Her mom flipped through page after page. Year after year. Family vacations. Happy memories. Moments from days long passed. Big smiles on everyone's faces.

The final picture in the book was of the last time they were all together at one of Aunt Sue's parties. Mom, Dad, Sadie, and Gramma were so cheerful. They all had such hope in their eyes.

Her mother cried. Sadie saw the tears streaming down and felt her pain. Her mother closed the album, hugged it to her chest, and sobbed. She rocked back and forth. Her tears streamed faster and heavier. Finally, her mom clutched the album even tighter and yelled up to the ceiling, "Help me. Please! Please help me feel love again. I beg you."

"Poor Mom," Sadie whispered, and wiped at her own tears.

Thelo patted her shoulder. "You aren't the only one who is lost, my dear girl."

CHAPTER FIFTY-TWO

Twist of the Key

"I T IS TRUE, old friend."

"You are right, Thelonious. The cloffuls never lie."

"Yet they can be tricky to read sometimes."

"This is not one of those times, though."

"No. I suppose it is not."

"I did not foresee this turn of events, but as with all things, they will go the way they will."

"There is no doubt about that, Banyan. No doubt."

CHAPTER FIFTY-THREE

Habnaws

"ALL RIGHT CLASS, we'll be starting in a few minutes. I'm stepping out for a second to talk with Principal Tennyson. I expect you all to be on your best behavior."

"Yes, Mr. MacNamara," they all sang in unison.

A few minutes went by in silence, and then of course Dave started in. "Whoa, who farted? Who let that awful stench out?" He waved a hand exaggeratedly in front of his nose.

More and more of the students were now gagging on what Sadie thought smelled like rotten eggs, sewer sludge, and a garbage truck. It was the stankiest fart she'd ever smelled.

"Yuck, it's horrible! I can't breathe. I can actually taste it!" yelled Dave.

"Eww, you just made me vurp, Dave," Kenny choked out.

"I bet it was Sadie," accused Dave. "I'll bet anything it was her."

"It wasn't me. I wouldn't do that. I don't smell like that. Leave me alone, Dave."

Dave smirked. "Oh, getting defensive? I'm one hundred percent sure of it now. I can see the green stink cloud coming from your chair. It's a good thing you wouldn't dare show up at the dance tomorrow, 'cause I'm sure that cloud would be your only date."

The whole class laughed hysterically. Soon the entire room followed Dave's lead, chanting, "Stink Bomb Sadie, Stink Bomb Sadie."

Sadie groaned and sank into her seat. Each day was getting more unbearable.

When the last bell sounded, she sighed with relief. She'd survived another day of humiliation, though the stink-bomb accusation ranked high today on her top ten list of worst "Dave Days."

Time to go home—Mystashan home, that is—after a quick stop.

Once she was home, she hurried to her room, tossed her book bag onto the bed, and retrieved her music box. She was halfway down the block and on her way to Banyan in less than ten minutes.

She sat in her spot among his vast roots and waited. Seconds later she stood barefoot on the sweet, soft grass that could only be found in Mystashan.

As Sadie picked her trail through the flowers, she heard "Sweet Sadie" calling to her on the light Mystashan breeze. Soon it became apparent who was singing. Sparks rose up from the flower petals. They were like tiny flecks of hyper-light.

"I recognize you. I thought I was seeing things, but you cheered me up when Dave gave me a mud bath. Thank you for that."

In response, the sound of tiny bells rang out, and they pronounced their name. The Silars whooshed by her in tight formation, hovering in the air.

Sadie noticed their movements were creating something. "Wow, I didn't know you guys could do that!"

They were forming pictures in front of her.

The Silars let out high-pitched laughter as they created their works of art. First up was what appeared to be Barnaby, but in his "earth wear." She recognized him by the iridescent blue that infused the image. The Silars appeared in various colors; their spectrum seemed endless. Their hues changed gradually or all at once.

"You guys are good." Sadie couldn't help but clap as they made several sculptures for her. "How wonderful."

They swirled through the air, sparkling away. This next piece took longer than the others. A face formed, one that at first looked like her own but then aged into that of her beloved Gramma Rose. Tears ran down Sadie's face. The Silars kissed her cheek and carried her droplets away.

"Thank you. That was incredible. It's truly special to see her again."

For their next masterpiece, the Silars whipped up Thelonious in precise detail. Shining from head to toe, he stood in the treeline before her. They painted the whole scene as a still life, with fruit hanging from the branches here and there for authenticity. Then the entire picture dissipated. Half the Silars went to the left, while the other half zoomed to the right, and in the now-vacant space stood the impressive real-life Thelo only a few meters away.

"Shall we take a walk, Sadie? There are so many places to see."

"Yes, please. I'd love to see more of Mystashan. I'd like to see all of it. By the way, where's Penelope? I haven't seen her in a while, and I need to talk to her."

"She is not here today, but I am sure you will be seeing her soon."

Darn it. I miss talking with her! I especially appreciate how nonjudgmental she is—the complete opposite of Mom. I have so much to tell her. Mostly about Sam. Of course I want to hear more about her too. "Maybe next time then."

As they walked, Sadie told Thelo about her day. "Can you believe Dave did that to me? He's still on me about taking Kylie's butterfly pin." Sadie turned to him. "Thelo? Not again. Thelo! I wonder why he loves doing this to me? He sends me places, and then he disappears all the time. Ugh."

She stood in a clearing, seeing nothing around her. As her frustration abated, she realized she was in the middle of her favorites: dandelions.

It was interesting that with how different Mystashan was from her world, white dandelions were still the same. True, these were bigger, wider, and fluffier, but they were pretty much the same as on earth.

"Okay. Where am I now?"

"Hello, Sadie."

"Huh . . . who said that?"

"I did."

"Uh, who? Uh, where . . . where are you?"

"Down here."

"Down here? Down where?" asked Sadie.

"Here. Right here, Sadie."

She looked down and around, but all she saw were dandelions. As she watched, they started to move. Swaying and wiggling, and then she realized they were part of something else—something larger.

Clustered in groups were dandelion people! Up out of the ground, with the pacing of a slow-motion camera, rose two residents of Mystashan. The only description Sadie could think of was that they resembled sparkly hedgehogs with full heads of dandelion hair. Hedgehogs that stood and walked like humans.

"Hellooooo. We're the Habnaws. I'm Mardin, and this here is Trina. We're responsible for the smooth underground operations of Mystashan, as well as mining crystals."

"*Under* Mystashan? I know there's that saying about learning something new every day, but I'm living it."

"Of course *under* Mystashan. There's a full underground travel system for the rest of the Habnaws," Mardin explained. "We don't like to stay in one place for too long, you know."

"Yeah. You get around all right," snipped Trina.

"What are you on about now?" Mardin cocked his head and squinted his eyes.

"You know, *dear*. You have wandering feet." That's why we call you 'the Excavator.'" Hands on hips, Trina scowled at Sadie.

Mardin threw up his paws and looked to the sky. "I have feet. I have to wander. It's my job."

Turning to Sadie he explained, "We like to get around, and this is the quickest way. We must keep *everything* in tip-top shape. Well, except that one time when Trina let that tunnel get filled up with dirt." Crossing his arms, Mardin gave Trina a sidelong glance.

"Me?" Trina glared with an air of offended innocence. "That was *your* mistake." She nodded vigorously, sending a wave of movement through her dandelion hair. "Yes. That was definitely your fault. If it weren't for you forgetting to remind me, I would have done it."

"Me?" bellowed Mardin. "Why should I have to remind you? You should know when it's your turn."

"Humph!" rumbled Trina. "You always remind me, but then you didn't. Therefore it's all your fault."

Mardin's jaw dropped. He threw up his paws again and muttered, "Ridiculous!" As he walked away from Trina, he motioned Sadie over to the side. Mardin whispered loud enough for Trina to hear, "Hey, you know what, Sadie? I could use a little change after all this nonsense."

Sadie glanced back at Trina, who had already started

wiggling underground. "Change?" asked Sadie. "What do you have in mind?"

"Could you do me a favor and make a wish? I haven't had a regrowing in a long while."

"A regrowing?"

"Yes, just blow on the top of my head, as you'd do on earth with your tribe of dandy lions."

Sadie tried not to laugh at his pronunciation. It brought to mind lions on the Savannah with bow ties and slicked-back hair. She took a deep breath and smiled instead.

"Favor? That's not a favor. I'd love to, but are you sure?"

"Of course I'm sure. We Habnaws love us some regrowing, and if Trina wasn't being a donkey's behind, I'm sure she would love one too."

Sadie felt a rumble underfoot, and the ground lifted a few inches next to her feet. She looked down and took a step to the left.

Trina popped up, wearing a three-inch cap of dirt, and grumbled, "Humph!" then lowered out of sight completely.

"Is she going to be all right, Mardin?"

"Yes. She'll get over it. Ignore her, Sadie, like I do." Mardin leaned forward.

Sadie, knowing her wish was silly, wished it just the same. She closed her eyes and concentrated, *I wish I were a princess.* Then she blew on Mardin's dandelion hair until it was all gone.

Each strand made a popping sound as it lifted up, swirling around one by one. He chuckled. His delight was evident on his face, and he danced in a circle as each new hair grew back almost immediately. "That tickles, but ahhhh . . . much better. I really needed that, Miss Sadie. Thank you."

She closed her eyes and said, "You're welcome" with a slight curtsy, then opened them to see Banyan standing before her. She was back in her world again. Sadie patted Banyan's trunk and let out a light sigh. "As amazing as the transport is, I don't think I'll ever get used to it."

Banyan rustled in the wind, and Sadie could almost hear the sound of his laughter.

Arriving home, she tried to close the front door with both hands so it wouldn't give her away, but the hinge creaked at the last second.

"Sadie? Is that you?"

"Yes."

"Did you clean your bathroom like I asked you to?"

"Uh, not yet, Mom." Sadie hurried down the hallway to her room. *Doesn't she know all the crap I've got on my plate? A reminder now and then wouldn't hurt, you know.*

Her mom continued from the kitchen, "I asked you three days ago to clean it. I shouldn't have to ask you twice, Sadie."

"Right, Mom. Because it would kill you to remind me of things once in a while. If you wanted it done so badly, why didn't you remind me?"

"So now it's my fault you didn't do as you were asked?" The anger began to bloom in her mother's tone.

Whoa. What? This is familiar. Suddenly it hit her. Sadie realized she sounded like Trina. *Oh, my goodness. Yuck. I'm Trina.*

Sadie headed toward the kitchen. "I'm sorry, Mom. You're right. I'll do it right now."

Mom raised an eyebrow. "Well, that's better. It's the exact opposite of what I thought you'd say, but I like it."

Sadie cleaned her bathroom, and when she was done, she tackled the closet her Mom had asked her to clean the week before. They'd both forgotten about that, but Sadie realized it was her responsibility to remember and not her mother's.

A short while later, Mom came to inspect the bathroom.

"Nice work, Sadie."

"Thanks. I cleaned the closet too, and I'll try to do better, Mom. I'll try to be more responsible and do what you ask me to the first time."

Her mother stared at her in disbelief.

Sadie shrugged and raised her palms. "What? Did I grow a third eye or something?"

"No . . ." Mom laughed. "I just wasn't expecting that." She moved forward and hugged Sadie.

Hesitantly, Sadie gave her a quick squeeze then went to her room to read before helping with dinner. When she entered her room, a new crystal sat in the middle of her bed, catching the light from the afternoon sun and projecting rainbows on the walls of her room.

ACCOUNTABILITY. *Yup. That's appropriate.*

Sadie helped with dinner, setting it on the table. She watched the clock, dreading the nightly tension that came with her father's arrival.

The car door slammed, and she heard her father's feet on the flagstones. Her entire body stiffened, bracing for what might come next.

He walked through the door.

"Hi, Sadie," he said with a smile.

Taken aback, she stopped, unsure what to do next. So she just blurted the first thing that came to mind. "How was your day, Dad?"

"Ah, you know. The usual. Come here. I have something for you."

"Really?" asked Sadie, surprised.

They sat on the couch. Mom watched from the kitchen archway. Dad reached into his jacket pocket. "Here, honey. This is for you. I've been so busy, and I know that hasn't been fair to you or your mother."

Too shocked for words, Sadie took the black velvet box. The

hinge made a small creak before snapping all the way open. Inside was a beautiful necklace with her initial. Gems sparkled all around the *S*.

"I love it! Thank you, Dad. Thank you so much."

"You're welcome, princess."

CHAPTER FIFTY-FOUR

In Like Finn

"**B**EAGLE!"

Finn looked around. Everything was dark, save for a single ray of sunshine that peeked through the slatted, broken window. It illuminated a small spot of peeling paint on the wooden floor.

"Beagle! Get in here this minute." He pushed off a rumpled pile of blankets and sat up, watching as the dust particles floated thickly in the light. It was hard to focus his eyes, but with a little time, he saw the room with its decaying floorboards and piles of garbage, made up of paper bags, candle stumps, and candy wrappers.

"Mr. Finn? You're back. Do you know where you are?"

"You're not Beagle!" he fumed. "Get me Beagle! Do you hear me? How did you get in here anyway?" Finn looked around the room again, trying to search out something familiar, but it was too dark.

"Beagle's not here, Mr. Finn . . . remember? It's me, Basset. I'm here for you like always."

"Really? You're always here for me? You want to know who's always been here for me until you took him away? Beagle! That's who. But I won't sully his name by speaking it in front of you."

Basset gulped back his tears.

Finn grasped at the memories that lingered in his mind. He stared at the wall, speaking with an unsteady voice:

"There was another place. Not here. I think it was from a long time ago, because I can't remember anything before then. That white-haired girl was there! She was there, and I hadn't seen her in so long. I saw light—it was too bright for my eyes. There was a buzzing sound, like bells, and I felt my eardrum burst, but no one believed me." Finn pulled on his left earlobe. Lights were flying around me, attacking me. "That girl—the same one from long ago! She chased me all around this cave. I know it was an important place, but they shouldn't have laughed. They were all so proud! Of everything. They told me I should behave. Don't do this. Don't do that. Always told me to be careful. Not to kick any rocks. I could see through them. They said they were special. Don't pull up the flowers because I hurt them. 'Stay away from the water!' So many rules.

"She laughed at me too. That was the worst part. The others were sitting around, watching. 'I'm going to get you!' she yelled, while everyone laughed and pointed at me. I was so scared. I kept running and running, but she chased me until I couldn't run anymore."

Finn felt wetness on his face. He tried to brush it away from his nose, but his hand came away smeared with blood. His head throbbed, and his vision began to fade. He could almost see it. The truth of his purpose was just beyond his reach. It danced on the outskirts of the darkness that clouded his mind.

"Mr. Finn? Can you hear me?"

Focus returned as pain faded.

"Mr. Finn?"

Finn opened his eyes and found himself cradled in Basset's arms, a damp towel pressed against his nose. "What are you doing, Basset? Get off me."

"Welcome back, Mr. Finn."

"Back? Where have I been?" Though the darkness remained, Finn's eyes were adjusting to it. "Where are we?"

Basset shook his head. "I'm not sure. You've been . . . How can I put this? Not like yourself for about two weeks, Mr. Finn. I've been worried. At first you seemed to know what you were doing. You brought us to this place. I tried to find out more and see how I could help, but you wouldn't respond."

"Well, we need to figure out where we are."

"I'd like to know too, Mr. Finn."

As Finn stood, the room began to swim. His knees buckled, and he fell back onto the bed. He waited for the room to stop spinning. "Why do I feel so weak? What did you do to me?" He shot Basset an accusatory glare.

"You're weak because you haven't been eating, drinking, or sleeping regularly."

Finn threw his hands up in the air. "Why haven't you fed me? I'm starving!"

"I've brought you food and drink, Mr. Finn. I make a sandwich for you every day. When you don't eat it, I do, so it won't go bad."

Basset scurried from the room then returned with a glass of water in one hand and a sandwich wrapped in a paper towel in the other. He brought them closer and offered them to Finn. "This one is smoked turkey with Swiss cheese and spicy mustard."

"Well, it's about time!"

Finn gobbled it down in just a few seconds. Though not yet completely recovered, he felt some strength begin to return. "Help me up."

Finn grabbed Basset's arm and allowed himself to be pulled to his feet. He took a tentative step to the window and looked outside. The light was bright, and his eyes watered. He spotted movement in the yard below: a girl. It couldn't be.

"It's her . . . the one with the signal . . . the one with the pigtails. Help me, Basset. I want to go downstairs and get a better look."

Basset half carried Finn down the stairs, careful not to go too fast and trip. When they reached the bottom, Finn pushed him away.

He walked to the back of the house, through the dilapidated kitchen, passing a chipped Formica table and two wobbly chairs on his left, against the wall. There was nothing else in the room except plumbing hookups sticking out horizontally to his right.

"Stay here, Basset. I don't want her to hear you." Finn opened the back door slowly, in case it needed oiling. It didn't. He peeked out in time to see the girl enter the woods and make her way through the underbrush.

Seeing the girl and hearing the signal intensify sent a necessary surge throughout Finn's body. Because of it, he was able to cover the length of the Fletcher yard in no time. It was clear where she had entered the stand of trees, and Finn plunged ahead. His strength renewed, he fought his way through the vines. The sunlight, filtered in the trees, now beat directly on the hill and the clearing as he approached.

Where is she? I should have stayed closer. Finn looked carefully at the ground. He spotted a trail where the grass was only just starting to spring back, as if some weight had recently stood upon it.

Which way have you gone, missy? Finn followed the places where the grass was flatter. They led him down to the stream. With still no sight of the girl, he picked his way along the stream, following the muddy imprints. He saw the large tree in the middle of the lowland. After reorienting himself, from where he stood he could see that the foot depressions ended there. *Why do this place and this tree seem so familiar?*

He heard sounds before seeing anything. Bright lights hijacked his vision, and then he remembered: the hospital, the electric shocks, the bang on his head in the cabin's bathroom. That tree!

Looking around for a place to hide, Finn ducked behind the closest group of cattails. Where there had been nothing next to the tree a moment earlier, that girl had appeared.

It looks like I'm in the right place.

She rubbed her leg and said, "How did that happen? Abrupt much?" She placed her palm on the tree. After a few minutes, she stepped out from beneath the branches and looked up. "Okay, I'm back. I guess it's time to head home. See you tomorrow, Banyan."

Finn waited quietly until she was up over the hill and out of sight to step out from the cattails. He deliberately walked in front of the tree and slapped its side. "See you soon . . . old friend."

CHAPTER FIFTY-FIVE

The Unmasquerade Ball

THEIR PLAN WAS to meet at their corner after school the day of the dance. Sam thought it would be a good idea to discuss any last-minute details. Sadie/Annie wondered if he'd show up since she hadn't seen or spoken with him since Wednesday, the day of the tree-carving incident.

She was nervous. *I hope he'll be there after the way I left him at the corner the other day. I might have scared him off.*

As she approached, she was relieved. There he was, pacing. He saw her, smiled, and met her for a hug.

"Are you feeling better, Annie?"

"Yes, Sam. Much better. It must have been a twenty-four-hour thing."

"Good. I've been looking forward to tonight for weeks." Sam took her hand and squeezed it gently.

Sadie felt the warmth in her face and knew she turned some shade of pink. "Me too. So we'll meet back here at seven?"

"I'd prefer to pick you up at your house, but yes, we'll meet here at seven. Remember, I expect that invitation. Tomorrow maybe?"

Sadie coughed to give herself time to think. "Um. Okay.

Tomorrow it is." *What am I doing? How can he come over tomorrow?*

"Sam, I have something to tell you." Sadie felt a fire in her face, but it seemed like the right thing to do, revealing the truth.

"Yes, Annie. What is it?"

"Um . . . well . . . it's hard to figure out the words."

"It's okay, Annie. You can tell me anything."

Hearing that name reminded her of her deceit. *No, I can't tell him yet! Stupid, stupid!* "I'm sorry, Sam, but I have to take off now. I have so much homework to do before I get ready for tonight."

Sam smiled, exaggerating a forehead wipe. "Phew. I got scared there for a second. Don't you have the weekend to do it?"

"It sounds like I might be doing other things this weekend, Sam. Like introducing you to my parents?" Sadie winked.

"Right! Gotcha."

"See you at seven, then."

"Sure." Sam leaned in, and Sadie turned her head to the side as she hugged him back.

She left for home, her guilt refusing to let her turn back to wave good-bye.

They met at the corner at seven on the dot. "Wow, Annie, you're breathtaking!" Sam exclaimed. "I mean you always are, but you look spectacular in that dress, that mask, and with your hair loose like that."

"Thank you, Sam. You look quite handsome yourself."

Sam wore a charcoal suit with black stripes, an unusual choice but quite dashing. He had a hat on, similar to the one Mr. Felix wore. Above his lip was a pencil-thin mustache, a shade lighter than his hair. As for Sadie, well, she had to admit the dress looked better on her than she thought it would. With Mom's help in the makeup department, she hardly recognized herself. Mom even helped curl her hair. Her mask was turquoise and gold, with pearl lining the inside of the eyes. Two black feathers extended from the sides, as if its eyeliner kept going. Not too shabby.

"I've seen that type of hat before. I forget the name, though. What's it called?"

"A fedora." Sam smiled. "Don't I look fedorable?" He nudged her with his hip.

Sadie laughed and nudged him back.

"I brought this corsage for you. I didn't know the color of your dress, so I picked out these light-purple orchids and baby's breath. I hope they're okay."

"Okay? They're incredible. Thank you, Sam!"

"Can I help you put them on your wrist?"

"Yes, please." She held out her left arm for him and smiled as he delicately slipped the flowers in place. *I feel amazing. More than . . . maybe ever.* She held out her wrist and admired it with a little smile.

"Shall we get going, Annie?" Sam offered his elbow, and she took it. They talked all the way to Sadie's school, and she realized it had been a long time since she had walked there with another human being. She didn't consider Dave one of her species.

Hand in hand, they made their entrance through the gym doors. Passing under the canopy of silver streamers and black balloons, they joined the party.

"This is so cool, Sam." Sadie couldn't believe her eyes. The gym had transformed into a magical wonderland, with lights, stars, and a turning kaleidoscope ball throwing colors onto the floor and walls.

All the girls wore masks, embellished with everything from feathers and gold ribbons to pearl chains and glitter. Some only covered their eyes, some included their noses, and some their whole faces. The boys wore mustaches, ranging from wide handlebars to thinner styles to full beards.

Sadie adjusted her full-face mask and let a little of her fear ebb away. *At least no one will know who I am.*

Sam led her farther into the room. Although she did her best to hide her excitement, it wasn't easy. "I've never seen anything like this before," Sadie exclaimed. "Have you?"

"Never. I'm glad we're here to see it together."

Sadie smiled. Heat rose up her cheeks, and she turned away, but then she remembered. The mask hid her blush as well as her identity. As a bonus, the lights were low inside the school gym. The stakes were high tonight, and she didn't want to take any unnecessary risks.

Her feelings for Sam were beyond her ability to express. When she first met him, it was his looks and charm that grabbed her attention. As they got to know each other better, she realized it was his depth and his kindness, which she fell farther for every day. She started to feel like her old self again—before Gramma Rose had died and Aunt Sue had moved away—but she needed to tell Mom about him tonight. *I can't believe he's supposed to meet her tomorrow.*

"Annie? Everything okay?"

"Yes. Sorry. I was taking it all in. By the way, that mustache suits you. You look very distinguished, Mr. Sam."

"Why thank you, Ms. Annie. And you look radiant." He touched her arm and leaned in to whisper in her ear. "Though I much prefer to see all of your pretty face. But I guess I'll just have to wait until the official unmasking."

"Unmasking?" Sadie took a step back. "What are you talking about?"

"This is how these kinds of dances work, Annie. I'm guessing this one will be the same."

Sadie's stomach did a triple flip twist, landing with a belly-flop thud. The thought of being unmasked—and having everyone know she was there—made her panic.

Sam must have felt something because he immediately took a step forward and held her hand. "Are you okay? We're going to have a fantastic time."

She wanted to be here so badly that she pushed away the thought that someone would recognize her. After all, she barely recognized herself, thanks to Mom's wizardry. She forced that uncomfortable—and possibly humiliating—image as far back in her mind as it would go. Being at the dance and dreaming that Sam was her boyfriend made it easy to pretend she had friends again.

"You're right, Sam. It's gonna be fine."

The other kids had no idea she was there. Sadie liked that people were smiling and nodding to her as she passed—even Melanie, whom she recognized by the birthmark on her neck, and her entourage, she guessed, of Ronnie and Jade. No one had expected Sadie to come tonight, so they weren't looking for her.

"Would you like some punch?" Sam asked her. "I've heard that's what I'm supposed to ask you first thing."

Sadie laughed, unable to hide how pleased she was. "Who told you that, your mom?"

Looking sheepish, Sam nodded and shifted on his feet.

"I'd love some punch. Thanks."

His bright smile returned. "You got it. I'll be right back."

She watched him maneuver across the room and focused on settling her nerves. Everything was going smoothly. *Yeah, until the unmasking.* She shook her head and forced the thought away once again. *Forget about it. Just have fun. You remember how to have fun? Yes, I remember how to have fun . . . I think.* She laughed at herself.

Her laugh instantly ceased when she spotted Sam. He was talking to Dave. *Oh, no. Come on, Sam. Get back here.* Sam turned back to Sadie and pointed at her, smiling. Dave, with his villainous Snidely Whiplash mustache, looked puzzled.

Sam returned to her side with two cups of punch. He handed her one. "Did you miss me?"

"Yes! Yes, I did." *Reel it in. Reel it in. Don't overreact!*

He looked at her sideways but didn't seem put off by her eagerness. "When are they going to start the music? I love to dance," Sam said. He nudged her gently with his elbow. "You're looking at a dance master." He swayed from side to side, dipping his shoulders and spinning around. "I'm going to be famous one day. You gonna be able to keep up with me, Annie?"

He's so confident. What I wouldn't give for even a tenth of his fearlessness. She was smitten but doing a darn good job of hiding it.

As if on cue, music poured out of the massive speakers at the far end of the gym.

"I'll do my best," Sadie replied, raising her voice just a bit to be heard over the thumping music. "Who knows? Maybe I'll be a famous actress one day. I mean, after this spectacular performance, I'm bound to be famous too."

"What?" Sam cupped a hand to his ear. "I couldn't hear you. Did you say you're going to be famous too?"

The smile faded from Sadie's face. *Did I say that out loud?* She tried to recover and shook her head. "No, I said I hope they play some good tunes," she yelled over the sea of echoing sounds. *Tunes? Really? Get a grip. I sound so childish. Definitely not what I'm going for. Come on . . . keep it together. It's Sam! I shouldn't be this nervous. What's happening to me?*

Bobbing his head to the music, Sam didn't seem to notice. "So should we start on a slow song or a fast one?"

"Uh, I . . . whatever you want, Sam."

"Okay, I say we start with a slow one then," he said with a wink.

Dave's still looking at us! Guess I should have said a fast dance. What if he tries to cut in? Now she was really nervous. *I thought my butterflies on this first date with Sam were intense. Now that Dave has zeroed in on us, I want to scream.*

"I'll be right back. Okay, Sam?"

Sam nodded. "Sure. Of course. See you in a few."

Sadie rushed to the bathroom. *Stay calm and don't screw this up. You can do it.* She was so nervous she fanned herself with a notebook someone had left in the bathroom. A couple of other girls entered, but they were so involved in their conversation that they didn't notice her.

"So do you think he's going to kiss you tonight?" the one girl asked.

"Oh, he'd better," raved the other girl.

"He's so cute. I can't believe how lucky you are."

"I know. He *is* cute. I bet he's a good kisser too." Both girls giggled loudly.

Sadie hoped Sam would kiss her tonight. The thought made her warm, happy, and scared all in the same moment. She closed her eyes and imagined their kiss: *Sam takes off my mask as he removes his mustache. He looks into my eyes and tells me how pretty I am, inside and out. Then he leans forward as we both close our . . .* Sadie felt a sharp jolt to her arm as one of the girls banged into her on their way out.

"Oh, sorry," the bumper girl said.

"It's okay," said Sadie. She was disappointed that her dream kiss was interrupted at the climactic point, but it served a purpose: she realized how long she must have been in the bathroom and hurried to get back to Sam.

"Sorry, Sam. There was a huge line." She hated not being honest with him. *But what's one more tiny fib when our entire relationship has been built on a lie?*

"You missed the slow song. I was bummed." He feigned a look of disappointment. "But hopefully they'll play another one soon."

A new song started, a fast pop song Sadie recognized from the radio.

"Oh, I love this song." Sam squeezed her hand. "Come on, Annie. Let's dance." He pulled her toward the dance floor. They weaved through the crowd and carved out a bit of room for themselves.

As they danced, he spun her around several times. Sadie kept up with him. Individual decorations became a seamless line of dazzling colors. Faces blurred, but she could make out their smiles.

"I'm having the best time," Sam shouted.

"*What*?" she yelled, trying to talk over the music.

Sam stopped dancing and leaned in close to her ear. "I said, 'I'm having the best time.'"

Sadie felt tingles all over.

Sam took her hand and led her to the far side of the gym, where only a handful of students lingered. It was quieter there, and Sadie didn't need to yell.

"You weren't kidding . . . you really are a good dancer," Sadie said.

"I told you." He twirled her around then dipped her. "You're not so bad yourself."

He pulled her against him and reached up to tuck a strand of her hair behind her ear.

She gazed deep into his eyes and saw whole worlds spinning there. Time slowed down until it stopped. The music and the other kids were gone. Everything disappeared except for Sam and Sadie.

"I want to see you without your mask, Annie."

Time started again and sped up so quickly that a fresh wave of panic slammed into her. Sadie backed up a few inches. She coughed a few times, trying to catch her breath. "But we aren't supposed to, Sam. We aren't supposed to do that until later."

"Come on." He placed his hands on her waist and pulled her close. "We can break the rules a little." He grinned mischievously. "I won't tell anyone if you don't."

He lifted her mask. The gym and all the students faded away.

With Sam's hands now on both sides of her cheeks, she felt dizzy and longed for that kiss.

He leaned in. She smelled the hint of fresh linen, felt his warmth. Everything slowed down, suspended in time as their lips drew nearer . . .

"Sadie? Sadie Myers! What are you doing at our dance? I knew something didn't seem right!" yelled Dave, who stood just a few feet away.

Sadie quickly put her mask back on, but it was too late. The damage was done. Within seconds a small crowd had gathered around them.

Sam stood in front of Sadie, protecting her from the barrage of accusations. "Go away!" he commanded. "Leave Annie alone."

"Annie?" Dave laughed in surprise and derision. "Is that what she told you her name was?" He laughed again—more of a cackle this time. "There's no Annie here. Only that thief, Sadie."

"Her name isn't Sadie," Sam shouted. Confused, he turned to her. "What's he talking about? Tell them. Tell them your name's Annie. Annie Cooper."

"Well, my middle name is Annie." Shaken, Sadie could hardly get the words out. "I tried to tell you . . . I *wanted* to tell you." She looked at Dave then back at Sam. "I was going to tell you when the dance was over, I swear. I just wanted this one night to—"

Sam took a step back. "You lied to me? All this time . . . you were lying to me?"

"It wasn't really a—"

Dave stepped in on that one. "Everything you know about

her is probably a lie. Not one honest word comes out of that thief's mouth."

"Thief?" Sam said.

Sadie grabbed Sam's arm. "Sam, it's not true," she managed in a whisper as tears streamed down her face. "It's not what it looks like."

"Come on, Sam. We'll fill you in." Dave laid an arm across Sam's shoulders and led him away. Sam glanced back over his shoulder, his expression thick with disappointment and a sense of betrayal.

Sam . . . Sam, come back!

Tears streaked down her face, soaking the inside of her mask as she headed for the nearest exit.

"Get out of here, Sadie."

"You should have known better, you freak."

But the meanest wound came from Melanie, hands down. "Look how far Stupid Sadie has fallen. Who would have thought she would leave her bedroom and dare to join our circle again?"

"*Hey!*" a teacher barked at her tormentors. "Knock that nonsense off or you won't be staying."

"Are you okay, Sadie?" asked Mr. Bartholomew.

Sadie shook her head and bolted through the door. *How could I be so stupid?* She yanked off her mask and ran to the front of the school, her heels clicking loudly on the linoleum. *How could I think I would get away with that? Stupid, stupid. Stupid Sadie. Yep, that name really does fit me.*

She sobbed loudly as she ran home. She ripped the mask to shreds, tossing it into the nearest garbage bin. By the time she reached the house, her feet screamed inside her shoes, and her dress had suffered several small tears. She pushed through the front door and ran down the hall.

"Sadie? Is that you? Why are you home so early?" asked Mom.

"It was awful, Mom. I shouldn't have gone."

"Sadie, what happened?"

She couldn't answer through her tears. "I met this boy, Sam. I really liked him. I really did, Mom. I was so stupid to think... to think..." Her tears swallowed her words

"Oh, sweetheart, come here." Her mother came up to hug her, but Sadie turned away and raced to her bedroom door.

"I'm here if you need me, honey," her mother called after her.

Sadie shook her head and went into her room. She didn't want comfort. Not from anyone, especially not from her mother. She didn't deserve it. She closed the door and collapsed onto her bed.

"I should have saved him for outside of school. I never should have taken him there. Why did I have to be so stupid? How could I ever think it would work?"

It hurt to breathe. Her chest burst open, and her heart fell to the floor. It rolled a few inches then exploded. "I didn't even get to explain it to him. I couldn't get my stupid words out of my stupid mouth."

Thirty minutes later, Sadie was all cried out. She crept out of her room and into the bathroom. She cleaned her face and stuffed the dress into the trash. *Mom's going to kill me, but I'll deal with that later.*

When she reentered her room, she saw a lump in her bed. *Huh?* Not much surprised her these days, but what she saw under the covers did. It was an opalescent-colored cat. *Angelic.* She had the softest fur too. *This must be Penelope.*

"Hi, sweet Penelope. Thanks for being here with me." Sadie crawled in as the kitty snuggled up to her. She felt Penelope's love as she purred her to sleep.

CHAPTER FIFTY-SIX

Dancing Blues

Sadie's eyes cracked open . . . just enough to take in the harsh reality of daylight, which immediately closed them again.

She heard the knock. Penelope jumped up and hid under the bed. Mom poked her head inside. "Sadie? Are you okay? It's almost two in the afternoon."

Sadie groaned and rolled over, turning her back to the door.

"A letter came for you. I think you'll be interested to see who sent it."

Sadie said nothing.

"I'll put it on the night table for you. Why don't you come out of your room and have something to eat? Staying in bed all day isn't good for you."

Sadie let out a long sigh. "I don't really care what's good for me, Mom."

"Okay, you have today to feel sorry for yourself, but tomorrow's a new day."

Whatever that means.

She waited until she heard the door close before looking to see who it was from. *Just what I need. To hear from him now of all times. Letter shmetter.* She dropped it, and didn't bother picking it up. *Who cares? My life is over.*

Penelope made several attempts to get her up and moving, but Sadie had no desire to do anything other than wallow in self-pity. She didn't blame Penelope for giving up and leaving, but now she felt completely alone. Last night she was certain she couldn't possibly feel any worse, but this new slap in the face from Christopher broke new ground, topping her chart of crap.

Sadie drifted in and out of uneasy consciousness.

There was a picnic on the crest of a hill. It took a bit of work keeping it balanced. She didn't recognize anyone there, but a bobcat attempted to bite her feet. Realizing it wasn't friendly, she quickly got into position with her feet tucked underneath her. Body strong, she used a towel for defense. She rolled it up and held it at arm's length, lodging it at the back of the creature's open jaws. The bobcat couldn't get at her, so it flew into the air, transforming into a vulture. She looked up and saw the detail in the maroon feathers as they came closer. They were tipped with knives. Some stabbed her arm, and she jerked away due to the painful punctures in her skin. The hideous bird flew into the air, reached its peak, and dove back. It tried to stab her again, but the towel shielded her from further damage. The vulture landed and transformed back into a bobcat.

Sadie shook herself awake. *What the heck was that?*

She remembered sleeping this long only one other time in her life. That was when Gramma had died.

Penelope was next to her again. Sadie knew it was now Sunday morning, and it was time to get back to herself. *I've done this before. I can do it again.* She stepped off the bed and onto the letter.   *Christopher.* She shook her head. *Your turn to wait, buddy.* Sadie picked up the letter and placed it back on the night table.

I need a shower. I have to wash away the Sams and Christophers.

Brushing her teeth, she caught flashes of the dance. *Shake it off*, she told herself. Then the unmasking. *Stop it.* Dave's big, ugly laughing face. *Eww, get out of my head!* That made her squirm. And of course, Sam. *I'll miss you, Sam. You could have heard me out, though.*

She made herself somewhat presentable and headed to the kitchen, which smelled like vanilla and sweet dough.

"Sadie, I made waffles with blueberries for you."

"Thanks, Mom, but I'm not hungry. I'll take a granola bar with me. Why don't you save them for Dad?" Sadie noticed he was out back in the hammock. *It's about time he relaxed.*

"He already ate, but that's a nice suggestion." Mom's spirits seemed lighter. "Are you feeling any better? Did you read your letter? I'm sure that helped."

"I'll be okay. The letter can wait. I'm heading out."

Mom's brow knitted. "Where are you off to?"

"Just for a walk around the neighborhood. I need some air."

"Okay, Sadie. I'll be here all day if you need me."

"Thanks. See you later."

Sadie's legs felt heavy as she slowly walked through imaginary cement toward the only place that might make her feel better: Banyan. She wanted to be comforted in a way only he could provide, with his soothing umbrella of branches surrounding her.

She arrived and had a mind to turn back when she saw him.

"Hello, Sadie."

"Ugh, not you!" Any hope that the day would bring her some peace disappeared the minute she spied Mr. Felix. "I could have lived my entire life without seeing you again." Sadie noticed he wore the same attire. "Why are you always in the same navy suit? What's up with that?"

"I'm a simple man. I found what worked for me, and I stuck with it," he explained as he drew closer toward her.

Sadie, curious as to what his face looked like, didn't back away. His nose was long with a squared-off end. His teeth were large but proportionate to his mouth. He gave a small smile, outlined by a neatly trimmed goatee, which eased some of the tension. His lilac eyes sparkled. As much as she didn't trust him, she was drawn to his eyes. They were enchanting.

Sadie, I think we got off on the wrong foot." Mr. Felix sat by Banyan's trunk, speaking in a soft tone.

Sadie backed up a few steps. "I think we got off the way we were meant to. All I want to do is sit here quietly with Banyan. I'm trying to forget a rough weekend, and you're in my way."

"You might like what I have to tell you." His voice rose a few notes.

"That's not possible."

"Give me a couple of minutes, and then I'll go. I have the answer to your question." He placed his Fedora on the grass.

"Okay. You have two minutes." Sadie folded her arms across her chest and leaned on one leg. She didn't make eye contact but squinted at the stream beyond.

"Do you know why this place is so special? Why Banyan chose to take up root here?"

Sadie stared at him then glanced down at her watch.

"We overlap the human world at this very spot. You, Sadie, come from a long line of individuals who protect both worlds from harm."

"Yeah, right, and how do you propose I do that?"

"Didn't you feel drawn here? Didn't you feel there was a purpose in it? In time you will see."

Sadie rolled her eyes and stared at her shoes. His words rattled around in her brain with a hint of truth. She *had* felt drawn to this place, and though she wasn't sure of its true purpose, she firmly believed she had been brought here for a reason.

"For now I will leave you." Mr. Felix picked up his hat and

tipped it toward her. "I respect your time, and mine has run out."

Sadie looked up. "Wait, I can spare a few more minutes. Tell me more. How am I supposed to . . ."

He was gone.

" . . . protect them?" Her hands tightened into fists at her side, and she stomped her foot. "Ooh, that Mr. Felix. He gets me so angry, Banyan."

Sadie, you'll have what you need when you need it. Let's sit and enjoy our day together.

Banyan surrounded her with dancing, shimmering leaves.

Sadie leaned against him and took a deep breath. "You're right, friend. What would I do without you?"

CHAPTER FIFTY-SEVEN

Slugs

THE DREADED MORNING had arrived. On Sadie's way to school, any vestiges of denial faded away. Sitting with Banyan helped her prepare herself as best she could, but she had a few guesses as to what was coming.

Students in the hallway, including Melanie and her groupies, pointed and laughed. *So the Monday fun has begun.*

She drew on yesterday's peaceful experience with Banyan and made sure to choose a seat close to each of her teachers as she progressed through the day. *One more subject to go: US history. Then I'm off to Mystashan. Finally, those longed-for words . . .*

"Okay. Class dismissed."

Sadie took the long way home, avoiding everyone from school.

An hour and a half later, she finished her homework then headed out. A year ago she'd been closed off to the natural world of her neighborhood. It was all about keeping her head down. Today, however, she looked up as she walked.

Barnaby seemed chipper as he leapt out of the azaleas. She sensed his glee at her reaction when she jumped back. Their game for the past week or so was that he would ambush her. She wouldn't know when, but it would be on her way to the Fletcher house. He didn't always cross with her into Mystashan, but she always appreciated his company.

Penelope waited for her on the other side of the straime.

"I'm happy to see you left your room, Sadie."

Sadie smiled at the taller woman. "Yeah, about that . . . Thank you for working so hard to get me out of my funk. I wouldn't have recovered as quickly without your help."

Penelope's long, elegant fingers stroked Sadie's hair with reassurance as she looked down into her eyes. "I'm here for you, Sadie. I want you to know that. You know you can talk to me about anything, right?"

"Yes, I know . . . and thank you. I really hope we can see each other more often—not just when I'm at my worst, I mean. I feel like I owe you one. Is there anything I can do for you?"

Penelope's laughter rang light and airy. "You do already, Sadie. You have no idea. You bring more to Mystashan than you realize."

"I do?"

Penelope smiled then kissed Sadie's forehead.

Remnants of her conversation with Mr. Felix returned to her thoughts. "Can I ask you a question . . . a question about Mr. Felix? Do you know him? He told me the oddest things yesterday, and honestly, I don't feel comfortable around that man. I'm concerned. He said I was—"

"I want to help you, but you'll get the most information from Thelo. He and Banyan are the only ones, I believe, who know the full story."

"The full story?"

Penelope nodded. "Come. Thelo is waiting for us as we speak."

Sadie decided not to push the issue any further, though she was hungry with curiosity.

"And here I am." Thelo materialized in front of them. "How are you, Sadie? How was your day?"

"Thelo, why is it you either pop in or pop out around the time I've asked a question?"

"Do I? I did not notice."

"Yeah, you kind of do. It just happened now. I asked Penelope about Mr. Felix, and she mentioned my importance to Mystashan, something Mr. Felix talked about yesterday."

"Leave those questions to me, Sadie. Some topics are not meant to spread too far afield." He placed a scaled hand on his heart. "Keep important things close."

"But . . . sometimes I don't know how to ask you or get you to answer. And I don't want to be too persistent." Sadie noticed Penelope had done her disappearing thing. However, when Penelope left, it didn't seem as rude.

"All knowledge comes when you are ready to hear it," he said matter-of-factly.

"That's what people keep saying. I'm ready—let me hear it."

Thelo was silent for a long moment. Too long, Sadie thought.

Sadie crossed her arms. "Fine. I'll drop it . . . for now. So you were asking about my day. It was more of the usual. Go to class. Avoid Dave. Go to my next class. Avoid Dave some more. Try not to die of humiliation." She kicked a small stone free from the dirt road. "We did a project, and no one liked my idea, so I stopped helping. Then they had the nerve to say I wasn't being a team player. Me? Not a team player? I had an idea that was out of the box, and no one would give it a chance."

As soon as "chance" left her lips, she transported to the edge of the treeline on the other side of the village. "Okay, great. Where did he send me now?"

She walked out from the tree cover into an open field. Many branches lay on the ground, while other branches were coming out of them at strange angles. They looked like they were covered with those fake candle flames she'd seen at the mall. They were ablaze with a deep mauve glow but not hot to the touch or burning the ground. It was a marvelous sight. She soon realized they were vines, with about eight tiny heads each. She realized they were not only alive, surprisingly, but also active.

Spectacular! They're all talking at once, but I can't understand what the heck they're saying.

"Hello," Sadie said. The group continued to talk over one another. "Hello," she said a little louder. Still no response. "*Hellooo!*" she finally yelled, waving her arms.

They all turned at once to look at her. "Well, you don't have to shout," they replied in unison.

"Sorry. You didn't seem to hear me. Who are you guys anyway?" asked Sadie.

"We're the Slugs."

"Slugs? Really?" Sadie pinched her face together as if she were smelling something foul.

"Yes, we're the builders of Mystashan," they said with pride, "although we haven't built anything in quite a while. We used to build all the time when Thelo was around. Now he's off doing so many other things, and we can't seem to get anything done."

Sadie relaxed her face, realizing that their name on earth had little to do with anything here. It was an experience listening to them speak the same words in many voices at the same time. Her ears rang while she adjusted to their high-pitched frequencies.

"He's asked us to build another Atrium, grander than the last one. He has some new crystals that the Habnaws found in their tunnels. He'd like to set up a new grid, but we can't figure out where to begin."

"Why not? You all seem to speak together. Why can't you build together?"

"Speaking and building are two different things. We may share the same voice, but when it comes to ideas, we each have our own opinion."

"Oh, boy." Sadie scratched the back of her head. *This should be interesting.* "You have to figure out how to work together."

"That's the problem. We can't. Not without Thelo. In the past, he'd tell us exactly what he wanted, and we would do it. Without him, we talk in circles and can't agree on anything. We don't like anyone's ideas. Except our own, of course."

"Maybe I can help," Sadie offered.

"You? How are you going to help?" They all swiveled their heads away from her and laughed derisively.

After their rudeness died down, she decided to try again. "How about you break up into groups and see if each group can come up with one idea?"

"Hmm." They argued back and forth about this for a while, but it didn't get them anywhere.

"Come on," said Sadie. "It's getting late. Can't you give it a try?"

"Fine. We'll try it your way, but we highly doubt it'll work."

As the sun began to set, their glow turned a fiery yellow. Each vine set off to its own section of land, away from the others, their light forming a giant circle.

Sadie stood in the middle. "There's only one rule to make this work," she told them. "You have to vote on someone else's idea. You can't vote on your own."

The vines bickered at first. Sadie roamed around, stopping to listen in at each group, reminding them of the one rule. Without being able to vote on their own idea, they were able to pick one at last. Each group held a vote, and its majority won.

It's working.

"I need every group's idea but not at the same time." Sadie took a stick and made a grid in the dirt with thirty rows. When

I point at your group, tell me your winning idea, and I'll write it down here."

When Sadie had all the new choices written down, she said, "Each group pick an idea from this list without picking your own."

Soon there were six ideas. Sadie worked with the Slugs to keep whittling away at the list until they finally had the winning solution. It had taken three hours of back-and-forth disagreements, but she finally had brought them all together. "Wow, you guys did it. See?"

Not one Slug had given up through the grueling decision-making. They didn't all concur at first, but they worked together and came to an agreement.

"We'll start on the Atrium tomorrow. Thank you, Sadie."

"You're welcome," Sadie said to . . . Banyan apparently.

"Hi, Banyan." Sadie wasn't fazed by her transportation. She was getting used to all the shifting around. She also had gotten used to the arrival of her crystals and celebrated each one. She felt that familiar weight manifest in her pocket. She loved getting them and finding out the word they sent her.

"Cooperation." *Nice. I've gotta remember I can't always get my way.*

Red flashes appeared in her periphery. She turned.

"Banyan, what are those flashes? I don't understand . . . When am I going to find out what they are? The blue and green ones feel good, but the red ones scare me."

A breeze lifted up the willow's branches, but no answer came.

"Banyan?"

CHAPTER FIFTY-EIGHT

What Would We Do Without Music?

FINN RAN HIS fingers through his thinning gray hair. "What did you say? I don't think I heard you correctly! You saw her and didn't wake me? That can't be true."

Basset cowered on his knees. "This was the first good night's sleep you've had since we left our cabin, Mr. Finn."

"Are you kidding me? Sleep? You think I need sleep? This is much more important than closing my eyes for a few hours. This is what we came here for. I cannot believe this . . . what with the magnitude of our situation. You are in serious trouble."

Finn's jaw began the familiar clenching. The heat rose in his face. He grabbed Basset by the neck and choked him with one hand, pushing him halfway up the wall. It was only when he looked into the smaller man's eyes—saw the strain and bulging, the silent pleading for his life—that he dropped him. Finn rubbed his hand, trying to ease the ache. "You're lucky I still need your assistance, or I wouldn't have stopped myself."

Basset shivered, still kneeling on the floor. "I meant the best for you is all. I always do." He coughed out his words.

"The best thing for me is figuring out how to get there. I need to know the second she passes this way again. We have to be quicker this time, or I won't be able to see how she goes. If one toe hits that driveway, I want to know about it."

Basset got up, and Finn grabbed the front of his shirt. "Fail to inform me of her arrival again, you sniveling saboteur, and you'll be in the ground."

Basset's shoulders slumped. "Yes, Mr. Finn. It was an unforgivable mistake."

"You bet your life it was. Where's breakfast?"

There was a tense silence in the house over the next two days.

Finn waited with growing frustration as Basset sat silently nearby.

"Damn it! Where is she?" I'm weary of all this waiting. I want to get there and get this done yesterday. All this rain doesn't help me either. If I hear one more plop on the roof, I will scream."

Basset sat on the dusty floor without making a sound.

Finn found Basset's face more disturbing than usual. It reminded him of too many things he didn't care to contemplate.

Another unproductive day passed.

It was Finn's turn to sit in the chair by the kitchen window and wait for the girl named Sadie. He had carved each dawn in the wooden wall. He knew it had been three days since Basset had made his near-fatal error.

It hadn't dared rain since Finn's threat. The predawn sky was full of dark hues, and this would be one of those horrid sunny days that bore into his eyes and pores. Sunglasses didn't do a thing to help him.

Finn played at being patient. The hours rolled by. Basset came downstairs for a few minutes then went back up. Finn heard the unmistakable sound of a foot on the driveway.

In a flash, he was on all fours beneath the splintered window ledge, edging toward the door. After scaling his way up by the handle, he turned it and eyed around the corner, where he saw her in the middle of the backyard. She hadn't heard him.

I'd rather she not see me, but if she does, I always have plan B.

He kept a respectable distance, but his primary goal was to keep her in sight. That way he could observe how she traveled.

With his best stealth on, Finn barely crunched the twigs and leaves that threatened to give him away.

He watched her sit by that mangy willow. He waited for the moment of revelation, and then *he* was there.

I know that hat! I should kill him where he stands. What is Mr. Felix doing here? I need to find out.

"Hello, Sadie."

"Ugh, not you! I could have lived without seeing you again."

You and me both, Finn thought. *Curious, though. I wonder what he did to you.* The acoustics were good, so Finn could hear everything.

"Why are you always in the same navy suit? What's up with that?"

Ha. Good question, Finn pushed his left ear forward.

"I'm a simple man. I found what worked for me, and I stuck with it. Sadie, I think we got off on the wrong foot."

"I think we got off the way we were meant to. All I want to do is sit here quietly with Banyan. I'm trying to forget a rough weekend, and you're in my way."

"You might like what I have to tell you."

"That's not possible."

Finn leaned so far forward on all fours that he nearly fell on his face. *They're about to spill it. Any time now would be nice.*

"Give me a couple of minutes, and then I'll go. I have the answer to your question." He placed his Fedora on the grass.

"Okay. You have two minutes."

Are you kidding me? Can't you see he's trying to get one over on you?

"We overlap the human world at this very spot. You, Sadie, come from a long line of individuals who protect both worlds from harm."

"Yeah, right, and how do you propose I do that?"

Really? All out of ideas already, little girl?

"Didn't you feel drawn here? Don't you feel there's a purpose in it? In time you will see. For now I will leave you." He picked up his hat and tipped it toward her. "I respect our time, and mine has run out."

Respect? That's fascinating, Mr. Felix. Not.

"Wait, I can spare a few more minutes. Tell me more. How am I supposed to . . ."

Where did . . . Oh, right. He never could give a complete answer.

" . . . protect them? Ooh, that Mr. Felix. He gets me so angry, Banyan."

"Angry" isn't really the best word for it!

Finn sat back on his heels and waited for her to transport. Any minute now he would know the secret. *Was it a password? A key? A knock on that stone over there?*

He watched how she sat there and spoke inanely to the tree. Maybe it was to herself. Difficult to know with Banyan.

It's got to be over an hour now. My eyes hurt from watching all this nothing. I need to move. It's either cross to the treeline or pull every last hair out of my head.

The girl got up and climbed the hill.

Does this mean you're not transporting? Come on now!

Finn closed his eyes for a second and saw red linings peppered with images of violence and mayhem: broken arms, twisted necks, and uprooted trees. His overheated brain threatened to blow any second. *Where the hell is Basset?* To be so angry without any release maddened him.

He moved into the shadows.

She froze, seeming to detect a change. She stared back, directly at him.

ACT THREE

Three Sides of the Story

Made of all shapes that flit and sway,
And mass, and scatter in the breeze,
And meet and part, open and close;
Thou sister of the clouds and trees,
Thou daintier phantom of the rose.

—"Shadow," Richard La Gallienne

CHAPTER FIFTY-NINE

The Night the Children Left

THE GIRL SMILED to herself and folded her gloved hands in her lap. She'd had her first lovely evening out with her parents in society. She wore her best dress with the crinoline peeking out underneath. Her bright-white gloves and the hat her father had bought her the last time he had traveled on business accentuated the outfit. The crinoline tickled, and the gloves took some getting used to, but it was her first time at the Eagle Lake Country Club, and she felt fancy and grown up now that she was eleven. Even the heavy rain couldn't dampen her delight.

The rain came down in torrents. She didn't understand how her father could see anything through the windshield with streams of water obscuring the glass.

The car's back tires swerved out of the line they'd been steadily following on the road. That was enough to wake her twin brother, who immediately turned his head to the left to observe her, his eyes wide. Her mother's breathing quickened, and the girl could tell she was nervous.

She understood why her mother reacted as she did, but the girl knew that panic didn't serve her own mind. It only drained her of her resources and ultimately her choices.

She silently called out for help, and a flash of *knowing* came to her. This was moments before her world changed. Her fingers tingled, and a calm strength flowed through her. She felt she might be strong enough to protect all the people in the car, the ones she loved the most.

The sound of the road changed to a muted grating, and she felt that telling little bump as the road shifted. They were headed onto the overpass known as Clover Bridge.

The car swerved, first once and then more often. Despite the girl's early decision to disregard her nerves and worry, they gnawed away at her stomach. It was no longer a conscious choice. Driving through this storm—after all was said and done, had this evening out been worth this harrowing experience?

She sang a soothing prayer song under her breath. She did it for her much-loved brother, who hid his face in his hands and burrowed under her arm. She felt his fear coming in pounding waves. By doing so, she somehow lost the ability to sense what her parents were feeling. Although she hadn't meant to separate from them, she felt a keen responsibility to care for her brother, whatever the eventual outcome. She tried her best to sneak a peek into the future—not very far . . . just enough to get to the other side of the bridge—but there was nothing. What a time for her sight to leave her.

A sweet giant of a white dog materialized behind her father's seat, almost in her lap. No one seemed to notice, but a wave of peace flooded through her again. She was amazed to see her brother's head pop up as he pointed a finger at the dog. He definitely saw it too. *What do you know? We're related after all.* She found herself letting out a little giggle despite the situation, which grew more treacherous by the second.

The headlights of the oncoming traffic penetrated the water-covered windshield. She wondered whether their end was near.

Was this why she saw the dog? Did it represent something about the grave or the afterlife? Before she finished that thought, the dog moved closer and encircled the two children with its expansive paws. Metal scraped on metal as the car crashed through the barrier. Gravity exerted its force within seconds.

They were floating through darkness. She heard her thoughts along with the beating of her heart. *Where are my parents? Are they in this darkness too?*

She moved through mist. Her brother's voice cried out in the distance. Truth be told, the softness of the white fur felt like all that stood between her and eternity. She put her head on the dog's chest and fell asleep.

When she opened her eyes, she was in a large bed, comfy as could be. The sun came with liquid-gold highlights through the slatted window, showing off her now-white hair. They somehow had lived through the night.

Her brother's anguished cries echoed from a nearby room. Were her parents with him? She couldn't sense them. She left the comfort of the soft blankets and ran to him. Fear rose in her heart when she saw the terror in his eyes. He didn't seem to know her at all.

The giant white dog that stood guard over her brother began to change shape. Moments later a shiny, jewel-laden, scaled creature stood where the dog had been. The scaled one had a kind face, assuring her that all would be well. "My name is Thelo. Do not be afraid. You are safe."

Where was she? Was she dead? Was this the long dream of the afterlife? Why was her brother so afraid?

As she tried again to comfort him, he scrambled from her arms and crumpled into the far corner of the bed and wall, as far away from her as he could get.

"Why are you so upset, Finn? Don't you know who I am? It's me: Rose."

CHAPTER SIXTY

This Man Needs a Melody

FROM BETWEEN THE broken slats, Finn and Basset took turns watching for the girl. They didn't expect her once it was dark, but who knew? The two men kept up their vigil even in the wee hours, though Finn forbade the use of light.

Finn thought she'd seen him the last time he followed her, but after looking right at him, not surprisingly she left. *Perhaps I'm beyond detection after all.*

Basset was on lookout. Finn hurried down the stairs and entered the kitchen. Basset's face still carried the faint traces of Finn's outburst. "Basset, go get four hours of shut-eye. If there had been any sign of her in the last four hours, I would have heard, correct?"

"Yes, Mr. Finn. I understand the magnitude of the situation now. I know I deserved my punishment," Basset said with a yawn.

"Good. She'd better come today, and if it's a colossal waste of time like it was yesterday, she won't be happy—or anything for that matter. What was that about? The girl didn't go anywhere. She just sat by that revolting tree, forcing me to creep about after her! I've just about had it. It's a good thing we're prepared with plans A, B, and C this time. Right, Basset?"

Basset nodded.

"It's a shame we'll be moving on from such a welcoming home, though. Don't you agree?"

Finn looked over at the worn Formica kitchen table where Basset sat, slumped down with his head on the cracked surface, sound asleep. Anger reared its head for a second, but there was no energy to sustain it.

Finn pulled a chair from the other side of the table and moved it closer to the window. She usually came by on his watch, and he was glad of it. He liked leaping into action without a middleman to delay things. They had switched once, twice, and then the sun was once again at the right angle in the western sky for her to grace them with her presence.

Her blond head passed by the window, and he took an extra beat to study her in that moment. She wore jeans and a light-pink sweater. A backpack was slung over her shoulder, and she held something in her hand. He leaned in a bit farther, but it was no good. He couldn't risk giving himself away, though he was more than a little curious about what she was holding.

He exited the Fletcher house in record time, with hardly a sound, but paused before following her into the underbrush, when he spotted a long feline tail. "She has that nasty blue cat with her," he whispered under his breath.

The cat's ears perked up, and its nose wiggled, sniffing the air. Finn pressed his back against the old house and waited, not moving a muscle. He'd have to use extra caution during today's pursuit.

By now, he knew the way, having followed her through the forest before. The signal that had been so strong when he first had seen the girl returned today. He wondered why.

The girl laid the package, wrapped in blue cloth, on the ground. Finn tried to contain himself. He was so excited he practically drooled.

This is it! She's going to show me any second, and I'll know the way. I'll finally know.

It was a box. She had unwrapped it and was doing something to the bottom of it. When she put it back on the cloth, she opened the lid, and he heard. Notes from a distant time . . . it was coming back. *Not that dreaded song!* It was the song his sister person always sung or hummed or whistled. It drove him right over the edge! The worst part of it? She knew and did it anyway.

The music played for a few more seconds. The willow's branches and bright-green leaves rustled in the still air. Then, before his eyes, they all disappeared: the girl, the cat, and the box. All that remained was that gnarled old tree.

That's how she does it! All this time I've been thinking there was an actual key, but this makes more sense. All I have to do is get my hands on that box, and I'm home free!

He felt the presence and heard that familiar voice. The one that had aided him regularly over the many years since that first vision in the cabin, the one where the girl had plucked something from the ground and held it out. He liked this voice much better than bossy Mr. Helpful, who'd deserted him over forty years ago.

Good to see you again, Finn. You should follow her home. Then you can get in and out with that box when everyone's gone for the day. You can take it for your own.

Finn looked around, but other than the shuddering of a few low-lying leaves, he saw nothing. "Why didn't you tell me if you knew the key was the box?" he demanded.

I thought about what happened when they first brought you over to the other side. Consider it a form of protection until the time was ripe. You're most welcome.

"Thank you . . . I suppose. You know what they did to me was wrong, don't you?" He listened for a moment or two, but there was no further conversation. He decided it had been his own idea to steal the box in the end.

Good idea, Finn, he congratulated himself. *Why, thank you. I am quite brilliant, aren't I?*

Finn sat on the ground, readying himself to wait for hours if need be. Not ten minutes flew by, and the girl was back: right where she'd disappeared.

He heard her say, "You're welcome." It raised him out of his reverie. *How long will I have to listen to her whine before we get going?*

"Hi, Banyan," she continued. Finn watched as she reached into her pocket.

When she uttered, "Cooperation," he almost lost it. His hands shook and reached out as if to strangle someone. Many a blade of grass died a gruesome death on the hill that day as Finn ripped them from their roots. He saw her looking around. *Could she be looking for me? If so, I bet that blue excuse for a feline tipped her off.*

It was quicker following her home than to the clearing. The cat wasn't with her, so he could stay closer. He memorized how he'd have to return to the house. Finn also jotted down her house number and the name of her street.

I've been waiting and planning for this my whole life, even when I didn't know it. I will breathe the air of freedom. I can almost taste it. Once I take them down, I'll take everything.

CHAPTER SIXTY-ONE

The Eyes That Stole My Heart

ADIE STROLLED TOWARD home. It had been two weeks since the disaster at the dance, and she'd made it through another busy, albeit grueling, day at school. Sam was still a featured player in her semiconscious daydreams, but she found that they helped her get through the loss, rather than make her obsessive.

Without everyone in Mystashan, it would've been unthinkably worse. Even Mom and Dad weren't bothering her as much these days. She'd overheard them whispering to each other about "giving her breathing room," which suited her well.

She turned onto her street and nearly bumped into a tall, old man in a dark-gray hat. His eyes grew large as their gaze locked. Sadie swore they had gone from brown to blood red as he nodded and skirted past her. Goose bumps erupted on her arms and at the nape of her neck. His eyes looked familiar in some way, but she couldn't put her finger on it.

She looked over her left shoulder, hoping another glance would help her pinpoint where she'd seen him, but the street was empty. She'd only taken three, maybe four steps. *Hey! He can't be off the street this fast. Where'd he go?*

Red flashes split the sky. Then it hit her. *Could they have something to do with this man?* An image of her music box flashed in her mind. Fear rose in her throat, and she broke out into a full-on run. She didn't stop until she was inside her bedroom with the door closed.

Breathing hard, she climbed her stepstool. From the top, she checked every inch of the shelf where she'd left it. Before totally freaking out, she checked the other shelves in case her mom was on a dusting spree.

It can't be gone!

After tearing her room apart, she sat on her bed, her head in her hands. She allowed big, heavy tears to plop straight down to the rug. *How could I let this happen? Gramma entrusted that music box to me. I've let her down. I've let everyone down!*

Looking up, Sadie thought she saw another flash of red where her music box used to be. *Again the red. That man and his eyes—is he the shadow man from my nightmares? He can't be real. No way. Not in my house anyway.* Beads of sweat formed on her forehead. The gravity of the situation gripped her heart. She collapsed onto the floor and begged, *Gramma . . . please help me. Show me a sign—it would make me feel a whole lot better. If you know where our treasure is, can you point the way, please? I was careful. How in the world could he know about our music box?*

CHAPTER SIXTY-TWO

It Was Plan C All Along

FINN WAS CONSUMED with maniacal glee. There were plenty of nice things to steal in that house, but this was a focused mission. He'd gotten only one prize out of it, but it was the one that mattered. Now he was on his way to that appalling tree. And from there . . . well, he knew where from there.

He laughed to himself as he thought about his recent encounter with the girl. *That was interesting timing. She's even more disturbing close up. But nothing else matters, now that I have the key.*

He had a feeling she would look for him, so he had darted behind a nearby shed until she ran in the house.

He stopped by the house to get Basset. It would have been fun to share the main event with someone, but Basset would have to stay behind to secure his return.

They headed to Banyan. He could tell that Basset was curious, but there wasn't a moment to waste. He'd been waiting far too long.

"Basset, I'll explain later. You'll see. Just wait here and hold up the rear guard. If I disappear, don't worry. It's all according to plan A."

Basset nodded; every strand of his salt-and-pepper hair stayed in place. "I will, Mr. Finn. Will you be gone long?"

"It's hard to tell, but you'll be okay. You're a resourceful man."

"You really think so, Mr. Finn?"

"I said it, didn't I? Now be still while I set up, won't you?"

Basset didn't answer; he did as told.

Finn set the stage for the ultimate moment of his life. He opened the music box.

Thirty seconds later . . .

He hurled the box toward the tree. Basset's left arm, a foot away from Finn, shot out without his asking his master's permission. His reflexes were quick enough to grab hold of the music box until his other hand caught up. He clasped it in front of the tree, having just saved it from total annihilation.

"Thank you, Basset."

The box fumbled in Basset's hands after those words, but then he steadied it as Finn marched toward him.

"That's it! That's it! It's been *her* the whole time." Finn poked Basset repeatedly in the chest. "We need her here, unfortunately. We'll have to retrieve her, that manipulative mutt. We must do this now. I can't let another sun set on this."

"What do you need me to do, Mr. Finn?"

A stick cracked across the clearing. Finn heard its echo.

"Shh! Someone's coming. It has to be her. Time to hide, here in the . . ." He gestured toward the cattails.

Once they were hidden, Finn turned to Basset. "Remember, you'll have to stay here and wait for me. She can't know you're here. I need her by that tree. She can escape if she's too far away. I want to enjoy this, and you should too. You played your part in making this happen."

Basset, his eyes filled with delight, looked at Finn and whispered, "I'm so happy for you, Mr. Finn. You'll finally have your reward . . . everything you've ever wanted."

CHAPTER SIXTY-THREE

Knock on Wood

SADIE WRAPPED HER arms around Banyan and sobbed. "Banyan, please let me in. Show me what I need to do," she pleaded. "I'll do whatever it takes to get back. Banyan! Thelo!" she cried out. "*Please.*"

Nothing. Not even a cricket chirped.

"Looking for this?" The tall, old man emerged from a thick growth of cattails and held up her music box. His clothes looked a few sizes too big and as though he'd gone weeks sleeping in them. He was a dusty mess, so she couldn't tell how much of his hair was actually gray.

"You! How could you?" She ran at him. Fists pounded, swinging away. She kicked. She yelled. But even though he was old, he was stronger, and his arms were long. He placed his right palm on the top of her head, keeping her at a distance.

She could see him from here. His brown eyes were small and narrow, like his face. His expression was one she'd never seen before, with his eyebrows high, as though his skin stretched toward his temples. There was a vague but frightening familiarity to him.

Pleading for her music box had zero effect.

"You're going to get me in!" the man roared.

She stopped swinging. "In?" She took a breath. "In where?"

"Come now, girl. Let's not pretend. We both know what I'm talking about."

Sadie stood, pale and defiant. "I have no idea what you mean."

"We'll see about that." He grabbed her arm hard and dragged her toward the tree.

He gripped her so tightly that she could feel the bruises forming. She kicked with all her might but couldn't gain any traction. "No!" she screamed, but no help came.

He pushed her to the mossy ground then pinned her down with a knee to her stomach. He rubbed his hands together and opened the music box.

Immediately Gramma's soothing, sweet song played, and Sadie became more peaceful, despite the growing pain. "No . . ." she cried weakly, but it was too late. The softness took hold as she and the man grew more and more transparent.

The music stopped. The darkness faded.

Sadie opened her eyes, saddened that this was how she finally had arrived in Mystashan again, with this . . . this wretched man. She looked at him, her eyes blazing, and immediately noticed he hadn't changed. There was no brilliance to him like there was with everything else that came here. He was just as dull as he was in their world.

They both turned to Banyan.

"Let me in, old tree."

"Finn, you know I will never do that."

"Yes, I figured you wouldn't . . . but she will."

"No, I won't!" Sadie yelled. "Never!"

Finn pulled his sawback knife from his ankle holster. In an instant Sadie knew what he planned to do.

He hacked away at Banyan's branches. Golden sap trickled out, a drop here and a few more drops from every wound.

"No!" screamed Sadie. "You can't." Tears streamed from her eyes.

Finn viciously stabbed Banyan over and over. He laughed as he stripped the tree of his bark and golden, shimmering leaves.

More and more sap ran freely.

Sadie heard Banyan's screams inside her mind.

"Stop! Please stop. You're hurting him!

"Let me in this minute, girl!"

When Sadie hesitated, Finn sank the knife into Banyan's trunk hilt deep.

"Okay," she said through choking sobs. "Okay, just stop. I'll do it."

"No, Sadie. You cannot." Banyan's voice was raspy and weak.

Sadie looked at the sap pouring from Banyan's eyes and couldn't take one more second of it.

"I'm sorry, Banyan," she said. "I can't let him hurt you anymore."

CHAPTER SIXTY-FOUR

Tied up in Knots

As Finn maneuvered Sadie onto the shore of Saponi Straime, the water tunnel rose. He noticed the silence immediately. The signal had been there, leading him to her, and now it was no longer there at all. It cut out once the water rose.

Holding on to Sadie's arm was a lot like steering a car. Twist it, and the whole body moved.

"That's more like it!" Finn laughed in her face. Overjoyed, he turned and waved to the tree. "See you later, ol' friend. If you're still *able* to see, that is . . ."

Sadie tried to run to Banyan, but Finn caught and held her arm, harder this time, and dragged her through the tunnel.

She sobbed uncontrollably, yammering on and on, screaming. "You monster. How could you hurt Banyan? How could—"

Finn dropped the rock he used. *Ah, silence. Finally. I thought she'd never shut up.*

He hauled her unconscious body to a small grove of trees. With a handful of vines, he tied her to a sturdy oak.

Finn stood up tall. It was his best posture in decades. He felt like howling his victory to the winds, but this was meant to be a surprise visit.

He backed up and surveyed the area. There was light up ahead, but here it was difficult to see through the tree's shadows at night. He could tell that Sadie hadn't moved. She was out cold, and the vines were more than secure. "Don't go anywhere. I might still need you for this or that." Finn bent over and whispered in her ear, "Piece of advice: if you have anything to do—inside your head, I mean—I wouldn't wait until later. Soon there won't be any later."

He crept through the woods with care, hiding behind trees. A quarter moon at its zenith spared a thin light, but another, fuller moon rose ahead, enabling him to see his forward path. As he drew closer, he saw more clearly. He headed toward a barely remembered village.

CHAPTER SIXTY-FIVE

The Reunion

ROSE OPENED THE door to the stranger. There was something familiar about the man who stood before her. She studied his face but looked away before it became intrusive. She noticed it was etched much deeper than her own, as if he'd spent all his time in the sun, yet he was pale.

"Hello. Can I help you?"

"What, Rose? You don't remember me? Don't you recognize your own flesh and blood?"

Rose's smile changed to confusion as she attempted to process his words. *Family?* They were all gone . . . her parents, and Finn, her twin brother. She could remember the night they'd told her he was dead as if it were yesterday. Rose looked long and hard at the man's weathered face. Then she saw it . . . in his eyes.

"It's impossible," she exclaimed. "My brother passed away a very long time ago."

Finn made a grand bow, dipping at the knees then returning to his full height; he was only a few inches taller than she was. "Nope. Didn't die. They must have lied to you, Rose. Still here. Still going strong." Finn offered her a strange smile.

It was then she saw the truth. It really was her beloved twin brother! She swayed on her feet a little. Holding on to the door for support, she burst out her welcome.

"I've got to be dreaming. Come in, Finn! Come in. It's a miracle, to be sure." Happy tears ran down her cheeks. She hugged him tightly. "After all this time . . . I can hardly believe you're alive. How is this possible? Where have you been all these years?"

Finn backed away and snapped his fingers at her eye level. "Hey, sister . . . get a hold of yourself. This isn't a social call. I have important business to discuss with you."

Somewhat amused by his serious tone, she teased, "Oh? Business? I just made a fresh pot of Earl Grey. Sit with me and have some tea." Her hazel eyes sparkled. "Don't you have a moment to celebrate with your sister after all this time?" Rose walked toward the kitchen; Finn followed.

"Oh, there will be a celebration," crowed Finn. "Tell me what I need to know, and I'll certainly be celebrating . . . by myself, thank you very much."

"Celebrate alone? When we're just now reunited?" Rose indicated the chairs so he could sit. "Tell me about this business of yours since apparently it can't wait for us to catch up."

"Have a seat, Rose." Finn pulled out two of the kitchen chairs. Once they sat down, he leaned in. "Exactly how do I get back to Mystashan?"

"Mystashan?" She was confused. "Why would you want to go there? I haven't been there in decades."

"Don't play coy with me. Tell me now!" Finn's foot tapped with an ever-quickening rhythm.

Rose reached out for his hand and clasped it in hers.

Finn allowed this.

"After Thelonious told me you had died, I locked myself in my room for weeks and couldn't eat. I grew disenchanted with Mystashan. They kept everything about you so quiet. I chose to leave as soon as I was old enough, because I couldn't stand being there without you. Everything about the place reminded me of you and how you suffered. I missed how we used to do everything together."

"Oh, boo-hoo, Rose. I'm sure you pined away. Look at you now—you're practically skin and bones." Sarcasm hung in the air between them, but he maintained his attention.

He halfheartedly tried to take his hands back, but she held on.

"I took care of you, and in your own way, you took care of me too. I've been there for you, just like I'm here for you now. I know Mystashan wasn't a good place for you." She noticed the corner of his right eye pool with enough moisture to create one small drop that never fell.

"I've been on the earth realm ever since. There's no passage back. You remember that, don't you, Finny? Once you decide to leave Mystashan for good, there's no memory of how to get back."

Finn sat for a moment. A heavy silence spread through the kitchen. He stood and sighed, then bent and kissed the top of her head. "I believe you."

He turned to leave. Then he stopped before he reached the door.

Rose stood.

Finn's right hand rubbed his neck.

"Which means you're of no use to me." He walked back to where she stood.

Rose's eyes teared as she placed a hand on his arm. "No use? I don't understand, Finny."

In an instant, his hands clutched her throat, lifting her up. Her feet kicked the chair, which clattered to the floor. Her teacup followed, shattering on the linoleum.

Shock and sadness flooded her face as he tightened his grip

around her throat. Tears ran down her cheeks, and she flailed around, grasping for anything she could find. Only her brother's arms were within reach.

Holding on to him, she felt an unrecognizable energy. She willed her hands to communicate all that she wasn't able to say aloud. She had loved and remembered him through many years: a lifetime.

Grasping the bit of hope that swirled along with the faces of her loved ones—her deceased husband, her daughter, her son-in-law—she reached her granddaughter. Sadie's face, her sweet Sadie, stayed with her the longest, and then there was only Finn.

She knew it was over. Her eyes locked on his and held them. In her final seconds, Rose mouthed, "I forgive you."

CHAPTER SIXTY-SIX

In the Heat of the Moment

EVEN AS HER body slowed and grew still, Finn felt Rose's life-force enter him through his palms and fingers. It was strong at first and pulsed with a soft blue light, but it slipped away with each passing moment. He felt her light dimming. He watched as her essence left her body and disappeared into his. It was brighter and broader than all the others combined. He took a deep breath and her energy followed. He reveled in its exhilarating power. He felt charged. Invigorated.

Then it changed. His body grew intensely hot. Excruciatingly hot. This was new and unpleasant. He began to panic. He'd never felt this uncomfortable before. This hadn't happened with the others. Rose's essence created unbearable heat throughout his body. That's when he saw that girl, her granddaughter—*his* grandniece. The image only stayed a second, but he knew.

After a tortured forever, the heat felt as if it were scorching his arms and legs before blazing like a cauldron in the center of his chest.

He didn't know what happened or why his eyes were tearing nonstop. He felt weak. Minutes ticked by. He sat on the floor, next to his dead sister. As he stared at her face, he tried to recall the last words she'd uttered to him. For the briefest moment, he felt almost . . . lost.

What was that? What the hell just happened? Shaking, Finn stood up carefully. He held on to the back of his chair until he stabilized. An inexplicable comet of blue flame left his chest, flew across the room, and set the curtains alight.

Absorbed in his inner world, Finn blankly watched the fire consume them.

This will take care of itself, I see.

As he walked out and closed the door behind him, he hesitated. Something compelled him to run back inside. He grabbed a throw blanket from the couch and batted the flames until they were extinguished. Black smoke swirled through the kitchen.

Finn took one last look at his sister before exiting her house.

Now rid of his internal inferno, he had returned to himself and regained his strength.

"I will never allow an intrusion like that again. This is the last time anyone will catch Finn Montgomery unprepared."

CHAPTER SIXTY-SEVEN

Say "Uncle"

AIR! I NEED *air!* Two hands pressed harder until only blackness remained.

Sadie blinked then closed her eyes again. She saw once more the lonely figure lying on the kitchen floor. *Is that Gramma? The curtains are on fire! Gramma! Get up! Get out of there!* She opened her eyes and did her best to focus on her surroundings, but her double vision and the throbbing pain in the back of her head made it a challenge.

There's no fire. Where am I?

As Sadie gave her head a few brisk wake-up shakes, dizzying nausea and confusion swept through her. With some trouble, she slowly remembered her vivid dream. *No. It wasn't a dream at all. It was real—and it was awful. That disgusting man who hurt Banyan and stole my music box killed Gramma. I saw the whole thing!*

Sadie struggled to stand up but couldn't move against her restraints.

What's happening? Why am I tied up? A familiar chill coursed through her. *That man. Where is he? I have to get free before he comes back. How could I feel what Gramma felt? Nothing makes sense, not unless . . . Was I at the Velluminator? How's that even possible when I can't move?*

Another wave of nausea hit her, and whatever had been inside her stomach forced its way out.

She panicked, pulling as hard as she could against the ropes. No use. They wouldn't budge.

Sadie couldn't absorb everything that was happening. Being tied up. That strange, hateful man. The fact that Gramma Rose had met with such an unimaginable end.

"Why didn't anyone tell me the truth? I was in danger too. I *am* in danger. Maybe they don't know the whole story? I mean, who would . . . except for Rose and that vile man?"

Then it hit her like a thunderclap.

That maniac is my great-uncle!

Her stomach somersaulted again.

Once her queasiness calmed, Sadie sobbed, feeling the last moments of Gramma's life. *It's like losing her all over again, and he's my uncle on top of it.*

I need to stop him! I need real answers from Thelo. I won't let him blow me off again.

Sadie struggled against her bonds. *What do I do next? I'm screwed.*

"Can anyone hear me?" she screamed. "Help! Help! I'm over here!"

CHAPTER SIXTY-EIGHT

Sideshow

FINN MOVED THROUGH the shadows, hiding behind boughs of dense leaves, as they provided good cover. As he drew closer to the village, its landmarks grew familiar. He immediately sought out the Atrium. It was hard to miss, taller than anything around it. *It represents everything I hate about this horrifying place.*

Finn waited behind the thick trunk of a chestnut tree, biding his time as several villagers strolled up and down the slate walkway. He waited until the path was empty then darted across.

Moving through the Atrium's archway, Finn sensed the beast's presence within the main chamber. He progressed slowly as his eyes adjusted to the low light. The beast sat quietly, his back toward Finn.

"You're much older, Beast. It hangs in the air around you like the putrefying rodent you are."

"Welcome, Finn. I've been waiting for you." Thelonious stood and turned to face him. "I knew you would find me."

"Of course I found you. Your treachery has clung to me these long years. It's always been there, boiling under the surface, although I didn't know what it was until recently. Once I knew its nature, its innate tracker led me right to you. Time to make things right. Unlike you, I finish what I start."

"I understand why you would see it that way. But maybe there is a chance you might see it differently? Perhaps you could sit with me for a few minutes?" Thelonious sat on the crystal bench and offered Finn the seat beside him.

Finn paced in a semicircle around him. The lines in his face deepened, as did his anger. "What good would sitting do? I don't want to talk. That's all you ever wanted to do, but it never helped a thing."

"We can sit in silence for a moment first. Maybe that will help?"

Finn shook his head in disbelief. "The way you speak is like a puzzle no one can understand."

"Do you have any questions for me?"

"No questions. You know why I'm here. I hate what you did to me, and I hate you. Period."

"Finn, I know you. You and Rose—"

Red exploded behind Finn's eyes at the mention of her name. "How *dare* you! *You* killed her, not me. I won't stand here and listen to this."

"Finn, I am so sorry. Mr. Felix brought you to this land with the sole intent of saving two young lives, but it was meant to be Rose alone. We read that in the cloffuls, but he couldn't leave you to die when he was capable of transferring you both." Thelonious looked up at Finn, pacing, following him with his eyes.

"Right away, you glitched. We could tell you were different. Your arrival was never meant to happen, and accordingly it did not go well. We had no choice but to send you back to earth with as normal a life as we could secure. We could not put Mystashan at risk."

"Who cares about your Mystashan? And you . . . who are

you to talk about me being different? You're the same as what exactly?"

Thelonious exhaled and lowered his head. "Most transfers to our realm have been successful. There was only one other who was like you. He began to fade with his first step into Mystashan. All that was left of him was his voice. Later that faded as well."

Crushing pain ricocheted through Finn's head and into his ears. He squinted, holding the sides of his head. It lasted half a second then was gone.

Thelonious looked at Finn without expression. "We are all a little damaged. That's why we have our lives, to grow and transform."

Finn pointed, stabbing the air. "What BS is this? I'll never believe a word you say. *Never*. You lie to everyone. You're nothing but a liar and a murderer. You snapped Beagle's neck. You strangled Rose. You even tried to drown me all those years ago. Admit it!"

"No, Finn. I tried to save you."

Behind him, Finn heard a throat being cleared, and he turned around, newly aware of his audience. *Oh, good. They're arriving. It's about time.* The numbers in the Atrium increased, surrounding the pair.

"I remember exactly what happened," Finn huffed. "Don't deny it. It was the day you showed me the island could change. We walked toward the water, and land grew beneath your feet." Finn gestured wildly with his arms. "You told me to try for myself, but the water didn't change for me, and I fell in. You knew I couldn't swim." Finn jabbed his finger pointedly at Thelonious. "Your arms held me down. Then others came. There were witnesses, and you had no choice but to save me."

"You are not remembering it correctly, Finn. It did not happen that way. I cared for you, but as much as I tried, I could not help you." Thelonious clasped his hands in front of him and looked up at Finn with moisture forming in the corners of his eyes.

"Cared for me? Really? I remember once thinking that might be true. A single solitary moment before I saw you for who you truly are. But now I've come to set things straight. There's no going back."

"Are you certain, Finn? There's always a way. You do have a choice."

Finn faced the growing audience and summoned his "big tent" bravado.

"Step right up! Don't be shy. Come one, come all to see the greatest ending on earth . . . Oh, pardon me! Not earth . . . Mystashan!" He paused for just a moment. "If you only knew what a gift I'm giving you today. Your deaths will transport you well beyond the misery that is this place."

All through the crowd, voices whispered: "What did he just say?" "Death? Does he mean *us*?" "I didn't sign up for this."

"Yes, we'll see soon enough. Before I take care of the rest of you, though, it will be an honor to dispatch your beast leader first. You don't mind waiting, do you?"

Thelonious spoke in a commanding tone. "I want all of you to know that there is no cause for alarm. In fact, it would be best if you remained calm and filed out of the Atrium."

"We aren't leaving you, Thelonious," cried one of the Mystashanians.

"How will you save us?" another voice called out, begging for reassurance.

"We've been over this. From what we've seen in the cloffuls, our choice is to let this play out. It is time."

"Cloffuls shmuffles. Enough with your ridiculous messages. Nobody cares." Finn spat at the floor in front of Thelonious.

A Freanwea grabbed Finn's leg, trying with all her might to

push the tall man to the ground. "Come on, everyone. We can take him!"

"No," Thelonious insisted with grounded authority.

Finn's hands tingled with newly awakened energy. He flung the knee-high Freanwea across the Atrium, into one of the crystal pillars, as if he were throwing a small stone.

Huh, would you look at that? I'm even more powerful than I knew. Well, it makes sense that power is on my side. Mystashan must agree that I'm in the right.

Before anyone had a chance to blink, Finn ran headfirst at Thelonious, knocking him off balance. The new energy gave him all the leverage he needed. They both fell onto the marble platform, with Thelonious on his back. Finn landed on top of him with an elbow to his face. He watched as Thelonious's large dilated pupils shifted back and forth.

"Please, everyone. Stay back," Thelonious croaked, pleading with a weakened voice. "You all know where to go."

Finn turned to the crowd, arms spread wide, and bellowed, "I hope you heard the lies your leader spun around my drowning incident, but yes, go ahead and trust him. This will be the last time you hear anything from him again. Stay and watch your 'fearless' leader's demise."

Straddling Thelonious, Finn turned and looked at his quarry. He heard encouragement from someone in the crowd: *Kill him, Finn.*

CHAPTER SIXTY-NINE

Bye the Glow

"HELP! HELP! I'M over here," Sadie called into the darkness, hoping someone would hear her.

"You don't have to shout. Always with the shouting."

It was the unmistakable unified voice of the Slugs. Sadie searched the ground nearby. "I can hear you, but I can't see you. Where are you guys? We have to hurry."

"We're right here. Just look down."

The warm yellow light grew into a brighter glow as realization dawned on Sadie. *You're the rope!*

"Let go of me already. There's a lunatic loose in Mystashan, and I'm not sure what he's going to do."

"A lunatic you say?" The Slugs released their grip and dropped to the ground.

"Yes, he's out of his mind. His name is Finn. Finn Montgomery. He killed my Gramma Rose." Sadie grabbed the tree for support as the realization hit her with fresh feeling.

Rose's and Finn's names whispered through the Slugs. Their lights went dark.

"Don't go back to sleep. I need you!" Sadie gained her footing once more. "I need your help."

Their lights flickered back on. They lowered their tiny heads. "We know where he's going."

"You do? Where?"

"To find Thelonious. Finn lived in Mystashan for a short while when he was a boy and didn't leave on the best of terms. In fact they weren't his terms at all. What can we do?"

"We need to think of a way to find Thelo and stay under Finn's radar."

The Slugs gave a collective shrug—well, as much of a shrug as vines can give.

Sadie kicked at a tuft of grass at her feet. The tender roots broke free, revealing the rich dirt below. *Dirt!*

"I've got it . . . the tunnels! Lead the way."

The Slugs' lights dimmed. "We'd rather not get involved. This isn't our fight."

Sadie knelt. "Don't you see? It's everyone's fight. We're talking about your home."

The Slugs murmured; it went on and on. "Just for the record, we're not sure that you know what you're doing, but we'll show you where to go."

"I'm not sure either, but I'm one hundred percent committed, and if you join me, together we can figure this out."

Tink.

Sadie reached into the left pocket of her hoodie as she felt the new weight. She closed her eyes for a second then held the stone up to the Slugs' glow. The stone read, LEADERSHIP.

"We have to hurry," Sadie urged. "Let's go."

The Slugs led the way to the mouth of the tunnels. They slithered across the ground, their light illuminating the opening. Once they were inside a short distance, the tunnel split in three directions.

Just when a Habnaw's assistance would have been useful,

there wasn't one in sight. "Which way, Slugs? Do you know which one to take?"

"No, we've never been down here before. Should we split up?"

Sadie considered her choices. "I think we need to stick together. There's power in numbers." A subtle scent of rose wafted from the middle passage. "Let's go through the middle one."

We'll follow you, Sadie, but what will we do once we get there?

"I don't know, but something tells me we'll know when it's time. Wait a minute! You can communicate telepathically like Banyan and Thelo?"

We can hear each other, and of course you're so loud, it's impossible not to hear you.

Really? You're going to go there? Sadie shook her head.

Sadie reached out to Thelo. *Thelo! Finn's loose in Mystashan. Be careful. He's already attacked Banyan, who's badly hurt. I'm going to try to find you via the tunnels.*

They continued deeper into Mystashan until they hit another split and then another. Each time, Sadie let her nose guide her and followed the scent of roses. It led to an unfinished stone wall they couldn't traverse. "This can't be happening." *I'm so frustrated.* She shook her head as if to clear it. *We can't give up.* "We have to get to Thelo!"

"You think on that while we rest. This spelunking is more than we bargained for!"

Sadie fought to keep her anger down. "Can't you see? If you don't help me figure this out, Thelo is going to die, and so could everyone else. Mystashan would be lost forever."

CHAPTER SEVENTY

The Main Event

*K*ILL HIM, *F*INN. *I hope you find your new power helpful.* This voice was crystal clear in his mind. He searched the crowd, looking for the one who had spoken. The owner of the familiar voice was here with him—recognition immediately coursed through him. *I did find it a pleasant surprise*, Finn replied. *Thank you.* They made eye contact for a second before his attention turned back to his prey.

The message further energized Finn. He punched Thelonious repeatedly, taking his lifetime of pain and anger out on the mighty creature. Jab after jab. Painful punches, kicks, and elbows. One after the other. Finn's hands were unstoppable. They needed no rest. Paying little attention to the blood dripping from his fists, he reveled in the sound of bones crunching.

Thelonious's saliva and blood stained the front of Finn's shirt as he continued to pummel him with first right, then left fists. He paused and wiped his knuckles across his chest, leaving a streak of dark-red blood.

"You're pathetic. You won't even fight back."

Thelonious moaned softly and lifted his hands to his face. Tiny lightning beams sparked from them to the affected parts of his body.

"Go ahead . . . heal yourself. I can do this again and again, all day long." He wrapped the fingers of his right hand around Thelonious's throat and raised his left fist, ready to launch the next round of blows.

A whisper rose in the crowd, and they collectively inched forward. Finn turned on them, glaring. His squinting eyes blazing with insanity, his voice boomed deeper than before. "Don't even think about it."

Still holding Thelonious by the neck, he raised his left palm and used the power of his rage to push the crowd back.

They couldn't budge; their feet were stuck in place. He watched as they tried.

This day keeps getting better and better.

Finn's deranged grin increased in size. He looked down at Thelonious, who lingered on the edge of consciousness.

"Why aren't you defending yourself? Not even one punch, beast? Is the fight out of you already? You know you deserve this. Is that why you're letting me beat the life out of you? Maybe the time has come for me to kill you at last."

Finn freed up his leg sheath and pulled out the knife. It hypnotized him for a moment. *This wasn't how it looked on earth.*

Here it wasn't simply an implement of destruction but an item of beauty in its own right.

"I bought this blade especially for you. Do you like it? It has a special point, one that I'll be making shortly. Why is it special? Because it can dig rocks out of any surface. Like, say, diamonds out of the hide of a beast. Isn't that exciting?"

Finn perused the glittering stones embedded in Thelonious, pausing at each one to estimate its weight and value. He smiled down at his quarry. Not only would he be a rich man, but also the fear he saw reflected in Thelonious's eyes was a gem he would treasure for the rest of his life.

"I have to admit, beast, you're even more stunning than I recalled. In all this painful madness you call Mystashan, after you tried to kill me and then cast me out, the one thing I've always remembered fondly is your treasure."

"I'm sorry, Finn. Even now I wish I could reach you." Thelonious's voice was weak and thready.

"But you can't, can you? Your arms are too damaged. Your words mean nothing. Know that I am going to enjoy this. Ready?" Finn stuck the tip into Thelonious's hide. It resisted at first, but he called upon the new strength he needed for this task. He pushed the knife in deeper.

Thelonious recoiled, struggling to move away from the blade.

"Ah, now you try to flee? I thought you were the powerful Thelonious? You're just a mouse. See this, everyone? Take note of your leader's cowardice. He tries to escape me now."

Thelonious managed to climb to his feet. He took several steps before collapsing to the floor.

"Oh, no, you don't, mouse. Our game has just begun." Finn knelt over him, his knees pinning Thelonious, making sure he couldn't escape.

The knife soon found its mark, just under a bright transparent stone.

Screams of agony echoed through the Atrium. Most people looked away.

"Don't miss the main event! Everyone must watch. It's a wonderful show I've put on for you, called, *Life Is Vengeance*. It's rude to turn away." Finn motioned again with his left hand, and the residents' heads swiveled to the scene before them. "That's better. Isn't this perfect? Wouldn't you agree, mouse?"

Finn took his time excavating the rest of Thelonious's diamonds. The smaller ones popped out easily. One by one they plunked into Finn's pockets. One large diamond on his abdomen gave him trouble; he worked up a sweat even with his new power. The radiance of the stone's multifaceted light transfixed him. *They'll be mine soon enough. I can't let their spell distract me now.* He dug in even deeper. When the jewel finally came out, a sucking reverberation resounded throughout the Atrium.

The assembled cries fueled Finn's joy at Thelonious's pain. Thelonious made no sound. The wounds seeped a multicolored muddiness, and many of the spectators closed their eyes. A brief electrical display lit the hall's interior until all that was left was dark syrup. Thelonious's fire was out.

With a menacing smile, Finn stood and faced the crowd. "Now for the rest of you."

CHAPTER SEVENTY-ONE

Step on Up

"WILL YOU PLEASE wake up!" Sadie told the Slugs. "I can't see a thing down here."

A voice called out from farther down the tunnel. "Yeah. Wake up already. I hardly think sleeping on the job is the proper thing to do."

"Who's here? Who said that?" Sadie called out.

The bouncing light of a lantern approached as the voice grew closer.

"It's me, Mardin. Wake up, Slugs. Thelo needs us, and you're wasting time."

"What's happened? How's Thelo? Have you seen him?" asked Sadie.

Mardin looked concerned. "He's the one who sent me. I hid in the Velluminator cave, so Finn was unaware of my presence. It's best you see for yourself." He lowered his voice. "Thelo couldn't risk telling the Slugs about Finn's arrival for fear their lights would give them away."

"Hey! We heard that! What does that mean?" they asked in concert.

"Never mind. Just keep your lights low. Let's get a move on before it's too late."

"Nice way to talk to us, Mardin. You always think you're better than us," grumbled the Slugs, but they moved forward.

Mardin didn't answer. Instead he felt along the rock wall in front of them. Two-thirds of the way up, he pushed where granite met marble, and a section swung inward, revealing a secret tunnel.

Sadie reached out and touched his arm. "Are we going to make it in time?"

"There's no telling, Sadie. We're taking the most direct route, but prepare yourself for the worst."

CHAPTER SEVENTY-TWO

The Echo of Impact

E VERYONE DID THEIR best to be quiet, but to Sadie's ears it was a cacophony of *shhh*. She whispered her entreaty to the near darkness. "Don't you realize that with every *shhh*, there's extra noise echoing in here?"

The Slugs singsonged in unison, "So how does a whole sentence rank on the Noise-o-Meter?"

"This is serious. Remember why we're here. That's it. Please. No more speaking."

"Look who's talking," the Slugs whispered.

Sadie wasn't sure her plea of silence would work, but to her astonishment, it did. They continued on a steady incline. The dirt turned soft going uphill, covering the sounds of their footsteps and other tracks. Up ahead a filtered light flickered through water, and they knew they were close.

A deep silence took hold of each heart. Sadie held an image of what the next moment might bring. *I have to be ready*, she reminded herself. The group came upon the Velluminator cave unnoticed, as the waterfall screen kept them invisible. Still, they were able to see out.

Sadie heard Finn's sickening laughter before she glimpsed the ramifications of his unwanted arrival in Mystashan.

All this devastation. I can't believe this is happening here. She was shocked to see the Atrium in complete disarray. *Slugs, I can't find Thelo.* At the mention of Thelo's name, the Slugs climbed on top of one another, extending themselves, and pointed directly at Finn.

"You see what I mean, Sadie?" asked Mardin.

Sadie couldn't believe what she saw. Thelo, devoid of his jewels, with hollow bloody pits dotting his hide, lay viciously beaten in the middle of the Atrium floor.

"Sadie?" Mardin turned to face her and noticed her head shaking.

"He's a monster. My uncle is a monster." Tears fell. She closed her eyes and withdrew inside herself to let the shock of it loose. She shook her arms and legs to bring herself back.

The Slugs held a collective deep breath then parted the watery curtain to get a better look.

Slugs, can I count on you to have my back? Sadie looked at them, pleading for their cooperation with her eyes.

Yes, we're with you. They yawned once in confirmation.

Sadie was about to respond when she heard it.

We know you're here.

This came from behind them in the tunnel. Everyone stopped where they stood.

"Did you hear that?" Mardin's forehead creased.

"I did." Sadie replied. *Slugs, keep your eyes on Finn.* She felt their level of concern rise.

First there was a scraping sound, and then a bang echoed in the high-ceilinged space near the back of the cave.

Everything has been set in motion, you outdated fossils. You can't stop him. We've already won.

Aware of the danger behind them now, she knew it was time to move ahead. She stepped out, and the second she emerged, Finn turned to face her.

"Who dares disturb my moment?"

Sadie's courage faltered when she noticed that his eyes flashed scarlet, as though his pupils were on fire.

She looked past him to Thelo, who lay still. A fire built within her; her fury filled her heart.

She ran straight at Finn, extending her arms. Blue light pulsed from her palms, pushing Finn back half a dozen feet. Sadie put herself between Finn and the immobilized Thelo.

"Stay away from him!" she roared.

She bent forward to check on Thelo when Finn's response hit her.

Her feet lifted off the ground, slamming her back into one of the Atrium's stone columns, knocking the breath from her lungs. Everything went dark for a moment. Her eyes opened to see two Finn Montgomerys standing in front of her. Her head pounded. She struggled to breathe. Everything blurred. *What happened?*

"Who do you think you are? You can't stop this. You're going to die with the rest of them." Finn stood a couple of feet away. His mouth hung open with viscous drippings at one corner. His eyes were way too wide.

Sadie looked over at Thelo. *Slugs, where are you?*

We're in the Velluminator.

Distract him, directed Mardin.

She glared at Finn, who seemed pleased. *All right, Slugs,* she thought, *be on your marks. Stay alert.* She returned her attention to Thelo.

"You're too late. He's mine to do with as I please."

"Are you enjoying yourself? When people are in pain?"

"What people? I don't see any people around here, except for your unfortunate self, and there are some who would debate whether you even fit that category."

Finn snatched a young Habnaw from the paralyzed crowd.

He held the boy up by one arm. "Like this, for example? Not a person." Finn hurled the whimpering child against the pillar to his left. An awful crunching sound echoed throughout the Atrium.

No one could help the poor boy, though many struggled to do so. They couldn't move; they were still under Finn's hold.

Sadie's hands curled into fists.

Sparkles of light rushed into the Atrium. The Silars had arrived, encapsulating the boy. These tiny beings carried the Habnaw high above the heads of the gathered crowd. With pained expressions, the onlookers watched as the boy's tiny seeds of hair burst individually into flames. Soon his light burned out.

"There. Are you going to cry? Over that thing you call a person?"

Sadie feigned detachment. "Maybe I'll cry or maybe I won't. What's it matter to you?"

She choked down the bile in her throat. *I can't allow him to hurt anyone else. I have to keep this fiend away from Thelo. I wish I knew what to do next.*

Sadie stared at Finn while her main focus remained inward. On her heart, where Thelo and Banyan lived. On her muscles and how strong they were. On her brain, where a thunderstorm picked up speed.

"Well? What are you doing? Are you going to stand there and stare at me? Let's see what you've got. I don't have all day."

Waiting for an inner answer, Sadie closed her eyes. The darkness inside grew lighter. Her crystals appeared in her mind's eye. Each had a signature quality, like its own song. At once, all five emitted tones of variously pitched frequencies. She felt them filling her body, mind, and spirit with a reassuring energy. Patience, appreciation, accountability, cooperation, and leadership—all were present and singing their songs.

Sadie opened her eyes and calmly looked at the sneering Finn, whose face glowed with feverish excitement.

"I've waited years to be here, to exact my vengeance." He kicked Thelo and laughed. "I have nearly everything I came for. Can you say the same?"

CHAPTER SEVENTY-THREE

Unconditional Conditions

SADIE STUDIED FINN for a moment. She couldn't believe there was anyone this evil. "Can I at least say good-bye to Thelo?"

The old man's face scrunched while his index finger tapped his lips. "Hmmm. That could be entertaining, seeing you fawn over a corpse. Go ahead. Say good-bye to the dead one. Why not? You're next."

Slugs, get ready.

Sadie turned to Thelo, dropping hard to her knees. "Thelo. Talk to me." She waited for an answer, but none came. "Wake up. It's me, Sadie. You have to wake up. Please." Muddy tears streaked her face. "Wake up right now!"

Finn laughed. "'Wake up . . . wake up and save us.'" He rolled his brilliant-red eyes. "I told you—you're too late."

Sadie ignored her uncle's gloating while she assessed Thelo. His brilliance was gone. Where his magnificent jewels once shone, there were now small maroon pools of something sticky. As gently as she could, she cradled Thelo's head.

She searched again for any vital signs, but all she heard was the silence of the night and occasionally Finn's booming laughter.

"Thelo, wake up!" she begged. "This isn't the way it's supposed to happen. You can't be dead."

Finn's falsetto voice mocked Sadie's grief once again. "'Oh, Thelo, you can't be dead. It's not possible. I need you!' It's about time you realized that you don't need him. Now you can't say your uncle never gave you any advice. Thelonious wasn't there for me either when I thought I needed him. And look how well I turned out!"

Sadie's tears dripped down onto Thelo's face. "You can't be gone . . . you just can't," she whispered.

Finn yanked her to her feet. "Enough! No amount of your bawling is going to bring him back." He stared her down, but he was the one who blinked and turned away first. "I'm going to enjoy killing her immensely," he announced to the crowd.

"Slugs! Now! Grab him!" *Make sure his hands are bound.*

Her outburst caught Finn off guard.

At Sadie's command, the Slugs snapped into action, twisting and binding Finn's hands tightly together behind his back. The Freanweas and Habnaws, now free of Finn's paralyzing hold, encircled him, while the Slugs elegantly wove their strong emerald vines around and through his arms and legs, leaving him standing bound. Even with his newfound power, Finn was no match for their united strength and was subdued. He was now the immobilized one.

He squirmed in his bonds then turned to look at Sadie. "You think you can stop me, wretched girl?"

"Slugs, take care of that yap trap, please." Sadie put her thumb and index finger together and motioned across her lips.

One set of vines crossed over Finn's mouth and silenced him.

Sadie focused her attention only on Thelo. A silver shimmer appeared over his chest.

She wiped her eyes to see more clearly, and an ounce of hope calmed her sadness. A crystal slowly formed over Thelo's heart, settling down gently. Sadie gasped, too afraid to touch it, for fear that it might disappear. She carefully read its message: UNCONDITIONAL LOVE.

"Thelo, come back to me. Please come back. I'm not sure whether this crystal is for me or whether it's supposed to help you."

She placed two fingers on his neck and checked his pulse for the tenth time.

Nothing.

CHAPTER SEVENTY-FOUR

Treasure and Travail

"Nice work subduing Finn, Sadie. I know it wasn't easy." Barnaby made his presence known.

Standing up, she asked him, "Where have you been?"

"It wasn't time yet."

"Wasn't time yet?" Her skin flushed bright red. She faced Barnaby, hands on hips, leaning in. "What does that mean? Thelo's dead. Where were you?"

"Sadie, you arrived first, and the damage was already done. I know it's hard to accept, but Thelo had faith in you," reassured Barnaby. "Trust his wisdom. He told me you would know what to do and not to get in your way."

She took Barnaby's words as a challenge. She held on to her leadership crystal, remembering what it represented. *I'm stronger than Finn*, she reminded herself. She looked at the treasure in her palm. She felt the pull of its power; it lurched from her hand toward Thelo's body and landed on the crown of his head.

She knew what to do. She called to the four crystals that were hidden in her sock drawer. One by one they slowly appeared over Thelo's body, aligned in a row from head down throughout his torso. With the six crystals levitating in place, Sadie waited, certain this was what Thelo needed.

Nothing happened.

I don't understand. I can feel their power. They have to work. This has to work.

Sadie held her breath, trying not to move. She willed the crystals to heal Thelo. The sensation of needles marched up her body, starting from her feet.

Nothing changed; Thelo remained motionless.

It's not working. How could it not work?

Heartbreak and frustration filled her, and all her emotions surged forth. Thelo was gone, and Sadie's murderous uncle stood bound and gagged by the Slugs just a few feet away.

The Slugs yelped and released the vine that covered Finn's mouth. "He bit us. Pull tighter."

Sadie's voice began softly, edged with tension. "You don't belong here, Finn Montgomery."

The closest vine smacked Finn on the back of his head.

Finn's head jerked forward as he spat, "You can't do anything to me here. I lived in Mystashan once. I know the rules."

Her eyes locked on his. "'Once' is a long time ago, and besides, who said I'm going to do anything to you here?" The needles subsided. Visible arcs of crackling electricity emanated with indigo fire from her fingertips.

As Finn struggled against his living bonds, the briefest expression of fear flickered in his eyes, but he quickly composed himself. "You're just a child. What could you possibly do aside from these weak carnival tricks?"

Sadie's voice picked up steam as electric energy fueled her body and the auric field around her. "When I say, 'Go,' you will leave!"

She kept the volume high. Her last words were thunderous,

reaching a crescendo that no being in Mystashan could ignore, especially the Slugs. She thrust her arms toward Finn.

"Here! You want Thelo's jewels so badly? Keep them. I'm releasing you from Mystashan. Get the hell out of here. *Go!*"

Clawing the air in front of him, Finn was sucked backward by such a powerful force that the Slugs almost didn't have time to let go of him. Before her last word died away, an enormous, black, swirling vortex opened up and swallowed Finn whole. There was no trace of Finn Montgomery anywhere in Mystashan.

CHAPTER SEVENTY-FIVE

Can't Keep a
Good Plan Down

"I'M VERY PROUD of you, Sadie," a strained voice called from behind.

She almost tripped over her own foot as she spun around. "Thelo? I can't believe this is real. Thank goodness. I thought I'd lost you forever." She knelt beside him and gently took his head into her lap.

"You cannot get rid of me that easily, kiddo," a frayed, raspy voice emerged.

A fresh crop of tears blurred Sadie's vision as her smile stretched as far as it could go.

Cheers from all quarters echoed off surfaces at every height. The populace of Mystashan gathered, speaking softly in excited tones on their way out of the Atrium.

"But how, Thelo? How did you finally come back?"

Thelo opened his shaking hand and held out a seventh crystal for her to take.

"This is yours now."

She held it up to see the life-saving word: COURAGE.

"I knew you could do it," Thelo congratulated her.

Sadie handed the crystal back to Thelo. "This belongs to you. You've shown courage beyond what I would have thought possible."

"No, Sadie. You earned it. It's yours."

"Then it's mine to do with as I will," she said, placing it in one of the vacant spaces in Thelo's wounded hide. Immediately the stone filled the void by expanding just the right amount.

Sadie stood and watched it happen, then shuddered and looked into his eyes. "Thelo, Finn could be back any second."

CHAPTER SEVENTY-SIX

Banyan's Offering

"WHAT ARE WE going to do?" Sadie asked Thelo. She leaned in to hear his strained words.

"Something tells me we do not have to worry about Finn coming back anytime soon."

Sadie looked long and hard at the courage crystal, now a part of Thelo. It represented a dark moment that she had helped turn to light. It would help her remember she always had the ability to face darkness.

Thelo tried to sit up, but Sadie placed her hand on his arm. "Should you be moving yet?"

In the next moment, he sat up, appearing stronger. His color returned, now a deep cobalt.

"How are you healing so fast?"

"Those were old wounds, Sadie. What happened with Finn was necessary in a way. It let that pain go so I could make room for what comes next. Once your crystals brought me back from the Calm, our Atrium crystals set the healing process in motion. We heal more quickly in Mystashan."

As Sadie nodded, her thoughts drifted to Banyan. "Banyan should be fine with a little time too, right? I need to see him. I need to know he's all right."

"Yes, I knew you would. I will go with you."

"Really? Are you up for that? I want you to take care of yourself."

"I can make it there for Banyan."

He struggled to find his feet.

"Thelo, please, you must rest," Sadie pleaded, reaching out to help him steady himself. "I've lost you once already today. I don't want to lose you again."

A gleaming walking stick made of polished ash materialized at Thelo's side. It was a sturdy branch, simple and unadorned. The top half spiraled in a gentle, sloping way that made the handle easy to grasp.

Thelo hobbled at first, but after several minutes of walking through the village, he learned to trust the staff and was soon able to keep up with Sadie.

Two moons illuminated the night sky, and the cool breeze tickled Sadie's hair. They saw a far-off golden glow that turned out to be their friend as they came near.

When they arrived, Banyan was resting.

His stab wounds were piteous. It was unimaginable how much golden sap he contained, as it still flowed like slowing lava from deep within the earth. His light was dimming by the minute. Many of his branches lay on the ground beside him; only a few stubs were left.

"Sleeping already, old friend? It is not even moondown yet."

Banyan opened his eyelids and gave a strained smile. Thelo sat on the grass beside him.

Banyan drew a slow, deep breath. All the while Sadie looked into his thoughtful green eyes. She used her intuition so she could see Banyan clearly: the wellspring of peace he contained and something else besides.

"Are you okay, Banyan?"

She waited for him to speak.

No words came.

"What can I do to help you? Do you heal quickly like Thelo?"

The silence continued. For clues, she looked to Thelo, who lowered his eyes and shook his head.

It struck her in the heart: the realization that something was seriously wrong with Banyan. In order to remain standing, Sadie planted her feet and paid extra attention to her balance. *As bad as this looks, everything's going to be okay. Everyone heals in Mystashan, right?*

The ground rumbled. At first she thought it was the sound of her world crumbling, but when she looked again, the cause was clear.

Where before Banyan had stood still and flush with the earth, now he rocked from side to side, slowly at first. With effort that was excruciating to watch, he heaved one of his deeper roots completely out of the earth, followed by another. Sadie was surprised to see how even the slenderest root fibers were undamaged by the process. Each lengthy root was intertwined with a variety of colorful crystals.

Come closer, please, Sadie.

"Oh, thank goodness. Of course, Banyan. Anything for you. I was afraid I might never hear your voice again."

May I hug you?

Sadie thought she saw the area around his face lighten.

"Are you sure I won't hurt you?"

Nothing can hurt me anymore, Sadie. Now, about my hug . . .

Sadie moved closer to Banyan's face. His eyes looked particularly bright and expressive, despite his wounds.

She wrapped her arms around his wide, cool trunk. Banyan's few remaining branches came down to embrace her. His crystal-laden roots rose up and around her. Soon Banyan's arms surrounded her from above and below.

Sadie closed her eyes and breathed in the ebbing green of

Banyan's essence. She placed a kiss under his left eye, where she thought his cheek might be.

They held their embrace for an extra-long moment, and then Banyan released her, holding her at branch's length.

I want you to have something. It might seem small, but I assure you it is not.

A low-lying branch reached down and scooped some of the warm liquid gold into a crystal vial the roots had fashioned.

Please take this golden sap. It has served me well, and I know it will treat you right too.

"Do you honestly think I would consider this a small gift? It's huge, Banyan. It's almost as incredible as you are. I guess it is you, in a way. But won't you need it all to heal?"

My body knows how to create more. Don't worry. Please take this gift from me. It is warm, so you can shape it tonight. Be as creative as you want. Think of me, and I will think of you. Please bring it with you when you return.

"But how can I get back to Mystashan without the music box?"

Meet me on earth, Sadie. I will show you how to transport back here at that time. Don't forget to bring what you made with you.

Sadie nodded. "I'll remember."

Whatever else has happened, good has come from today's events, and you were crucial to most of it. Never doubt that you are a part of our family . . . as well as your own. Be happy, dear Sadie. We all must rest. I will see you in a few days.

Sadie wiped a tear from the corner of her eye. "Good-bye for now, Banyan. Please take care. I love you. I'll definitely see you soon." *He has to be okay. He just has to.*

Good night, Sadie. Good night, Thelonius, old friend. Find me on the inside if you need me.

She did all she could not to cry. She wanted to stay, to help bolster Banyan's recovery with her love and friendship.

As Thelo and Sadie moved toward the Saponi Straime, she stopped to take one long look back. Banyan appeared so odd with his large roots out of the dirt, spread topside with shimmering liquid gold all around. His eyes were already closed, and she wished he breathed like humans so she could see that he was alive.

A scream rippled the air in front of them.

"What was that, Thelo?"

"It happens from time to time through the different dimensions. It is most audible here since this is the gateway."

"Why haven't I heard anything like it before?"

"That is a discussion for another day. Let's get back, Sadie. The others will wonder where we are."

Once through the Straime, Sadie stopped again to face her companion.

"Thelo, I know Banyan will be okay, but I'm worried. I wish I could do more."

Thelo nodded with understanding. "It could go either way, Sadie. I think we will know more in a few days. For now, the way we can help him most is by letting him rest."

Sadie gently shook her head. "I helped you, Thelo. I know I can help him too."

"You *can* help. You're right about that, although it might not be in the form that you are imagining."

CHAPTER SEVENTY-SEVEN

Back to Basics

FINN LANDED HARD on the ground. He took a tumble, almost hitting his head on that leaking tree. He lay still, assessing each part of his body to make sure all of him was still there. He glanced up at the broken branches above him and admired his handiwork. The tree looked nearly dead.

He pushed himself to his feet, only to stagger backward as Basset embraced him with enough momentum that they toppled over.

"Get the hell off me!" Finn growled.

Basset stood and retreated a few steps. "Sorry, sir. I'm glad you're back safely."

Finn's tone softened. "I have good news to report." He dropped a hand into one of his pockets and smiled, the last remnants of pain from his reentry fading away. "Basset, come look at what I brought back for us!" He pulled out two handfuls of the stunning diamonds that he had dug out of Thelonious. "I won. After all they did to me, I came out on top. I won. *We* won."

"How did you do it, Mr. Finn?" Basset's face brightened, in part from the glow of the jewels in Finn's hands.

"That purple-haired one really thought she had me. To think

some flea-bitten girl could overpower everything I've done and can do. But she was sadly mistaken."

The mood took a sudden turn as Finn threw his head back and burst into high-pitched laughter.

"*Yes!* I did it. I did it! I killed Thelonious *and* retrieved his jewels," he yelled to his devoted man. "Can you believe how lustrous these are? How many I got? How much they'll be worth? Never another thing to worry about."

He watched as sunlight danced from one gem to another. They were even more marvelous than he'd remembered from long ago.

I finally did it. Their glow mesmerized him. Then, even as he looked at them, he thought their brilliance faded a bit. *Must be a trick of my eyes.*

Now they were clearly fading. *This can't be happening.*

The diamonds lost all radiance. They turned dull, dark, and finally were no more than common granite.

"*No!*" he howled. "It isn't fair! They can't be gone!" Yet even as Finn debated the outcome, the stones turned to a fine powder. The last specks blew away. They were gone.

Finn dropped to his knees, tears of disbelief streaming down his face. "It isn't fair. It isn't . . ."

He tried but couldn't finish his last word. Something was happening. He could no longer speak. He stood frozen, a silent scream echoing inside.

CHAPTER SEVENTY-EIGHT

Oh, Mission!

As Sadie stepped out from the straime, she looked up at Thelo. "I need to ask you something. It's been on my mind, and after all that's happened, I want to know."

Thelo smiled and nodded. "I will do my best to answer any questions you might have. Go ahead."

"All this time, and you've never explained why I'm here. Mr. Felix mentioned something about it, but he never gave me a straight answer I could understand. What does it mean that I'm part of a long line of individuals? Who are these individuals? How does what I did today fit in with Mr. Felix's explanation about protecting both worlds?"

"Come over here, Sadie."

Thelo motioned toward a couple of boulders off to the right so they could sit. The ground was covered with ivy and periwinkle, visible by moonlight and the Silars, who had returned to Thelo's side, should he need help.

Tingles of excitement mixed with anxiety scurried over her skin. Even with everything she'd been through today, she had no idea what this talk would reveal. She settled herself and looked up with anticipation.

"Sadie, the cloffuls tell us who will fill that role." Thelo rested his chin on his walking stick. "They let us know who is next. Your grandmother was one in line to protect us."

"Gramma Rose came here? When?"

"As a child, of course, with her brother, Finn."

"And she was one of . . . the individuals?" Sadie shook her head in disbelief. "But how could Gramma protect anybody's world?"

"The same way you're going to. Rose lived here for a while. She came here when she was a little younger than you are now. Many times our crossovers come from the same family line but not always. It's a long story, but ultimately your grandmother chose to return to earth. Many years after her departure, the cloffuls began showing new signs to give us direction. They led us to you."

Sadie sat quietly, absorbing this revelation.

"You asked about Mr. Felix's line of individuals," Thelo continued. "They were all people like you—each with his or her own strengths—who were called upon to protect the balance between Earth and Mystashan. Each world is critical to the other. They overlap at the Saponi Straime and the spot Banyan occupies."

"In what way do they balance each other, and what am I supposed to do?"

"I understand that you have many questions, but each experience you have will make that clearer. No one here can tell you your mission, because each person's mission is distinct." Thelo gingerly stepped down from the boulder and offered Sadie his hand, while he used his walking stick for support. They continued on their stroll.

"I have so many questions," Sadie admitted. "I appreciate you talking with me about them."

Thelo smiled. "Of course. Now come with me. We have something very special planned for tonight, something just for you."

"It's all wonderful and I appreciate it, but I wish Banyan could be with us." A burning sensation flooded her eyes again.

"He will be, Sadie. You will be bringing his gift with you. In a way, it is very much the same thing."

Sadie nodded. "I like thinking of it that way." She reached into her pocket and pulled out the small crystal vial of sap. It still felt warm in her hands. "I wonder what I'll create with it."

They came to a fork in the road. Since Thelo continued on the right side, she asked him if she might take the left fork and visit Penelope before meeting up with him again for the celebration.

"Of course, Sadie. Enjoy yourself, and we'll meet up soon."

"Thanks, Thelo. I won't be long. Hopefully I'll find her. I'll reach out to you telepathically when I'm on my way back or need anything."

Thelo's wave was nonchalant, and he was soon out of sight.

CHAPTER SEVENTY-NINE

In the Meanwhile

O<small>N</small> T<small>HELO'S</small> <small>WAY</small> back to the village, he reached out to Banyan. *Yes, I told her, but I have not told her everything. Just what she needs to know for now.*

She will need to know more over time, Thelonious. Of course, it is not possible for anyone to tell her the future completely. We might have misinterpreted the cloffuls. We have done it before. We can hope that she will be spared some of it.

Indeed. Spared and thriving is the way we would like to see Sadie. Sweet dreams tonight, Banyan. I will see you again, yes?

It is entirely possible. We have been at this a long time, my friend. You were the first one I saw in the cloffuls.

Long time gone since then and such a kick in the pants.

Long time, it is true. I will miss Mr. Felix as well.

Now wait a minute. You will see him again. Thelo searched his mind for what he could see of Banyan's face.

A moment's hesitation, and then Banyan replied, *Yes, I suppose you're right.*

CHAPTER EIGHTY

To Err Is Human

S ADIE REJOINED THELO in the village. She had hoped to share her experience today with Penelope, but it would have to wait.

"Everything looks better than I could ever imagine, even here in Mystashan. Speaking of spectacular, your diamonds are coming back more radiant than before. Are they all in?"

"Yes, they are, Sadie."

Sadie couldn't help but smile as everyone ran around streaming decorations through the trees and over the houses. They had set up benches throughout the village. Flowers of every sort and color came of their own accord, to beautify and define where the festivities would take place. The moonlight was bright now as the fuller one reached its peak. Some of the Silars took up residence in the lanterns, helping everyone see their way clearly. Many fire pits and torches had been set up as well.

"Thank you for the party, Thelo, but it really wasn't necessary. This place, you, everyone in Mystashan—they're like family to me. I just did what had to be done to protect you."

"It is a delight for all of us to do this for you. We have many things to celebrate tonight. It is likely that neither I nor any of us would be here to have this conversation, let alone decorate for a party, had it not been for you, Sadie. Thank you for saving my life and in turn everyone else's."

"He was so evil, Thelo. I thought he killed you. I couldn't let him hurt anyone else."

Thelo's brows creased together while his mouth tightened.

"What? What is it?"

"Take a walk with me, Sadie. There is something I wish to share with you."

"Okay. Where are we going?"

"To the Atrium, but do not worry—we will be back before long."

"Are you up for this tonight?" Sadie asked.

"Yes, thank you. I am feeling much better. In fact, I am ready to go dancing." Thelo twirled around and flashed Sadie an impish smile. "Care for a spin?"

"Sure. My mom taught me. I hope I can keep up with you."

"Once the music starts, you might be stunned at how accomplished I am. I have not danced in many lifetimes, but I am sure it is something I will never forget. I dance in my memories. Does that count?"

"I'm sure it does."

Several minutes later, Sadie stood in front of the Atrium. The disarray was a sad reminder of today's events. Stones and crystals were out of their careful placements. Chips had been blown into the crystal walls. Many flowers were trampled and dead. Silars tended the living. She and Thelo made their way to the Velluminator cave.

"I need to show you a few things in the Velluminator that words cannot explain," Thelo said, as they stood in front of the device.

"That reminds me," Sadie cut in.

Thelo paused, "Yes, Sadie?"

"I have a question about the Velluminator. Is it possible to come here when I'm dreaming? When Finn knocked me out, I saw Gramma's murder and felt everything as if it were happening to me. How can that be?"

Thelo tilted his head and raised his index finger to his mouth. "Huh . . . It does happen on occasion. Not many can do that, Sadie. Your subconscious mind traveled here and allowed you to see and feel that unfortunate event from inside the Velluminator. It means you are even stronger than we first thought."

Sadie trembled, remembering Gramma's last moments alive.

Thelo put his arm around her before continuing. "I can understand why you would think of Finn as thoroughly evil, but there is more to that story. You see, Finn was never supposed to come to Mystashan. It was a decision Mr. Felix made to save Finn's life when he was a boy."

The Velluminator lit up. Images came quickly into focus. Thelo showed Sadie the night on the Clover Bridge and how they both were brought over when it was only supposed to be Rose.

"Finn did not meld with the frequency of Mystashan. It short-circuited his brain, in a way, transforming all the joy and wonder of this place, of any place really, into pain and misery for him. It twisted him, restricting what typically brings happiness until he could no longer see the good in anything or anyone. We tried to help him, but he began to hurt himself as well as others."

Sadie narrowed her eyes. "I don't believe it. There must have been something in him, something in his personality that made him that way. How could our enchanted Mystashan do that to him?"

"You can judge for yourself." Thelo directed her attention back to the screen.

CHAPTER EIGHTY-ONE

Lots of Luck

"FINNY, LOOK WHAT I found."

A young Finn rushed over to where his sister pointed. "What is it, Rose?"

She gestured toward a patch of bright-green clover. "See it?"

"Yes, clovers. So what? We see clovers all the time."

"Look closer. You'll see."

Finn squatted, arms on his knees for support. He looked at the clovers as hard as he could. Finally he looked up at his sister. "I don't know what I'm looking for."

Rose squatted next to him. "There, Finny. Right there." She pointed closer.

Finn gasped, eyes growing large. "Whoa. I can't believe it. That can't be a real four-leaf clover, can it?"

"It's real. It's a perfect four-leaf clover." Rose gently pulled the clover from the dirt. The soil was a fine powder, and it released the plant without harm. "Here, you take it."

Finn shook his head. "I can't take it. You found it—it's yours."

Rose stood up. "I want you to have it. That way, when I'm not with you, you'll always be safe. I want you to have all the luck in the world for all your days. I know . . . why don't you bring it tonight when we go out with Mother and Father? Remember,

Father's being honored by the mayor, so that would be a perfect time to take it with you."

Finn leapt up and hugged his sister tightly. "I love it! Thank you. You're so good to me. You're the best sister ever."

"It's only because you're the best brother. I love you, Finny."

"I love you too, Rose."

The screen went dark. Sadie wiped her tears on her sleeve. She didn't want to admit to Thelo how affected she was by what she saw.

Thelo's voice came out of the darkness. "How are you holding up? Are you okay?"

"It was bittersweet watching them together, knowing what he became. I see now how difficult it must have been for you. It breaks my heart knowing they loved each other the way they did and how everything turned out afterward. Thelo, would you do things the same way with Finn if you could do it all over again?"

"That is not an easy question to answer, Sadie. It is something Mr. Felix asks himself every day. We did what we did based on what we knew at the time, and that led us to who and where we are right now. Ultimately, it was a tough call. What do you think you would have done?"

"I have to think about that. It's a lot to take in. You said Finn was no longer a threat. How can we be sure?"

The Velluminator light came back on.

Finn stood in front of Banyan.

Poor Banyan. He looks awful. Sadie put her hand on her heart and focused her love on him. She watched Finn, who appeared upset.

Thelo's diamonds turned to sand, which blew away. A weight of overwhelming despair washed over Sadie.

"*No!* It isn't fair! They can't be gone!" Finn dropped to his knees, tears streaming down his face. "It isn't . . . fair. It isn't . . ."

He couldn't finish his last word. He clearly tried to speak, but no sound came out. She felt his fear mounting as his body turned to stone. It began with his feet and worked its way up.

A stiffness overtook Sadie's body as she tuned in more and more to Finn's emotions. It was getting harder for her to breathe.

Thelo reached out and placed a hand on her shoulder. *Remember, Sadie, you are reacting to what Finn is feeling. It is not your pain.*

Finn's vision seemed to blacken gradually as his eyes turned to stone along with the rest of him. Sadie felt his helplessness, disbelief, and a second conflicted presence in his last moments as Finn Montgomery.

A teary-eyed stranger ran up and broke off one of Finn's fingers right before Finn crumbled and was gone. This only made the man cry harder.

The screen went to static instead of its usual black.

"What happened to the picture? And who was that crying person?"

Thelo sighed. "I do not know who that was. The static happens sometimes. We have our best people working on both things."

"That man certainly cared about Finn and seemed to be waiting for him. Should we be concerned about him coming here?"

"I think the answer must be yes. Until we get more information and get the Velluminator running properly, we will have to stay alert. The word is already out to Penelope and to other helpers living on earth."

"Why didn't you tell me that Gramma Rose had a brother?" Sadie asked.

"It was not mine to tell."

"What does that mean? You could have stopped all the

horrible things he did from happening. And Gramma might still be alive."

"We cannot know that or see everything." Thelo motioned to the screen. "The static is one example of how our vision is sometimes blocked.

"Sadie, you asked me earlier if I would do anything differently, knowing what I know now. I do not think I would change anything, because whatever we choose has its own set of consequences. If Finn had died that day on the bridge so many years ago, we do not know what new obstacles would have emerged on that other road, that new road."

Sadie looked at the darkened screen. *Dark, dark . . .* "Thelo, there were others coming up behind us in the tunnel. They made it clear they're on Finn's side. Do you know anything about that? About who they are?"

"We suspected Finn was not acting alone, but we could not pinpoint any accomplices. There are powerful people here, and unfortunately many have veils to hide behind."

CHAPTER EIGHTY-TWO

Changing of the Guard

"Mr. Finn. What's happening to you?"

Basset reached out for his hand and broke off one of Finn's fingers. The younger man swallowed a scream and sat down heavily, his tears flowing.

He watched in horror as the only father he'd ever known crumbled to the ground. Finn Montgomery was no more.

He opened his hand, hoping to find the finger intact, but instead his palm filled with shards of stone, which turned to powder and blew away.

The rest of the dark pile swirled into a dusty tornado of smaller and smaller pieces.

"No, Mr. Finn. You can't be gone. What do I do now? I need you. Please come back." Tears blinded his vision.

As he spoke to the empty pile of clothing, his words drew the breeze toward him. Heat invaded his throat.

Basset swallowed fire. Finn's whole life entered his consciousness. Pictures of Finn's world spun through him, including ones of himself at various ages. He finally felt Finn's love for him, something he'd kept hidden all their life together.

"Oh, Mr. Finn! Why didn't you tell me?" Basset sobbed.

Others came after—strangers with their own sets of images. *What's happening to me?* The last thing Basset remembered before spiraling out of control was a Voice calling him, "Kiddo." He fell to the ground, his mind awhirl with images and voices. He stared up at a set of puffy white clouds and then only darkness.

The twinkling blanket of the night sky stretched out overhead, but then Basset realized his eyes were still closed. He opened them.

I must have passed out. He sat up. Finn's dusty clothes lay on the ground beside him. They moved. Basset kicked backward like a crab then jumped into a kneeling position.

"Mr. Finn?"

A paw emerged from under the sleeve.

The clothes lifted off the ground as a small object Basset had seen before moved toward him.

The music box emerged, pushed out by the snout of a cat, whose rich coat shimmered, changing from one bright hue to another.

"I know you from somewhere, but I can't think from where. How do I know your name?"

You know many things now. There is much we need to do, Basset. Grab the music box and let's go.

Basset stood, picked up the music box from the ground, then put it in his pocket. He brushed off the dirt from his clothing and out of his hair before addressing the feline. With eyes flashing a scarlet flame, he commanded, "I'll decide what we need to do." *Wait a minute. Was that me?*

Now you're talking, kiddo.

"Did you hear that, Penelope?" Basset asked.

Yes, I heard your rudeness, and after all I've done for you too, she told him. *You and I make decisions together, if you'd be kind enough to recall.*

She's never made decisions with you, the Voice told Basset. *She made them with Finn. Don't let her play for power here. And no, she won't ever be able to hear me, Basset.*

"The name's Derrick."

CHAPTER EIGHTY-THREE

The Celebration

As Sadie and Thelo walked back to the village from the Velluminator, paper lanterns rose slowly into the night sky, brought to life by the Silars. The festivities had begun. The musicians grew jubilant at their approach. People stood and smiled as Sadie and Thelonious walked by. Many shook hands or bowed. Sadie and Thelo returned their welcomes.

The pair settled in their own private nook where a bonfire crackled to life.

"I know Banyan said I could return to Mystashan without the music box, but he's not well. Can I really get back without it?" It was very warm as Sadie stood in front of the fire pit. She put her hands in her pockets and rocked back and forth. She moved more out of nervousness than anything else.

"You will no longer be needing the music box. I think you will find a way all by yourself."

Sadie gave him a sidelong glance. "Could you be more specific?"

"I thought you had a certain assignment to do for Banyan?"

"I knew you were going to say that, but don't you really mean I have to figure this out by myself?"

Thelo placed a gentle hand on her shoulder. "You are never completely alone, Sadie. You will find help as you need it, and it will not always come from the places or people you expect. Keep an open mind and listen carefully, to yourself as well as others. Trust me. Your awareness will then grow and serve you well."

Sadie smiled. "After all we've been through, I trust you. It was as if I held your heart in my hands today. As the day progressed, I understood the meaning behind your words. Before, you rarely made sense."

As she glanced at Thelo, the color rose in her cheeks as she realized what she'd said. "I'm sorry. That must have sounded awful. I didn't mean it the way it came out."

Thelo gave her a half grin. "Not to worry. I know what you meant. I can read you better now too. There is something else we need to talk about, Sadie. It has to do with one of the reasons you are here." He motioned for her to sit beside him. "After everything that happened with Finn and Mystashan, your grandmother chose to break her oath and return to earth permanently."

"What do you mean by 'her oath'?"

"These individuals sign up for the great honor of protecting Mystashan at all costs. They do this by giving their assent. Are you prepared to do the same?"

Euphoric from the day's events and ultimate victory, Sadie couldn't answer fast enough.

"Yes!" She leaned over and hugged Thelo's neck.

"Then it is done."

Sadie heard a click inside her mind. She noticed an immediate change but didn't know what it meant.

Thelo gave her a solemn nod before continuing. "That's what we call the Shiffderrence. You'll get used to it soon. Now, young lady"—he winked—"go find someone to dance with. I am sure they will be lining up."

Sadie's shoulders slumped a little. "I thought you and I were going to dance?"

"I will in a little while." He took a seat on the grass. "I am going to rest here for a bit."

He's worried. I can feel it.

"Okay, I'll be back for that dance. Don't think you're going to get out of it."

This time he gave her a full smile. She felt a little better and had more confidence that he'd be okay if she left.

Sadie walked slowly through the crowd. She took her time, absorbing the sights and sounds around her. *The lights, the music, the Silars in the trees . . . this is what Mystashan is all about. I'm relieved it's getting back to normal. Almost normal. Everyone looks happy, as if nothing's wrong in the whole world.*

A small Habnaw ran right into her without looking.

"Hey, slow down there, kid. Why are you in such a rush?"

"Sorry, Sadie. I'm just happy to be here tonight. Is that a good reason?"

"Yes, it is. Do you have time to tell me your name?"

"Hanley."

"Nice to meet you, Hanley." *Whoa. Could it be? I thought he died.* Sadie realized it was the child Finn had hurled against a pillar in the Atrium.

I'm right here. He didn't kill me. I'm tough. The young boy looked up at Sadie with resolve.

"Don't you know it's impolite to listen in?" Sadie teased. "Have you had a regrowing lately? Want me to make a wish?" She laughed to herself. *Like I'm doing him the favor.*

Hanley gasped, his paws flying to his mouth. "Yes! Yes, please. I've never experienced a regrowing before." He danced around her with excitement. He couldn't stop his jiggling.

"You're going to have to stand still. Otherwise I won't be able to do it."

He looked as though he were trying to calm himself but lost out. Hanley wiggled nonstop in front of Sadie. "I'm trying as hard as I can."

"Are you ready?"

Hanley nodded, his eyes glowing with anticipation.

"Okay, here goes."

As she made her wish, her little friend giggled with the lifting of his dandelion hair.

"Ooh." He clapped as each seed pod flew off into the night. He watched until they disappeared. Once they were out of sight, Hanley hopped from side to side as each new strand grew back. "Hahahaha. That tickles."

Sadie bent her head forward and wore a smile of her own.

"What did you wish for?" he asked with his joyful grin.

"Something I wish for every day." Sadie's smile slowly faded. "To see my Gramma again."

Sweet Sadie.

Sadie felt the breeze on her neck and heard Gramma humming the song from the music box.

"Gramma? Gramma, are you here? Where are you?"

"Who are you talking to?" asked Hanley.

"You don't hear the humming? The song?"

The boy shook his head and stilled himself for a moment, leaning forward as if straining to hear whatever it was he couldn't. "I just hear the sound of fun! C'mon, Sadie."

"You run along. I'll be there in a minute."

"Okay," he squeaked. "I'll see you later. Thanks again."

"Thank you too, Hanley."

They hugged, and then Hanley scuttled off.

Gramma's humming returned. This time it came from the distance. Sadie looked to a path on her right, where a swirling patch of fog formed. She froze. *Is my wish coming true already?*

It's not exactly what I meant, but any Gramma is better than no Gramma.

The patch was in motion, slipping behind a hut. Sadie had to move fast to keep up with it. It flew in and over the homes of the village. For a moment, she lost sight of it, but then it reappeared above the hut in front of her and shot back down and around. *Where is she taking me?*

The fog found its place in front of a larger dwelling and bounced lightly while it waited for Sadie to catch up. When she stood in front of the building, the patch dispersed and left behind a door in its place. "88B" was etched into the wood. *Hmmm. I guess I have no choice.* Sadie turned the knob and walked into the dimly lit room.

"Hello? Is anyone home?"

"In here, sweetie."

A wave of warm familiarity infused Sadie at the sound of Gramma Rose's voice.

"Gramma!" she called out. Sadie ran into the room, but no one was there. She searched the whole dwelling, but it was empty.

"Gramma? Where are you?" The hut remained silent. *She wouldn't do this to me.* The excitement waned. She lowered her head and let the tears flow.

As Sadie turned to leave, she caught sight of her reflection in an antique mirror that hung on the wall. The mirror's framework was elaborate, with a wooden column on each side. With some hesitation, she walked over and stood in front of it.

She couldn't believe the sight before her; she'd never seen herself in Mystashan. Her violet hair, which she'd already seen on her shoulders, was longer and more lustrous than she could imagine. Her ivory skin almost glowed and offered a soft, striking contrast to her luminous emerald eyes and fiery pupils.

"Wow, if they could see me back home, they'd never mess with me again."

It was difficult to turn away. She was entranced by the radiance deep within her green eyes. The mirror shimmered. She blinked. It shimmered again. Squinting the way she had all those months ago in her bathroom at home, she braced herself. The face in the mirror began to transform. It looked like her but a little different.

Hello, Sadie. It's time to go back home. You'll be late for dinner. She almost tripped over herself stepping backward when the reflection's lips began to move and spoke with Gramma Rose's voice.

"No! Don't go away. *Please.* Not again."

She stared longer at the mirror, but nothing changed. The vision didn't return.

After another long glance at her own reflection, she turned to leave. "I'll be back soon, Gramma. Thanks for letting me know it's dinnertime on earth. Love you."

She left the little house marked "88B" and headed back to where she'd left Thelo. "You're still sitting here?"

"Yes. There is much to think about, but I have done as much as I can for tonight. Is it time for our dance?"

Sadie shook her head. "Sorry. I can't. I have to get back. Gramma told me it was dinnertime."

"What do you mean? Rose told you that? That is not possible, Sadie."

"I know, right?" Sadie shrugged. "All I know is there was this mist, and then I was in this house. There was a mirror there, and I finally saw what I look like too. Then Gramma told me I needed to go home now. I wish I could look this way back home." She gave a toss of her long violet hair.

Sadie looked at Thelo; his concerned expression had returned.

"What? What is it? You've got that worried look again."

Thelo shook his head. "It is nothing. We had better get you back then."

"You're doing that thing again, Thelo."

"What thing would that be, Sadie?"

"The thing where you don't answer a straight question. But never mind that now. Would you please thank everyone on my behalf for throwing such an amazing party for me?" Sadie gave Thelo a long hug. "Thank you too, by the way!"

His eyes sparkled in response. Thelo clinked his glass to get everyone's attention.

"Fellow Mystashanians, Sadie has done us an enormous service today. Ever humble, she has asked me to thank you all for tonight's festivities on her behalf. I would also like to thank you for putting this party together on short notice and for keeping hope alive in Mystashan."

There was a roar of applause from all corners of the celebration.

Thelo offered Sadie his arm and escorted her to Saponi Straime. "I am proud of you, Sadie. You showed your true strength today, and it will keep expanding."

Sadie smiled. "Thanks. I'm excited to see what happens next. Just do me a favor. No more dying, okay? Once was enough."

He merely nodded. "Good night, Sadie."

"'Night, Thelo. I'll be back soon. There's a couple of things I need to take care of back home."

"We all need our rest. Banyan too. I will see you in a couple of days' earth time. If anything happens of importance, I will inform you."

"Thank you, Thelo. For everything." They hugged good night.

Banyan looked like he was sleeping. Sadie whispered, "Good night, sweet Banyan. Heal quickly. I'll see you soon."

CHAPTER EIGHTY-FOUR

The Return

SADIE WALKED THROUGH the front door and closed it as quietly as possible. Her mother stood next to the kitchen counter, flipping through a cookbook.

"Oh, hi, Sadie! Where did you come from? Thin air?

If you only knew how right you are. She ran over and gave Mom a hug.

"Whoa, what's that for?"

"Nothing. I just missed you."

"You've only been gone a couple of hours, but I'll take it," Mom said, her tone brighter than usual.

"I love you, Mom."

She stepped back to survey her daughter. "I love you too, honey." She brushed a few strands of Sadie's loose hair out of her face. "Something's different about you. For starters, your hair is down. And the bottoms are purple! When did you do that?"

"Um, they're purple?" Sadie pulled some of her hair around to where she could confirm what her mother said. "I guess it was during art class? I didn't realize. But what do you think of it? I kind of like it."

"Yes. It's different in a good way, but there's still something else. I can't put my finger on it. I'm sure it'll come to me later."

They hugged again, a little longer this time. "Can I help you with anything?" Sadie asked.

"Where is my daughter, and what have you done with her?" teased Mom.

Sadie smiled. "Right here. Right where I've always been."

"I guess so." Mom pointed to a recipe in the book. "Come on. Let's get dinner started. Dad will be home soon."

Sadie enjoyed every bite of their dinner together that night and even got Dad to smile a few times at her jokes. Mom made Sadie's favorite: eggplant parmigiana with angel hair pasta and salad.

After kissing both her parents good night for the first time in ages, Sadie headed to her room.

She briefly wondered how she would find her way back to Mystashan, but that was a challenge for another day. First she had to do what Banyan had asked. She wanted to make him the most brilliant creation.

She flipped on the bedroom lamp. Penelope, with her shimmering fur, was fast asleep on the bed. Sadie plopped down beside her. "Where have you been, sweet one?"

There was no reply except for unabated soft snores and purring.

No matter. I'm excited to start working on my gift. The feeling of calm from the sap has been sublime, even though it's been wrapped in cloth inside my pocket.

The sap was intact within the small crystal vial, the consistency of molasses yet not sticky. She brought it over to her window seat and began to work with it. Sadie decided to use her hands, as neither instructions nor tools had been provided. Her hands shook with the excitement, energy, and responsibility of creating something special for Banyan. Even so, she picked up the sap as gently as possible. The amount was generous and filled her palm.

As her hands worked, she concentrated on her breathing, which helped alleviate the shaking.

The sap still felt warm all these hours later. It was pleasant to shape and mold it. She glanced at Penelope and whispered to her, but there was no movement except her quiet, steady breath.

A montage replayed in her mind. It was the scene with Finn in the Atrium. She'd done what she had to do, what she knew was right, but it wasn't until that moment that Sadie realized her life had seriously been in danger. Was it odd that it hadn't occurred to her at the time?

Hours passed as she molded and shaped the sap. She fell asleep with her project in her hand, her head leaning against the window.

In the morning, she awoke with a paw on her arm and the soft brush of Penelope's tail around her back.

What do you have there, Sadie? Can I see?

Sadie looked down at her hand, amazed to find a perfectly formed egg settled in her palm as if it belonged there. The sap had grown overnight in volume and size . . . It was *still* warm.

She rubbed one of the sides, revealing a crystal world that had grown within it.

"Look! A crystal somehow formed inside the sap overnight!" She held it up to let the morning light reflect off all the facets within.

Curious. What else do you see?

"I see Banyan's eyes and a green mist that seems alive."

Penelope pawed at the egg, bringing it close to her, but stopped as Sadie asked her a question.

"Where were you yesterday while everything erupted in the Atrium?" Sadie unconsciously pulled back the egg from Penelope's grasp. "I looked all over for you—there, in the village later, and at the celebration."

They're calling me. I have to go. See you soon, Sadie.

"Who's calling you?" Sadie looked to her left, but the cat was no longer in her room.

Must have been super important, I guess, to blow me off like that.

Sadie turned the egg over in her hands. She loved what she'd created and its inner world. She felt closer to Banyan as she held it.

Her smile disappeared at once, and she felt very afraid.

Banyan, please tell me you're okay.

CHAPTER EIGHTY-FIVE

Le Confession

SADIE HID HER creation with the rest of her crystals, wrapping it in a pair of socks for extra safekeeping. Even with all she'd been through, there was still school in an hour and a half. She dressed and prepared for what she had to do today. She put on her S necklace, Dad's gift. This was the first time she had felt safe to wear it to school. It satisfied her to finally be able to wear it without fear.

Sadie sat down on the bed and slid on her shoes. She reached for her keys on the nightstand and noticed a crystal on top of Christopher's letter. *Hmm. Thelo, is this the courage crystal I gave you? How could that be? It was embedded in your body last I saw. Could this be a new one? Do we each have one now?*

She realized why it was on top of Christopher's letter. She knew she would need everything the crystal represented to read it. It must be time.

Sadie tore open the envelope and unfolded the paper. The three words written there shocked her. Paralyzed, she let go, and it fluttered to the carpet. *After all this time? What am I supposed to do with this now?*

Her shoulders tensed, and she shook her head. "No!" *He can say whatever he wants. He did before. It means nothing anymore.*

His words stared up at her. "I'm coming home." *What was he thinking? I'm not going there.* Sadie stood and glanced one last time at the note on the floor, stepping on it as she left her room.

* * *

The school day passed quickly, rushing toward the moment Sadie raised her hand. It was five minutes before the final bell. "Mr. MacNamara, would you mind if I spoke to the class for a few minutes? It's very important."

Her classmates mumbled under their collective breath. Although Mr. MacNamara didn't usually grant this type of request, he let her speak. Maybe he was having a good day or something.

Sadie walked up to the front of the classroom and looked around at her classmates. Her eyes stopped on Kylie Allen.

"I had a music box once," she began. "My Gramma Rose gave it to me."

Bursts of laughter erupted. Kylie alone remained serious.

Unfazed by the laughter, Sadie continued. "It was very special to me, and it played my grandmother's favorite song."

The laughter grew even louder than before.

Sadie's eyes locked on Kylie's. "Someone took it from me, and it hurt my heart badly."

"Oh, Sadie. You're killing me," clucked Dave. "I haven't laughed this hard in . . . forever. More, please! And by the way, your hair looks ridiculous."

Again, laughter erupted throughout the room.

All Sadie saw were Kylie's brown eyes. "I realized then how much it must have hurt when someone stole your pin, Kylie." The room went silent. Sadie reached into her pocket and pulled out the butterfly pin.

"I knew it," yelled Dave. "You're in serious trouble, Sadie."

"Yeah, your days are numbered, Myers," Kenny chimed in. "If I were you, I'd hide in a cave for the rest of the year. You're such a loser."

Sara cautioned, "Hide your stuff, everyone. I wish you went to another school, Sadie!"

Sadie looked down at the pin for a moment and walked over to Kylie. With calm confidence, she placed the pin on Kylie's desk.

"I'm so sorry, Kylie. I didn't think about what I was doing. I was angry that everyone forgot about my birthday. Even my own parents. I didn't realize it would hurt you when I took it, but I definitely know now."

Kylie looked shocked and didn't say a word.

Mr. MacNamara remained silent throughout the exchange.

"May I be excused?" asked Sadie.

It felt like Mr. MacNamara had temporarily lost the power of speech, but after a few seconds, he finally said, "Yes."

Sadie gathered her things and headed for the door.

"Yeah, you'd better leave, Sadie!" yelled Dave. The rest of the class hollered after her as well.

Warmth spread through Sadie. *Wow. That felt really good.* She was buoyant. *I feel amazing now; I'm so glad that weight is off my shoulders.*

She took her time walking down the hallway and noticed student artwork on the walls. *I never realized how talented some of my classmates are.*

"Sadie . . . Sadie."

Kylie ran after her.

"Sadie, that was really brave of you." Kylie caught up to her. "I was so upset when my pin was stolen. I guessed you took it, but after what you just did, I can't be mad at you. I don't know how I'm able to do this, but . . . I forgive you, Sadie."

Sadie looked down at her feet then back up. "Thanks, Kylie.

I know what I did was totally wrong, but I promise I'll never do it again—to you or anyone else."

Kylie smiled. "You know what? I believe you. Do you want to walk home together?"

Sadie nodded. "Sure. I just have to stop at my locker first."

CHAPTER EIGHTY-SIX

Testing 1, 2, 3 . . .

NOW WHAT?

Dave and his goons marched up the hallway toward Sadie and Kylie.

Surprise, surprise. She knew they were going to retaliate in light of her confession. *Sigh.* Sadie readied herself.

"Hiya, Sadie. You think you're gonna just give that pin back without any consequences? I warned you."

"Dave, leave her alone," Kylie demanded.

"It's okay," Sadie said. "I can handle them."

"Ha-ha! You can handle us?" Dave scoffed. "Yeah, I don't think so."

Sadie ignored him and concentrated on opening her locker.

"I'm talking to you, stupid, or are you too dumb to understand?"

Looking around, Sadie pretended they weren't there. She finally spoke to Kylie. "I know I'm hearing something. I'm really not sure what it is. Could it be caveman speak, or maybe it's what cockroaches sound like when they cry."

The hallway traffic stopped. All eyes were on Sadie and Dave.

"What did you say? Who do you think you are, Myers?" Dave shook his head in disbelief.

"That's exactly who I am: Sadie Myers."

He grabbed her arm and spun her toward him. "What did you say, Stupid Sadie?" He looked at the chain around her neck. "I know what that *S* stands for on that ugly necklace of yours: stupid. It belongs to me now."

Dave reached for her neck, but Sadie was faster. In one smooth motion, she brought her history book up to block his hand. His fingers jammed and bent backwards.

"*Ow . . . Ow!*" Dave bent over in pain, cradling his fingers with his other hand. "Damn it! I think you broke my fingers."

"You'll live." She turned to Dave's friends. "And by the way, I'm not afraid of any of you."

Kenny and Alex looked at her and backed away. She saw her reflection in the window. Her eyes held a powerful energy she'd only seen in Mystashan.

Dave looked up at Sadie. "Come on guys. Get her."

When Dave's cronies backed off, he slowly straightened up and moved away. When he got to a safe distance, he whispered, "This isn't over, stupid."

Sadie knew they wouldn't be bothering her anymore. The familiar weight of a newly acquired crystal pulled at her pocket. She didn't have time to look, since she wanted to give Kylie her full attention, and she was pretty sure she knew what it would say anyway.

"Wow, Sadie. That was really something."

Sadie grinned at Kylie as they headed out the door.

CHAPTER EIGHTY-SEVEN

Consequence of Truth

"I'M IMPRESSED WITH how you handled yourself back there. It's about time someone put them in their place." Kylie and Sadie began their walk home together.

"Thanks, Kylie. I appreciate you saying that. The timing felt right."

"It's like that, isn't it? Timing counts for so much."

Sadie nodded. "Yes, and every moment is important in its own way."

"True. I remember once being so disappointed because I had my first date all planned out. I went to the movies with this boy, but the theater was completely full except for the first row. I was almost willing to give myself neck cramps just so my plan would actually pan out. But that wasn't the way it went, luckily."

"Why luckily? What happened? Did one of you end the date?"

"No, we went out to dinner and had the best talk. Then we walked on the beach and joined a fire pit and danced in the sand. Things worked out better than I ever could have imagined."

"Where's he now?"

"He goes to a different high school," Kylie explained, "but

he left three weeks ago on a junior-year exchange program in Japan. He took the six-month option because he didn't want to be away from me any longer than that. He's the youngest of four brothers, and his parents are very nice to me.

"We write letters back and forth at least two times a week, and I've received two of his so far. It's a long distance for the mail to travel. So yes, we're still seeing each other, if that's what you're asking."

They gave each other quick smiles. Kylie's eye contact wavered for a second then came back.

"I love your new look, Sadie. It suits you. Hey, is that guy over there waiting for you?" She pointed behind Sadie, who turned to see Sam standing on the corner.

As soon as Sadie saw him, he headed their way.

"Kylie, would you give me a minute, please? I'll be right back."

Kylie nodded. "Sure. I'll wait here for you."

Sadie met Sam and walked him back to the other side of the street.

"Hi, Sadie. I hope you're doing okay. I want to apologize for the way I behaved at the dance a couple of weeks ago. I was caught off guard and very confused by the whole situation. There's no excuse; I shouldn't have left you there by yourself. I should have waited to hear everything you had to say. I'm so sorry."

"Thanks for saying that, Sam."

"Do you want to hang out by the creek later?"

"I'll have to give that some thought, and anyway I don't think I can do it tonight."

Sam looked at her with sad eyes. "Sadie, give me a chance to make it up to you?"

"I'll think about it, but right now I have a friend waiting for me. I have to go. Bye, Sam."

Sadie walked away without looking back. From behind she heard Sam call after her.

"Sadie. I'll be there in case you change your mind. I hope it's not too late."

"Who's that?" Kylie asked. "Is that the guy from the dance?"

"Yep. That's him."

"I felt so bad for you, but I didn't think there was anything I could do. There was so much pressure from everyone to be mean to you—I just tried to avoid the situation all together. I'm really sorry. What did he want?"

"He wants me to meet him later."

"What are you going to do?"

"I'm not sure. Right now I'd just like to walk with you and not think about him."

Kylie smiled. "Sounds good to me."

The girls discovered they had a lot in common. They both loved to read the same kinds of books. They loved animals and taking discovery walks around the neighborhood. Their conversation flowed easily. They shared the same route home until they stopped to turn toward their own side streets.

"Hey, Sadie, I have to check with my parents, but would you like to come over on Saturday?"

Sadie gave her a warm smile. "I'd like that a lot."

Kylie looked down at her pin and smiled. "Bye, Sadie. See you tomorrow."

Sadie waved then turned toward home.

A tug in her pocket revealed another new crystal. Grateful to receive it, she read her newest addition. She especially liked this message: FRIENDSHIP.

What a turn of events today. Who would've thought?

I guess I'll have to figure out what to do about Sam and Christopher at some point. For today, I'm going to enjoy my clear conscience.

A few large clouds parted to reveal the sun.

Wait a minute. I got another crystal after my fight with Dave. I haven't even read it yet. Sadie pulled it out carefully and tried to read the word embedded on it, but it was too bright outside.

She looked up at the sky and eased her face into the warm sunshine. *What a day it's been . . . and there's so much to look forward to.*

She studied the unique, shape-shifting clouds as they traveled across the sky.

After a while they began to interrupt her thoughts. The clouds were stretching and twisting, like handkerchiefs of silk and velvet in hues of green and blue.

Hmm. I've never seen them look like this before.

Wait! It can't be.

"Cloffuls? What are cloffuls doing here? They aren't supposed to . . ."

Oh.

Flashes of red burned the sky.

* * *

About The Authors

ANDREA AND LESLIE are two sisters collaborating on writing through obstacles and illness. It is an entirely new way to know each other while working on their mission of Peace and Empowerment.

Andrea earned a culinary degree and worked as a chef and general manager for many years. She now focuses on her passion for writing. She writes short stories and continues to work on additional collaborative writing projects.

Leslie earned degrees in Literature and Education. She taught elementary school as well as writing and technology to teachers. A successful grant writer, she later evaluated incoming grants for the Bill & Melinda Gates Foundation. More recently she worked on her certification in Life Coaching. She's drafted four novels and various short stories.